BLACK HUNTERS' MOON

STOKER'S DARK SECRET BOOK TWO

A SUPERNATURAL VAMPIRE THRILLER

P.G. KASSEL

Storyteller Works

ISBN 13: 978-0-9967919-4-6

Library of Congress Control

Number: 2019900861

Storyteller Works

Los Angeles, CA

Cover Design by Derek Murphy

"But when these things begin to take place, straighten up and lift up your heads, because your redemption is drawing near."

Luke 21:28

CHAPTER 1

There was something disturbingly familiar about the place. More unsettling was the feeling of being drawn through time and space. It was as if she were an iron nail within the reach of some powerful, unseen lodestone. The stone drew her forward, always tugging, never loosening its grasp. She fought the force of it, struggled against it, but never with any effect.

Tree-covered hills faded into view from the darkness. Now the landscape grew more formidable, the hills giving way to mountains and the trees becoming forests. The stands of timber parted to reveal an open meadow, and there was an isolated hillside village.

The village sparked her with the hope of refuge, shelter from the thing wrenching her into this foreign world. But even though smoke curled from the stone chimneys, wooden shutters covered the windows and the doors remained latched. She attempted to call out to those who might be inside but found herself incapable of voice.

The village was soon left behind and the forests grew so dense that they shadowed the landscape with an ominous darkness. The trees assumed an unnatural animation, their limbs twisting and reaching for her. A dull terror welled up from deep within, her primal instincts urging her to flee, but the drawing force made it impossible to turn back.

The dark forests funneled up the mountainsides and the terrain became more rugged. Precipices forged of sharp, jagged rock dropped off into blackness. Black, threatening clouds covered the craggy peaks at the utmost heights of the mountaintops and swirled down into the narrow passes.

She could hear muted, distant thunder and the hollow whistling of the wind blowing through the trees. The flurries carried another sound as well, blended with the timbre of the wind. It gradually became distinguishable, a soft voice, a whisper, really. A soft but harsh, metallic whisper, horrible and familiar. The memories it carried sent chills to the core of her soul.

Most of the words were too low or too garbled to make sense of and were lost in the hissing of the wind, but she could make out her name. The voice beckoned and invited; it urged and encouraged and attempted to dispel doubt. And ebbing in and out of it all was a chilling, subtle tone, ominous and threatening.

Now she found herself on a crude, and ancient narrow road. It climbed upward through the mountain pass, winding through the saw-toothed formations of stone and precariously skirting the sheer drops into the valley below. The road's terminus faded into view, a high, rocky bluff shrouded in shadows and mist.

She found it impossible to make out any details of the place through the haze, but it was a place of timeworn stone and wood, and death. And helpless, she was being pulled toward it.

Her fear was numbing as she felt her body pulled into the vortex. She strained and fought futilely against the drawing force, but a chilling blackness soon surrounded her.

In the darkness, she was no longer moving. There was no whispering of the wind or rustling of trees. There was no thunder, only silence. And in that silent blackness, she was not alone.

She made out the intense, glowing eyes. They drew near, their gaze never leaving her, and then the pale, drawn face faded into view around them. The lips were pursed in a horrible grimace, showing those sharp, prominent teeth.

As he drew near, he pulled apart his great black coat and tore open the top of his shirt, exposing his bare chest. She tried to retreat but could not, her legs feeling as if they were weighted with blocks of lead. He reached out, his long fingers encircling the back of her neck. As he pulled her to him, he raked his finger across his chest, opening a vein with the long, pointed nail. Blood trickled from the wound as he pulled her face closer and closer, forcing her mouth down toward the open gash.

She closed her eyes and tried to scream, but could muster no sound.

And then she no longer felt his grasp and the blackness returned. Another sensation, the sensation of hunger replaced the terror.

She hungered not for a roast or a rich pudding. She did not yearn for fine cheese or a baked pastry. It was not a hunger she was familiar with. And there was a scent as well, an aroma that roused the hunger. It was a faint, coppery smell.

Pale hints of light penetrated the darkness. The dim rays pushed back the blackness enough for shadows to form. And through the shadows, she could make out the form of a man. He was lying on his side, sleeping. The man was familiar to her, but she still could not make him out well. She approached him and the hunger inside her grew. She was next to him now, gazing down at him. In his sleep, he seemed so helpless. So very helpless.

Bram Stoker was only half-asleep when he sensed that something was off. It was as if some ghostly hand was shaking him awake. He had become a light sleeper in recent weeks, so it was with little effort he opened his eyes.

Driven by instinct, he turned his head toward his wife's side of the bed. The covers were thrown back. Florence was gone.

He glanced at the wall clock, almost three in the morning.

"Florence!" he called out, rolling out of bed. By the soft, amber light of the smoldering embers in the grate, he pulled on his trousers and donned his slippers.

"Florence," he called again, hurrying from the bedroom.

He headed for the stairs leading to the lower floors of the house. As he reached the second floor landing, he could see the front door standing wide open.

Stoker sprinted down the last flight of stairs, rushed through the open doorway, and down the three steps to the short walkway leading to the street. In another moment, he was through the gate and on the sidewalk.

The late February morning was bitingly cold, and the heavy fog had covered the paving stones of Cheyne Walk with glistening moisture. There she was, three doors down, wearing only her nightclothes, walking barefoot in the middle of the street.

"Florence," he called out, hurrying after her.

She continued walking in silence.

"Florence," he called out again as he caught up to her.

He placed his hand on her shoulder. She pulled away from his touch and moved on.

He stood in front of her and put both hands on her shoulders.

Her long, dark hair framed her lovely but pale face and fell down over her breasts. The silver cross that she was never without hung below her throat, reflecting what little light there was. She was staring at him, her gaze empty and distant. There was something disturbing about the way she was looking at him, the way her mouth was set and the way her eyes seemed at once both empty and intense.

"Florence," he repeated louder than before.

She didn't hear him.

"Florence."

Her eyelids fluttered and her body swayed. Awareness suddenly returned to her gaze, and then confusion as she recognized him.

"What is it? Where, where am I?" she blurted, panic in her voice.

She shivered, now aware of the cold.

"It's all right. You're on Cheyne Walk. You've gone out again," he told her.

She reached out to him. He pulled her close.

"Another dream?" he asked.

She nodded vigorously and sobbed. "Yes."

"But where were you going?"

"Going?" She seemed disoriented.

"Why did you leave the house?"

"I was going—" she paused and her sobs increased.

"You're here with me, none the worse for wear. You're safe," he assured her. "But you're going to catch your death of cold out here. Let's get you home."

She shuddered in his arms as he began walking her back to their home at number 27, the mist glowing pale in the soft light from the street lamps.

"I'm sorry," he said. "I'm so sorry."

Being sorry seemed so inadequate. He was responsible for her nightmares and the misery that came with them. It ate away at him every moment of every day.

The dreams had begun some three months earlier, following Vlad Tepes' escape from England. The man, if it was correct to call him a man, had murdered the Stokers' maid, Tillie, and several other innocent people. And it was all because of Stoker's selfish pride.

After many weeks of interviews with this powerfully charismatic man, the only conclusion Stoker could arrive at was that Tepes was undead, a vampire.

He had never believed in such things, but certain evidences could not be ignored, and what Tepes had done to poor Lucinda Westen, Florence's best friend, was the absolute proof. He had seen Lucinda dead, his friends had seen her dead, and then they had all seen her again, animated with life. Undead.

If after these experiences he found his sleep something less than sound, he could certainly understand Florence's nightmares. She had lived a nightmare because of Tepes. For reasons Stoker never understood, Tepes had turned his attentions to her. He had kidnapped her, intending to lure Stoker and his friends to their deaths, and almost succeeded. They all came perilously close to dying that night in the Zoological Gardens at Regents Park.

They reached number 27 and he opened the gate for her. Moments later, he closed the front door behind them, locking it behind him.

"Let's get you back upstairs," he said. "I'll get the fire burning again so we can get the chill off you."

Florence hesitated.

"Bram, you've nothing to be sorry for," she assured him. "I don't blame you for any of it."

He nodded, not feeling consoled at all, and then placed a gentle kiss on her lips.

"Let's get to that fire," he said.

As they walked up the stairway her words echoed in his mind. They were kind words, encouraging words.

If only he could see a reason not to blame himself.

CHAPTER 2

A rthur Conan Doyle arrived at the Lyceum Theatre shortly after 10:00 in the morning and made his way to Bram Stoker's office. The door was open and he could see Stoker at his desk, his tall, athletic frame bent over stacks of papers and files on his desk, his brow furrowed. He straightened the coat of his brown tweed business suit, tapped his knuckles against the door, and stepped inside.

"Mr. Doyle," Stoker exclaimed with warmth, getting up from his chair.

"Mr. Stoker," Doyle smiled with equal warmth.

"It's been, what, six weeks since I saw you last?" Stoker wondered.

"More, I think. I do apologize for just dropping in like this," Doyle said.

"Nonsense. You know you're always welcome here," Stoker assured him.

Stoker waved Doyle into the chair in front of his desk. Doyle sat down, placing his hat on his lap.

"Judging from your desk, I'd say you're overloaded with work," Doyle commented. "What gives you the most trouble, managing the theater or managing Sir Henry?"

"They've both rather blurred together," Stoker answered with a smile. "Though I think managing Sir Henry *always* takes more effort."

"I thought he was on hiatus."

"I suppose hiatus is as good a word as any," Stoker chuckled.

"Yes, I'd heard that it wasn't, well, by choice," Doyle said.

Stoker sighed. "No, and I shouldn't be laughing about it. We produced two plays in a row that didn't do well at all. The box office receipts were less than admirable."

"Sorry to hear it."

"And then he couldn't seem to choose the next play for production," Stoker explained. "With all the indecision, too much time passed without income."

"I know too well his difficulty in making decisions," Doyle said with a wry chuckle.

"All in all, I'd have to say that 1896 has begun rather roughly. Though I still believe *The Adventures of Sherlock Holmes* would be very good for the Lyceum," Stoker said. "At any rate, the chain of circumstances has put us into something of a minor financial crisis."

Doyle felt a momentary twinge of guilt. "I am sorry to hear *that*," he muttered.

"We're making out all right for the moment. One of the visiting theater companies that leases the Lyceum agreed to settle in until we get our next play into production, whatever it might be. They provide us with a small percentage of their box office along with the monthly leasing fee," Stoker told him.

"Good," Doyle responded, settling back in his chair. "Now, how are you doing?"

"I'm well," Stoker replied. "Busy, but well."

"You don't appear all that well to me."

"I suppose I have my worries," Stoker said, running his fingers through the auburn whiskers of his neatly trimmed beard.

"I assume these worries are centered on your wife?"

Stoker's pleasant smile disappeared. "There's that deductive reasoning of yours."

"How is she doing?" Doyle inquired.

"The nightmares, they're worse," Stoker answered.

"How so?"

"At first, her dreams were nothing more than just reliving the events with Tepes that last night in the Zoological Gardens. And there's no mystery about that. She was certain she wouldn't live through the night," Stoker explained. "But now it's, it's something else. It's as if she's being called somewhere, and she's actually trying to go."

"What do you mean?" Doyle queried.

"She leaves the house. I'll wake up in the middle of the night and she won't be there. The first time it happened, she got almost to the end of the block before I caught up to her."

"So it's happened more than once?"

"Four times in the last month," Stoker answered. "And she describes herself as traveling, flying across some strange land toward a destination that seems to terrify her."

"Troubling, indeed," Doyle said.

"Seeing Florence so frightened and seeing her pain, well, I can't stand it," Stoker said.

"You mean you can't stand yourself, don't you?" Doyle asked.

"What?"

"You're still blaming yourself," Doyle said.

"Who else should I blame? My stupid pride and ambition brought this curse upon all of us."

"It wasn't your fault," Doyle said.

"Nonsense," Stoker almost spat. "I saw signs, clues of what he was, but I didn't stop. I kept listening to his stories, his deceptions. Maybe I tried to get out from under his influence, but I kept with it because I wanted to be more than I am. I wanted the success and celebrity that men like Sir Henry, Shaw, and even you enjoy."

"You were just as much a victim as anyone," Doyle reasoned. "Tepes sought you out."

"The beginning and the end of it is that people ended up dead because I wanted to write a brilliant book. I'm still alive, though, aren't I? All of it just so I could gain recognition."

"Perhaps your book began with selfishness, but you've turned that around. You're writing it now to serve as a warning," Doyle said.

"If I can ever finish it," Stoker grumbled.

"Writer's block? It happens to all of us. It'll pass."

"I don't know, most of it is done, but I can't seem to devise an ending. I suppose because, for me, it never really ended. He got away," Stoker said.

"Well, you must stay with it. I'm looking forward to how you handle it all."

"I'm so worried about Florence I can barely think."

"My Louise, with the consumption eating away at her, is always a great concern to me," Doyle said. "At least there are some things we can do to ease her discomfort. I can't imagine how it must be for you trying to combat such an intangible malady."

"I'm not doing anything, because I haven't the slightest idea what to do," Stoker said. "That's what tortures me."

"There's more to it, I think," Doyle said.

"How do you mean?"

"Don't let guilt drain you. Guilt can take every good thing from you if you let it. Your joy, your strength, even your ability to perform daily tasks, writing, for example."

"I don't know what I can say," Stoker said.

"You made a mistake, but you came to your senses and took action," Doyle said.

"But the damage that was done."

"I'm saying you have to get over it. Fight your way through it," Doyle told him. "If you don't, you won't be any good to anyone. And Florence needs you now more than ever. She needs your strength."

"But how? How do I do it?" Stoker's voice trembled.

Doyle gazed at him for a long while and then leaned forward.

"I'm afraid that's something you'll need to discover for yourself," he said.

They sat in silence for a while, Stoker gazing at the papers on his desk. After several moments, he looked up.

"Forgive me. I've gone on like this about all my problems and I didn't even ask you why you've come," Stoker said.

"I was hoping to have a word with Sir Henry," Doyle replied. "Would he be in yet this morning?"

Stoker glanced at his wall clock.

Stoker checked his watch. "Yes, I would think by now. Is it something where I might be of service?"

Doyle shifted uncomfortably in his chair.

"I'd like you to sit in with us, if you would," Doyle answered.

"Well, then, let me lead the way." Stoker rose from his chair and headed over to the door.

Doyle pulled himself out of his chair and they reached the doorway at the same time. The author paused and turned to Stoker.

"I have a suggestion," Doyle said.

"Yes?"

"Why not take Florence to see Professor Vambery? He knows more about Tepes than anyone else. Perhaps he can shed some light on these nightmares."

For the first time that morning, Stoker looked hopeful.

"That's an excellent idea!" he said. "I can't believe it didn't already occur to me."

"Well, your mind's been occupied elsewhere. Let me know once you arrange something with the professor," Doyle said. "I'd be very interested to hear what he has to say on the matter."

"Certainly."

"Now, Sir Henry?" Doyle gestured toward the stairway.

"Indeed."

CHAPTER 3

Sir Henry Irving could not hide his indignation. "You're doing what with your play?"

"I've made arrangements to have it produced elsewhere," Doyle answered.

Irving's bushy eyebrows raised a full notch. "You're taking your play elsewhere?"

Doyle nodded. "I had an offer that fits my needs, an excellent offer."

On their way to the Beefsteak Room, Stoker had a feeling of foreboding about the business Doyle intended to conduct with Irving. It was not so long ago when the two men had not been so chummy. Each were successful, widely celebrated men, and used to having their own way. Their initial clash of egos had been a constant threat to any ongoing relationship. It wasn't until they joined him, banding together in the hunt for Tepes, that the two men recognized qualities in one another that they truly admired. There was still competition between the two men, but for the most part, camaraderie had replaced animosity.

But now, in the time it took Doyle to accept an offer of tea and pastries from Irving's longtime valet, Walter Collinson, there it was, the crashing down of months of negotiations, and perhaps even a friendship. Stoker had done his best to get Sir Henry to secure Doyle's play, but he had dragged his feet. Now it was too late.

"I hope you understand," Doyle said. "Our negotiations here appeared to have sunk into the mire."

"May I ask with whom this arrangement is?" Irving inquired in an icy tone, swinging his long legs off the ottoman and unfolding his tall, slender body from his leather wing chair.

"Of course," Doyle shrugged. "It's going to make its way to the press soon, anyway. William Gillette will be taking it on."

Stoker winced as he watched Irving's expression darken.

"William Gillette, the American?" Irving asked through very thin lips. "The American actor?"

"He's quite popular, I understand," Doyle said.

"You think *he* would make a better Sherlock Holmes than I?" Irving challenged.

"My opinion has nothing to do with it. You didn't want to do the play," Doyle retorted.

Stoker could see that Doyle was a bit taken aback by the intensity of Irving's reaction.

"What was your objection?" Doyle continued. "You didn't feel you wanted to play the role of some common policeman?"

"I never really had the chance, did I?" Irving said, staring at his half-eaten breakfast on the table beside his chair as if it had offended him.

"Sir Henry, in all fairness, we failed to make a commitment regarding Mr. Doyle's play," Stoker reasoned. "And it's been months."

"Anything worth doing takes the time to do it correctly," said Irving. "I suppose that since Gillette is involved, the play will be produced in America."

"Yes, though if it's a success I assume it will find its way here."

"I'm sure it will," Stoker interjected.

The comment drew an icy glare from Sir Henry.

"An English character in a play that takes place in England produced in America with an American actor. Oh, that's just fine," Sir Henry growled.

Doyle took another sip of tea, gazing up at Sir Henry from his chair. "Honestly, Sir Henry, I didn't think you wanted to do it. On the other hand, Gillette arrived for our meeting in full costume. He's enthusiastic and so are his backers."

"Well," Sir Henry pointed his finger accusingly at Doyle's broad chest. "If you believe an American can play Sherlock Holmes more convincingly than an English actor, more convincingly than I, then so be it."

Without another word, Irving strode out of the room with a dramatic slam of the door.

Doyle looked over at Stoker. "I'm not sure what I expected, but that rather exceeded it."

"I'm sorry. He takes these things rather personally," Stoker explained. "He'll come around."

Doyle sighed, put down his tea and rose from his chair. "I am sorry for you in all this," he said. "The hours you spent in negotiations, trying to make this work."

"Well, I can't say I'm overjoyed, but business is business," Stoker replied.

Stoker escorted Doyle to the door and into the hallway.

"I can find my way from here," Doyle assured him.

"As you wish."

CHAPTER 4

S tochelo would have liked to have been riding faster. His horse was a handsome Nonius, healthy and swift when spurred. He had stolen him some two years before from a large farm near the mouth of the valley. But his job this day was to make certain the wagon kept moving, and the wagon could only move slowly with its load of new lumber.

"Somebody tighten the ropes," Jardani, the man driving the oxen team, called out to the two men riding with the load in the wagon. "I can feel it shifting."

As a man looked to the task, Jardani removed his wide-brimmed hat and pushed his long, dark hair back from his face. After making sure the bright green feather was secure in the band, he returned the hat to his head.

"Heaven help us all if he ever lost that feather," Zache said, riding beside the wagon on horseback, his hand resting on the hilt of the big Kukri knife that he always carried in his wide black belt.

Stochelo chuckled. Zache was a tough, hardened man, but also his friend and trusted lieutenant. He often found Zache's remarks humorous.

"Where did you get it?" Stochelo asked.

"It was part of a payment," Jardani answered. "I built some shelves for a tailor in Bistrita. He paid my fee and then threw in this feather after I admired it. I suppose my work pleased him."

It gratified Stochelo that Jardani's experience had been a good one. It wasn't always so. The Szgany people walked something of a narrow path with townspeople and villagers. They were generally viewed as not much better than common criminals.

The civilized gentry extended no trust at all toward the Szgany, but neither did they wish to go without the gypsy skills. The Szgany's abilities with carpentry, livestock work, and even sewing by the women were highly touted and sought after.

"Well, you make quite the pretty peacock," Zache joked.

"You both have envy," Jardani told them.

"Envy?" Zache asked.

"That I cut a better figure than either of you. I know how to dress," Jardani quipped.

They all laughed. Laughter was good; it made work easier. And they had had more work than usual over the past ten days.

Stochelo and his men had spent a full week gathering the lumber. What they couldn't steal, they cut and milled themselves. The amount of wood needed, how it should be milled, and how it should be used were described in the instructions provided to them.

He had found a good stand of trees for the job in the center of the valley and instructed his people to make camp in a nearby clearing. The camp site was sheltered from the eyes of travelers on the road, yet close to the place where the work would be done. Stochelo didn't consider his business to be the concern of outsiders, especially townspeople or villagers.

Some of the Szgany people lived in towns on the outskirts in hovels since they were not allowed to own property. Stochelo saw no reason to live in a village; he saw no reason to become one of them.

The nomadic tradition of his people that reached back hundreds of years was, and always would be, his life. If there was work to be done in the foothills at the base of the Carpathians, then their wagons would journey there. If there was money to earn at the mouth of the valley, then that is where the wagons would encamp. Perhaps they did not have the comfort of a warm brick house, but they had the freedom to live as they pleased.

The trees began to thin beside the road as it steepened and narrowed. The only sound was that of the horses and oxen's hooves crunching through the large patches of snow that spread along the road. By the time they were well into the Borgo Pass there was no longer enough road for Stochelo and Zache to remain beside the wagon. They urged their horses ahead of the oxen to lead the way. The other two men on horseback fell in behind the wagon.

The temperature dropped with the gained altitude, and the chill in the air was especially noticeable within the shadows cast by the tall, jagged rocks. They reached a crossroads where the most traveled and best maintained road was marked by signs on an ancient wooden post. Stochelo led his men onto the unmarked road that showed little sign of use or maintenance and climbed higher into the mountains.

The old, pitted road wound between rugged outcroppings of stone that towered over the men. Their route alternated from traveling through the rocks on either side of them to the sharp contrast of a steep downslope into the gorge on either side of the road. And then back into the shadows of more stone walls.

It was just after noon when they reached the point in their route that Stochelo knew well. The road pushed out of the cliffs onto a large, rocky plateau peppered with small groupings of trees. Above them, built upon the very peak of the mountain, rested the fortress ruins. The castle's crumbling stone walls had been built hundreds of years before as a stronghold against the Turks. The Ottomans had not been the only threat, of course, but every invader had been fiercely beaten back.

Jardani pulled his sheepskin vest tighter around his large, powerful frame. "Why do you think he returned?" he asked.

Stochelo glanced back to see Jardani gazing up at the castle. All the men were looking up at the place.

"I don't know," Stochelo answered.

"He was with the English?" Jardani asked.

"England is where we sent the boxes," Stochelo confirmed, straightening the ends of his prominent moustache.

"I wonder why he came back."

"It's not our place to question a boyar, and especially not the Voivode," Stochelo scolded. "He has returned and that's all there is to it."

"I liked it better when he was gone," Jardani said.

"Better?"

"The air was not so heavy. Fear makes the air heavy and the nights long."

"We have nothing to fear from him," Stochelo said, sounding a bit surprised.

"Don't we?"

"Do you even know what you're talking about" Stochelo challenged. Jardani was still young, with maybe twenty-four years, but he was a thinking man and sometimes that could prove vexing.

"It's foolish to think there is no danger to us in what we do," Jardani answered.

"Our people have served his house for centuries, and profited well for it," Stochelo pointed out.

"Yes," said Jardani. And then after a few moments, "Do you ever wonder what the price might be for that?"

"What are you talking about?" Stochelo asked.

"You know what he is. We all know what he is."

"It does not concern us," Stochelo insisted.

"Perhaps it should," Jardani mused.

Stochelo noticed that now Zache and the rest of the men were following the conversation.

"It concerns me to keep our people fed," Stochelo answered, irritated.

"If I murder an innocent man, and you've helped me by giving me a weapon or hiding me, are you, too, not guilty of the same murder?" Jardani asked.

"Innocent? Would you prefer he fed upon us instead of the villagers?" Stochelo asked. "Do you think any villager or townsman has any concern for us? Do you think they had any concern when our people were nothing but slaves? We've been free now for over thirty years, but they still treat us less than human."

"Not all of them," Jardani responded.

"It's of no matter to me if all of them do or not," Stochelo snapped. "What matters to me is that we survive, that we make a living."

"There is danger in working for him." Jardani's tone was firm, unequivocal. "Anyone should be able to see that."

"You talk like an old woman," Stochelo barked. "Life is full of danger. We might as well profit from it."

Jardani sighed. "I'm sorry. I didn't mean to cause anger. All I'm saying is that it was better when he was gone."

"You should be careful what you say here lest he hear your words," Zache cautioned.

"He sleeps now."

"You're a fool if you think his hearing is bound only to his waking hours," Stochelo snapped.

The last seventy-five feet of road leading to the castle narrowed onto a natural stone bridge with a two hundred foot drop into the craggy gorge on either side. Jardani kept a tight hold on the lines as they made their way across.

The wagon rolled into the shadow cast by the great barbican to the left of the castle gate, several stones in its corbel broken and crumbling. Jardani guided the oxen under the archway, its walls a solid four feet thick, and then under the spiked lower tips of the iron gate, chained open in its recess within the rampart.

The animals' hooves clattered against the paving stones and echoed off the stone walls. Jardani circled the courtyard until the oxen were facing the gate again and then pulled them to a stop, with the wagon positioned in front of the oak door. The door appeared small in the towering stone wall, only some six feet high and not quite three feet across. It hung on crude, rusted hinges and was banded together by iron straps secured with large, hand-formed nails and bolts. It had been built for defense, so only one man at a time could pass through it.

The courtyard was substantial, with years of weeds pushing up from between the paving stones and through the snow. Ancient vines snaked high up the walls, with many of them creeping into the castle through the windows. A deteriorating tower flanked the castle to the north, overlooking a precipice that no human army could ever breach. Two small turrets faced the courtyard, each strategically placed for observation and defense. A parapet ran along the top of the walls, originating from each end of the main building.

Stochelo and the other horsemen climbed down from their mounts.

"We'll take our midday meal then unload," Stochelo announced.

They took less than an hour to rest and eat, enjoying the jumări and goat cheese, washing it down with a strong local wine. Soon they were back at work, unloading the wagon, stacking the wood on the covered outer walkway leading to the ancient chapel.

As they worked, Stochelo noticed Jardani often looking at the windows of the main building and towers. It was as if the man was trying to peer into the interior of the castle, or perhaps he was being watchful should something suddenly come soaring out of one of them.

It wasn't only Jardani; he caught each of the work party glancing around the place, doing their best to hide their nerves. Despite better intentions, Stochelo found himself glancing up at the towers and the windows of the great hall.

As they worked, the silence of the place was broken now and then by the voice of one of the men asking some question or another, or someone offering direction. They had all the lumber unloaded and stacked under the cover of the walkway in under an hour.

Stochelo scrutinized the finished work and nodded his approval. "We'll go now, before the sun drops any lower."

"I thought you said there was nothing to fear," Jardani remarked.

The remark angered Stochelo, but he quickly overcame it. This place had a way of putting a man on edge. "I know what I said, but *he* is not the only thing dwelling here."

"Then let's be gone," Zache encouraged. "My daughters will have a meal waiting."

The men readied to leave.

"We'll come back in the morning," Stochelo advised. "Get an early start."

As they passed under the great spiked gate and moved onto the road, Stochelo glanced back at the decaying ruins. He felt a slight relief that they were leaving. Afraid or not, this was a place of death.

CHAPTER 5

The men were mostly quiet on the trip back down the mountain. Jardani watched Stochelo ahead of him, sitting straight and proud, and very sullen in the saddle. The long knife he always carried was in its scabbard on his belt. His hunting rifle hung from a leather tether secured to the saddle horn.

Stochelo's outward appearance was no different from any of the other Szgany men. A wide-brimmed hat shaded his head. His baggy, dirty white trousers were tucked into high, black boots. A wide leather belt studded with tarnished brass nails encircled the blousy linen shirt covered by a heavy fur-lined coat.

But Jardani knew Stochelo was not like most of the men of his clan. His physical strength, combined with an imposing strength of will, had established him as their leader. A keen and calculating mind had enabled him to keep a firm grip on that position for more years than Jardani could remember.

Zache pulled his horse up beside the wagon and nodded toward Stochelo.

"He's angry with you now, but it will pass," Zache said.

"He's a good man," Jardani answered. "But I wish he could see things more than just black and white."

"Perhaps if you someday come to lead our tribe, you'll understand his ways," Zache said.

"You'll be leading long before me. Besides, I'm not sure I'd want to. I don't know if I could," Jardani said.

"You could."

"When I was a boy, the money that service to the Voivode brought us impressed me," Jardani said. "I even felt proud, you know, that our people served a boyar."

"It's always been so," Zache said. "The Voivode has many protectors, but we are his protectors in the home country. I suppose there is some reason for pride in that."

"Yet, my father still warned me against straying out of the camp after sundown, especially alone," Jardani said. "And my mother taught me all the protections against the evil eye. It always puzzled me and made me wonder. If we were truly safe, then why be concerned?"

"I can't say that none of our people ever died by his hand, but it was only the ones who betrayed the Voivode's trust," Zache commented.

"My wife and I can live without fear. Your family can, your wife and daughters. But don't you ever think about the families in the villages, the towns? Husbands mourning for their murdered wives, mothers grieved to death over their children taken."

"There are times I do," Zache replied. "But this has been the way for many centuries."

"What about him?" Jardani gestured toward Stochelo. "I wonder if he's ever had any feelings for those preyed upon."

Zache was slow to answer and Jardani could see the older man choosing his words with care.

"I think, over the years, his ability to feel has slipped away," Zache said.

The sound of voices up ahead drew their attention. They had left the mountainous section of the Borgo Pass behind and were now in the high foothills. A few farmhouses spotted the countryside along the road and he realized they were close to the village of Poarta de Munte.

Up ahead, he saw Stochelo shift in his saddle, turning toward the source of the voices. A few yards farther up the road, they came into Jardani's view, a group of six Székely men from the village working in the cold slush to clear an irrigation ditch running along the edge of a small apple orchard.

The village men noticed them and stared. Jardani could see the distrust in their faces. It was always this way with people from the towns and villages.

Stochelo waved at the work party. "Hello, do you need any of our men to help you?" he called out. "A fair wage will bring you any help you need."

A tall, rugged looking fellow in a sheepskin vest, about Jardani's age, stepped forward. He had straw colored hair covered by an old, uneven hat.

"Not today," the fellow said pleasantly, leaning on his spade. "We're almost done."

Another older man gestured with the spade handle. "You can keep on moving," he called out, no kindness in his voice. "There's nothing here worth stealing."

Stochelo reined his horse to a stop. Jardani braked the wagon close behind him.

"I offer nothing but help and you speak to me with the respect of a swine," Stochelo challenged.

Jardani thought Stochelo looked more amused than annoyed as the villager pointed the spade handle at him. The man was middle-aged and of average height, his baggy pants caked with mud, his hat stained with sweat.

Again, the man jabbed the air with the spade. "We don't need you here. Just move along."

"Branko," the younger man called to him, his tone admonishing.

"Don't you speak to me like that," Branko barked at the young man. "I'm old enough to be your father."

"It's a public road," Stochelo called back. "I think we'll move on it as we like."

The man with the spade responded by spitting with contempt.

Jardani watched as Stochelo surveyed the orchard with exaggerated interest.

"It looks like it will be a fine year for apples," Stochelo said. "Perhaps we come back when the trees are full."

The man with the spade glared at Stochelo, and then the younger man stepped up to him and placed a gentle hand on his shoulder.

"Branko," the man said. "We have work to finish."

"I know there's work," Branko hissed, pulling away from the young man's hand, his eyes still fixed on Stochelo. "Show me respect, boy."

The younger man looked up and caught Jardani's gaze. Jardani saw no anger or hate in his eyes.

"They're just passing through," the rugged fellow said. "They've caused no trouble and we have to finish before the sun goes down."

Branko spat again and then turned his back to the road, returning to the work in the ditch. The rest of the men did the same.

Stochelo laughed and then coaxed his horse forward.

Jardani snapped the lines and his oxen pulled the wagon into motion with a lurch. They were almost past the orchard when Jardani glanced back. The rugged man was back at work with the others, digging in the dirt and mud in the ditch. Suddenly, he paused and glanced back up at the road. Again, Jardani met the man's gaze. Jardani nodded. The man nodded back and then returned to his digging.

CHAPTER 6

Doyle observed Florence was uneasy, but that was understandable under the circumstances. She sat in a comfortable chair in front of Professor Vambery's desk at his flat on Gordon Street. The professor, too, sat in front of the desk, having abandoned his regular chair in order to sit closer to, and facing Florence. He looked quite comfortable in a well worn green lounging jacket and old slippers. His thinning hair was unruly in contrast to his full, neatly trimmed beard.

"I hope you don't mind that I've invited Clarise to join us," Professor Vambery said to Florence. "I'd like her to take notes."

Clarise Vambery, her clear, smooth skin glowing, sat in her father's desk chair with pen and paper at the ready. She was dressed for work in a simple, practical white blouse and brown skirt. Her chestnut hair was tied back, hanging down past her shoulders.

Florence smiled at her. "Not at all. I think it's lovely we can all spend some time together, even if it's to examine my shortcomings," she said.

"If you ever had any shortcomings, I'm certain I never noticed them," Clarise said.

Doyle and Stoker had found seats among the stacks of books, papers and artifacts that filled most of the disorderly, but warm wood paneled room. Once a Professor of Oriental Languages at the University of Budapest, Vambery considered himself an adventurer and traveled whenever he could. His study was packed with mementos from his journeys.

Doyle watched Vambery chatting with Florence about nothing in particular for almost ten minutes, understanding that the professor's intent was for Florence to become more comfortable before they got to the business at hand. But the longer they chatted, the more anxious Stoker became.

Doyle leaned over close to him. "I'm very pleased you took my suggestion to come here," he whispered. "I'm sure it will prove worthwhile."

"I wasn't sure how Florence would take the idea, but she embraced it wholeheartedly," Stoker responded, also in a whisper. "She was just as enthusiastic about you being present. She's desperate to be rid of these nightmares and thinks you might have valuable insight to offer."

Doyle smiled. "I hope I won't disappoint her."

"She has a great deal of admiration for you," Stoker assured him.

The professor's voice drew their attention.

"Very good, very good," he said to Florence. "Now, Mrs. Stoker, I would be quite interested in hearing about these dreams you've been having."

Florence let out a long breath and then began. Vambery listened without comments or questions while Clarise jotted down every word in shorthand. Once she had finished, Vambery stared at his intertwined fingers for several moments.

"Your dreams? Are they always the same?" Vambery asked.

"I think I see a bit more detail each time. And in the distance covered as well," she answered. "When the dreams began, they didn't seem as long as they do now, and they didn't take me quite so far."

"How so?" the professor followed up.

"At first I'd be taken only as far as the valley," Florence explained. "And then I'd wake up. The next time I went far enough to see the village in the hills."

"And then, the next time you might see, the road beyond the village, and so on." Vambery added.

"Yes."

"Forgive me," the professor began, "but the point at which you see Tepes, are you able to tell me where that takes place?"

Florence considered the question before answering. "I can't say for certain, but I suspect that it's at those ruins, or whatever they are. I've never been able to really make it out."

"This is the place where he forces you to, to ingest his blood?" Vambery probed.

"Good God," Stoker blurted out. "Is that what he's doing?"

Vambery held up a quieting hand to Stoker.

"Is that what's happening, professor?" Florence shuddered.

"You described him opening his shirt and then opening a wound in his chest," Vambery said. "And then pulling you down toward the bleeding wound."

"But I don't have any recollection of actually," Florence couldn't finish the horrible thought.

"Is this a significant point, professor?" Doyle asked.

"It will depend."

"Upon what, father?" Clarise asked.

"There's no question in my mind that Vlad Tepes still has some kind of influence over Mrs. Stoker," Vambery explained.

"But how? In what way?" Stoker asked.

"You'll have to forgive me. I won't have many specific answers for you," the professor replied. "When you first contacted me about these dreams I assumed we'd be dealing with common nightmares. But the dreams you're describing aren't simply reliving an old terror."

"They were at first," Florence volunteered.

"As you said. But what you've described here today goes well beyond that. These dreams are consistent and progressive. I suspect some kind of outside power to be in play, though I cannot understand how."

"That's not very encouraging," Doyle sighed.

"Well, we aren't done as yet," Vambery replied before turning back to Florence. "My dear Mrs. Stoker, I believe we have more to learn here, but we need to go further in order to learn it."

Florence shuddered. "I've told you everything I can recall."

"No doubt, no doubt," Vambery assured her. "But I believe hypnosis might help you recall even more."

"Hypnosis," Doyle repeated. "Fascinating."

"I'm not sure I like the sound of that," Stoker added.

"It's perfectly safe," Clarise assured him. "I've watched father do it on several occasions, and he even did it to me once when I was having trouble sleeping. It was very relaxing."

"I wouldn't suggest it if I weren't certain that there is more going on here than we are currently aware," Vambery explained. "I believe Mrs. Stoker is telling us every detail she can remember, but dreams can contain many levels of consciousness. It's very possible that she is blocking or is being blocked from seeing all that there is to see."

"Being blocked?" Stoker repeated, surprised.

Vambery nodded.

"What would I have to do?" Florence asked.

"There is nothing for you to do," Vambery answered, reaching out and taking her hands in his. "Just sit as you are and relax, and worry about nothing. You are completely safe in this place."

"All right, then let's get on with it," Florence said. "If it'll help end these awful dreams, then I must do it."

"That's the spirit," the professor encouraged. "Now, I just want you to relax. Think about resting your entire body."

As the professor spoke, his voice became soft and soothing. Still holding Florence's hands, he raised them up to chest level and drew them apart so there were perhaps eight inches between them.

"I'm going to release your hands now, but I want you to keep them just where they are," he instructed.

Florence nodded, following the professor's instructions.

"Very good," the professor encouraged. "Now relax. Focus your mind on sinking back into your chair."

The professor raised his hand, open palm facing him, positioning it in Florence's line of sight in the space between her outstretched hands.

"You see the ring on my finger with the silver crest? I want you to look at it. See nothing else but the ring," Vambery urged. "You are relaxing. Your body is comfortable and relaxed in your chair. You feel your legs relaxing, sinking down into the chair. You feel your back, relaxed and comfortable. Your arms are relaxed."

Stoker, Doyle, and Clarise watched, absorbing the process.

"Now," the professor continued. "Your arms are comfortable now, relaxed. Your arms are growing heavy. They grow heavier and heavier with each passing moment. They will soon grow so heavy that their weight will draw them gently downward. When this happens, you will continue looking at and seeing only the ring. Your arms are so relaxed, so heavy."

After only a moment, Florence lowered her arms into her lap. Her eyes, now distant, did not waver from the ring.

Doyle, delighted with such an excellent demonstration of hypnotic induction, glanced over at Stoker. Stoker looked back at him with a face drawn in worry. Doyle placed a reassuring hand on his shoulder.

Vambery continued speaking to Florence in soothing tones for several minutes. Once he was satisfied with the depth of her trance, he looked across the desk at Clarise. "We are ready to begin," he announced in a soft whisper.

"Now, Mrs. Stoker," Vambery began, his voice soft. "You have been taking a journey."

"A journey," Florence repeated.

"Yes, journeying in your dreams," Vambery elaborated.

"Yes."

"I would very much like to see what you see on your journey," Vambery continued, maintaining his voice in a gentle, even tone. "You will describe it to me."

Florence hesitated a moment, then said, "Yes."

"Excellent, we will leave this very minute."

Professor Vambery prompted Florence through her dream journey. He never asked for any location or description, but formulated what he wished to know in his mind, and then instructed her to tell him about it.

Florence described the journey as starting with water; she could see nothing, but heard water lapping against the hull of a ship. This was a detail that she had never before voiced. There were other elements never before revealed as well. She heard more than one foreign language being spoken on the various legs of her journey, but German was the only one she could identify. There was a brief portion in her narration chronicling landscape moving past a train carriage window. This was quite different since Florence had repeatedly described her movement as floating or soaring through the air.

By the time Florence began describing what appeared to be a fortress or castle at the peak of a mountain, everyone in the room was leaning forward in their chairs. When she described the figure of the man blended with the darkness, her body shuddered, and it took Professor Vambery some effort to keep Florence calm enough to continue. Even though she never mentioned his name, they knew of whom she was speaking. The sharp teeth, the eyes so intense it was as if they glowed. It could only be *him*.

"He is opening his coat," Florence told them. "And he's torn open his shirt." She pushed her body back in her chair, as if trying to retreat from something horrible.

"You are safe," Vambery assured her. "We are all here with you. None of this is real."

"He's taken hold of me," she whimpered.

"We are here with you."

"His nails are like claws. He uses them to open one of his veins. Blood, blood. He's pulling me to him."

The anguish in her voice started Stoker out of his chair, but Vambery held up a hand to him and he stopped.

Vambery leaned closer to Stoker and whispered, "You must keep hold of yourself a few minutes longer. This is a critical point in her dream and we must see it through."

Stoker settled back in his chair, but Doyle could tell he was far from calm.

"Mrs. Stoker," Vambery continued. "He speaks to you, does he not? Tell us his intentions."

"I don't know, I don't know," Florence cried out. "I can't get free of him. No, no. He's pulling me to him. I can taste the blood on my lips. No."

Vambery recoiled at this detail, and concern flooded his face. Clarise was so rattled by the description that she dropped her pen and had to recover it.

Stoker sat frozen while an expression of horror spread across his face.

The professor appeared lost in thought for several moments before addressing Florence again. "Where are you now?"

"It's dark," Florence said, her voice trembling.

"You are in the fortress with him?"

"It's so dark," she repeated.

"Yes, it is dark. But there is moonlight to help you. Look, let the moonlight help you see."

Florence squinted.

"Details of your surroundings are becoming visible," Vambery prodded. "Do you see them?"

Florence cocked her head to the side and nodded.

"What do you see now?"

"Pathways," Florence responded.

"Pathways, excellent. Can you see anything else?"

"Pathways, signs."

"Signs?" The response obviously puzzled the professor.

"Does she mean road signs?" Doyle asked in a whisper.

Again, Vambery held up a hand.

"Tell me what the signs say," Vambery instructed.

Florence strained to see through the darkness. "I don't know. I can't see."

"There are paths and signs. There is more. Tell me what more you see."

"Bars."

"Bars," the professor repeated. "I don't understand. Tell me more about bars."

"Bars," she repeated. "Cages. Cages with animals."

"The bandstand," Doyle whispered again. "Ask her if she can see the bandstand."

"There is more to see," Vambery told Florence. "A small structure. You see it, don't you?"

Florence cocked her head again. "I'm on the steps."

"You are on the steps. And he? He is on the steps with you?" Vambery inquired.

"Yes," Florence moaned, tears forming in her eyes. "He won't let go. I can't get free."

The depth of concern in Vambery's eyes was unmistakable. "Oh my," he muttered, leaning back in his chair. "Oh, my."

CHAPTER 7

I t took Professor Vambery only a few moments to remove Florence from her hypnotic state. She seemed relaxed and even refreshed, none the worse for wear. Vambery, though, appeared shaken.

Doyle saw it, and he observed Stoker noticed it as well.

"What is it, father?" Clarise asked, concern in her voice.

He glanced at her without responding, his eyes troubled.

"Professor?" Stoker began. "Please, tell me what you think?"

"Perhaps the ladies would care to step out and make us all some tea," Vambery suggested. "We can discuss it then."

"I assure you, if I can tolerate these dreams and the things we all saw last year, I can hear whatever you might have to say now," Florence stated, her tone firm.

Vambery looked to Stoker for reassurance. Stoker nodded.

"It troubles me greatly," Vambery began. "All of it is of great concern."

"The worst must be behind us," Doyle offered. "Just come out with it."

"Mrs. Stoker," Vambery took her hands in his. "I must ask you this outright, though I'll find it painful to do so."

"Just ask, sir," Florence said. "I know you mean me no harm and only wish to help."

The professor nodded. "Do you specifically remember Tepes forcing your mouth to his wound on that bandstand in the Zoological Gardens?"

Florence gave the question some thought before answering, but then shook her head. "No, not really."

"Under hypnosis, you told me you tasted blood. Do you have any conscious memory of tasting blood in your mouth that night?"

Florence began to answer, but caught herself. Her brow wrinkled in concern, and then a look of dread filled her eyes. "Oh, no," she managed. "Oh, no."

"What is it?" Stoker asked.

Florence looked into her husband's eyes. "I thought I must have bitten my tongue when I fell on the steps, or cut my lip," she admitted, her voice heavy with despair.

"Why didn't you mention it then?" Stoker asked.

"Why would I? Compared to everything else that night, it seemed like nothing."

"Indeed," Vambery agreed. "The question is now, why did he stop?"

"Stop what?" Doyle asked.

Vambery adjusted his position in his chair and gathered his thoughts. "Do you recall our discussion once it was determined Miss Westen's corpse had traces of blood in the mouth?"

"It *was* several months ago," Doyle shrugged.

"I haven't forgotten a word of it," Clarise blurted. "It still gives me shivers."

"The vampire can kill their victim outright or turn them," Vambery continued.

"That's what happened to poor Lucinda," Stoker volunteered.

Florence lowered her head and stared into her clenched hands.

"In the case of Miss Westen, Tepes took her to the point of death, but before killing her, forced her to drink his blood. It wasn't until she had done so he took her life," Vambery said.

"You're saying he had the same intentions for Florence?" Stoker's face grew pale.

"I am," the professor answered. "And I ask again, why did he stop? Why didn't he kill her when he had her?"

The room remained silent for several moments.

"The cross," Stoker blurted out.

"What cross?" Doyle asked.

"I gave Florence the cross I'd been carrying," Stoker explained. "Tepes wanted nothing to do with it."

"I put it on right after you gave it to me," Florence assured him.

"That could be our answer," said Vambery.

"The cross stopped him from, well?" Clarise asked.

"If the cross had come into his sight, it would be very difficult to bear," Vambery explained. "The cross represents the purity of Christ wherein he is pure evil. For him, there is no reconciliation."

"I recall the cross and chain being outside my dress when Bram and the others found me," Florence said.

"Then we thank God for it," said Vambery. "But my greater concern is that Tepes was successful in getting you to ingest his blood at all."

"What does it mean?" Stoker asked.

"I can offer no exactness in any of this," said the professor. "When Mrs. Stoker first related her dreams to us, I believed we were hearing of events that could happen. Possible events in a possible future. But this terrible thing has already happened. It happened that night in Regent's Park. His blood now runs through her veins. If Mrs. Stoker dies with his blood running through her, she will become like him."

"Like Lucy," Florence said.

"Then what's to be done?" Doyle asked.

"We must kill him. We must kill Tepes," answered Vambery. "It's the only way. If we're to believe the legends. And at this point, it would be wise to do so. If he still lives when she dies, her soul will be lost."

"That's enough!" Stoker almost shouted. "Can't you see you're frightening her?"

"Bram, you're being rude," Florence reprimanded. "I insisted on being present and if I'm getting more than I asked for or expected, then I have only myself to blame."

"Killing him is one thing. But how can we even find him?" Doyle asked. "He left the country for God knows where months ago."

"God indeed knows where," Vambery said. "And if I am correct, so does Mrs. Stoker."

"What?" Florence sat upright with surprise.

"I've no explanation for it, but Tepes has somehow extended his reach to her. Mr. Stoker has stopped his wife from leaving the safety of her home on more than one occasion. And Mrs. Stoker is unaware she is even attempting to do so. Her dreams contain landmarks, and they progress in clarity and the distance they cover with each occurrence. Perhaps the phenomenon is because of his blood in her veins, perhaps not. But this is more than simply the symptoms of a traumatized victim."

"But what does it all mean, and can we do something about it?" Doyle asked.

"If I am correct, he is attempting to draw Mrs. Stoker to him," Vambery explained. "I can't imagine why, but he wants her. Perhaps he is just vindictive enough to see her as unfinished business."

"Revenge," Stoker said.

"Perhaps, but I don't believe he will stop as long as they both live," Vambery responded. "It's imperative we hunt him down and kill him before anything can happen to Mrs. Stoker."

Vambery turned to focus his attention on Doyle. "You asked what can be done about it. I believe Mrs. Stoker can lead us to him if we allow it."

"What on earth are you suggesting?" Stoker asked, horrified.

"We allow Mrs. Stoker to follow her dreams, and we make sure we follow her," Doyle explained.

"You're proposing using my wife as bait?" Stoker asked, tensing with astonished disapproval.

"I believe every man here to be too much a gentleman to refer to me as *bait*," Florence assured him.

"If I'm right," Vambery remarked, "Tepes will continue to draw Mrs. Stoker to him. If we keep her close every moment, all we must do to find him is follow where she leads."

"But father," Clarise protested, "He could've gone anywhere, anywhere in the world."

"We know he ruled Wallachia, so it's not unreasonable to assume that he'd take refuge there or nearby," Vambery answered.

"His homeland would logically provide him the best sanctuary," Doyle agreed.

"He's familiar with it; he'd have the most protection there. Wallachia merged with Moldavia, Transylvania, Bukovina, along with a few other territories to form the Romanian United Principalities. That might blur the lines a bit, but we can make our way to that general region and then follow Mrs. Stoker to the precise location."

"Absolutely not," Stoker fumed. "She was almost killed the first time. Curse me to hell if you think I'll allow her anywhere near that murderous animal again."

"But friend Stoker," Professor Vambery answered. "What if something happens, God forbid it, in the meantime? An illness, an accident? It could be anything. You must think of the eternal consequences."

Stoker looked miserable. He gazed at Florence, dazed and fearful, sunk low in her armchair.

"You can count on my help," Doyle offered. "It never rested well with me. Tepes getting away from us like he did."

Stoker rose from his chair, and taking Florence's hand, helped her from hers. "I won't do it," he stated with great bitterness. "I cannot do it."

He led his wife to the door and then turned back to the room. "I'm grateful to you, professor, I really am. But I've already come too close to causing my wife's death and there is no circumstance that will make me repeat that kind of foolishness."

With a final nod to all, Stoker ushered Florence through the doorway and closed the door behind them.

CHAPTER 8

He could feel the strength ebb slowly into his body well before he awakened. It was the same sensation each evening as the burning sun dropped in the sky until the blackness of night overwhelmed its heat. As the light faded, his strength returned.

Now fully awake, Tepes remained still for a few additional moments, sensing his surroundings, listening for any unfamiliar sound. With little effort, he pushed open the heavy lid of the coffin and rose. The blackness of the vault was complete, but he could see well enough.

Nearby, his surviving two wives stirred and climbed from their sleeping places, their long, dull white gowns slithering over the edges of the coffins behind them. His two wives in life were long dead. The first from suicide, the second from plague. His union to these two was a marriage of blood. He did not bother acknowledging them, and they watched in silence as he walked across the burial chamber to the stone stairway.

The others were rising now too; he sensed them in the other lower regions of the castle. These were souls brought into the eternal night by his wives, used for a time as playthings before being cast away out of boredom. Some of them then turned others they knew from life. Friends and family were the easiest to deceive.

They were uneducated peasants, fools who had not possessed enough sense to protect themselves from his kind. In their reborn existence, they functioned as mindless animals, resting, hunting, killing, and feeding. There were perhaps a dozen of them in the castle now, all of them forbidden from the main vaults, allowed to rest and seek refuge from the daylight hours only in the lowest chambers of the castle.

He had always been more discerning when creating another of his kind. It was serious business, with eternal consequences. Without exception, it was always part of a greater purpose, and always to further his immediate plans.

He felt the hunger churning in him as he made his way to the upper rooms. Conditions had not improved since his return; he had not expected them to. He had not expected to be forced to return.

The windows of the south tower provided a strategic view. Off to the west was the valley, containing farms and villages. Since he had returned, the people had become more cautious than ever. And in his absence, some had become emboldened. A farmer in one of the foothill villages had even dared to take his third wife from him.

He realized it was her own doing. She had been young when he took her as his wife; she had always been young in mind and spirit as well, often foolish from the combination. The centuries of life had done little to remedy this.

In her hunger, she had become careless, lingering too long into the night. Not heeding her instincts, she had allowed herself to be trapped in a barn, cornered until sunrise. Weakened by the heat of the morning sun, the farmer and his two sons overpowered her. While the sons pinned her to the ground, the farmer drove a sharpened fence stake through her heart. In a final outrage, one son removed her head with a wheat scythe.

He felt no loss or remorse, no sadness at learning of her death. He was incapable of such emotions. It was of no matter, but he could allow no one to take such liberties with his house or its members. He would see to it the farmer paid for the murder. And if it came to be he could not locate the farmer, then the village would pay in his stead.

Besides, one wife might have been lost to him, but the English woman would be his soon enough. Powers were already in motion to make it so. He would have her, and in having her he would satisfy his revenge on the men who forced his unplanned departure from England.

He would kill them all, but the woman would remain his through eternity.

A tingling awareness swept through him, the instincts that had kept him alive through many lifetimes. He smiled to himself, a pleasureless smile, and wondered if they'd be so bold if they knew he was already aware of their presence. He sensed three of them climbing the tower wall at the opposite side of the structure. His mind visualized them in their climb, like monstrous rats, their clawlike fingers gripping the moss covered stones, their toes digging into the crevices as they ascended toward the window behind him.

The soft scraping sound as they slithered over the window sill told him they had arrived. Turning to face them was unnecessary for him to know they were standing in front of the window some twenty steps away.

"You enter my house uninvited," Tepes challenged, his voice as sharp and hard as steel.

"We would speak with you, Voivode," one of them responded uneasily, in a high pitched voice.

Unhurried, he turned to face them. They stood in the soft beam of light from the half moon streaming through the window. Two of them were barefoot, attired in filthy, threadbare clothing, almost rags, stained copiously with dried blood. Their hair was long and matted, one dark headed and the other with locks the color of straw. They had been very young men when they died, not even as old as twenty.

The one whom had spoken had managed somewhat better. He was older, both in the age when his life was taken, and in the years he had existed in his current life. His tattered, ancient military jacket covered a dirty tunic, also caked with dry blood. Filthy breaches were tucked into riding boots, their leather dry and cracked. An old cap adorned his head, strands of greasy, tangled hair escaping from beneath it.

Tepes gazed upon them, his disdain infinite. They were not familiar to him, but he knew their kind well. These fools were little better than the near-animals he allowed to rest in the lower catacombs. They were only slightly more aware than predatory animals and not much smarter. Incapable of blending in with the inhabitants of a village or town, their only hope to feed would be to ambush or run down some careless prey. It was remarkable to him they had managed to survive at all.

"It must be a matter of great importance," he replied. "For you to come here with such impudence."

"We would speak with you," the one in the military jacket repeated more nervously than before.

"Then speak."

All of them shuffled with discomfort, and then after a few moments of silence, the military jacket fool took two uneven steps forward. "You have returned," he declared.

He remained silent, seeing little reason to respond to the obvious.

"You have returned. Things have become hard again," the military jacket lout hissed.

"Hard," the straw-haired fellow repeated.

"Ah, two of you speak," Tepes observed.

"You have returned and the people are frightened again," military jacket elaborated.

"And what is that to me?"

"They were not so frightened, they were not so cautious, when you were away," military jacket continued. "They take more care and it is hard now, more difficult to feed."

"And you," the straw-haired man growled. "You take many for yourself. Little is left for us."

"You leave little for us and make it harder," military jacket hissed again. "When you are gone again, it will be better."

The military wretch pulled a long and well preserved dagger from a scabbard under his jacket and leaped forward, his sharp teeth bared in a snarl. His companions withdrew crude, short spears sharpened from forest wood from under their rags and rushed after him.

Tepes avoided the leader with little effort. None of them saw him move, only a blur of motion. He applied a vice-like grip to the man's forearm with one hand and ripped the dagger out of his fist with the other, tearing two fingers off the hand as he did so. The fellow screamed as Tepes threw him across the room, where he landed in a heap against the wall.

The other two foolishly charged. Tepes slashed the dagger through the air, removing the head of the dark-haired one. A dull thud echoed through the room as the head hit the floor and rolled several feet before coming to rest face down on the stones. In only a moment, the head was nothing more than a skull, and as the body twitched, it decomposed until all that was left was a heap of bones spotted with rotting flesh.

Seeing two of his companions dispatched, the straw-haired peasant turned to flee. He moved faster than any living human could, but it did him little good. The fool wore a confounded expression when Tepes appeared between him and the window.

In a single movement, Tepes pulled the makeshift spear from his hand, spun the point around and drove it deep into his chest. A hideous scream escaped the creature's throat before being strangled by the blood flooding his lungs. Tepes dragged the body to the tower window and tossed it out as casually as if he were disposing of a piece of rotten fruit. He heard the bones clattering against the rocks below moments later.

In the few moments it had taken for his friends to be destroyed, the leader of the unlucky band pulled himself to his feet. Leaning against the wall, he watched as Tepes advanced on him.

"Your companions have deserted you."

The man wiped his bleeding hand across his military jacket. "Great Voivode," he spat. "Stories of your strength and power are ancient, but we are starving."

"By your own blundering," Tepes responded. "And now this folly."

"What else was left to us?"

The leader's eyes fell on the discarded wooden spear. He rushed over to the crude weapon, picked it up with his thumb and remaining two fingers, and readied himself in a defensive position.

Tepes walked toward him, observing the dismay on the man's face as he discovered he was incapable of movement. So great was his fear that his wits had all but abandoned him.

Tepes reached the man and effortlessly pulled the wooden spear from his hand, throwing it across the room. Gazing upon him as if he were a grotesque, but fascinating insect, Tepes took the man in an iron grip, raised the dagger and thrust it deep into his chest. The leader screamed pitifully as Tepes sawed a jagged opening with the blade. Dropping the dagger to the floor, he drove his hand deep into the wound. The screams increased as he found the throbbing heart and gripped it in his fist. With brutal strength, he wrenched it from the man's chest. He was sure the fool glimpsed it before he died and his body rotted away.

Tepes studied the blood staining his hands and clothing. His coat and shirt would require cleaning, another annoyance resulting from his three visitors. It would have to wait for another time. He became aware again of the hunger gnawing at him.

Looking out across the valley far below, he stepped up onto the window ledge. It was probable that he would have to travel farther than the foothill villages, but he would visit them first, anyway. With his long, dark coat billowing around him, he leaped out into the night.

CHAPTER 9

Eduard held the recorder at arm's length, admiring his work in the lamplight. The polished wood felt smooth and cool in his hands. The center bore was perfect, and he had chiseled out the windway by hand. His father's trade was carpentry and Eduard was now more appreciative than ever before for the skills his father had taught him. He had spent most of his evenings working on the recorder in his father's shop, a small barn behind their house converted for the purpose.

It had taken several weeks to complete the instrument, but Valeria was worth it. She was the most beautiful girl in the village. He had admired her for months, but she didn't seem to even notice him. And then one day he caught her looking at him. Instead of turning away when she knew she was caught, she smiled. It was then he knew Valeria liked him as well.

They were both sixteen, so it wouldn't be long before they could formally enter a courtship. But Eduard had to act with haste. Valeria was a popular girl and there would be other suitors. When he learned she loved music and knew how to play the cobza, he decided to make the recorder. It would be impossible for Valeria to mistake the seriousness of his intentions with a gift so special.

Each day he spent working on Valeria's gift, the anticipation of seeing her receive it increased. He felt like he would burst if he didn't put the recorder into her hands this very moment. He placed the instrument on a nearby table and went to the rack beside the front door to get his coat.

"What do you think you're doing?" his father asked from across the room.

"I finished the recorder for Valeria," Eduard answered as he slipped into his coat.

His father took a puff on his pipe and rose from the rocking chair he had placed in front of the hearth. "Valeria, the Banik's girl."

"I'm going to give it to her," Eduard explained.

"Now?"

Eduard noticed his mother had stopped cleaning the dishes in the kitchen. She was looking at him with a little smile on her face and he felt embarrassed.

His father crossed the room and picked up the recorder, examining the craftsmanship. "This is very fine work, Eduard. You did an excellent job."

"It's beautiful," his mother added.

"Thank you."

"Valeria will love this," his father said, handing the recorder to him. "Give it to her tomorrow."

"Tomorrow?" Eduard protested. "But I must see her now."

"The sun set an hour ago," his father said.

"Her house is just across the square. I'll be fine," he argued.

"You'll be fine because you won't be taking foolish risks. See the girl tomorrow." With that, his father returned to his chair by the fire.

Eduard recognized the finality in his father's tone well enough to know that arguing would be fruitless. As a last hope, he looked at his mother.

"She'll still be there tomorrow." His mother smiled and then returned to her kitchen.

He felt a little sick inside as he returned to his room at the back of the house. Not bothering to remove his coat, he shut the door and sat down on his bed, rotating the recorder in his hands. What if someone else made their intentions known to Valeria before he did? He had to see her tonight.

He rose from the bed and went to the window. Valeria's house was so close; it wouldn't take long. He would slip out, give her the gift and tell her how he felt, and he would be back in his room before his parents knew he was gone. The string of garlic hanging from the window latch swayed as he pulled open the sash. A few moments later, he was outside.

He stayed close to the houses as he made his way around the square toward Valeria's house. Her front door faded into view through the darkness, and a shiver of anticipation swept through him. He picked up his pace. A soft rush of wind suddenly blew over him and he heard a flapping sound behind him, like the sound a sheet made when his mother snapped it before folding. Eduard turned around to look.

Standing before him was an older man, tall and thin, wearing a long, flowing black coat. His complexion was pallid and a gray moustache drooped around his thin, red lips. His eyes were penetrating, glowing like dark embers in the night gloom. But more disturbing was the expression on the man's face. He looked like a hungry animal.

Eduard knew in that instant he was gazing upon the Voivode, nosferatu. He felt the recorder slip from his fingers and heard it clatter upon the paving stones. And then he felt the urine spread across his pants and trickle down his legs.

Alexander Ciernik patted his stomach and then thumped his fist on the table.

"That was the best tochitură I've ever eaten," he stated, spooning up the last of the stew.

"You say that every time." Tatiana picked up the bowl and carried it to the kitchen.

"And I mean it every time."

Tatiana laughed, and he watched her as she went about her business in the kitchen. She was twenty-four and Alexander thought her the most beautiful woman in the village. They had been together since they were both seventeen, working hard to build a life together.

"All of you," a voice shouted from outside. "Come out."

The voice was unfamiliar to Alexander. It had a harsh, metallic ring and penetrated the walls of his house with an unnatural clarity.

Tatiana abruptly stopped what she was doing. "What was that?"

"I warn you all," the voice came again. "Come out!"

Alexander pushed back from the table and hurried to the door.

"Alex," Tatiana breathed his name, alarmed.

He pulled back the bolt on the door and pulled it open an inch. Peering through the opening, he gasped in horror.

Standing in the middle of the village square was a tall man dressed in black from head to toe. His hair was iron gray and fell to his shoulders.

Alexander knew right away what he was looking at, and it sent a chill through his body. Even more terrifying was that the monster had Eduard Tesar in his grasp. The boy was limp with fear, his mouth hung open, his breath coming in quick gasps. His eyes were open wide but seemed to see nothing. The Voivode held him upright, the long fingers of his left hand wrapped around the boy's neck.

"Come out, all of you," the nosferatu shouted again.

Slivers of light appeared around the square as doors cracked open. Alexander looked toward the Tesar house. Eduard's father, Marek, stood in his doorway, a look of pure anguish on his face.

Lenka Tesar appeared behind her husband and pushed past him.

"No, no," she wailed.

Marek grabbed hold of her as she tried to run to her son. As he pulled her back, she fainted. He lowered her to the floor inside the door and then turned back to face the horror in the square.

Alexander could hear the terrified utterances seeping out from the half-open doors around the square.

It's him!

God protect us.

The Voivode, it's the Voivode.

He has the Tesar boy.

Why? Why is he here?

"Yes," the Voivode called out. "Now you see."

"Oh, God," Tatiana said, crossing herself as she looked out the window.

"Release him," Marek called out across the square. "Please, please let him go."

Alexander saw the Voivode turn his gaze upon the boy's father. His mouth formed a perverted smile, a smirk of superiority and disdain.

"Did my woman ask for release?" the nosferatu asked. "Was she given mercy?"

"Please," Marek begged.

"Which of you dared to kill her? Which of you dared to murder a member of my house?"

Alexander knew that the farmers who had done the deed didn't even live within the village boundaries.

"Will no one come forward?" the Voivode taunted. "Is this a place of cowards?"

"My son had nothing to do with her death," Marek yelled.

"Your son?" The monster looked at the boy as if he was a choice cut of beef.

There was little time and little hope for Eduard. Alexander looked helplessly at Tatiana and she looked back with tears welling in her eyes. If anything was to be done, it would have to be done quickly.

Lenka Tesar began regaining consciousness. She pulled herself up to her knees and steadied herself on the door frame. With a loud, anguished moan, she began weeping.

"No one will come forward," the Voivode growled. "It is of no matter. But know this, all of you. Cause harm to one of mine and you will enjoy more of my visits."

Alexander's eyes fell on the cross Tatiana had hung between the door and the front window. It was almost two feet long and hand-painted in muted colors. He pulled it from the wall and ran through the doorway. Tatiana screamed his name as he left the safety of their home.

Alexander saw the Voivode level his hateful gaze on him as he charged, the cross extended in front of him. He was relieved to see that he was not the only one with the idea. At least two other men had left their houses and were racing straight for the monster, crosses or crucifixes in their hands.

The nosferatu saw them all. Its mouth curled in a terrible sneer and it hoisted Eduard up straighter.

"I will begin with this one," the Voivode said.

Alexander ran harder. He was almost there.

The Voivode whirled around. His great coat fluttered out around him, and Alexander thought he saw the monster move forward and upward in a single blur of motion. He heard Eduard cry out and then they were gone.

The other men gathered around Alexander, all of them still holding their crosses. They stared at the spot where the Voivode and the boy had been standing only a moment earlier. It was as if they had never been there, and the only sound to be heard was the wailing of Eduard Tesar's mother.

CHAPTER 10

"You never mentioned what the occasion is?" Florence asked as they climbed down from the brougham at the Lyceum Theatre's stage door in the alley off of Wellington Street.

"I don't believe Sir Henry mentioned anything specific," Stoker answered, helping her down from the coach step. "He just said he'd appreciate it if we could join him for dinner tonight. He rarely has these small gatherings, so I thought it good to accept."

"Of course," Florence said.

She looked lovely in a long, simple, deep blue gown with a modestly low neckline and short sleeves. A silver broach accompanied her silver cross this night, and white gloves completed the outfit. Stoker was dressed for dinner as well in the traditional black dress suit with white neckerchief, and open waistcoat.

"We're not late, are we?" she asked.

He pulled his watch from his waistcoat pocket and flipped open the lid. "No, it's just eight."

Stoker paid the driver and escorted Florence to the stage door. Holding it open for her, he glanced at the brougham clattering away. The coach passed a man in a well worn boilerman cap leaning against the wall in the shadows at the opposite end of the alley. It was an odd place for anyone to sit, so Stoker observed the man. The fellow glanced his direction, tipped his hat and then looked away again, not moving from his position. He was probably waiting to meet his mates for an evening of drinking, Stoker thought as he stepped into the theater.

He greeted the doorman and led Florence through the wings, guiding her through the bustle of actors and stagehands involved in the evening's entertainment. The company leasing the theater offered entertainment ranging from plays of light comedy to variety shows that Sir Henry deemed "Only one rung up from burlesque on the ladder of poor taste." Tonight it was a play.

Entering the Beefsteak Room, Stoker was surprised to be greeted by not only Sir Henry Irving, but Arthur Conan Doyle, Professor Vambery and Clarise. Clarise was radiant in a simple but elegant pastel yellow gown.

"Goodness," Florence exclaimed after greetings had been exchanged. "I had no idea that you'd all be here. How nice."

"Nor did I," Stoker added, a hint of suspicion in his voice.

"That's my doing, I must admit," Sir Henry answered, stepping forward and ushering the Stokers into the room.

"And mine," Doyle added.

"Mr. Doyle stopped by and filled me in on the situation with Florence," Irving continued.

"So you two are speaking again, as long as it's about my business," Stoker scoffed.

"Bram," Florence squeezed her husband's arm.

"Our differences aside, we all share a concern for Florence's well-being, and yours for that matter," Irving returned, his eyes narrowing and an edge in his voice.

"It's as they say, Mr. Stoker," Clarise offered. "We're all very concerned."

"We appreciate that," Stoker answered.

"If there's something to be done, then I think it's the best course to give it proper consideration," Professor Vambery said.

"A conversation over a nice dinner can't do any harm," Doyle added. "And you might even see things differently."

"That's unlikely," Stoker muttered.

"Well, I'm quite hungry and have been looking forward to dinner," Florence declared.

With his customary excellent timing, Collinson stepped into the room just as she finished her sentence.

"Dinner is ready to be served," he announced.

"Ah, excellent. Shall we, then?" Irving invited with enthusiasm.

They took their seats at the table. Collinson, along with two servers in full livery, made certain the food and drink flowed efficiently.

From the watercress soup, to the poached salmon with sauce mousseline, everyone kept the conversation to general topics. But as the boeuf bourguignon and French green beans were placed on the table, Sir Henry drew everyone's attention with a nervous cough.

"From what I've been told, there's little question that Florence is still at considerable risk," Sir Henry began.

Stoker frowned but remained silent. Florence put down her fork and gave Irving her attention.

"The long and the short of it seems to be that, whatever this hold Tepes has on our dear Florence, it's certain that he won't stop his advances on her," Sir Henry continued.

"He's gone now," Stoker said. "He's no longer even in the country. She's in no physical danger. She just needs time to heal, and to forget."

"I fear there's more to it than that," Vambery said.

"I'm aware of your opinion," Stoker responded.

"It will not stop, he will not stop," the professor insisted.

"No one can say that for sure," argued Stoker.

"Denying the facts repeatedly won't change them," Doyle said. "But at any rate, why take the risk? If we take the offensive, it gives us some control over the situation."

"Your idea of taking the offensive is to use my wife as bait."

"There's no question it's dangerous, but it's the only chance we have of finding him," Vambery said.

"We'll take every precaution. At least one of us will be with Florence every moment, and we now know his weaknesses," Doyle asserted.

"We'd be on his ground," Stoker challenged. "We'd be in his territory. God knows what we'd be walking into."

"But we'll all be there," said Irving. "I remember too well the things he did. I saw what he did. And in the face of all that I'd still like to go; I'd like to see this through so he can do no more harm."

"You'll need someone to help with the various languages, so I will be useful along those lines," Professor Vambery volunteered. "And you know, I'm well versed in the customs of Romania, Transylvania, wherever we might find ourselves."

"I'm not sure I like the sound of that," Clarise said. "Father's health hasn't been what it should be."

"Your concern is noted, my dear, but I'll be fine."

"And I was thinking about Morgan Quincey," Irving interjected.

"The American cowboy?" Florence asked.

"Indeed, he was quite fond of Miss Westen, and I think he might want to be in on this. Besides, he's younger than the rest of us men, and I'm sure that kind of energy would come in handy. I could wire him."

"I've already explained," began Stoker, "that I have no intention of placing Florence in danger again. And it's not just dangerous as Professor Vambery said, it's outrageously dangerous."

"But it's still the best solution, and possibly the only solution," Vambery countered.

"I'd ask none of you to walk into such a dangerous situation," Stoker declared.

"That's very noble of you, Mr. Stoker," said Clarise. "But I saw how you all worked together and fought together when that terrible creature was in London. It gives one great confidence in you all. If there's even a small possibility that you can free Mrs. Stoker from these dreadful circumstances, then you must act on it."

"It's not that I don't appreciate what all of you are willing to do, but I simply can't allow it. I've put Florence through enough already and I won't put her through anything more," Stoker insisted, his voice weak.

"Bram, perhaps we need to consider it," Florence said.

"Florrie, no." He sounded miserable.

"What if Professor Vambery's right? What if there's even more to it? What if he won't stop?"

"You're safer in London," Stoker said. "I promise you."

"It's not as if we don't understand the risks," Irving added. "We've discussed the matter at length and believe we have a workable approach."

"I think it's best that we drop the subject this evening. Please." Stoker felt terribly awkward in the silence that followed. Everyone was staring at their plates.

Sir Henry broke the silence by ringing for Collinson. "Well then, I think I'm looking forward to some dessert," he announced.

The conversation over a tasty dessert of dried oranges and figs, and an ice cream nut cake, centered on Sir Henry's boredom with not having a play to produce. Stoker realized several of the remarks were aimed at Doyle, but if the author noticed, he did not react.

After coffee and cordials, the evening had run its course. Stoker noticed that Doyle, Irving, and Vambery exchanged a few furtive, frustrated glances between one another, but no one again brought up the topic of Tepes. The last sip of coffee seemed like the final nail in the coffin as far as Stoker was concerned.

"Thank you so much for a wonderful evening, Sir Henry," Florence said, planting a kiss on the actor's cheek. "Everything was lovely."

"My pleasure, I assure you," Irving replied graciously as Collinson and one of the servers carried in the men's coats and ladies' cloaks from the adjoining room.

"I have to be on my way as well," Doyle said.

"I'll see you all out," announced Irving, opening the main door.

During dinner, Irving and Doyle united in their cause. But walking together through the theater, Stoker noticed they barely glanced at one another. Only the ladies filled the awkward silence, chatting about the evening's menu.

Making their way through the wings, the sound of applause rose from the auditorium.

"I didn't realize it was so late," Stoker commented. "This play always ends at ten-thirty."

"We're just in time to get a cab, then," Doyle observed. "Before the crowd gets out."

The doorman saw them coming, got up from his stool and opened the stage door.

Irving stopped in the doorway as his guests moved into the alley.

Stoker was providing Sir Henry with some small detail about the following day's schedule when the sound of an approaching coach drew his attention. He looked up to see that Florence had wandered away from the group and was already almost thirty feet down the alley.

"Florrie," he shouted.

Bearing down on her fast from the Burleigh Street entrance to the alley came a four wheeler pulled by a team of two horses. The driver was nothing but a silhouette in a bowler hat, and hanging on in the open door was a tall man wearing a boilerman's cap.

Fearing the coach would run her down, Stoker broke into a full run toward Florence. Doyle took in what was happening and followed Stoker while Irving ushered Professor Vambery and Clarise back into the safety of the doorway.

As the four-wheeler reached Florence, the driver reined up the horses, neighing and snorting, their breath puffing from their nostrils in white plumes. The tall man swung down off the coach, and grabbing Florence around the waist, dragged her toward the coach door.

"Florence," Stoker screamed.

The tall man lifted Florence into the four-wheeler with little effort as the driver whipped the horses. Stoker and Doyle had to leap out of the way as the coach galloped by. It clattered up the alley, turned onto Wellington Street, and was gone.

CHAPTER 11

F lorence Stoker disappearing inside the kidnapper's coach rendered her
husband paralyzed. After his initial shout, Stoker did not call out. He
did nothing but stare at the space where the coach had once been. Doyle
gave Stoker a rough shove and broke into a full run up the alley toward
Wellington Street. The shove did the trick; he could hear Stoker running on
his heels.

"Send for the police," Irving shouted at Professor Vamberry. A moment
later, Irving was running up the alley behind them.

Doyle reached Wellington Street and came to a dead stop. The after-
theater traffic was already growing heavy and the street was busy. They
strained to spot the coach that had taken Florence among the growing
number of hansoms, four-wheelers and several bicycles.

"There," shouted Doyle, pointing down the street as Irving joined them,
out of breath from his sprint up the alley.

Weaving in and out of traffic, the bowler-hatted driver whipped the
horses around the corner onto the Strand, disappearing from view.

Doyle started to a run again, this time heading toward a hansom cab
parked at the curb, its driver standing beside it. Stoker and Irving trailed
closely behind him.

"Get in," Doyle bellowed to Stoker and Irving as they reached
the cab.

The driver began climbing up to his seat. A surge of disbelief contorted his face as Doyle shoved him aside, climbed into the seat, and seized the reins.

"Here now!" the driver roared.

"My name's Arthur Doyle," he called down to the driver.

"I don't care who you—"

"I'm renting your cab," Doyle interrupted as Stoker and Irving climbed aboard and folded the doors closed.

"I'm calling the police," the irate driver screamed as Doyle snapped the reins and the horse bolted down the street.

"We've already sent for them," Irving called out.

Doyle drove with a manic determination to overtake the kidnappers. Cutting off another cab, he guided their horse around the turn that put them onto the Strand.

"Do you see them?" Irving shouted through the open trap on the roof.

"No," Doyle shouted back.

Doyle found it a substantial challenge keeping control of the horse while trying to survey the road for the kidnapper's coach. Weaving in and out of the traffic, he spotted them. They were a full block ahead and creeping along, their path blocked by a horse bus turning in front of them from a side street. Doyle allowed himself a smile; perhaps they had a chance to rescue Florence after all.

"They're just ahead," Doyle called down through the trap.

Irving raised himself up in his seat for a better view. "I see them," he called out.

Through the open trap Doyle could see Stoker, gripping the door, staring straight ahead, silent. He whipped the horse and swerved to the middle of the street, narrowly avoiding an oncoming coach. The driver shook an angry fist at him as they sped by.

From his vantage point atop the cab, Doyle could see the driver of the kidnapper's coach struggling to get around the bus. The angle of the bus and the oncoming traffic made it difficult, but he was making headway.

The kidnapper glanced back over his shoulder. Doyle saw the look of alarm on the driver's face before he turned forward again and whipped his horses with a renewed energy.

Doyle raced to close the distance between them before the other fellow broke through. He snapped the reins again and guided the horse through a narrow opening in the traffic.

"Try not to break our necks," Irving called out.

The driver in the bowler hat forced his way past the lumbering bus and the coach and picked up speed again. Doyle could see the buildings of the King's College in the near distance. The kidnappers' coach veered back from the center of the road to the right. The driver reined his horses into a sharp turn, taking the coach onto the college property.

Doyle turned onto a side street.

"What are you doing?" Irving shouted. "They're getting away."

"They're cutting through King's College," Doyle shouted back. "Heading for the river, I think."

"But they turned down there ahead," Irving argued.

"I can close the distance by cutting across to the college."

Not having the kidnappers in sight created an unpleasant tightness in Doyle's stomach. He knew he had taken a risk. The King's College property was on his left and the hansom rocked as he guided the horse into the first lane leading into it.

Doyle peered through the darkness ahead, hoping for good fortune. As the hansom approached the first intersection, the kidnapper's coach raced through it, heading for the river.

"We've got them," Doyle yelled in triumph.

He steered the cab through the turn and now the kidnappers were only fifty yards ahead of them. They had a team of two horses, but they were hauling more weight pulling the larger coach. The hansom was lighter and more maneuverable.

The bowler-hatted driver turned on to the River Road and whipped his horses. The road was bordered by the Thames on the right, with scarce traffic at this hour. Doyle wasn't gaining on the kidnapper's coach, but he wasn't losing any ground either.

The coach veered right and disappeared from view down an access road leading to the riverbank. Doyle spotted the road and as soon as he had the cab on the incline, the coach was in view again.

"A boat," Irving called up to Doyle. "They must have a boat."

Several small but workable piers and storage buildings populated the area ahead. The four-wheeler had to slow down in order to make the turn onto one of the piers.

Doyle reined up his horse, bringing the hansom to a stop at the entrance to the pier, and jumped to the ground. Irving scrambled out of the passenger seat with Stoker, and as Stoker's feet hit the ground, he again found his voice.

"Florence," Stoker shouted.

The kidnapper's coach, parked on the pier, was next to a pile of large crates. The man wearing the bowler was already on the ground, helping the tall man in the cap pull Florence from the passenger compartment. She did not appear to be resisting.

A few oil lamps hung from the pilings along the pier, their low flames casting dull, dancing shadows along the deck planks. At the end of the pier waited a small steam launch, grayish smoke billowing up from its stack. A third rogue, obscured by the shadows, manned the vessel. The kidnappers hustled Florence along the pier toward the launch.

Doyle and Irving rushed in pursuit, with Stoker trailing behind. The steam launch was small and sleek, and would make good speed through the river currents. They could not allow the kidnappers to get Florence into that boat.

As Doyle closed in on the kidnappers, the tall man halted and whirled around. Doyle saw the revolver in the man's hand just in time.

"Look out," he shouted, diving to the ground as the man fired.

A split second later, Stoker and Irving were down beside him.

As the echo of the shot died out, the kidnappers continued moving Florence toward the end of the pier.

Doyle and Irving were on their feet again. Doyle reached into his coat and pulled his Webley revolver from the inner pocket.

The kidnappers were now only forty feet from the launch.

Doyle raised the Webley and took aim, firing a shot into a barrel six feet to the right of Florence and the men holding her.

"Stop. Stop now," Doyle shouted.

Irving dived for the ground again, and Stoker and Doyle scattered, as the tall fellow whirled around and fired another two shots. The gunman then snapped a hasty order to his companion. As the man in the bowler hat continued toward the launch with Florence, the tall one fired another shot.

This time, the bullet buzzed perilously close between Doyle and Stoker.

The man with the gun was preparing to fire again.

Doyle raised the Webley and took careful aim. Florence was too close to the tall man, but that would change as her captor moved her forward. He waited, feeling his heart pound in his chest.

The kidnapper fired another shot. The bullet plowed into the wood deck only inches from them. Doyle waited and watched. Yes, Florence was just out of the line of sight. He squeezed the trigger and the Webley roared.

The tall man screamed as the bullet struck him in his upper left chest and spun him around. His gun went flying, bounced off the pier and then into the river.

At the sound of the scream, the man in the bowler hat looked back in time to see his friend crumple to the ground. He pulled Florence along, then thought better of it when he saw Doyle, Irving, and Stoker racing down the pier toward him. He pushed Florence away, ran the last several feet to the launch and jumped in.

Doyle, Irving, and Stoker reached Florence as the bowler-hatted man untied the lines and pushed the boat away from the pilings. The man operating the launch opened the throttle, and the little vessel sped up, moving away from the pier, hissing and chugging.

Doyle fired another two shots at the launch, now about forty feet from shore. With the vessel's brisk speed, it seemed unlikely his bullets found a target. He soon lost sight of the launch in the darkness.

"You just happened to be armed?" Irving asked.

Doyle shrugged and led the way back along the pier. He was relieved to see that Stoker appeared to have regained some of his senses.

With a gentle touch, Stoker shook Florence. She did not appear harmed or any worse for wear, but her eyes were dull and distant.

"Florence," Stoker called to her. "Florence."

She gradually gained awareness and then seemed surprised to see him.

"What is it?" she asked. "What's happened?"

"Thank God," Stoker sighed.

Florence surveyed the immediate area, confused by her surroundings.

A low groan attracted their attention.

Doyle hurried over to the tall man sprawled on the pier, his revolver pointed and ready.

"He's still alive," Doyle announced.

Irving joined Doyle while Stoker followed with Florence.

The man was trying to raise himself up on his elbows. His cap had fallen from his head, and his coat had dropped open, revealing the stain of blood still spreading across his chest.

"Who are you?" Doyle asked.

The kidnapper responded with a grimace.

"Tell me who you are," Doyle demanded.

"I'll tell you nothing," the tall man sputtered, a thin trickle of blood oozing from the side of his mouth.

"You're from Manchester, if I'm any judge of your accent," Doyle said. "From the slight swelling of the veins in your nose and the puffiness in your face, I'd wager you drink too much. There's a lack of any one distinguishing mark on your hands, so I assume you earn a living doing odd jobs, but nothing too strenuous. Running errands, light carpentry, lifting and carrying, that sort of thing. Your clothing is cheap and your shoes shabby, so it's obvious you don't earn a lot for your labors. So, who paid you to do this?"

"Go to hell," the man returned, coughing up more blood.

"He doesn't have long," Doyle informed his friends. And then addressing the dying man, "What did you want with this woman?"

"I'll say nothing. I'm loyal, I'll say nothing."

"Loyal? Loyal to whom?" Irving questioned.

The tall man glared up at them, a crazed gleam creeping into his eyes.

"Who sent you? Who told you to do this?" Doyle demanded.

"You know nothing," the kidnapper hissed.

"I asked who sent you?" Doyle pressed.

"You will not best *him*," the man babbled.

"Who? Name him, man," Doyle shouted.

The crazed look grew more intense on the man as he twisted and strained, trying in vain to rise.

"He will see it done," the man wheezed, his body beginning to convulse. "His will, it will be done. The woman."

The convulsions abruptly overwhelmed the man's body. With a final groan, he coughed up more blood and his body went limp. A final, wheezing breath bubbled the blood pooled on his lips.

They all turned away from the gruesome sight.

"What did he mean?" Irving asked. "Who is *he?*"

"Tepes," Stoker answered. "No one else."

CHAPTER 12

The door of the hansom hung open. Florence sat inside on the leather bench where she could rest more comfortably while waiting for permission to return home. Stoker watched her, feeling only concern, numb to almost every other sensation.

Beside him waited Doyle and Irving, all of them watching with impatience as Lestern examined the body while his men walked the length of the pier several times, looking for anything that might shed light on the incident. After a few minutes, Lestern strolled purposefully back to them.

"I was at the Lyceum when word reached me about this," Lestern explained. "When the report came in that it was Mrs. Stoker taken, I went over there myself."

"I appreciate that," Stoker mumbled.

"So, how did that bloke end up shot?" Lestern asked.

"I shot him," Doyle volunteered. "After he began shooting at us."

Stoker, Doyle, and Irving related the events of the evening. Lestern listened, occasionally interrupting with a question while stroking his impressive moustache. Once all the details had been related, Lestern turned and pointed to the body lying on the pier.

"You're certain you have no idea who that fellow is?" Lestern probed.

"No idea," Doyle said.

"We never saw any of them before," Stoker added.

"And you have no idea why they'd want your wife?"

"No," Stoker answered. He could see Lestern was far from convinced.

"This is probably nothing more than a few ruffians seeing a beautiful woman and thinking they'd like to have a bit of sport with her," said Doyle.

Stoker glanced at the cab window, concerned that Florence might have heard the remark. If she had, she showed no signs of it.

Lestern began pacing. "You know, if I were you, I'd be inclined to think it might have something to do with that other unpleasantness that occurred last year with your maid and Miss Westen."

This time Stoker saw Florence wince.

"I don't see why you'd suggest that, inspector," Irving said. "The murderer, or murderers, were never caught or even identified."

"True," Doyle added. "What connection could you possibly see when you don't even know who was behind those murders?"

"So, you all see this as little more than a coincidence?" Lestern asked.

"What else could it be?" Irving responded.

"You'll forgive me for being direct, gentlemen," Lestern began. He stopped his pacing and leveled his gaze at them. "But I've always felt that you knew then and know now who was behind those killings."

"I didn't appreciate that suggestion at the time, Mr. Lestern, and I find I appreciate it even less now," Doyle growled.

"Are we under suspicion?" Stoker asked.

"As I said, it's just a feeling," Lestern responded.

"Well, your feelings aside, Mrs. Stoker has had a trying evening, and I think she'd appreciate the safety of her own home about now," Doyle said. "And we've got a cab to return to its owner."

"Yes, by all means," Lestern agreed with some reluctance. "Stevens, Marsten," he waved over two of his men. "The hansom won't hold the four of you. Stevens here will drive it back to the theater and help you smooth things out with the cabbie. You can use the kidnappers' coach. Marsten will drive you."

"Thank you, Inspector," Florence's voice issued from inside the hansom. "You're very kind."

Lestern tipped the brim of his hat to her. "Not at all, Mrs. Stoker. I'm sorry for all this unpleasantness tonight."

Stoker helped Florence down from the hansom as the bobbie climbed up to the driver's seat. The hansom rolled away as they walked the few feet to the other coach.

Stoker helped Florence into the coach, and then held the door open as Doyle and Irving joined her inside. He then climbed in himself and turned to shut the door. Before he could get his hand on the handle, Lestern stepped forward, took hold of the door, and then locked his eyes on Stoker.

"I don't want you to worry," Lestern said. "We'll be keeping a close watch in case there's anyone else who might intend Mrs. Stoker harm."

Lestern closed and latched the door and then signaled his man.

As the coach lurched into motion, Stoker settled into the seat beside Florence. Her body was stiff with tension and an odd, distant look shone in her eyes. He took her hand in his.

"Are you all right?" he asked.

She nodded. "I just want to go home."

"I'm sorry, so very sorry."

"It's not your fault, Bram."

He was responsible for every bit of this situation, and everyone knew it.

They rode along in silence for a few moments. Finally, Irving looked up at Doyle.

"Do you think we handled Lestern the right way?" he asked, keeping his voice low lest their driver overhear.

"Denying any knowledge of what might be behind what happened tonight?" Doyle asked. "Of course we did."

"Ah, I forgot that you always know the best course," Irving responded, his sarcasm obvious. "He didn't buy what we told him."

"Perhaps not," Doyle said. "But we had little choice. To admit we know who orchestrated tonight's events, and why, would be admitting that we know who murdered Tillie and Miss Westen. We'd be hard pressed to explain it."

"You're right, of course," Irving agreed.

"The real question is, what's to be done now?" Doyle said.

Stoker listened in silence, his mind overwhelmed with all that had happened. He hoped it had all ended with Tepes' escape from England. But deep within, he had always known that as long as Tepes lived, there would be a shroud over his family and friends. He just didn't want to face it. But now, in the light of Florence's kidnap attempt, he could no longer afford to pretend that everything was all right. But what was to be done?

Stoker turned the question over and over again in his mind as the coach rolled through the dark London streets, the horses' hooves clattering hollowly on the bricks. Fifteen minutes later they turned into the alley beside the Lyceum.

The coach rolled to a stop behind the hansom with Officer Stevens standing dutifully beside it. Two other bobbies stood outside the stage entrance and one of them stepped forward to open the coach door.

As Stoker helped Florence down from the coach, the stage door swung open. Professor Vambery and Clarise hurried out into the alley. Collinson and Harry Loveday, the Lyceum's stage manager, followed close behind them.

"Thank the Lord," Clarise said, rushing to Florence and enveloping her in a firm embrace. "Are you all right? Did they hurt you?"

"I'm fine," Florence assured her. "Just a bit rattled is all."

"I can only imagine," Clarise said. "Come inside and we'll find you a nice glass of sherry."

"It won't take a moment," Collinson said, hurrying away to fetch the sherry.

"I'd just like to go home," Florence sighed.

"And you will," Stoker assured her. "Just give me a few minutes. I have something I have to discuss with our friends."

"Where is the cab driver?" Doyle inquired.

"My office," Loveday answered. "I explained the entire matter to him."

"And that substantial slice of roast beef Collinson supplied him went a long way in calming him down as well," Professor Vambery added.

"Of course he still wants to be paid," Loveday added.

"I'll take care of that and be right back," Doyle said.

They all followed Doyle into the theater. Once inside, Loveday retrieved two chairs from the stage set for the women. By the time they were seated, Collinson had returned with a tray carrying a decanter of sherry and several glasses.

No one wanted the sherry, not even Florence, but Collinson poured a glass for her anyway and placed it in her hand. By the time Doyle rejoined them, she was taking polite sips.

Stoker stood by in silence for the next few minutes as Doyle and Irving updated the professor and Clarise as to the night's events, and answered their questions.

"So, you're certain about all this?" Vambery asked.

"We are," Doyle answered.

"But how is it possible?" Clarise asked. "He's not even in the country."

"Tepes must have wealth acquired over the centuries," her father explained. "With such resources, he can enlist agents to do his bidding. And then there's the possibility of the occult."

"How do you mean?" Sir Henry asked.

"There are many lost and troubled people who look for meaning and purpose in dark places," the professor explained. "Satanists are the most obvious example."

"You think we might be dealing with satanists?" Sir Henry asked, alarmed.

"I'm only speculating. But Tepes has lived a long time and has undoubtedly developed more than one way to acquire followers, or disciples, if you will."

"No matter how he's doing it, it all boils down to all of us being in danger again," Doyle said. "Mrs. Stoker most certainly is."

The room became silent and Stoker could feel their eyes on him. He had considered the possibilities in his tortured mind. He knew there was only one solution. But now the thought of Florence being at risk any longer was almost unbearable.

Stoker looked up at his friends. "Professor Vambery, I think it's time we discuss the plan you presented at dinner."

CHAPTER 13

On a cold but pleasant morning two days following Florence Stoker's attempted kidnapping, Doyle sat at the end of the massive table in the Beefsteak Room. Sir Henry proposed the location as the perfect headquarters for expedition planning and everyone unanimously agreed.

Doyle took the initiative and get down to business. "We know the Czarina Catherine sailed to Varna with Tepes and his last earth box," he began. "With any luck, we can pick up his trail there."

"But he told me his home was in Romania," Stoker said.

"If he told you the truth, then he could be anywhere in the country. My thinking is that by beginning in Varna we have a chance of acquiring information that will establish a solid trail," Doyle explained.

"Do you think there'll be a trail after so many months?" Irving asked.

"There will almost certainly be a bill of lading for the earth box," Professor Vambery said. "If we can gain access to it, it should have at least some of the information we need."

"And then we can set out from Varna in whatever direction is indicated," Doyle added.

"Let's not forget," began Vambery, "that Tepes' hold on Mrs. Stoker will draw her to him."

Stoker winced.

"I sent a wire off to Morgan Quincey this morning," Irving said.

"I'd certainly welcome Quincey's help," Stoker said. "Anything that might better assure my wife's safety."

"I will be going along as well," Professor Vambery said. "I've traveled extensively through Eastern Europe and my services as interpreter will come in handy."

"Yes. Very good," agreed Sir Henry.

"Then I'll be going, too," Clarise stated.

Professor Vambery straightened in his chair. "No. No, my dear. You will not."

"I have to agree," said Doyle.

"I've always been father's traveling companion," Clarise explained, her face set doggedly. "I'll not have him roaming all over God-knows-where without someone to look after him."

"My dear, all of us, of course, will be very mindful of your father," Sir Henry assured her.

"And I'll be there to make sure you are," Clarise said.

"You understand, Miss Vambery," Doyle began. "It's going to be difficult enough keeping Mrs. Stoker safe. But having another woman along to worry about—"

"Mr. Doyle," Clarise interrupted. "My mother passed away when I was still quite young. My learning experiences have extended well beyond the areas of training typically afforded a woman. I've traveled often with my father. I'm fluent in three languages, an expert rider, and I'm more than proficient with both a rifle and revolver. Oh, and I also took the second place ribbon with a long bow two years ago at the Grand National Society archery tournament. All things considered, I don't think you'll have to spend much time holding my hand."

"I'll have her along as my personal bodyguard," Sir Henry chuckled.

"As a Christian woman, I have faith that God will look after me. After us all," Clarise continued. "Besides, I've a feeling that Mrs. Stoker isn't overjoyed at the prospect of being the only woman on this trip. There may be times when she'll require or welcome the company of another woman."

Doyle noticed Mrs. Stoker smile for the first time that morning.

"Well, there's something to that," Florence said. "But I don't want you putting yourself in danger on account of me."

"I don't want you putting yourself in danger for any reason," the professor exclaimed. "But I must admit, Clarise has always proven herself to be more than capable."

"Thank you. I'll take that as your acceptance."

"All right. But I still don't like the idea," Doyle scowled.

"I don't know how I can do this," Stoker said, his voice uneven.

Doyle turned to look at Stoker. The man was staring at his hands resting on the table top, his complexion pale, a light sheen of perspiration spotting his forehead.

"Stoker?" Doyle prodded.

"I don't know if I can do any of this," he almost moaned.

"It's become a matter of doing what must be done," Doyle said.

"When I first met Tepes, I did everything in my power to keep him away from Florence. And from you, my friends," Stoker explained. "Now we're talking about delivering her to him."

"Our main purpose always will be to keep her safe," Doyle responded. "We all know what's at stake."

"Without question," Professor Vambery agreed.

"When I think about what could happen, should I ever misjudge him again… what could happen to my wife, to any of you," Stoker said. "I can't stand it."

"Once we're there, it's very likely he'll be hunting us," the professor said.

"But he's hunting us right here, right now," Irving commented.

"My point is, what I should have said is that once we're in his country, he can hunt us more efficiently," the professor explained.

"Then even more reason to find him and kill him," Doyle said. "Beat him at his own game."

Stoker sat still, his eyes fearful, his body stiff. Florence placed her hand over his.

"You have to decide whether you can do this," Doyle advised Stoker. "If you can't, you won't be of any use to us."

"All of you have already extended yourselves well beyond what Bram and I could ever hope to expect," Florence said. "Through all that ugly business last year, you stood by us. And now you're all willing to do it again. I can't even comprehend such compassion and courage." She paused, retrieving a handkerchief from her handbag to blot away tears. "If you're willing to put yourself in such danger again, for us, then you can expect both of us to do our part." Florence squeezed her husband's hand tightly. "Isn't that right, Bram?"

Stoker turned his gaze to Florence. "Yes, of course," he said. "I apologize, my behavior, shameful."

"It's all quite understandable," Sir Henry said.

"Well, I don't understand it," Stoker mumbled.

Doyle led the rest of the meeting for another hour, doing his best to cover every detail he could think of. Stoker, still not himself, took part the least, but everyone else contributed a good deal, and Doyle appreciated it. He generally found "leadership by committee" to be a frustrating waste of time. But in this case, the dedication and determination of everyone at the table produced efficient results.

Doyle agreed to procure weapons for their protection. Irving, recalling the events of the previous year, thought it wise to include weapons of faith as well. He took on acquiring crosses for everyone and a supply of holy water as well. The Stokers and Vamberys joined forces to book tickets and lodging, and to buy maps.

"Of course, precise planning for travel and lodging will only be possible as far as Varna," Professor Vambery pointed out. "We don't know where the trail will take us from there."

"But we shouldn't have much trouble finding accommodations along the way," Clarise added. "Father's knowledge of the region is impressive."

"All right, then, it's agreed," Doyle said, concluding the meeting. "We leave eight days hence, Monday, March third."

"Right," Clarise confirmed. "The Orient Express departs from Gare de l'Est station each Tuesday evening at 6:30. We'll be in Paris by Monday night. We'll have to wait out the day, of course, but that shouldn't be too bad."

"There's a good deal to accomplish by then," Doyle stated. "So, let's get to it."

Doyle lingered behind as everyone made their way from the room. Now only he and Sir Henry remained.

"I appreciate your being able to put our differences aside to be a part of all this," Doyle said.

"We all do what we must do," Irving responded, his demeanor icy.

"Did you notice Stoker during the discussion?" Doyle asked.

"He wasn't himself," Irving answered. "I mean, he's been a bit off ever since the murders last year, but he seemed particularly morose today."

"I'm not sure that morose is the word," Doyle muttered.

"What's your view, then?"

"He's eating himself alive with guilt, and now that there's been a renewed threat to his wife, it's become worse."

"And this worries you," Irving observed.

"Because it seems to have incapacitated him," Doyle stated.

"Any suggestions as to a remedy?"

"I'm inclined to think the only remedy is the kind he's going to have to find within himself," Doyle answered. "What I do know is that if he freezes up when he's needed, he could end up getting himself, or one of us killed."

CHAPTER 14

Jardani made his way through the forest carrying a wood auger he had taken from a farm in the lower foothills. Stochelo had commented that they could use such a tool in their work at the castle. Jardani thought little of it at the time, but later the same evening he recalled that he often saw men using such a tool at this farm where he was hired to tend livestock. He visited the farm to have a look and was rewarded. Jardani could have taken other valuable tools as well, but he made it a practice to only take what he needed.

Jardani walked at a fast pace to assure he'd be back in camp in time to leave for the castle with the others for another day of work. Early morning light glowed through the trees and reflected off the ice and snow clinging to the branches. The forest was heavy with early morning dampness and the air was cold. The woods were eerily quiet, amplifying the sound of Jardani's footsteps on the soft earth. An animal sound drifted through the trees.

Jardani stopped to listen. Almost immediately, he heard it again. The bellowing of a cow came from somewhere ahead. A stray cow would be a nice prize to take back to the camp.

Several minutes later, following the cries of the unhappy cow, he came to a hollow. The bellows were coming from down in the hollow and through the thickets that lay ahead. But now he heard something else, the voice of a man. Jardani felt a momentary sting of disappointment. The cow would not be his if it was attended. He was about to turn away, but his curiosity got the better of him.

Jardani moved through the foliage until he came to a break in the trees. A large cow was stuck in a bog at the bottom of the hollow. A man, his back to Jardani, was at the edge of the bog, pulling on a sturdy rope he had thrown around the animal's neck. He was making little progress, and Jardani saw why. One of the cow's hind legs was entangled in the branches of a fallen tree.

"How did you get yourself into all this?" The man asked the cow in frustration. "This is the kind of trouble that comes from wandering off on your own during the night."

As the man adjusted his position to better his progress in freeing the cow, his profile presented itself. Jardani had seen this man before. This was the rugged fellow from the irrigation ditch, the villager with the straw colored hair.

The man was as tall as Jardani remembered, his handsome face darkened by the sun, and his hands calloused from hard work. His pants, tucked into well-worn boots, were damp and muddy from his struggle with the cow. The fellow's coat was open and Jardani could make out a light linen shirt and sheepskin vest underneath.

The villager let the rope go slack but kept a firm grip on it as he stopped to rest. While catching his breath, he turned toward Jardani. He looked startled for a moment, but then just stared up at him. Jardani stared back. He could see suspicion in the villager's face.

A few moments passed, and Jardani saw a flicker of recognition in the man's eyes. The cow sounded another series of gloomy bellows, but the man ignored them. He nodded at Jardani. Jardani nodded back and then, seeing no reason to waste any more time, turned to leave.

"You were driving the wagon," the fellow called out, his voice mellow.

Jardani paused and turned back, looking down at the fellow in silence.

"The other day, on the road. you were driving the wagon," the man repeated.

"Yes," Jardani answered.

"I was sure of it."

With that, the man turned away, planted his feet and began tugging at the rope again. The cow bellowed yet again.

Jardani pivoted away and took a few steps, but then stopped again. He gave the matter some thought, and then turned back and started down the slope. He had no particular concern for the villager, but he hated to see a good cow suffering.

The villager turned toward him.

"That downed tree there in the mud has hold of her," Jardani pointed.

Realizing that Jardani had come to help, the villager looked surprised.

Jardani placed the auger on a fallen log and then began looking around for something he could use. He found it in a limb about as big around as an ax handle. It was a good seven feet long and had a thick, short branch jutting off it close to one end. Jardani lifted the limb and carried it to the edge of the bog. Its length was just a little short; he would have to get closer. Jardani waded into the bog until the sludge was almost to the top of his boots.

The villager took up the slack on the rope as Jardani used the limb to probe in the mud around the fallen tree.

"I am Ciernik," the villager said between the cries of the cow. "Alexander Ciernik."

"Jardani."

The villager nodded acknowledgement but said nothing more. A few minutes later, Jardani felt the limb take hold of something solid under the mud. He pulled back on the limb and saw the tree in the bog move a few inches. Putting more effort into it, Jardani strained to pull the tree back about a foot from the cow. The animal's leg came free from the branches and it bellowed again.

Alexander began pulling hard on the rope and the cow moved toward dry ground. With some effort, Jardani waded out of the mud and threw the limb aside. He took a position on the rope behind Alexander. The two of them put their backs into it and a few minutes later, the cow was on dry ground.

Jardani sat down on the log beside the auger to rest. He felt satisfaction that he had done a kind service, but he knew his people would not approve. Stochelo would be annoyed with him if he knew.

Alexander removed his hat and wiped his brow with his forearm. "This cow is more trouble than she's worth," he said.

"She was this morning," Jardani agreed.

"She's wandered off in the night three times in the last two months," Alexander continued. "But this is the worst thing she's managed."

Jardani shrugged. He picked up the auger and got up from the log.

The villager's eyes fell on the auger. "You work with wood?" he asked.

"I must go," Jardani said. He turned and started back up the slope.

"Hey," Alexander called out.

Jardani paused and looked back down the slope.

The villager put his hat back on, a friendly smile on his face. "Thank you."

Jardani managed a smile of his own and nodded. He offered the man a parting wave, turned and hurried on his way.

CHAPTER 15

"You say you stumbled into a bog?" Stochelo asked for the third time.

"Yes," Jardani answered.

"It must have been a terrible bog, seeing how long it took you to get free of it," Stochelo growled.

Stochelo was fuming by the time Jardani, his boots crusted with mud, returned to the camp twenty minutes after they were supposed to have set out for the castle. They were all gathered around the wagon waiting for him, and the wood auger he brought with him as a prize did little to bring any calm.

Jardani was again driving the wagon, but this time pulled by a team of two sturdy work horses. They had completed their trips carrying the heavy lumber loads, so the slower oxen were not required. His cargo on this trip consisted of tools and men.

Following Stochelo and Zache, he turned the horses onto the natural bridge. The castle keep cast a shadow over them. They were soon through the gate and into the courtyard. As the men jumped from the wagon and gathered their tools, Jardani wondered at how, even in morning daylight, this place appeared foreboding.

They had completed the exterior work on the castle, and today they would begin work inside. Jardani watched the other men transferred the remaining lumber from the courtyard stockpile, carrying it through the main door into the shadows beyond. He shuddered at the thought of going inside, but moved forward to join his companions.

The main entrance opened into the great hall where Stochelo directed them to stack the wood against the outer wall. Dust carpeted the stone floor and rose into the air when they walked over it. The pitiful amount of light in the hall found its way in through the tall windows set high in the walls. The diffused beams, alive with the ancient dust, streamed downward through the gloom, disappearing before they reached the floor. Heavy cobwebs spanned every corner and hung off the old, heavy wood beams that supported the roof.

Two doors flanked the room, with one positioned beneath a wide stone staircase that curved upward twenty feet to a passageway spanning the room's length. He could make out the tops of two additional doorways on the second level through the gothic arches that adorned the length of the balcony. Two doors stood in the back wall of the room, past the pillars that upheld the passageway. One was set in the middle of the wall and was slightly ajar, as if daring one to venture beyond. The other was just below the main floor level, with three steps descending to it.

After looking the room over, Stochelo and Zache went back to the wagon and returned with several oil lanterns.

"We look around now to see what must be done. Then we make a plan of how to best go about the work," Stochelo said.

Jardani felt his gut tighten at the prospect of venturing any deeper into this place of darkness. Judging from the faces of his companions, he was not alone.

"There are several levels below us, down into the mountain. We're to go no lower than one level down," Stochelo told them.

"You've been in here before?" Zache asked with surprise.

"None of our people have been inside before now," Stochelo responded, his tone impatient. "But I've been told by *him*, and we would be wise to do as we're told."

"I'd be happy to go nowhere else but here," Jardani said. "But if I have to, I'd rather start with the upper floors."

Stochelo shrugged. "Then we'll start with the upper floors and work our way down if it calms your nerves."

Jardani was certain that nothing would calm his nerves as long as he was in this place, but he kept silent as he followed Stochelo and the others up the stairway. From viewing the castle outside, he knew the main structure was four stories high, with two of the towers extending at least another twenty feet above the highest rooftop. Once they reached the passageway overlooking the great hall, Jardani saw stairways at each end of the passage continuing upward. They headed for the closest one and it took them to the top floor.

"Take half the men and look through the east rooms," Stochelo instructed Zache. "I'll take the west. Check the doors. Make note of passages that might lead outside."

Weary of Stochelo's grumpiness, Jardani moved alongside Zache and the four other men who already stood near him. His lantern held high, Zache led them from room to room. The lanterns proved to be less necessary in the outer, windowed rooms, but every man was grateful for them in the inner chambers and passageways. But despite the lanterns, the gloom seemed to squeeze in around them, and the stillness was oppressive.

The purpose of some rooms was obvious. Jardani identified the sleeping apartments by their fireplaces and the wood remaining from bed frames or headboards. They entered three other spacious rooms that Jardani thought might have been sitting rooms. One apartment served as a woman's sewing room, evidenced by the remains of a spinning wheel. Several other rooms were not so obvious.

They were standing in one of those featureless compartments watching Zache examine the hardware on a deteriorating door. Zache glanced at Jardani.

"You'd like to get out of here," Zache stated.

Jardani answered with a shrug, not wanting to appear afraid or weak.

"I don't blame you," Zache continued. "With the fever taking my wife, I am all my two girls have. I need to return to them at the end of each day."

"Do you believe as Stochelo does?" Jardani asked. "That we are safe in this place, safe from the nosferatu?"

Zache glanced at the other men.

"Maybe yes, maybe no," Zache answered. "Our people have served the Voivode for many generations. A smart man knows there will be benefits as well as risks in such an arrangement. A smarter man will know it is best to always keep the risks keen in his mind."

It took almost forty minutes to explore the entire wing. They returned to the stairway landing and waited for Stochelo's group to return. In just a few minutes, Stochelo appeared with his men close behind him.

Together, they descended to the third floor, repeating their inspection routine. The third floor was very much like the fourth, and in a half hour, they began on the second floor.

They had looked through several rooms when Jardani discovered an archway opening onto a small balcony. He approached the stone balustrade and looked over. Below him was the chapel, the stone of its altar and some small sections of the outer wall crumbling. Overlooking the altar was a stained glass window, rectangular in dimension, its top adorned with a decorative gothic arch.

The window depicted the Crucifixion of Christ with the Virgin and Saint John the Evangelist kneeling at the foot of the cross. But the image of the cross itself was missing. The upper portion of the window had been shattered and the only section of the cross that remained was a small bottom section with Christ's feet.

There were no other crosses in the chapel, not in image, stone, or metal. The absence of the most powerful symbol of faith in heaven and earth in this place did not escape his notice. He crossed himself and hurried back to join Zache and the others.

A short time later, they were all gathered together on the main floor of the great hall. It was necessary to replenish the oil in the lanterns, a task that was accomplished quickly.

"Only the lower level remains and then we can plan out our work," Stochelo announced. "Remember, go down no more than one level."

Again, the two groups set out in separate directions. Zache then led them to the door set under the stairway at the far end of the hall. The door was open a few inches and the hinges creaked painfully as he pushed it. He stepped through the portal onto a landing and then stopped in his tracks. As Jardani and the rest joined him on the landing, he saw why.

They stood within the west tower, and the narrow stone stairway descended along the curve of the wall into the blackness below. The stairway had no guard wall or railing; a misstep would find a man hurtling down into that unknown blackness.

With lanterns held low to illuminate the stone steps, they descended with caution, hugging the wall, their senses alert. Large, rotting beams spanned the diameter of the tower, supporting the heavy stone walls, and a smell of dusty decay hung in the air. To Jardani, the descent seemed endless, but by the time they reached the bottom of the flight, he guessed they were only some twenty-five feet below the main floor.

The light from the lanterns unveiled another door in the wall before them, closed tight in its frame. Zache moved to the door, drew the latch and attempted to push it open. Warped wood or rusty hinges made the door stubborn, so Jardani stepped forward to help him. Together, they put their shoulders to the door and pushed. With a scraping and screeching that echoed through the tower, the door gave way.

It opened onto another broad landing, but this time in the lantern light Jardani saw only three wide steps dropping to the floor. The room was round, about thirty feet in diameter, and there was no doubt it was the castle armory.

Rotted oak racks lined the walls and occupied the floor in the center of the room. Most were empty, but some held the broken remains of forgotten weapons.

Walking along one of the rows, Jardani kicked something that rolled across the stone floor with a clatter. A rusted helmet came to rest next to a rusted breastplate.

"We're done here," Zache said. "Let's go back up."

They reached the top of the stairs, grateful to be free of the total blackness below. As they stepped back into the great hall, Jardani spotted Stochelo's group, their lanterns casting dancing shadows, approaching along the passageway under the balcony. Suddenly, a man beside Stochelo at the front of the group tumbled forward. Jardani heard the man's lantern clatter on the stone floor and then a loud scream. The other lanterns appeared to scatter away from the spot where the man went down.

Jardani and Zache ran across the hall toward the commotion. Reaching the passageway, they saw Stochelo's man scrambling away from a pair of legs that jutted out from an alcove in the wall. The other men were again moving closer, adjusting their lanterns to see better.

Jardani stepped up to the alcove as Stochelo leaned in with his lantern. The legs belonged to a boy of perhaps fifteen or sixteen years. His face was frozen in terror. His shirt had been ripped from him and bite marks covered his chest and arms. The most terrible wounds were at his throat, which was little more than a bloody mess. The men crossed themselves.

"One of the villagers," Stochelo observed.

"He's just a child," Jardani said.

"A foolish child," Stochelo said. "If he managed to be caught like this."

"May he be with God," Zache muttered.

"There's nothing we can do for him now," Stochelo said. "We go." Stochelo began walking away.

"Someone help me get him to the wagon," Jardani said.

Stochelo turned back. "What? Leave him where he is."

"We can't leave him here," Jardani responded.

"He's a villager and of no concern to us," Stochelo argued.

"If he were your son, would you want him left here? In this place? We're taking him back with us," Jardani yelled, the anger bubbling up inside him.

Jardani held his gaze as Stochelo glared at him. Stochelo's face softened, and he gestured to the other men.

"Give him some help," Stochelo ordered.

Jardani pulled the body from the alcove as two other men stepped forward. Death overwhelmed this place, he thought, death prevailed in this country. And it had been accepted without question for far too long.

CHAPTER 16

S toker held the stage door open wide as Doyle, aided by Harry Loveday, wheeled a cart from the alley into the backstage area. The cart carried a large rectangular shipping crate.

"How did you do?" Stoker asked as Doyle and Loveday removed the top of the crate.

"Rather well, I'd say," Doyle beamed.

"Ah, I see I'm just in time," Sir Henry announced, approaching through the wings. "I trust Mr. Doyle wasn't going to move forward without me again."

In one hand, Sir Henry held a beautiful, ten inch Bowie knife with a stag horn hilt, a gift from Morgan Quincey. In his other hand, he held a canvas bag. Aside from his sarcastic remark, he barely acknowledged Doyle.

Stoker peered into the crate. It was stocked with rifles, revolvers, and an ample supply of cartridges. Several short spearlike weapons were also present.

Ignoring Irving's rudeness, Doyle reached into the crate and withdrew a Lee-Enfield carbine and slid the bolt open.

"A friend of mine in the Essex regiment managed to pull a few strings," Doyle explained. "These have been converted for smokeless powder cartridges, .303 caliber with a ten round magazine. There's one for each man, and one for Miss Vambery, since she claims to be proficient with firearms."

Doyle replaced the rifle and picked up a revolver. "I've always favored the Webley, so I got one for each of us, even Mrs. Stoker. We'll show her how to use it, of course."

"These will be excellent for defense against any human adversaries."

"That's what they're meant for," Doyle said, placing the Webley in the crate.

"Normal men won't be our primary threat," Stoker said, unable to disguise his worry.

"It goes without saying," Doyle agreed. "Which is why I arranged for these."

The author withdrew one of the spears from the crate. It had a sharp blade in the shape of an elongated teardrop. The broad, rounded end of the blade fitted over a stout, hardwood shaft reinforced with a tight wrap of brass wire. Stoker estimated the overall length to be forty-five or fifty inches.

"What *is* that?" Loveday asked.

"It's an iklwa, a Zulu weapon designed for short range stabbing," Doyle explained. "I've got an authentic one in my collection and with the wooden shaft, it occurred to me that it might be just the thing for a thrust to the heart. I took it to a fellow I know in Clerkenwell and he made these replicas for me."

"And these should provide some defense as well," Irving said, untying the drawstring of the canvas bag and holding it open.

Peering into the bag, Stoker saw a collection of crosses and crucifixes.

"These should work well if we have any close confrontations," Irving said. "I purchased some smaller ones for all of us to wear around our necks, too."

"A sound precaution," Doyle affirmed.

Irving ignored Doyle's affirmation and placed the canvas bag in the crate. "These can travel in here and I'll pass out the necklaces to everyone on the train," Irving said. "This I'll just keep with me," he motioned with the Bowie knife.

"This crate should be the most unwieldy thing we're taking. Everyone should strive to pack efficiently so we can make haste in our travels," Doyle stated.

"I spoke with Professor Vambery yesterday afternoon. He'll have a list of guidelines and packing suggestions tailored to the region we'll be traveling for everyone by tomorrow," Stoker said.

"The weapons can stay here," Sir Henry gestured at the crate. "Loveday will make sure it's at Charing Cross for the train on Monday."

"I'll go and make the arrangements now," Loveday assured them. "No reason to wait."

"Thank you, Harry," Stoker said as Loveday hurried off.

"I'm afraid the only loose end lies with Quincey," Irving said. "He hasn't responded to my telegram. I sent a second along with our itinerary, but still haven't had word back."

"We still have some time. At any rate, we've made excellent progress these past days," Doyle said. "I think we're as ready as we're going to be."

Stoker felt the gnawing fear and guilt well up within him. "I don't feel ready at all," he said.

"You'll feel better once we're on our way," Doyle encouraged.

"Will I?"

"It's the waiting that wears us down," Doyle continued. "Taking action will make you a new man."

"Perhaps," he said. "I just wish Florence didn't have to be involved."

"Professor Vambery believes—" Sir Henry began.

"I know what he believes," Stoker interrupted, immediately embarrassed by his snappish tone.

He saw the looks Doyle and Sir Henry exchanged. They couldn't manage to get along, but were in total agreement viewing him as a handicap. He couldn't blame them; he viewed himself even worse.

"I apologize," Stoker sighed. "I'm worried for Florence. That's my only excuse."

"Of course," Sir Henry said.

"Do you believe we have any chance of killing him, Tepes?" Stoker asked. "Do you think it's even possible?"

"All I know is that we must try," Doyle answered. "The alternative is too horrible to consider."

"That's what haunts me," Stoker admitted. "What if we fail? What if I'm killed and Florence is left to that, that thing?"

"Tepes possesses a terrible strength and powers we don't fully understand, but there are things he fears," Sir Henry said. "The sunlight, the cross, and remember how he was wary of that pointed gardening tool you parried against him at the zoological gardens."

"I couldn't have said it better," Doyle agreed. "If he has fears, then he has vulnerabilities."

"We should pray we have at least a chance to exploit them," Stoker murmured.

CHAPTER 17

The first of the villages on the road leaving the mountain pass lay just ahead. Jardani knew the boy lying dead in the back of the wagon, covered by the old tarpaulin, might not be from this village and he was prepared to visit as many of the hamlets as he could before the sun set. The sun was already low in the sky. Dense, detached clouds drifted lazily across the sky, casting mottled shadows over the trees and village rooftops.

Astride his horse, Zache said, "Here is the first one."

"Poarta de Munte," Jardani replied.

When Jardani asked for help with the boy's body, Zache was the only man willing. The very idea of doing anything to help the villagers annoyed Stochelo and the other men appeared to fear the body.

They rode past the orchard where Jardani had first seen the villager, Alexander. The few men working there stopped what they were doing to watch them travel by. Their gazes reflected curiosity and wariness.

Jardani glanced over at Zache. "Why did you want to come along for this?"

"My two children. If something happened to one of them, I'd want to know what it was, even if it was a bad thing."

Jardani and his wife had not yet been blessed with children, but he understood. He turned onto the wagon path leading into the village. Up ahead, an old woman was pulling laundry from a drying line strung between her little house and a post. At the sound of the wagon, she turned to gape at them.

The closer they drew to the village, the more people they encountered, and more wary stares. Several of them strained to see what was in the back of the wagon.

Zache looked at the sober faced villagers. "We'd see a different welcome if they needed a barn repaired or livestock tended to."

"With a little good fortune, this will be the boy's home," Jardani said.

"God willing."

Several villagers gathered as Jardani drove the wagon into the village square. He brought the wagon to rest in front of the communal well. Several village men surrounded them, staring up at them and peering into the wagon bed.

Zache was alert and watchful, but kept his hand away from the large knife carried in his sash.

"Jardani," came a call from behind the crowd.

Jardani shifted his position and saw the man, Alexander, weaving his way through his neighbors.

"What brings you here?" Alexander asked, a curious smile on his face.

"That's what we'd all like to know," a voice came from out of the crowd.

"What's carried in the wagon?" another voice sounded.

Alexander turned toward the villagers and raised his hands. "Quiet! At least hear why they've come."

The grumbling subsided.

"Welcome, Jardani," Alexander said.

"You know this gypsy?" asked a man pushing to the front of the crowd.

Jardani recognized him as the man Alexander had called Branko.

"Not well," Alexander replied to Branko. "He gave me help once when I needed it."

Alexander turned back to Jardani. "Now, tell us, why have you come?"

Jardani swiveled around on the wagon box and stepped into the wagon bed. He knelt down beside the body.

Jardani pulled back the blanket from the dead boy's face. "We found this boy early today. Is he from this village?"

A collective gasp rose from the villagers crowded around the wagon, and Jardani saw the sadness cloud Alexander's eyes.

Alexander nodded, and still staring at the body, called out, "Someone go get Marek Tesar."

"Perhaps that," Jardani pointed to a two-wheel cart on the far side of the well.

As one of the men wheeled up the cart, Zache climbed from his horse into the back of the wagon.

"Where did you find him?" Alexander asked.

Jardani hesitated, fearing his own answer.

"Where?" Alexander insisted.

"The castle."

Another gasp went up from the villagers, followed by declarations of disapproval. A flurry of motion swept through the crowd as each person crossed themselves.

"You were at the castle?" Branko asked, the anger in his voice unmistakable.

Jardani nodded.

"What business would you have there?" Alexander probed, his face dark with suspicion.

Again, Jardani hesitated.

A commotion erupted at the rear of the crowd. A man of middle age and thinning hair moved through the throng that cleared a path for him. He stopped short of the wagon and a terrible grief contorted his features.

"This is Marek Tesar," Alexander explained. "Eduard's father."

"So that was his name," Zache muttered.

Marek Tesar pulled his gaze away from the body to look up at Jardani and Zache. His eyes were glazed and moist with tears. He said nothing.

Jardani and Zache helped Alexander and the man who had gone for the cart transfer the body off the wagon.

"We are sorry this has happened," Jardani said to Marek Tesar. "Sorry this has happened to your son."

Marek Tesar turned, and weeping, followed the man with the cart back toward a house at the edge of the square.

Branko moved closer to the wagon and shook his fist. "You are at the castle and then you come here. You bring evil with you," he hissed.

"All I saw them bring today was Eduard," Alexander said. "And we are all grateful for that."

Jardani acknowledged Alexander's affirmation with a silent nod.

"Grateful?" Branko spat. "You commune with the devil. We don't want you here."

Zache pulled his horse close to the side of the wagon and climbed into the saddle. Jardani returned to his seat on the wagon box.

"Go on, get out," Branko yelled as he stomped away.

Alexander walked around to the front of the wagon and extended his hand to Jardani.

"They are upset," he said. "But they are still grateful you brought Eduard back. It is what they would want, whether or not they can see it now."

"Yes," Jardani said, shaking Alexander's hand.

Alexander turned and offered his hand to Zache. Zache appeared a bit surprised by the gesture, but accepted the hand.

"I don't know what you might be doing at the castle," Alexander said, turning back to Jardani. "But I know, whatever it is, it will do your soul no good."

"Go on, get out of here!" a shout came from a villager.

"We just wanted to bring the boy back," Jardani answered, defensiveness in his tone.

Alexander stared up at him for several moments. Jardani held his gaze.

"I think our people and your people could use a little more trust between us," Alexander said.

Jardani shrugged. "A hard thing."

"Perhaps it can begin with you and me. Thank you for bringing Eduard back to us. You'll be in my prayers." Alexander turned and walked across the square.

With a nod from Zache, Jardani snapped the reins and drove the wagon away from the village.

CHAPTER 18

At 9:30 in the morning, a crowd had congregated on the Charing Cross platform for the boat train. Two porters had taken charge of the luggage and had already placed it aboard. Professor Vambery had kept a small satchel containing maps and travel guides with him. He and Clarise stood near the edge of the platform chatting with Sir Henry, who had just completed passing out simple crosses on necklace chains to everyone. A few feet away, Stoker was standing protectively close to Florence. Doyle made his way over to them.

"I trust Mr. Loveday got our crate of weapons on board?" Doyle asked.

"I just came back from the baggage car and saw it there myself," Stoker answered.

The train superintendent announced boarding and they all headed toward the train. Doyle stood beside the rear entrance of their car, ushering his friends aboard. He was just about to follow them on when he noticed two men standing near the platform entrance gate.

One was a bookish looking fellow wearing a black bowler hat and wire rim spectacles with thick lenses. He was neatly dressed, albeit in inexpensive clothing. He held an open newspaper in his hands, which he appeared to be glancing through. The second man was thickset and of average height. His complexion was dark, his clothing casual and of a higher quality than those of his companion. On his head he wore a wool tweed cap, a cigar dangled carelessly from his mouth.

Doyle had a distinct feeling that the men were watching him. He boarded the train, but instead of joining his party in the forward car, crossed into the car behind. He hurried to the back and peered out a window.

The two men were still standing where Doyle had first seen them, although the newspaper was now folded under the bookish fellow's arm. The men were looking at the car Doyle and his friends had boarded. He was about to explain it away to his being excessively cautious when the two whistle blasts signaling the train's departure sounded and both men hurried toward a car near the rear of the train.

With a long hiss from the releasing brakes, the train lurched forward. Doyle couldn't be certain about the two men, but if they were interested in him and his friends, it would become clear soon enough.

The train was picking up speed when Doyle entered the forward car to join his friends. Stoker and Florence sat together. Across the aisle from them sat Professor Vambery and Clarise, facing Sir Henry. Doyle sank into the seat beside the actor.

"I was beginning to think you might have missed the train," Sir Henry said, the coolness in his voice obvious.

"No, I was just watching some of the other passengers board," Doyle responded.

"A pastime, Mr. Doyle?" Clarise smiled.

"Something like that."

They spent most of the journey in idle conversation, and almost none of it related to the task at hand. The one exception was because of Doyle's curiosity regarding Florence's ability with a revolver. He moved across the aisle and sat opposite Stoker and Florence. "Did you have an opportunity to instruct Mrs. Stoker with the Webley?"

Stoker nodded. "We took a drive into the country and spent a few hours practicing."

"I didn't like the idea of it." Florence offered a mock shudder. "I didn't feel comfortable about the whole thing at all. But after a while, I think I started to get a knack for it."

Stoker smiled at his wife. "I thought she did quite well."

"I'm glad to hear it," Doyle said.

"I rather enjoyed the shooting," Florence said. "Of course, I hope I never have to use the gun. I'd be mortified at the thought of shooting a person."

Doyle shrugged. "Well, it's just a precaution. It's our job to make sure you're never in a situation where shooting is necessary."

"Amen to that," Stoker said.

The train was an express, so they made excellent time rolling across the English countryside. Doyle watched the homes and business places of Tonbridge slip by, and a while later, Ashford came into view and was just as quickly gone. The superintendent walked through the car announcing arrival in Folkestone in five minutes.

The train slowed as it approached the harbor terminal and slowed even more when it entered the tight curve that brought it in line with the pier. Once the brakes brought the locomotive to a full stop, Stoker and Doyle took charge of seeing the luggage and supplies transferred to the boat. Sir Henry and Professor Vambery escorted the ladies onto the pier.

Several minutes later, they reunited at the foot of the gangway. Doyle scanned the travelers moving about the pier. If the bookish fellow and his friend were preparing to board, they weren't being obvious about it.

"Is anything wrong?" Sir Henry asked.

Doyle considered the question. He had only the most shallow of suspicions concerning the two men from the Charing Cross platform. If they had any malicious intentions, there was no hard evidence of it. At this point, it was probably best not to cause any undue alarm. "No. Everything's in order and we're ready to board."

Twenty minutes later they were aboard the boat steaming for France, and in just under two hours were docking in Calais. Aside from the channel being a bit choppy, the trip was uneventful.

Doyle and Stoker repeated their duty of seeing to transferring the luggage and then rendezvoused with the others waiting quayside beside the French train for Paris. It took only a short time to board and find seats.

The train pulled out of Calais on time and Doyle dozed off as the landscape raced past his window. He was awake and alert by the time the train pulled into Gare du Nord. Just six hours after leaving London, they had arrived in Paris.

After disembarking, they all gathered outside the terminal while porters loaded their luggage into two cabs. The station was busy this late in the afternoon, and a bustling throng of people moved past them.

"After a day of travel, all I want to do is take a bath and have an early supper," Clarise said.

Florence bobbed her head. "I feel the same way."

"You'll both have your wishes fulfilled in a short time," the professor said. "Our rooms are booked at the Hotel Saint-Etienne. It's a twenty-minute cab ride."

"The Hotel Reynaud is right across the street and it's excellent," Sir Henry said.

"Clarise booked us rooms at the Saint-Etienne because it's right next to the Gare de l'Est station. It'll be most convenient for our departure tomorrow evening," Professor Vambery explained.

"You're most efficient, Miss Vambery," Doyle said, drawing a brief scowl from Sir Henry.

"Ah, it looks like we're ready," Stoker said, tipping the porters.

Sir Henry climbed into the second coach along with the Stokers. Doyle provided both cabbies with the name of their hotel and then joined the Vamberys inside the first coach. With the horses' hooves clattering on the paving stones, the cabs pulled into the Paris traffic, leaving the Gare du Nord behind them.

The Hotel Saint-Etienne had proven to be an excellent choice. Clean and comfortable, it offered every amenity.

The Orient Express had an established departure time of 7:08 each Tuesday and Friday evening. It displeased Doyle, wasting an entire day doing nothing, but it couldn't be helped. They passed the time exploring in the neighborhood around the hotel, interspersed with a few leisurely meals. At 6:00 pm Stoker coordinated with the hotel staff to have their luggage transported to the station. Now, just short of 7:00 pm, they were all gathered on the platform. Stretching down the tracks before them was the long, gleaming train.

Stoker and Vambery had secured first class accommodations, something Doyle was grateful for considering the length of the journey. The Stokers, of course, shared a compartment while everyone else took individual quarters. They had all seen their luggage secured and inspected their compartments by the time the locomotive's whistle sounded and the train began gliding out of the station. Some forty minutes later they gathered in the restaurant car for the evening meal.

Sir Henry watched the shadows and occasional flickers of light rushing past outside the window. "Well, we're committed now."

"It does feel more real," Stoker said.

Doyle leaned forward. "We'll be all right as long as we use our heads and don't take any foolish risks."

"We all must be watchful," Professor Vambery said. "Tepes had agents watching us in London. We have to assume that scrutiny will continue."

"Yes," Doyle agreed, his thoughts going to the two men he observed on the platform at Charing Cross. "From this point forward, none of us can be alone, especially Mrs. Stoker. And if she and Miss Vambery are together, at least one of us should always be in their company."

Stoker picked at his roasted chicken. "Clarise has her own compartment, but the professor's room adjoins hers."

Vambery nodded. "There's a connecting door as well. Very convenient."

"We won't be shy about calling for you at even the hint of a threat," Clarise said.

Florence smiled. "Indeed. I intend to return to Cheyne Walk in one piece."

Doyle admired her spirit, but could hear the underlying fear in her voice.

The rest of the meal passed with light conversation as the train sped across the French countryside toward Strasbourg. Once the waiter had cleared the plates, no one was tired, so they moved on to the salon car for an after dinner drink.

They found a convenient conversation area equipped with comfortable chairs and a small sofa. Over glasses of sherry and brandy, the talk continued. Doyle was relaxing for the first time since leaving London when a slight movement at the opposite end of the car caught his eye.

Two wing chairs, their backs to Doyle, faced a small sofa. Someone sitting in the chair had placed their left arm on the armrest and held up a pair of wire rim spectacles with thick lenses. As Doyle watched, the right hand appeared from behind the chair grasping a white handkerchief which was tasked to cleaning the glasses.

Beyond the wing chair, resting on the couch, Doyle made out a wool tweed cap. The chairs blocked the owner from view.

He had hoped that he was being overcautious on the station platform at Charing Cross, but now there could be little doubt. The bookish man and his thick set companion were on this train. Doyle couldn't fathom how he had missed them.

He turned his attention to his friends. "I need your attention for a few moments. There's something you all should be aware of."

CHAPTER 19

S toker had felt anxious ever since Doyle had revealed that the two men were on the train. At Doyle's suggestion, they remained in the salon car until the two men left. Once they did, just before midnight, he and the rest were able to get a good look at them.

Professor Vambery suggested they make the chief train superintendent aware of the men, but Doyle pointed out that all they had at this point was suspicion. Until someone infringed upon their privacy or committed a crime against them, they had no grounds for a formal complaint.

Stoker spent that first night sitting next to the compartment door, his Webley next to him, watchful and listening as Florence slept. He retrieved his manuscript from his bag, along with several sheets of fresh paper. He was close to finishing the story, but so far, an ending had proven elusive. Tepes had disappeared from England, leaving a wake of death in his tracks, and those circumstances had left him with a sense of failure and confusion. It muddled the task of guiding his story to its proper conclusion.

Now he scribbled down his observations on the journey, hoping the exercise might help ease his nerves and free his mind for writing of a more creative nature. At the sound of any activity in the passageway, he would put aside his paper and pen, take hold of the revolver, and inch open the door to see who might be present. The only sounds came from the porter delivering extra blankets and pillows, or the occasional traveler returning late from the salon car.

Around four in the morning, the train slowed as it approached Munich. Stoker increased his vigilance when the train pulled into the station and kept it while the French locomotive was detached from the train to be replaced by the German engine. It would be next to impossible for anyone to leave a train traveling sixty-five or seventy miles per hour. But he worried someone would attempt to remove Florence from the train by force while it was stopped at a station. Thirty minutes after arriving in Munich, the train departed for its passage across Germany. No threat presented itself that night. He dozed off before dawn and managed to get a couple of hours of sleep.

Florence betrayed him at breakfast as they steamed into the station at Ljubljana. "He stayed up the entire night."

"I was doing a spot of writing," Stoker said.

Florence leaned toward him. "You were keeping watch over me."

Doyle gave Stoker his best reproving frown. "You'll be no good to any of us if you don't get rest."

"It was my intention to keep watch as well," Sir Henry said. "But I'm ashamed to say I fell asleep."

The metallic clanking of a coupler detaching drifted into the car. Then the sound of hissing steam and Stoker watched as the Austrian locomotive backed onto a siding beside the restaurant car.

"I walked through the cars before bed," Doyle said. "I was hoping to discover where our two shadows might be residing, but there was no sign of them."

"What could they possibly do on the train?" Florence asked. "There are so many people and no easy escape."

Stoker leaned back in his chair. "I don't know what their intentions might be, but we'll take no chances."

Doyle nodded his agreement. "Indeed. And on the subject of not taking chances, once we're finished here, you need to get some sleep. Perhaps Mrs. Stoker can stay with Clarise in her compartment this morning while you rest in yours."

Clarise brightened at the suggestion. "We'll get to know one another better."

Florence nodded her agreement.

"And I'll stay with them as well," the professor said.

"I'm open to anything that will get my husband to do what's best for him," Florence said.

"All right," Stoker said. "But I want to walk the train again first. I'll feel better if I know where those two men are."

The train experienced a slight lurch as the Slovenian locomotive was attached to it. Fifteen minutes later, the whistle sounded and the train lumbered out of the station, heading for Croatia only an hour away.

With breakfast concluded, Doyle accompanied him in inspecting the other cars. They went forward first, stopping just short at the baggage car door, and then worked their way back toward the rear of the train. They passed through the second class sleeping cars, then the restaurant and salon cars, and made their way along the first class sleeper cars with no sight of the mysterious men.

Once Florence was situated with the Vamberys, and Doyle and Irving had both assured him they would stay on watch, Stoker returned to his compartment and lay down on the berth. With his mind filled with worry and doubt, he was still awake when the train pulled to a stop in Zagreb. Once the train was on its way again, he drifted off into a fitful sleep.

The clatter of the car wheels passing over a track spur awakened him. Stoker was surprised to discover he had slept over five hours, and as he looked out the compartment window, he saw the train was already coming to a stop at the Belgrade station. After tidying up and changing clothes, he made his way to Clarise's compartment to check on Florence. The professor opened the door at his knock and Stoker was glad to find Doyle inside as well.

Grateful to see her well, Stoker kissed Florence on the cheek. She smiled, but otherwise scarcely acknowledged him.

"Is anything wrong?"

"I think we all may be a little tired." Clarise said.

Professor Vambery folded his arms in front of him. "Probably from being penned up in here all day."

Concern showed on the professor's face, and then Stoker noticed the same concern from Doyle and Clarise.

"We've seen no sign of them," Doyle said, changing the subject to the two men. "Sir Henry's been sitting in the salon car most of the day keeping watch, and I've been up and down the passageways."

"Perhaps we should be grateful they've kept their distance," Professor Vambery said.

Clarise frowned. "Although it is worrisome not knowing what they're up to."

A moan rose from Florence. The sound was short and soft, but obvious enough to draw everyone's attention. Stoker sat down beside her. "Florrie?"

Florence turned toward him. A hint of a smile shown on her face, but her eyes were dark and faraway. "I'm fine. Clarise and the professor are very fine company."

Stoker looked up to see everyone watching them with concerned expressions. Something wasn't right, but this wasn't the time to make a case of it with Florence present.

"Perhaps if we all move to the salon car," he said. "A little food and drink would do me some good."

They all agreed to join Sir Henry in the salon car and then move on to dinner once their appetites warranted it. Doyle went on ahead to find Sir Henry while Stoker and the professor escorted the ladies back to their compartments.

"You're sure there's nothing I can do for you?" Stoker asked Florence as he opened the compartment door for her.

She didn't bother to look at him. "You mustn't worry about me so much. I'm fine."

Once Florence closed the door behind her, Professor Vambery and Clarise moved closer to him.

"You saw?" The professor gestured after Florence

"She's not herself."

The professor nodded. "It began gradually, just after you went to take your nap. She became less and less engaged with us."

"If one of us asked her a question, she'd answer it, but only in a way that took the least amount of effort. And her eyes, just staring off at nothing," Clarise said.

"Why don't you go on ahead and freshen up while I finish bringing Bram up to date," Vambery said.

"I can take a hint," Clarise said. "You want to talk man to man."

"We'll wait for you here," her father said as she walked away.

The professor waited until Clarise was inside her compartment. "I assume what we're seeing has to do with proximity. The closer we draw to him, the more influence Tepes has over your wife."

"But how?" Stoker asked, his voice laden with worry.

Vambery shrugged. "I don't know. But we have to watch her closely from this point on."

"Do you think she might harm herself?"

The professor drew a deep breath. "I can't say anything for certain, but right now I'm more concerned with her harming one of us."

CHAPTER 20

The stop in Belgrade was lengthy. The train superintendent announced they would have two hours there and passengers were welcome to disembark. He concluded with a warning the train would depart on time, with or without all its passengers.

The Stoker party ventured off the train, but ventured no farther than the station platform for the sake of their own security. The two hours flew by and as the train pulled out of the station, they all made their way to the salon car. They spent what remained of the afternoon in conversation, enjoying hors d'oeuvres and aperitifs served by the salon car's attentive staff, and gazing at the Serbian countryside.

Stoker found himself preoccupied with worry for Florence. She inter-acted with everyone, but was reserved and picked at the food only when encouraged. As the train sped toward the Bulgarian border, they moved to the restaurant car for dinner. Again, Florence showed little interest in her food.

They finished up dinner while the train was stopped in Sofia to attach the Bulgarian engine. This proved to be another long stop. They spent the time in the salon car with the men enjoying cigars and brandy while the women sat nearby, each with a magazine and a glass of port. The train had been underway again for only twenty or thirty minutes when Florence closed her magazine. "I think I'd like to go to bed now, Bram."

"The reading has made me a little drowsy as well," Clarise said.

The men rose to their feet as the women gathered their things.

Doyle consulted his watch. "Eleven forty. I didn't realize it was so late."

"Do you think we should take another look along the train before joining them?" Sir Henry asked.

"A good idea."

"I'm gratified," Sir Henry responded, his sarcasm obvious.

"Why don't I escort the ladies back to their quarters?" Professor Vambery said. "I'll keep watch in the corridor until you return."

Sir Henry stepped toward Vambery. "I'll go along with the professor and walk to the back of the train before I return to my compartment."

"That leaves the front of the train to us," Stoker said to Doyle.

He kissed Florence on the cheek and watched until she had left the rear of the car with the Vamberys and Sir Henry. Doyle then led the way as they strolled through the front cars. They said little, choosing to focus on their search for the two men. The expedition proved unfruitful. Whoever the two men were, they were proving to be experts at elusiveness.

They made their way through the forward second class car. Only the baggage car remained ahead. Reaching the front, Doyle took hold of the door latch and pulled it open. At the same moment, the train superintendent stepped out of the baggage car, securing the door behind him. When he turned and saw them, the fellow was momentarily startled.

"Can I be of service, messieurs?" the superintendent asked, his English accented.

Doyle looked past the man to the baggage car entrance. "No, thank you. We're just stretching our legs before bed."

"Ah, oui. I enjoy the evening walk myself from time to time," the superintendent acknowledged. "You must turn back from here, though. Only railroad personnel est autorisé, are permitted in the baggage carriage."

Doyle smiled. "We were just turning back, anyway."

Stoker led the way back with the superintendent tagging along behind, leaving them once they passed through the restaurant car.

Reaching the end of the coach that connected to their sleeper car, Stoker opened the door. As he did so, a man pushed past him. Stoker caught only a glimpse of the wire rim spectacles on his face, and then noticed the bowler hat carried in his hand.

"My pardon," the fellow mumbled with the hint of an accent as he hurried away.

"Stoker," Doyle said in a hushed tone.

Stoker nodded, casually turning to see the man exit through the front end of the car. "I saw him. He's just come from our car."

"Hurry on then."

Together, they rushed through to the sleeper car, and both came to an abrupt stop. Professor Vambery was nowhere to be seen. Stoker ran forward, his heart pounding.

Reaching the compartment he shared with Florence, he pulled the door open. Florence, dressed for bed, stood at the end of her berth folding an item of clothing. She started at his sudden appearance.

A wave of relief washed over Stoker. "Are you all right?"

"Of course. What's happened?"

"Lock the door behind me. Don't open it unless you hear my voice or another you recognize from our group."

He stepped back into the corridor and shut the door. As soon as he heard the lock catch, he went to Professor Vambery's door where Doyle joined him.

"Professor," Stoker called out.

No reply.

"Professor Vambery," he called again.

When no answer came, Doyle stepped forward and opened the door. Lying on the compartment floor, a bloody gash across his temple, lay Professor Vambery. They hurried inside and moved the professor from the floor to his berth.

Doyle placed his ear to Vambery's chest and listened. "He's alive."

"Sir Henry," Stoker shouted. "Sir Henry, hurry!"

Stoker heard movement from Sir Henry's quarters and a moment later the actor, still dressed except for his coat, appeared in the doorway.

An instant later, Clarise, wearing a robe, opened her door and looked out. "What is it?"

"Your father," Stoker said.

Clarise hurried to the compartment door with Irving on her heels. Her complexion paled as she stepped inside. "Father, no!"

"He's alive, Clarise, he's alive," Doyle said.

"Dear God," Irving said. "What happened?"

As Doyle continued looking to the unconscious professor, Clarise pushed past him to the shelf where there sat a water pitcher and washbasin. Retrieving one of the towels at the edge of the shelf, she wet the corner of it and then dabbed the blood away from her father's wound.

"Allow me, Miss Vambery," Doyle said, taking the towel from her hand. "Sometimes my medical education comes in handy."

"Who did this?" Sir Henry asked.

"The man with the bowler. We passed him in the corridor." Stoker rushed out the words.

"Did you see him when you walked through to the rear of the train?" Doyle asked Irving.

"I saw no one," Irving responded.

"If the one we saw went toward the front, then where is his friend?" Stoker wondered aloud.

"He could still be nearby," Sir Henry said.

"We need to make sure. Mr. Doyle needs to attend to the professor. You check the rear of the train. I'll go after that fellow with the hat," Stoker said to Irving.

Stoker reached into his pocket to make sure he had the Webley.

"Don't take any chances," Doyle advised.

"Stay close to Florence," Stoker called out as he hurried back toward the front of the train.

He made his way back through the salon and restaurant cars with no sign of the man with the bowler or his companion. He slowed his pace somewhat in the second class sleeping cars, doing his best to look past the curtains. Again, there was no sign of either of the men. Soon, Stoker found himself facing the door of the baggage car for the second time that night.

Stoker stepped through on the connecting platform and tried the door. The handle turned.

He eased the door open, slipped inside, and then squeezed himself behind the nearest crate. The only illumination came from the moonlight seeping through the four narrow windows set in each of the two sliding side doors. Stoker could make out the dark shapes of boxes, trunks, and crates. The sound of something scraping across the floor reached him.

He strained to see through the darkness and listened for the sound again against the click clack of the steel wheels rolling along the tracks. As the train rounded a curve, the light coming through the windows shifted, revealing the silhouette of a man pushing a large crate across the floor toward the sliding side door at the far end of the car. The man straightened up, walked around the crate, and unlatched the door. He slid the door open and the noise of the locomotive poured through it.

The man's back was to him, so Stoker moved deeper into the car, slipping behind another crate just as the man turned back toward his crate. The fellow bent over the crate and began pushing it toward the open door.

Stoker peered out from his hiding place as the light from the open doorway shifted again. He could see better now, his eyes adjusting to the gloom, and what he saw confounded him. This wasn't the man with the bowler hat he'd seen leaving the sleeper car. This man wore a wool tweed cap and was pushing the crate of weapons Doyle had assembled through the door. Stoker felt a tremor of dread.

Without a moment of hesitation, he charged forward, throwing his full weight into the tweed cap man. They both tumbled across the floor and slammed into a rack of luggage secured to the far wall. They rolled away from the rack, each trying to gain control over the other. Stoker got onto his knees, pulling his revolver from his pocket. But tweed cap jumped to his feet and kicked the gun from his hand before he could take aim. The gun clattered across the floor and out the open door.

His wrist throbbing from the kick, Stoker charged again, slamming his fist into tweed cap's jaw. The man staggered backwards and tripped over several pieces of luggage. He reached into his coat and withdrew something. A sharp click sounded and Stoker saw the glint of a knife blade.

Tweed cap climbed to his feet and advanced on him, the knife now an extension of his arm. Stoker looked for something he might use as a weapon. Nothing useful caught his eye, but he snatched a leather satchel from a nearby rack and held it in a defensive stance.

The man crouched and leaped forward while bringing the knife up. Stoker parried the thrust with the satchel and then clubbed the fellow with it. Tweed cap fell back but only for an instant before lunging forward again with a vicious thrust. This time, the knife penetrated the leather satchel and held steadfast. Stoker twisted the satchel, wrenching the knife from the man's hand.

In the blink of an eye, his opponent was on him again. Tweed cap's fist connected with his chin, and then Stoker felt himself propelled backwards by the man's weight. His back and then his head slammed into something hard. There was a flash of light, and then everything went black.

The first hint Stoker had that he was still alive came with a stabbing pain in the back of his skull. Then the throbbing hiss of the locomotive and the clicking of the wheels against the rails grew in volume. His eyes opened and he realized he was lying on his side facing the baggage car's open door. As his vision cleared, he saw tweed cap once again leaning over the crate of weapons, inch by inch pushing it through the door. The crate was almost halfway out.

Stoker forced himself up and leaped forward. This time, tweed cap saw him coming and rose to meet him. They grappled and Stoker realized in a fresh flash of terror that the man was dragging him toward the door. Stoker saw the blurred shadows rushing past in the night and the crate inching forward with the movement of the train.

The gaping opening loomed closer and Stoker fought with every bit of strength he had. But he felt his strength waning and the pain in his skull increasing. Tweed cap had dragged him within a foot of the opening. He felt his sense of balance failing him. He heard his own voice cry out as he felt his footing slip.

Stoker suddenly felt himself pulled backwards and away from tweed cap's grip. Doyle leaped into view and hurled himself at tweed cap, slamming his fist into the man's jaw. Tweed cap staggered backwards and lost his footing. Doyle rushed forward to grab the fellow, but it was too late. With his arms flailing, tweed cap tumbled through the doorway with a terrible scream. He bounced off the side of the weapons crate and disappeared into the blackness.

The crate, its precarious balance upset by the falling body, slid through the door. Stoker and Doyle scrambled to grab hold of the end of the crate, but they were both too late. With a terrible scraping sound, the end of the crate angled upward and fell into the night.

CHAPTER 21

"It's not too bad." Doyle studied the back of Stoker's head. "The professor ended up with a slight cut, and you with a nasty bump. Fortunate, both of you."

Doyle had helped Stoker back to the sleeping car. Not wanting to disturb Florence, he had taken him to his own compartment. Now, except for Professor Vambery who was sleeping, everyone was gathered there.

Stoker gingerly touched his head. "It throbs like the devil." Stoker said.

"Go straight to bed and stay there until morning. Rest should help," Doyle said.

"But one of them is still out there."

"Mr. Doyle and I can take turns keeping watch," Sir Henry said from the doorway, scarcely acknowledging the author.

"Yes." Doyle nodded.

"You needn't use me as an excuse," Florence said. "And I'll never understand what possessed you to confront that man on your own."

Doyle thought Florence seemed a bit more like herself. At least she appeared to be more engaged.

Stoker shrugged. "There was no choice. A lot of good it did, though."

"Spilled milk," Clarise said. "What matters is you're all right."

"So what are we left with?" Sir Henry asked. "We still have the crosses around our necks, at least."

"I'm certain we can buy more of the large crosses," Florence said.

"I still have my revolver," Doyle said.

Stoker looked down at his shoes. "Mine went out the door of the baggage car."

"I have my Bowie knife," Sir Henry said. "I don't suppose we could purchase more guns in Varna?"

Doyle thought it doubtful. "It could prove difficult, being foreigners."

"How did you think to come after me?" Stoker asked Doyle.

"I'd done all I could for the professor when Sir Henry returned from the rear of the train."

"There was no sign of either of the swine," Sir Henry said.

"The reasonable conclusion was that both of them must be in the front of the train. I was afraid you might be walking into something you couldn't anticipate. I decided to go look for you. When I reached the baggage car, I heard the fight."

"But you never saw the other fellow, the one with the bowler hat," Sir Henry said.

"No, and I still have no explanation as to how he managed to avoid us," Doyle said.

"I wish I'd gotten to that thug sooner," Stoker said.

Doyle pointed a reproving finger at Stoker. "It's no good talking like that. You did everything you could."

"I must admit, for the first time since we started all this, I felt like I was truly making a fight of it," Stoker said. "Feeling my fist pound into that fellow, for once, it was something tangible."

"I believe I know what you mean," Sir Henry said.

"You did well, Stoker," Doyle said. "No one here thinks otherwise."

"Did I? Thanks for that." He looked down at his feet again and then said, "I'm not feeling so well. I'm going to try to get some sleep."

Doyle watched Florence follow Stoker out of the room. He waited until he heard the compartment door click shut. "He's taken all this on himself."

"I think he's come around a bit," Sir Henry said.

"Perhaps, I hope so," Doyle said.

"You must remember he came very close to losing his wife last year," Clarise said. "And now circumstances force him to risk her life again. I think we can afford to give him some grace for that."

"You're right, of course," Doyle said. "My only concern is if every one of us isn't at the top of our game, we could all end up dead."

Clarise aimed a mock frown at Doyle. "If those are your concerns, then I suggest you try praying instead of predicting doom. I wouldn't be here if I were trusting you alone for my safety, as capable as you've proven to be. My life is in the hands of God, and so is my trust. Philippians tells us 'I can do all things through Christ which strengthens me.' My prayers for Bram are that he'll find that strength. Yours should be as well."

Doyle had put little credence in God over the years, but he'd been compelled to question his own disbelief when he saw Tepes repulsed by the cross. It was obvious as well that they had emerged unscathed from conflicts with the monster where the more reasonable outcome should have been that they ended up dead. His companions' faith was strong, and they had credited God with the protection that had seen them through.

"Miss Vambery, once again your counsel proves to be strong and appropriate. You're right, we should be placing our faith in something beyond our own abilities," Doyle said.

Clarise answered him with a smile. "Well, I've scolded the both of you enough for one night. I'm going to look in on father."

They bid her goodnight and watched her disappear into Professor Vambery's compartment.

Doyle consulted his watch. "It's almost twelve forty-five. We should arrive in Varna around four this morning. We'll have to be off the train no later than seven, so we'd better get some sleep."

Sir Henry gestured in the general direction Clarise had taken. "That is one formidable woman."

"Without question."

The Orient Express slacked its speed as it approached the northeast corner of Bulgaria and the Black Sea coast. Just after four thirty in the morning, with brakes moaning and loud hisses of steam colliding with the cold air, the train slowed to a stop in the station at Varna.

A faint noise emanated from a corner of the baggage car as the train crew made preparations for the passengers to disembark. The man stepped from the large crate he had prepared for this trip.

His instructions had been to look for any opportunity to disrupt the Stoker party's journey. Once in Varna, if he saw an opportunity to remove the Stoker woman from the train, he should take it. And if he had to murder any of her escorts to do it, so much the better.

But the train had proven difficult with the confined spaces, and passengers and crew ever present. As the train entered Bulgaria, he had grown anxious. The end of the journey drew near and they had done nothing. He had no desire to report nothing to his master.

His mistake had been in trying to make his own opportunity. Bludgeoning the man, Vambery, had been rash and a foolish risk, but he had thought it necessary to draw attention away from the baggage car so his partner could do his work. But their timing had been poor and Stoker had reacted faster than anticipated.

He decided it would be most prudent to conceal himself after his attack on Vambery, so was uncertain about what had taken place between his associate and Stoker. Whatever happened, he had concluded that his associate was dead. He had found his partner's knife lodged in a leather satchel. He removed it and placed it in his coat pocket.

The death of his associate was inconvenient, but of little concern; there were others waiting for him in Varna. Others like himself who served for the promise of an eternal life and power over mortals. When the master called, they would carry out whatever errand or assignment he required to spread the cleansing darkness that would eventually eliminate the weak from the earth.

The Stoker woman would leave the train in a few hours, and then there would be many more opportunities. He would watch and wait.

The man placed the bowler hat on his head and adjusted his glasses, picked up his small travel case, and walked the few steps to the nearest side door of the car. He pulled back the latch as quietly as he could manage and then slid the door open a couple of inches. There he waited until there was no one in view, then opened the door wider and stepped out onto the platform. With a final, cautious look around, he hurried away and disappeared into the shadows.

CHAPTER 22

The sun was still low in the morning sky. Jardani, seated in front of his wagon on an overturned washtub, watched Miri use a folded rag to remove the kettle of boiling water from the hanger over the crackling fire. He admired her slender figure as she squared down next to the porcelain teapot he'd given her the year before. She poured some of the boiling water into the pot to warm it, and while returning the kettle to its place over the fire, noticed him watching her.

"What?" she asked.

"I said nothing."

"You're looking at me."

"You're nice to look at."

Miri laughed and shook her head. Her long, dark hair fell across her eyes and she swept it back into place. She emptied the water from the teapot and retrieved the wire basket of tea she had prepared from a little table next to the wagon stairs. She placed the tea basket in the pot and then filled it from the kettle.

"Just a few minutes more." She hiked up her long skirt enough to sit down next to him on the low folding stool he had made for her.

They sat in silence, watching the activity in the camp. Smoke rose from the cooking fires outside each of the wagons. Women were cleaning up after breakfast while children played at their feet. One man was seeing to some improvement on his wagon. Others tended to livestock at the edge of the encampment or organized goods they had acquired. Across the clearing, Zache sat with his two teen-aged girls, admiring some needlework each of them had just finished. At the wagon next to Zache's sat Stochelo with three other men, deep in conversation while enjoying their pipes.

Miri rose again and poured the tea into cups. "What does your day hold for you?"

"I'm not sure."

She hesitated. "You're not going back to the castle?"

"I think our work is done there."

"I don't see why anyone should need to go there," Miri said.

Miri placed the teapot back on the table and picked the two cups she had just poured. He leaned forward and took hold of the end of the long, red sash tied around her waist. He began slowing drawing her back with it as if he had hooked a great, beautiful fish.

"Jardani!" She scolded him with a laugh. "Be careful. You'll make me spill the tea."

He took hold of her and gently pulled her down onto his knee.

"You know how I feel about our pact with the Voivode?"

Miri's smile faded. "You haven't approved for some time now."

He nodded as he reached up and stroked her cheek.

"It's important to me that you know that."

Miri kissed him on the cheek and then handed him his tea.

He took a sip. "Good. Thank you."

At that moment, a commotion arose on the opposite side of the camp. Stochelo and his group were on their feet staring at the edge of the clearing and several other members of the tribe were walking in that direction. Zache was on his feet now, too. He caught Jardani's eye and nodded toward the source of all the interest.

"What business do you have here?" Jardani heard Stochelo ask from across the camp as Miri moved from his knee so he could rise. He didn't hear a distinct reply.

"Jardani? This man asks for you," Stochelo called out.

Jardani made his way through the small crowd. Half way to the edge of the camp he recognized the villager, Alexander. Standing beside him was the father of the murdered boy.

"Alexander," Jardani greeted the villager.

Alexander acknowledged the greeting with a polite nod.

"How do you know this man?" Stochelo asked him with suspicion.

"He's from the village where Zache and I returned the boy."

He glanced at Stochelo, who glared at him and then turned back to the villagers.

"Why have you come?" Jardani asked.

"I was trying to tell him." Alexander gestured toward Stochelo. Then, turning to the boy's father. "This is Marek Tesar. It was his son you were good enough to bring down from the castle."

Several of the onlookers gasped.

Jardani remembered the man.

"You are Jardani?" Marek Tesar asked, stepping closer.

Jardani nodded.

"I fear I treated you with rudeness when you were last in our village."

Jardani remained silent as Miri came to stand beside him.

"My neighbors treated you badly as well."

Silence hung over the clearing as Tesar looked down at his shoes.

"When you brought my son to me I was overcome with sadness. My heart was breaking. That is my only excuse for the way I treated you. And it is a poor excuse."

Jardani could only nod his understanding.

"But you must know how much it meant to me and my wife that you brought our son home to us," Tesar continued. "You must know how terrible it was not knowing where he was and imagining horrible things. You'll never know what it meant that you brought him back to us."

Jardani watched Stochelo's stern expression soften.

Tesar looked up and saw Zache watching him. "You, you were there, too."

"Yes," Zache said.

"I want to tell you both I am sorry. Sorry for my rudeness, and for any good it does, the rudeness of my neighbors. And I want to thank you for returning my son to me and his mother."

Tesar was looking down at the ground again and Alexander placed a comforting hand on his shoulder.

Asena, Stochelo's wife, approached from where she had been listening at their wagon. "You can stay for some tea if you like. Sit for a while," she said.

Only after extending the invitation did she look at her husband. Stochelo was frowning, but shrugged his consent.

Tesar shook his head. "Thank you, no. I've said what had to be said. Now it's best we return home."

The two villagers turned and began walking back toward the trees.

Miri made her way around Jardani and caught up to the villagers. She took hold of Marek Tesar's arm to stop him. Jardani watched as the man turned and looked into his wife's eyes.

"We're sorry for what's happened," Miri said to him. "Jardani and I are sorry, and we will remember you in our prayers."

Marek Tesar took Miri's hands in his and gave them a tender squeeze. She pulled away and returned to Jardani's side as the two villagers continued on their way. The tribe watched them in silence until they had disappeared into the woods.

Jardani realized many eyes were now on him. Stochelo approached him, his expression hardening again.

"I told to leave the body at the castle, but you would not listen," Stochelo hissed. "And now villagers come into our camp."

"The man was grateful. All he wanted was to tell us so."

"They called you by name. How do they know you?"

"I helped the younger one free his cow from a bog. You remember, I told you of it," Jardani said. "I only saw the father in the village when we returned the body."

"You said only that you'd been stuck in the bog. You said nothing of any villager."

"Knowing how you feel, why would I?"

"You know how I feel, yet you go against my wishes."

"I saw no harm in helping a man who needed it," Jardani said.

Stochelo closed the distance between them. "Do you think one of them would bother helping you?"

"That one who just left would." Jardani toward the path the visitors had taken.

"If you wish to live here with us, then you'll do as I say," Stochelo said. "We do work for them when they have it. We take their money, but they are not our friends. They've never been our friends. You'll keep your distance."

"And why is that? Because you say so?"

"That should be enough!"

"Would you not welcome help if you needed it, even if it came from a villager?" Jardani asked.

One of the oldest members of the band, a wizened fellow named Babik, stepped forward.

He addressed Stochelo. "Too many times I've come across those who I would never have intended to meet. No one can avoid anything or anyone completely."

"They see us as nothing but animals or criminals. They'd see us again as slaves if they could," Stochelo roared.

"Not all of them," Jardani said. "There are decent men among them just as there are among our people. And there are evil men among them just as there are with us. We're all the same."

Stochelo spit in disdain and pointed a finger in Jardani's face. "We don't need them. We don't need their distrust or their scorn."

Miri stepped up to Stochelo and placed her hand on his shoulder. Jardani recognized the gesture and knew she hoped to calm him, but Stochelo looked at her with surprise and contempt.

"Jardani gave help to a man who needed it," she said. "Maybe that is all that's needed to heal some of the distrust. Maybe we should all do as my husband has done."

"This doesn't involve you, woman," Stochelo said, shoving her away.

Miri stumbled backwards, lost her footing and fell to the ground.

Jardani stared in disbelief. It was one thing for Stochelo to bully him, but to lay hands on Miri. A fury boiled up inside him. He hurled himself forward, throwing himself into Stochelo and knocking him to the ground.

Jardani had seen the shock in Stochelo's eyes as he charged him, but by the time they were rolling in the dirt, the older man's fighting instincts were fully engaged. As they both staggered to their knees, he wrapped his arms around Jardani in a crushing hold. With a bellow of rage, Stochelo tightened his grip. Jardani felt the air leaving his lungs as the pain spread through his shoulders and chest. He slammed his forehead into Stochelo's chin.

With a cry of pain, Stochelo loosened his hold and Jardani twisted away from him. He found his balance and charged again, this time swinging his fist at Stochelo's head. Stochelo threw up an arm and deflected the punch, and then threw one of his own. Jardani tried to get out of the way, but Stochelo's fist slammed into his chest. The force of the blow knocked him backwards and Stochelo rushed toward him. Again Stochelo's arms locked around him as they tumbled to the ground.

Jardani had the strength of his youth, but Stochelo fought with cunning honed from years of experience. He pinned Jardani under him and pulled his fist back. The blow landed on Jardani's jaw. Jardani couldn't take another blow like that. As Stochelo drew his arm back for another strike, Jardani struck upward, landing a blow under Stochelo's chin. The man's head snapped back and Jardani delivered another punch. Stochelo tumbled off him, and Jardani scrambled to his feet. In only a moment, Stochelo regained his footing.

They faced each other, fists clenched and at the ready, each looking for an opportunity to attack. Suddenly, Zache was standing between them. "Enough!"

Jardani wasn't about to drop his guard, and Stochelo didn't appear that he would either. Zache pushed them away from each other.

"Stop, stop it now. We live with the scorn of the townspeople, and now we fight amongst ourselves? No!" Zache said.

Stochelo lowered his fists but stood his ground, trying to catch his breath. His wife approached from their wagon and stood behind him, concern lining her face.

Stochelo pointed at Jardani. "This is not done."

"It's done for now," Zache said. "We'll all talk later. As for now, both of you go clean yourselves up."

Jardani kept his eyes on Stochelo as he made his way over to Miri who was standing nearby between two protective women, both glaring at Stochelo. Stochelo pivoted on his heels and stomped off toward his wagon with Asena following behind him.

Miri took Jardani's arm and they headed back to their wagon. His mind raced with all the implications of what had just happened. He had openly opposed the leader of their tribe.

Jardani was uncertain of what might happen next, but he knew everything would be different. It had all changed in the passing of only a few minutes. The traditions of his people were strong and important, but he knew that from this moment forward he would no longer follow them blindly.

CHAPTER 23

Doyle watched, his impatience strained, while the clerk worked his way through a messy stack of documents laid out on a small, wooden table. The clerk was a dark complexioned, rough looking fellow with enormous arms that had once carried a good deal of muscle. Doyle deduced he had been a dock worker in his younger years. Aging, or perhaps an injury, had placed him in the Harbor Administration office. There were two other staff members, both men, going about their various tasks. In the twenty minutes he and Vambery had been waiting, several other men had been in and out of the busy office.

Doyle turned to Professor Vambery sitting next to him in the line of uncomfortable wooden chairs. The cut on the professor's head had scabbed and he had reported no lingering malaise from the attack. "Are you certain he understands what we're looking for?"

"My Bulgarian is excellent," the professor answered.

After disembarking from the Orient Express, they had made their way directly to the Grand English Hotel. Stoker had wanted to question the Varna port officers himself about the Czarina Catherine and its cargo, but Doyle argued it would be best for everyone if he stayed at the hotel along with Sir Henry to assure Florence and Clarise's safety.

He was still worried about Stoker's state of mind and thought it would be more calming for the man to stay close to his wife. Besides, with his knowledge of the city and his language skills, Professor Vambery was the logical choice to accompany him.

Vambery rose from his chair and Doyle noticed the clerk was walking toward them holding a few papers in his fist. The fellow dropped the papers on the front counter and exchanged several words with Vambery.

"He can't find any information about the Czarina Catherine," Professor Vambery translated.

"How can that be? Is the record keeping here in such disorder?"

The professor shrugged. "He says he has the schooner's transit papers showing its departure from England, but there isn't anything documenting an arrival here."

While Doyle was considering this information, the office door opened and a young man, perhaps thirty, with auburn hair, strolled in carrying an armload of papers. He looked curiously at them as he made his way around the counter and placed the papers on top of a row of file cabinets. The fellow opened one of the cabinet drawers, began leafing through the papers and filing them away.

Doyle shoved his hands into his coat pockets. "This is very disappointing. We've only just begun and we've already reached a dead end."

Professor Vambery turned back to the clerk and again they engaged in conversation.

"What did he say?" Doyle asked as soon as the exchange ended.

"He's sorry. He has no explanation."

"That's it then. We'll have to rethink this."

Vambery turned to the clerk, thanked him, and bid him a good day.

They were turning toward the door when the young man with the auburn hair called out to them.

Vambery turned toward the counter. "He's telling us to wait."

The fellow began a discussion with Professor Vambery. The professor's demeanor turned from disappointment to excitement.

Doyle joined them at the counter. "What?"

"He heard the Czarina Catherine mentioned while we were in the office. He didn't mean to eavesdrop but couldn't help—"

"Yes, yes, but what's he want with us?" Doyle interrupted.

"He knows the Czarina Catherine. His brother crewed on it a few years ago. Once our friend here heard what we were looking for, he realized the clerk wasn't searching in the right place."

"What in blazes does that mean?"

The young man said a few more words to Vambery. Vambery answered him and then turned back to Doyle.

"He says this other fellow has only worked in the office for a few months and isn't familiar with all the procedures. He explained that ships are quite often diverted to other ports because of unpredictable weather. The transit papers for diverted vessels are filed in a different location."

"So, there may be something, after all?"

The auburn haired fellow joined the older man at a group of cabinets at the back of the room. Together they leafed through one grouping of papers after another.

A short five minutes later, the young fellow gave a shout and hurried back to the front counter, waving a piece of paper. The older clerk followed on his heels.

Professor Vambery asked the young man what he had and Doyle waited, his patience no better than before, while the fellow spoke. The older clerk followed along, nodding at whatever the other fellow was saying.

"The Czarina Catherine never docked here. It docked in Galatz," the professor said.

"Galatz?"

"It's about two hundred miles north, across the Romanian border."

"Give them our sincere thanks." Doyle presented each of the men with a twenty leva banknote.

The men beamed over the gift as Vambery thanked them.

Doyle ushered Vambery out of the office and set off at a fast walk across the wharf.

"We'll return to the hotel with the information, but on the way I want to check the train schedules," Doyle said.

"Bulgarian train schedules can be somewhat haphazard," Vambery replied. "But perhaps we'll get lucky."

"Train schedules be damned. We've got the trail again."

CHAPTER 24

The first available train to Galatz did not depart Varna until nine thirty the following morning, and the Bulgarian railroad proved to be no Orient Express. There were several station stops, with the longest delay being in Bucharest. It took almost four hours to cover less than two hundred miles. Now they were only a few minutes away from their destination.

Doyle noticed Irving appeared a bit low. "Weary of all the travel, Sir Henry?"

"No, not so much. I was just thinking about Morgan Quincey. I was hoping he'd be able to join us, but the itinerary I sent him only detailed our whereabouts as far as Varna."

"Perhaps he wasn't able to come," Stoker said.

Sir Henry shrugged. "I thought of that, of course."

"I met Mr. Quincey first at Miss Westen's funeral," said Clarise. "But I don't think we spoke a dozen words between us while he was in London."

"All I know is that we'd be better off having him and his Colt with us," Sir Henry said.

"Speaking of guns, once we've spoken with the harbor authorities, we need to see about replacing our weapons," Stoker said.

"We will," Doyle said. "But I doubt we'll have much more luck than we had in Varna."

Varna had revealed itself to be a large, bustling city with a light frosting of snow. They made their way through the narrow, winding lanes flanked by closely clustered wooden buildings. By sunset, they had found only one source for weapons, a hardware store that had a small inventory of guns, just shotguns and rifles. Vambery did his best with the negotiating, but the proprietor, suspicious of foreigners, made some vague excuse why he couldn't part with any of his stock. They returned to the hotel empty handed.

As their train pulled into the station at Galatz, Doyle called for everyone's attention. "Does anyone have any objection to going directly to the harbor?"

"Perhaps the ladies would prefer finding a hotel first," Sir Henry said. "Especially after this long train ride."

"That could take some time since we don't know where we'll be staying yet," Doyle said.

Clarise leveled a very cross look at them both. "Goodness, when will you two stop taking up opposite sides and try being friends again? I'm fine with finding a hotel after we've done our detective work."

"And Mrs. Stoker?" Doyle asked.

"Yes, of course," Florence said.

"And for the record, I'm not the one being unfriendly," Doyle muttered.

Irving began forming a response, but a stern look from Clarise silenced him.

With a squealing of brakes and the hissing of steam, the train came to a stop at the station platform. Eager to follow through with their new clue, Doyle led everyone off the train and expedited the gathering of their baggage.

The sky was a drab, dark gray and a light snow began falling as they made their way to the line of cabs waiting on the street.

He lifted the bowler from his head and dabbed his forehead with a dirty handkerchief. Replacing the hat, he then removed his spectacles and used the same handkerchief to wipe the thick lenses. Staying close to the wall, he took a cautious look around the corner.

The Stoker woman was just climbing into a cab. The other woman climbed in with her while the men secured the luggage. He had been waiting for them. His master had been right in predicting that the English would follow the same path he had already traveled returning from England.

He cocked his finger at the four men waiting for him and they came forward. They were common men, rough men, but obedient to the cause. The darkness they served had enveloped them and they toiled with enthusiasm for the eternal carrot dangled before them. He pointed toward the street and all the men peered around the corner of the building.

"You and you," he singled out two of the four. "Follow them. Note where they go for the remainder of the day. Once they settle somewhere, report back to me at the tavern."

The two men nodded and started on their way, but one of them paused and turned back.

"Will we kill them?" he asked, keeping his voice low.

"We are to kill them if the opportunity arises. Those are our instructions, but not the Stoker woman. She's not to be harmed. Whether the others die by our hands here or reach the destination they seek, they will still die."

"I think I'd like to kill them," the man responded.

"As would I, so we will see. Now get going, and don't let them see you if you know what's good for you."

The two men disappeared around the corner of the building.

He remained at his vantage point, watching as the cabs containing the Stoker woman and her friends departed. Once they were on the way, his men hurried to the street and secured a cab of their own. One of his men gave brief instructions to the driver and then climbed aboard. He watched until the cab disappeared into the traffic and then turned back to the two remaining men.

He nodded toward one of them. "Go to our Szgany friend at his place on the wharf. Tell him to take the message up river that they are now in Galatz and the woman is with them. Then find us back at the tavern."

The man nodded and hurried away.

He watched until the fellow was out of sight. Gesturing to the remaining man to follow, he walked from the station. He looked forward to a pleasant afternoon in front of the tavern's warm hearth, and a glass or two of dark lager while he considered just how he might kill as many of the English travelers as possible.

CHAPTER 25

Professor Vambery translated. "He says he has nothing detailing the arrival of a large box on the Czarina Catherine. Not within the time period we provided."

Doyle noted Stoker's muted impatience as the very old, very slight fellow behind the service counter swept a wisp of thinning white hair off his forehead and shrugged. He looked through the several papers spread out on the counter before him for the third time and then said something to Vambery in Romanian.

"He has the arrival date and time, and he says they removed cargo from the ship, but it consisted of barrels of grain, some textiles, and a variety of food items imported from England," Vambery said.

Doyle dug inside his coat pocket and produced the shipping transfer papers drawn by Smyth and Pierson, Carriers that they had discovered in one of Tepes' hideaway houses. He passed the papers to Vambery. "Ask him if he's familiar with the shipper."

Vambery placed the transfer papers on the counter in front of the old fellow and translated Doyle's question.

The fellow looked over the papers for what seemed an interminable amount of time and then shook his head. Vambery asked a follow-up question. This time, the clerk nodded and answered while gesturing and pointing.

"He tells me that they don't file anything by the name of the shipper,"

Vambery explained. "But he knows this shipper and says they keep an office here."

"In Galatz?" Stoker asked.

"Here at the harbor. It's just down the way."

Doyle headed toward the door. "Then let's not waste further time here."

Vambery thanked the clerk and they hurried outside to the cabs where Sir Henry was waiting with the ladies. Stoker explained the latest developments to them while the professor gave instructions to the drivers. Less than five minutes later they were in front of the office of Smyth and Pierson, Carriers. The office, a somewhat weatherworn structure, was near the riverbank and connected to a larger warehouse. Florence and Clarise expressed weariness at sitting in the cab, so they all entered the office.

The interior of the building proved more comfortable than the exterior suggested. A fellow countryman named Jasper Randolph, the office's managing director, greeted them with genuine warmth. Once he realized he was being visited not only by England's best known actor, but by its most popular author as well, Mr. Randolph offered his services with great enthusiasm.

Doyle handed Randolph the transfer documents and explained what they wanted. Randolph called one of his people over and showed him the paper. The fellow hurried off and began rummaging through one of the filing cabinets. A few minutes later, he was back with the news that he had found nothing related to a box being offloaded from the Czarina Catherine in November or December of the previous year.

The lines on Randolph's forehead deepened. "It's very odd. We should always have records of any cargo loaded onto our ships, and corresponding paperwork upon delivery. I don't understand what's gone wrong in this case."

Stoker shook his head in frustration. "Another dead end."

"Perhaps the captain can shed some light on it," Randolph said.

The response surprised Doyle. "The captain?"

"Captain Donley, master of the Czarina Catherine," Randolph said.

"He's here?" Stoker asked.

Randolph bobbed his head. "The Czarina Catherine's been in port for four days. Supposed to depart yesterday, but had to be held over for repairs."

"What excellent luck," Sir Henry said.

"I'll take you to her and introduce you to Captain Donley," Randolph offered. "It's just a short walk."

Randolph escorted them from the office and led them along the wharf.

On the way, Clarise used the time to get the name of a decent hotel from their host.

In only a few minutes they were at the gangplank of the Czarina Catherine. The sidewheel steamer was majestic in an industrial workhorse kind of way. It might carry the occasional passenger, but it was clearly designed for freight transport. Until now, Doyle's only sight of the vessel had been from above, viewed from a bridge crossing the Thames. He still had a vivid image of Stoker plunging downward from that bridge, missing the deck by a narrow margin and landing in the steamer's wake.

Jasper Randolph went aboard and soon returned to the deck rail with Captain Donley. They were all ushered aboard and introductions made. Randolph advised them of his busy afternoon and excused himself. The captain invited them to join him in his cabin.

Doyle noticed Florence moved along at a slower speed than normal for her, forcing Stoker to slow his pace in order to escort her. Her eyes appeared distant once again as she gazed around the ship.

The captain's cabin turned out to be quite comfortable. They all found chairs and focused on the business at hand.

"Of course I remember that passage," Captain Donley said once Stoker explained their business. "I'll never forget it."

"What made it so memorable?" Clarise asked.

"Well, ma'am, if I was to say, in all my life I've never seen a more favorable passage, at least when speaking of speed. Not natural at all for the time of year. We made such good time it was as if the devil hisself was blowing us along."

"The devil, indeed," Vambery muttered.

The captain's expression darkened. "But then, well along, we found ourselves steaming blind. Still moving swift, mind you, but a fog rolled in and stayed with us for many a league. I was inclined to slack off steam and sail until it passed, but the crew complained loud against it. We ran by Gibraltar without being able to see or signal and it just never left us."

Stoker leaned forward. "You said your crew objected to slacking your speed in the fog?"

"The fog put the edge on their nerves, it did. But if I was to say, their grumblings caused me many a burden. Once we got past the Bosphorus, some of the Romanians came to me demanding that I heave a great box overboard."

Florence leaned toward the captain with extreme interest as he spoke, her eyes fixed unwavering on him.

"And did you send it overboard?" Stoker asked.

"You did not," Florence stated in an odd tone.

"I didn't, no. Though I've wondered many times since if perhaps I should have. But seamen are a superstitious lot and you can be sure I sent them about their business," Donley said.

"Your transit papers had you sailing for Varna," Doyle said. "Why did you put in at Galatz?"

"Well, there's one of the troubling parts of it all. The fog didn't let up for five days. The men were almost crazy with fear over it, so I kept up speed and posted lookouts, telling them to look sharp. When we finally came free of the fog, we found ourselves in the river across from Galatz."

"But you didn't correct your course for Varna," Stoker stated.

"The Romanians were fearful they were. Once the fog broke, mind you, they'd already dragged the box on deck ready for flingin'. I had to argue with a handspike in my hand. The only way I could stop any bloodiness was by agreein' to unload that damned box at Galatz." At that, the captain turned to Florence and Clarise. "Beggin' your pardon for my poor language, ladies."

Both women nodded.

"It took us all day to clear for the harbor, seein' that our papers were written for Varna, so we had to pass the night at the wharf," Captain Donley continued. "A little more than an hour 'fore sunup a man came aboard with orders written to him from England to receive a box. Only one name was on his papers and marked on the box. Dracul."

At the mention of the name, Doyle exchanged glances with Stoker and the rest of their party. Captain Donley noticed.

"This is a name you know?" the captain asked.

"We know it," Stoker said.

Donley adjusted his position on his chair. "I can tell you my Romanians didn't like it. The man said he'd come at that hour as to not have to transact with the customs officer."

"If you please, who wrote the orders carried by this man?" Professor Vambery asked.

"Ah, Smyth and Pierson," Donley said. "They came direct from the London office. I was already feelin' much uneasy about that box, so I was happy to get rid of it. The crew felt the same way, so they got right to the task, but all the while crossin' themselves agin' the evil eye and such. I can tell you I felt much better once that box was on the back of the wagon the fellow brought."

"Do you have the name of this man?" Stoker asked.

"I'll be gettin' that for you in no time." The captain got up from his chair and hurried to a desk built into the cabin's starboard bulkhead.

The interruption gave Doyle the time to observe Florence. Stationary in her chair, her eyes distant and her lips slightly parted, she was looking over every inch of the cabin as if trying to absorb some unseen power.

Donley returned, waving a paper in his hand. "Here I have it. One Issac Mandelbaum received the shipment."

"Is there an address?" Doyle asked.

"Burgen-strauss 16."

"Thank you, Captain, thank you." Stoker shook the man's hand. "You've been of immeasurable help."

CHAPTER 26

The hotel recommended by Jasper Randolph was English-owned and operated under the name of The Hotel Galatz. It was clean and comfortable and afforded them all a much needed rest. Stoker, Doyle, and Professor Vambery set out after breakfast to interview Isaac Mandelbaum.

Doyle had informed Professor Vambery about his observations of Florence. It didn't surprise him the professor had also observed the change in her. The men decided, for the sake of her safety, that Florence remain in the hotel with Clarise.

The hotel kept a private coach for guests and was more than happy to make it available to a famous author. Vambery was familiar with the city, but Galatz proved a pleasant surprise to Doyle and Stoker. The snow dusted thoroughfares were paved and lined with gas lamps. They saw evidence of electricity as well, with electrical cables leading to a few businesses along the way.

It was just nine o'clock when the coach turned onto Burgen-strauss, a moderately busy street occupied with small offices and a variety of shops. Number 16 proved to be one of the smaller offices on the block with a small window facing the front. A tarnished brass plaque mounted beside the door read *I. Mandelbaum, Forwarding Agent*.

"How may I be of service?" a portly fellow asked in accented English, rising from behind his cluttered desk as they entered the tiny office.

"We're looking for a Mr. Mandelbaum," Stoker said.

The man gave a curt little bow, causing the tassel on his fez to whip back and forth. "Indeed, I am he," he answered. "How can I help you?"

"We understand that late last year you were the receiving agent for a large box carried to Galatz on the steamer Czarina Catherine," Doyle said.

"And who do you understand this from, if I may inquire?"

"Captain Donley, master of the Czarina Catherine," Doyle said.

Mandelbaum took on an air of suspicion. "Are you with the British authorities?"

"No," Doyle said. "We're just British citizens looking for information." He turned to Stoker and Vambery. "I believe Mr. Mandelbaum has some concerns regarding his removing cargo from a vessel without the required customs inspection."

"I was paid handsomely to follow instructions," Mandelbaum said.

"So you remember the transaction," Stoker said.

"Distinctly. And please take seats, gentlemen, if you will."

Stoker shook his head. "Thank you, but no. We're in something of a hurry. You said the transaction was memorable?"

"I remember it for the ungodly hour required and because of the unsavory fellow I was compelled to complete the business with," Mandelbaum said. "And it was also the only time I've had any business with the Czarina Catherine."

"What unsavory fellow?" Stoker asked.

"Grigor Ivankov." Mandelbaum spit out the name with disdain. "My instructions were to turn over the crate to him. By previous arrangement, he came to me early that morning. He insisted that I take him to the ship with me, to save porterage fees, he said. We drove in the cart he'd brought and he paid me in gold for the trouble. The scum stayed in the shadows as the crate was put in the cart. He didn't want anyone seeing him. Once we had the cargo, he returned me here and then went on his way."

"Why did you dislike this man so much?" Stoker asked.

"He's a rodent known for dealing with the Slovaks and gypsies who trade along the river."

"Gypsies, you say," Professor Vambery said with great interest.

Mandelbaum nodded. "A disgusting man dealing with thieves and cutthroats."

"Were gypsies involved in this transaction?" Vambery asked.

"I've no idea," Mandelbaum responded. "Nor would I want to know. But if they were, it would probably be the Szgany. Ivankov dealt much with the Szgany."

"Do you have an address for Ivankov?" Doyle asked.

Mandelbaum slid from the desk, walked around it and flopped back into his chair. "He conducts business out of a hovel near the river."

Mandelbaum scribbled down the address on a scrap of paper and handed it across the desk to Doyle. "Of course you obtained no information from me."

"Of course. You've been most helpful," Doyle said.

Mandelbaum shrugged indifferently.

After looking at the address Doyle handed him, the hotel coach driver assured them in his broken English that he was familiar with the neighborhood. He also assured them they would find it unpleasant.

The surroundings indeed become more unpleasant with each block they traveled. Well tended shops and offices gave way to industrial buildings, each more grimy than the last. Even the considerable patches of snow spotting the streets were dirty.

"I feel encouraged," Stoker said, over the clatter of the wheels on the paving stones.

"I agree," Doyle said. "If our luck holds, this Ivankov fellow might tell us what we need to know. Professor, I noticed you found some interest in Mandelbaum's mention of the Szgany."

"Yes."

"Why is that?" Stoker asked.

"Many Szgany tribes live in the areas of Romania, Transylvania, and Moldavia," the professor explained. "It would make a good deal of sense if a band of them were somehow involved in transporting the box into those northern regions."

The industrial buildings began to share the neighborhood with shabby residences. Most of them looked like shanties that appeared to be tacked together with whatever materials could be scrounged.

As they drew closer to the river, an icy wind blowing off the water chilled them. The coach came to a stop and they climbed out, pulling their coats tighter against the cold.

Their driver pointed across the street. "That is the place you want," he said.

The shack was one of the larger structures on the block and appeared to be abandoned. But as they approached the front door, they could hear a woman talking inside. Stoker stepped up to the door and knocked. A few moments later, a ragged, middle-aged woman opened the door and peered suspiciously at them. Two young children were at her feet, holding on to her dress. When she spoke in a tired, abrupt tone, Doyle assumed she was asking about their business there.

Professor Vambery began a discussion with her in Romanian. Doyle observed the woman, but could not tell if the interview was bearing fruit.

While Vambery conducted the interview, the door of the house next door opened and a man appearing to be in his mid-sixties leaned casually in the doorway, smoking a pipe. His drab work clothes well matched the surroundings.

The woman finally shrugged, retreated into her shack, and closed the door.

"What did she say?" Stoker asked with impatience.

"She's never heard of Grigor Ivankov," Vambery told them. "She's lived here with her husband and children since just after Christmas and she doesn't know who had the place before them."

"Grigor Ivankov, rotten scum," the man next door said in halted English.

"You know him?" Stoker asked. "We were told he lived here."

"That fellow no good," the man told them. "What do you English say, a ragbag?"

"So you know Ivankov?"

The man took a leisurely draw on his pipe. "I am landlord here. I have this house, the one on the other side there, and this one you just come from."

Stoker couldn't hide his impatience. "Then you do know him."

"That one no good, always late with rent. Every time I have to go demand him for it. Every time."

Doyle stepped forward. "Sir, it's important that we find this man."

"He comes and goes at all hours of night. Up to no good, I tell you."

"Yes, yes, he is not a good man," Stoker said, too loudly. "But it's important we speak with him."

"Can't speak with him," the landlord said.

"Why is that?" Doyle asked.

"Dead."

"What?" Stoker asked, not wanting to believe what he heard.

The landlord shrugged. "Last November they find Ivankov in the churchyard at St. Peter, his throat torn out like some wild animal did it."

CHAPTER 27

They returned to the hotel after leaving the late Grigor Ivankov's shack. After checking in on Florence, Clarise, and Sir Henry, everyone agreed that lunch was required. There was a significant amount to discuss. So, for the sake of privacy, they avoided the hotel dining room, eating instead in Professor Vambery's room.

During lunch, Stoker brought everyone up to date regarding the morning's investigation, and once the hotel staff cleared the table, Professor Vambery covered it with one of his maps.

"With Ivankov being murdered, we have no way of knowing the precise destination of Tepes and his earth box," Vambery said, peering at the map.

Sir Henry stretched in his chair. "That's probably why Tepes killed him."

"Yes, but he'd made the passage on the Czarina Catherine molesting none of the crew," Professor Vambery said. "He didn't want to put his escape at risk."

"You're saying Tepes may have murdered Ivankov because he needed nourishment?" Doyle asked.

Vambery shrugged. "Yes, he could have simply been hungry."

Sir Henry leaned forward, his elbows on the table. "But what did Tepes do without Ivankov to move his box?"

"If I were to guess, I'd say after feeding on the unfortunate Ivankov, he moved the box himself to the next point of departure. He'd be in his own form and completely visible at that point, so whoever he met had to be someone he trusted, and who felt secure with him."

"The Szgany?" Clarise asked.

The professor smiled at his daughter. "Very likely. Some of their bands have had questionable alliances over the centuries, and we've already seen what enough gold can do to secure loyalties."

Doyle tapped his fingertips on the map. "You mentioned knowing where the Szgany are located."

Vambery nodded. "It's a good deal of territory, but if we can reason as closely as possible the route Tepes may have taken, then our chances of success should increase."

"Well then, we need to think as the monster thinks," Clarise said.

"Exactly right," Doyle said. "How would he have set his plans?"

She rose from her chair and leaned over her father's map. Following her lead, everyone gathered around.

Stoker studied the map. "Leaving the city by road would present countless problems. Too many people along the way and people are curious. Anyone choosing to investigate the box could undo him. And if he was traveling under the charge of the Szgany, they'd be sure to attract more attention than would be safe for him."

"Yes, and then there are still the customs people and octroi officers to avoid," Sir Henry said.

"I doubt he'd have chosen to flee by rail," Clarise said. "There's always the chance of delays with trains."

"Yes," her father agreed. "And a delay could prove fatal to him."

"He traveled by water," Florence stated with a gentle confidence.

They all turned and stared at her in stunned silence. She gazed vacantly at the map.

"Why do you say that?" Stoker moved closer to his wife.

"The river," Florence murmured.

"Yes, but how do you know?" Stoker asked.

"I feel it."

"Do you know what river he traveled?" the professor asked.

Florence offered Vambery an empty smile.

Vambery turned to the others. "It does make sense. Transporting the box on the river is in one regard the safest route, and another the most dangerous."

"What do you mean?" Sir Henry asked.

"The vampire cannot abide the living water, the moving water. He'd be helpless if his boat was wrecked."

Doyle adjusted the map. "He'd direct a troubled boat to take him to land."

"Yes, but if it were unfriendly land, his position would still be threatened," Vambery said.

Clarise traced a river on the map with her finger. "He's already chanced passage by water. First on the schooner that brought him to England, and then on the steamer that aided his escape. His traveling from Galatz by river makes the most sense."

"All right, but which river?" Stoker glanced at the map and then turned to Florence. "Can you tell us, darling? Do you know?"

Florence turned to meet her husband's gaze and smiled an odd, eerie smile that unnerved him for a moment.

Vambery again leaned over the map. "He'd have had his choice of the Pruth or the Sereth. The Pruth would be the most easily navigated, but the Sereth joins the Bistritsa River here at Bacau."

"Is that significant?" Stoker leaned in closer to see where the professor was pointing on the map.

"Only because the Biatritsa flows down from around here." Vambery pointed. "A place called the Borgo Pass."

"Do you know the place?" Doyle asked.

"I've never been there," the professor said. "But I know at least a few Szgany tribes make their home in the area. They work and trade along the foot of the Carpathian Mountains. I'd wager my money on following the Sereth River."

"So what do we do? Engage a boat?" Clarise asked.

Stoker shook his head. "Horseback would be faster. I suspect the only reason Tepes chose the river was to avoid outside interference."

"Yes, he'd choose safety over speed," Doyle agreed.

"Then we can follow the river by road," Vambery said.

"Florence is quite capable in the saddle." Stoker put his arm around Florence. "I assume you ride, Clarise."

"Like a member of the Fifth Dragoon Guard, Mr. Stoker."

The response brought much needed humor into the room and the sound of laughter refreshed them all. Even Florence smiled.

"Then our next step should be finding mounts," Stoker said.

Doyle consulted his watch. "It's too late in the day to do any good now. We can look for horses first thing in the morning."

"There will be hotels and inns along the way. But I think we should carry provisions in case we find ourselves in open country." Professor Vambery sat down in his chair.

"It's settled, then," Stoker said.

Clarise stepped away from the table. "The best thing for the remainder of the day is to get some rest. Tomorrow is going to be full, and I predict the days to follow will become even more taxing."

With everyone agreed, they retired to their rooms with plans to gather again for dinner.

"May I have a word with you gentlemen before we go?" Stoker asked.

"Of course." Vambery answered for them all.

"That gives you and me a few more minutes together." Clarise placed a hand on Florence's arm.

Florence smiled at Clarise, but said nothing as they left the room.

Stoker waited until Clarise shut the door and then turned to Professor Vambery. "Florence's knowledge of the river route."

"Yes. I believe she knows it as a fact," Vambery said.

"It frightens me," Stoker said.

Vambery nodded in agreement. "He has some telepathic link to her, though I can't say how. It explains how the closer she is to him, the stronger the connection."

"If Tepes does have some way of knowing her mind, then it would be prudent for us to exclude Mrs. Stoker when we're making our plans," Doyle said. "I'd feel better if any move we choose to make comes as a complete surprise to him."

"Is there nothing we can do about it?" Sir Henry asked. "I mean, about this influence he seems to have over her. I hate to see the poor woman that way."

Professor Vambery's expression set in determination. "The only thing we can do is make it our business to find Tepes and kill him."

"We will kill him," Stoker said. "On my life I swear it."

CHAPTER 28

The night was cold, but not intolerable. Large gray clouds moving across the sky sporadically blotted the murky light from the partial moon. As the gathering clouds thickened, the moonlight disappeared altogether.

Stochelo kept his horse moving at a walk along the main road. Zache, vigilant in scanning the trees for potential threats, rode beside him. The only practical light illuminating their path came from the oil lanterns each of them carried, the glow from their flames reflecting off the snow-patched ground. They rode in silence, the blackness of the night and the purpose of their ride making them watchful.

The howl of a wolf sounded somewhere in the distance up ahead; a mournful cry that echoed off the mountains and then was lost in the frosty air. A second howl soon followed.

Stochelo carried a well-used hunting rifle suspended from a sling on his saddle. Hidden under his coat was a large wooden cross hand painted by Asena with flowers and vines. He wore a much smaller, silver crucifix around his neck on an old chain and hidden inside his shirt. Zache, besides his big knife, carried an old military revolver tucked in his sash, and had also protected himself with a hidden cross.

The guns were a precaution against the wolves. The crosses were of greater comfort than the guns. Guns would be of little use against the undead creatures that infested the area.

Of course, their safety was declared to be guaranteed. A nosferatu doing harm to any Szgany of Stochelo's band would pay a horrible price under the Voivode's hand. But Stochelo was realistic about such a guarantee. Many of the creatures that stalked the towns and villages, and hunted these forests, were more than animals. Certainly, any such creature, driven and crazed by hunger, posed a vicious threat.

A light snow began falling, and from somewhere in the woods up ahead, another wolf howl drifted eerily through the night. Zache rested his hand on the grip of his pistol.

They entered the crossroads at the Borgo Pass and reined in their horses near the old signpost. They rested in their saddles, watchful and silent as the minutes passed. The breath from the horses turned to vapor in the cold and lingered in the lanterns' glow. The beasts began snorting and grew skittish.

"He comes," Zache whispered.

A soft wind began blowing, moving the snowflakes along in swirling clusters. In only a few seconds, the wind lessened and the snow once again fell.

"Good evening to you both." The voice cut through the cold night air like a knife.

The Voivode stood on an outcropping of rock not six feet above the road. Enveloped in his long coat, he appeared to be a part of the darkness, with only his pale face distinguishable.

"Voivode." Stochelo returned the greeting, offering a curt bow.

The Voivode said nothing more for several seconds, standing motionless on the rocks, gazing down on them, his eyes seeming to look into their souls. After a time, he withdrew his gaze and looked up at the falling snow. "The night is bitter."

Stochelo knew the nosferatu felt nothing of the cold and wondered why he had bothered mentioning it.

"The work is good," the Voivode said, this time looking at him. "You and your men have done well."

"I'm glad you're pleased," Stochelo answered.

The Voivode jumped from the ledge. A mortal man would turn his eyes down to see where he would meet the ground, but the Voivode's gaze remained on Stochelo. The great coat billowing out around him seemed to slow his descent, and he landed softly on the ground beside the signpost.

Stochelo passed his reins to Zache and dismounted, then stepped toward the Voivode. They both advanced, meeting in the middle of the crossroad. With the nosferatu closer to the lantern light, Stochelo could make out a smear of blood at the right corner of his mouth, and smudged across his cheek.

The Voivode reached inside his coat and withdrew a leather bag, bulging full and tied shut with a leather thong. He extended his arm to Stochelo and opened his hand. Stochelo took the bag, nodding his gratitude, and hefted it in his grip.

The weight came from the gold coins inside and the feel of it always warmed Stochelo. These were not average coins. They were ancient and worth far more than their face value.

"I trust you will find the amount generous," the Voivode stated.

"There's no doubt," Stochelo responded. "Thank you."

The Voivode gazed upon Stochelo for several seconds in silence and then, "Men are coming here."

"What men?" Stochelo asked.

"Englishmen. They will come soon in search of me."

Stochelo nodded.

"They come to do me harm, and they come with something I want. I will trust you, as in times past, for your protection in the daylight hours when I am disadvantaged."

"Of course."

"The time nears when I will require your help in eliminating these enemies," the Voivode said, the grimness in his tone overpowering.

Stochelo didn't like the sound of that and remained silent.

"We will speak again and you will know what is to be done," the Voivode said.

Stochelo again nodded.

"Now, return to your wives before the night grows colder."

Stochelo offered another curt bow, returned to his horse, and climbed into the saddle. Zache handed over his reins. They were about to depart when the Voivode suddenly appeared in front of the horses. The animals skittered, but the men brought them under control.

"There is another matter before you leave," the Voivode said.

Stochelo and Zache shifted in their saddles, their nerves beginning to show.

"Something was removed from my castle. After one of your visits."

Stochelo and Zache exchanged glances.

The Voivode's eyes bore into them. "I see you know of what I speak."

"The boy," Stochelo said, fighting the fear beginning to overtake him.

"Why was it taken?"

"One of my men. One of my men insisted on it."

Confusion appeared on the Voivode's face. "Insisted? Under your charge?"

"He was overcome with compassion for the boy's parents," Stochelo said. "He wished to bring them comfort by returning the body."

"An admirable fellow." The Voivode sounded almost sincere.

"He is a good man. But headstrong."

The Voivode's eyes narrowed. "I gave the boy to my wives. He was a great amusement to them, though they were disappointed he lasted such a short time."

Stochelo felt his stomach turn, but held his eyes steady on the Voivode.

The Voivode smiled a thin, satisfied smile, and then backed away from the horses. In the blink of an eye, he was back up on the ledge, the snow flurries swirling around him. He glared down at them from his perch, his eyes cutting through the night blackness.

"Know this," he hissed. "Anything in my castle, living or dead, is mine. And nothing, alive or dead, will leave or be taken from it unless I deem it so."

There was no mistaking the threat. Stochelo and Zache urged their horses around in the direction they had come. The wind gusted again and the snow fell heavier than before. A flapping sound came from behind them. Unable to fight their better judgment, both of them swiveled in the saddle to look.

Barely visible in the darkness, a large bat flew several feet above the ledge where the Voivode had stood moments before. The creature circled twice over the crossroads signpost and then disappeared into the night.

Without urging from their riders, the horses bolted down the mountain road. Behind them, a wolf howl sounded. Another wolf answered, and then another, each reverberating howl building upon the other to form an unholy harmony.

CHAPTER 29

The morning launched a flurry of activity. Sir Henry again good-naturedly agreed to keep watch and company with Florence while the rest of them set out from the hotel to gather what was required for the journey north. The professor and Clarise set out in the hotel coach to purchase supplies for the road while Stoker and Doyle found a cab and went in search of riding horses.

Finding horses proved to be difficult. After visiting several liveries within the city, they discovered no one would lease them horses for travel beyond the city limits. Stoker and Doyle soon concluded that purchasing horses and tack would be necessary and then set about finding a seller. That alone presented its own challenges. Without Vambery along to translate, their communication was spotty, and the stables they visited were unwilling to sell more than one or two horses. In some cases, the horses for sale were less than desirable.

Just after eleven, a livery owner with a smattering of English directed them to a farm outside the city where he said the horses were for sale. After hiring two mounts from the livery owner, they dismissed their cab and set out on their way. Before leaving the city, they stopped for a hasty lunch of sausage, cheese and bread, which they washed down with a local beer. They made a second stop at a known bank where Doyle used his letter of credit to withdraw the funds needed to purchase the horses.

Following the livery owner's directions, Stoker and Doyle found the farm about three miles beyond the outer edge of Galatz. After their lack of success that morning, they were apprehensive about what they might find, but the trip proved to be worthwhile. One of the farmer's three teenaged sons spoke adequate English and showed them over a dozen horses, all in good health and excellent condition. As an unexpected boon, the farmer had acquired a large supply of surplus tack from the army and was eager to profit from some of it. The saddles, saddle blankets, harnesses, and bridles were all well used, but in good condition.

Working together, Stoker and Doyle evaluated the stock and soon cut out seven horses, one for each of their party plus a horse to carry supplies. While Doyle completed the sale with the farmer, Stoker worked with the fellow's sons to ready the stock for travel. Since there was only one packhorse, they saddled each of the riding horses with all tack in place.

Leading the horses back to the city required little effort, but upon arriving at their hotel an hour before sunset, they learned that the hotel's stable was not large enough to board their horses. The hotel clerk directed them to the first livery they had visited that morning, only a short block away. The livery took in the horses and an employee guided Stoker and Doyle through the barn to an open corral at the rear of the property.

An employee informed them in painfully broken English that the livery would close at seven that evening, but they could check on their stock at any time by using the alley that ran along the side of the building. With the horses corralled and the tack stored in the livery barn, they walked back to the hotel.

"How is she doing?" Stoker asked Sir Henry as he entered his room and stooped to kiss Florence on the cheek.

Sir Henry smiled. "Just fine. It's been a quiet afternoon."

Stoker discerned a deeper meaning from the actor's tone.

"Did you enjoy your day?" He took Florence's hand.

She looked at him with an odd expression on her face, not normal for her, but one that he was seeing more frequently. "I'm feeling rather cooped up."

"I can imagine, and I'm sorry for that. But we'll be on our way tomorrow, so you'll have a wonderful change then."

"Were you successful today?" she asked.

He was about to answer when he remembered Doyle's caution about speaking too much of their plans in front of her. "I'm sure everyone will want to hear about it, so I think I'll answer that question over dinner this evening. But first I'm going to walk Sir Henry to the door and then take a bath. I have more dust on me than I care to admit."

Florence didn't acknowledge his response and didn't seem to notice as he walked Sir Henry to the door and stepped into the hallway with him.

"It went well?" Sir Henry asked once Stoker had closed the door behind them.

"We got everything we needed. She's been like that most of the day?"

"It's odd business. She'd be quiet for a good deal of time, not seeming to even care that I was in the room with her. And then in a blink she'd be her old self, engaging and in good spirits."

"I appreciate your watching over her. More than I can say."

"It's my privilege. Now I suggest you see to that bath. You've got a bit of a horse smell to you."

Once Sir Henry returned to his room, Stoker heeded the suggestion of a bath. It proved to be exactly what he needed. Less than an hour later, feeling quite refreshed, he was relaxing in a comfortable chair across from Florence.

He attempted to engage her in conversation, but she had little to say, and soon grew more distant. Adjusting to her mood, he picked up his paper and pen and began jotting down his thoughts.

His mind revisited the fight he'd had with the tweed capped man aboard the Orient Express. Writing a dramatic narrative of the battle, it pleased him to find the smallest details rekindled in his memory. He remembered the feel of his hands on the man in the luggage car. He could almost feel the sting of his fist hammering into the fellow's jaw.

For the first time since Tepes had fled England, recounting that hastily fought brawl, he felt he was truly fighting back against the evil that had cursed his family and friends. And it felt empowering. As the words flowed from his pen, he realized he had more strength than he had imagined. It felt good to be writing, and in the writing he realized he had the potential of being a formidable adversary.

CHAPTER 30

B y seven thirty that evening, they had gathered in the hotel's dining
room. They all enjoyed an excellent dinner, with the courses served at
a leisurely pace. Stoker was glad about it. The day had been long, and he
was grateful for the opportunity to slow down and relax. Everyone had
accomplished their tasks and Clarise was particularly pleased she had
purchased crosses to replace those lost from the train. She had one for each
of them, all different, ranging between seven and ten inches.

Despite the relaxing setting, Stoker wrestled with the anxiety that had
plagued him from the moment he made up his mind to embark on this
expedition. At least Florence appeared to be back to her old self, charming
and present, enjoying the food and drink, and taking part in the
conversation.

"My goodness, it's just nine thirty," Sir Henry said, glancing at the
dining room clock.

Professor Vambery folded his napkin in his lap. "This may be the last
casual meal we enjoy for a while. Tomorrow we'll be heading for rougher
country, and amenities may prove harder to come by."

"Then I suggest we at least enjoy a solid breakfast before we set out,"
Clarise said.

Stoker nodded. "Yes, but an early one. I'd like to cover as much ground
as possible while the sun is up."

"Agreed," Doyle said. "And ladies, we need to caution you about the saddles."

"Caution us?" Florence asked.

"He means we have no sidesaddles," Stoker explained. "The fellow we purchased the horses and tack from had only military equipment. Cavalry saddles, in this case."

"Riding astride," Clarise chuckled. "How indecent!"

Florence laughed. "At long last, a justified opportunity to be indecent. I suspect with the long ride it will prove more comfortable."

"I'm glad you understand," Doyle said as he rose from the table.

Everyone followed his example and they made their way back into the hotel lobby.

"I want to check on our horses before retiring," Stoker said. "Would you gentlemen mind escorting Florence up to our room? I won't be long."

"Not at all," Doyle said.

"Do you mind if I join you?" Clarise asked Stoker. "The fresh air would do me some good."

"Fine," Stoker said.

Doyle reached into his coat pocket, withdrew his revolver and passed it to Stoker. "Take this. It's a dark night."

Stoker accepted the gun with a nod of thanks, placed it in his waistband, and covered it with his coat.

"I'll just run up to my room for my coat and be right back, and I'll bring yours as well. Florence can get it for me," Clarise said. She hurried up the stairs.

Stoker bid everyone goodnight and watched as they climbed the stairs. A few minutes later, Clarise rejoined him. He put on the coat she brought him as they made their way outside.

The night air was brisk, but not uncomfortable, and the soft light from a half moon filled the shadows neglected by the gas street lamps. The street was deserted except for an occasional cart or pedestrian, and their footsteps echoed along the block.

"I appreciate your attention to Florence," Stoker said.

"She's a fine person. I enjoy our time together."

"I would think, in her current circumstances, it could be difficult."

Clarise glanced up at him. "Nonsense. The malady isn't her fault. There are moments when it's a bit trying, but then all friendships have those moments, don't they?"

Stoker nodded but said nothing.

"She's still the woman you fell in love with and married Bram. Don't lose sight of that."

"Never. I'm just afraid for her. I don't know if I'll ever be able to forgive myself for putting her in this position."

"Now you're just speaking nonsense. God will see us through this as He did when Tepes first plagued our lives," Clarise said.

Stoker was about to respond when a movement in the darkness farther up the street caught his attention. He stopped walking and peered into the shadows.

"What is it?" Clarise followed his gaze.

"I thought I saw something."

In another moment, he was certain of it. A man leaned against the wall of the livery stable, his shadow cast across the snow powdering the street. No sooner did Stoker make him out than the fellow disappeared around the corner of the building into the alley.

"I saw him," Clarise confirmed.

Stoker reached inside his coat pocket and pulled out Doyle's gun. He broke it open, checking to make sure it was fully loaded.

Clarise couldn't hide her alarm. "Heavens. You really think you'll need that?"

"It's could be nothing, but he just headed up the alley toward our horses." Stoker locked the cylinder back in place and returned the weapon to his pocket. "You should return to the hotel."

"I will not." Clarise took a step forward. "Let's see if the fellow's up to anything."

They proceeded up the street toward the livery. Upon reaching the corner, Stoker stopped and peered up the alley. He heard movement, but could just make out the outline of the corral fence. The horses whinnied, and the sound of their hooves stomping the ground drifted down the alley.

"Stay behind me and, for God's sake, be careful." Stoker began running.

Reaching the rear of the livery building, he saw the man, a rough looking fellow who looked as if he hadn't shaved in a week, pushing open the corral gate.

The man spotted Stoker at the same time. He hesitated only a moment and then rushed to push the gate wide open.

"Stop," Stoker shouted, rushing forward.

Removing his cap as he ran into the corral, the man waved it in the air, shouting at the horses. The spooked animals ran around the corral, snorting and whinnying, and then the fellow managed to chase one of them through the gate. In a heartbeat, the other animals raced after the leader, bolting through the gate and galloping toward the rear of the alley. The horses turned onto the adjoining street and were gone.

Stoker reached the gate just as the ruffian rushed out of the corral. Without hesitation, the fellow swung. Stoker tried to dodge it, but the blow struck him hard in the shoulder and spun him around. Clarise cried out behind him.

The man charged and swung again. This time, his fist landed in a solid hit on Stoker's jaw. Stoker dropped to his knees, stunned, his skull throbbing.

The fellow produced a knife from inside his coat, a long, beveled blade that glistened in the dim moonlight. He advanced on Stoker, grinning with morbid satisfaction.

Stoker tried to get the revolver from his pocket, but the fellow was almost on him. He heard Clarise yell as she jumped on the man's back, locking her arms around his throat.

"Clarise," Stoker yelled as the fellow began thrashing about.

Stoker got to his feet as Clarise loosened her hold on the man's throat and raked her fingers into his eyes. The fellow screamed and dropped the knife, bringing both hands up to his face.

Stoker rushed forward as Clarise pushed off of the man's back, lost her footing and tumbled to the ground. Stoker pulled Clarise back to her feet and herded her behind him. Freeing the Webley from his coat pocket, he advanced on the groaning man, now doubled over in pain against the fence. The knife lay on the ground near the fellow's feet. Stoker kicked it away into the darkness.

He leveled the revolver at the beaten man. "Who are you?"

The fellow glared in silence at Stoker as he used his sleeve to wipe away the trickle of blood running from his eyes and down his cheeks.

"I asked, who are you? And who put you up to this?"

"I had something to do with it." An accented voice came from behind him.

Stoker whirled around and froze.

Not a dozen yards away, leering at him, stood the bookish fellow in the bowler hat. Seen through the thick lenses of his wire rim glasses, his eyes appeared freakishly magnified. Dangling from his right hand was a long, thin, ugly stiletto.

Next to him was Clarise, her eyes wide with fear. A tall man with hardened features and rough clothing gripped her by the arm. Stoker could make out the outline of a revolver stuck inside the waistband of his trousers.

Stoker raised the Webley, but the man in the bowler hat shook his head as if reproaching a small child. At the same time, Stoker heard something behind him.

He turned as two men, both holding revolvers, walked into the alley behind him. They walked up beside him, and one of them relieved him of the Webley. The man stuck the Webley in his belt and stood his ground.

Stoker felt his stomach turn over in a wave of nausea and silently cursed himself for his foolishness. The fellow who had stampeded the horses had wanted to be seen outside the livery. He had wanted them to follow him, and they had played right into this trap.

The bookish man ran his eyes over Clarise as if sizing up a tasty meal. "I think it will please me most if you watch while I kill her. I won't be able to take the time I'd like, of course. Her screams might summon help before I can finish properly."

"No," Stoker pleaded. He started forward, but the two men near him took hold of him. He tried to twist away; they held him fast.

The bookish man gazed at Stoker and smiled a twisted, perverted smile. He then turned back to Clarise. Taking hold of her arm, he leaned closer to her. Parting his lips, he ran his tongue up and down her throat. Clarise shut her eyes and shuddered.

Stoker struggled harder than before. "Stop it!"

The bookish man smiled at him once again, and then, turning back to Clarise, raised his knife.

CHAPTER 31

The sound of hooves clattering on the paving stones thundered down the alley. Looking toward the main street, Stoker saw a silhouetted rider in a wide brimmed hat and a long coat that draped over the back of his horse. Behind the shadowy rider was a second horse, packing supplies. The rider reined his mount to a halt.

The bookish man, surprised, turned toward the rider, the point of his knife remaining at Clarise's throat. The tall man flanking Clarise turned as well and pulled the revolver from his waistband.

In an instant, a long object appeared in the hands of the rider. Then the quick mechanical sound of a rifle cocking. A sharp loud crack filled the alley and Stoker saw a tongue of flame cut through the blackness.

The tall man cried out and crumpled to the ground.

Stoker heard the rifle cocking again and the rider fired. The side of the bookish killer's head burst open in a splatter of blood. He dropped to the ground, the stiletto still gripped in his hand.

Clarise, blood splattered across her face and eyes wide with shock, stared at the two dead men at her feet.

The assailant Clarise had wounded bolted up the alley and disappeared into the night. The two men holding Stoker released their grip on him. One of them raised his gun; Stoker charged and tackled him to the ground. He heard another shot ring out and then the sound of a horse galloping toward him.

Stoker twisted the revolver out of the man's hand and heaved it deep into the corral. The thug took advantage of him being off balance and jammed a knee into Stoker's chest. Stoker hurtled backward and landed on his side. He saw the fellow jump to his feet and begin running toward the street intersecting the back of the alley.

Stoker watched the other man raise his gun, but this time it was pointed at the rider. Again Stoker heard the loud report of the rifle and saw the muzzle flash.

The man screamed and his hands flew up to his chest as he fell over backwards, a plume of blood spreading across his shirt.

The rider pulled up his horse. Morgan Quincey swung from the saddle, holding a Winchester in his right hand. He cut an impressive figure in his tall boots, and the long coat that Stoker believed was called a *duster*. As Quincey walked forward, the duster opened and Stoker saw a gun belt underneath with a long barrel Colt in the holster.

"Are there any more of 'em?" Quincey asked, peering into the shadows.

"Mr. Quincey!" Stoker exclaimed. "Thank God."

"Are there more of 'em?" Quincey repeated.

"I don't think so. Aside from the three you've killed, there were just the two that ran," Stoker assured him as he turned and began hurrying toward Clarise.

"You okay?" Quincey asked, following him.

"Fine, thanks to you."

Clarise was standing in the same spot, her hands held up to her mouth, cupped together as if in prayer. Her eyes, wide with horror, fixated on the two dead killers at her feet. Stoker took her gently by the arm and led her away from the bodies.

"It's over," he told her. "Are you all right?"

Regaining some of her composure, Clarise nodded. "You?"

"Thanks to Mr. Quincey here, yes," Stoker answered.

Her eyes narrowed as Quincey approached.

"Ma'am," Quincey greeted her. "I trust and hope you stand uninjured."

It surprised Stoker to see Clarise's expression transform from one of shock to anger.

"Those... men... were... they were only inches from me," she stammered. "Both of them."

"Yes, ma'am," Quincey agreed.

Clarise stepped up to Quincey and punched him in the chest with a girlish swing.

The blow surprised him. Stoker thought it looked as if the strike hurt Quincey's feelings.

"You might have killed me." Clarise glared at him.

Quincey looked at his shoes, as if overcome by a moment of shyness. "Well, it's true that I *might have*, but those scum there that had hold of you, they were most certain of doing so."

"But you shot them with me right next to them."

"I didn't see much of a choice in that," Quincey said, a defensiveness creeping into his tone. "It wasn't likely I'd have hit you though, ma'am."

"And stop calling me *ma'am*. My name is Clarise Vambery, as you should well remember, and you'll address me as *Miss Vambery*."

"Yes, ma'am, uh, Miss Vambery." Quincey shuffled his feet.

Clarise's eyes drifted to the rifle in Quincey's hand. "And why would it be so unlikely?"

"I'm a fine shot."

Stoker stepped closer to Clarise. "No matter how he managed it, we owe Mr. Quincey our lives."

With a fearsome glare, Clarise removed a handkerchief from her coat and began blotting the blood from her face.

Morgan Quincey looked down at the dead men. "Who were they?"

"Agents working for Tepes," Stoker said.

Quincey reacted with surprise. "He has that far a reach, does he?"

"He does. We saw the one there with the bowler hat on the Orient Express. We were hoping we were free of them, but it appears they've been watching us the entire time."

Quincey nudged one of the dead men with the toe of his boot. "They won't be watching you anymore. Least not these here."

"Where on earth did you come from, and how did you know we were here?" Stoker asked.

"I'm sure it would be delightful hearing of Mr. Quincey's journey and catching up." Sarcasm laced Clarise's tone. "But did either of you notice there are three dead men lying here on the road? I suspect we'll have some explaining to do to the local authorities."

"She's right about that," Stoker said. "We should get Miss Vambery back to the hotel. And I need to tell our friends that we've lost the horses. First the guns gone, and now this."

"What about guns?" Quincey asked.

"We left London with a crate stocked with guns and some Zulu spears Mr. Doyle had thought prudent to bring along. The dead fellow there, he had an accomplice on the train who pushed it all out of the baggage car. I tried to stop him but," Stoker trailed off.

Morgan Quincey gave Stoker a formidable slap on the back.

"Now don't you worry 'bout the horses. I'll get those rounded back up for you before we bunk in tonight," Quincey promised him. "And no need for concern over guns."

Quincey walked over to the packhorse, with Stoker and Clarise following. He loosened the straps holding a long wooden crate.

"Give me a hand with this, if you would."

Stoker helped him lower the crate to the ground.

"Here you go," Quincey said as he pulled the lid of the crate open.

The crate contained lever action rifles and boxes of cartridges.

"Winchesters." Clarise looked at the guns with some admiration and then re-assumed her anger.

"Brand new, Model 1892 carbines, all with saddle rings, just like this one," Quincey held up the rifle in his hand. "And I've got Colt sidearms in that other box there, and plenty of .44-40 cartridges. They load into both pistol and rifle."

"Mr. Quincey, you've saved us tonight in more ways than one," Stoker said.

"Let's get this back together," Quincey said as he lowered the lid on the crate. "Then I'll go round up your horses while you take Miss Vambery back to the hotel."

"You don't need help?" Stoker asked. "There's seven animals in all."

"I can do it quicker alone," Quincey answered. "But if you wouldn't mind taking my pack animal back to the hotel, I'd appreciate it. He can board in the stable there, and these guns'll be safer stored inside for the night."

"I'll see to it."

As soon as they secured the rifle crate back on the pack horse Morgan Quincey hurried to his horse and mounted up. A few moments later, he rode off into the darkness.

CHAPTER 32

The officer leading the investigation for the Galatz police, a man named Nicolescu, had received a portion of his education at a small Northern England university and spoke proficient English. Officer Nicolescu sequestered Stoker and Clarise in the hotel dining room, now closed, with one of his men at the door. He then left with the other three of his men to investigate the scene of the shooting. All the while, Doyle, Irving, Florence, and the professor waited with considerable anxiety in the hotel lobby.

A short time later, Nicolescu returned to the dining room alone. He was suspicious of them and rather unhappy that Morgan Quincey, now identified as an American who did the shooting, was not yet present.

While still awaiting Quincey's return, one man dispatched to the alley returned with a report that lessened Nicolescu's suspicions. The policeman reported they knew nothing of the dead man with the bowler hat and thick glasses, but recognized his two dead accomplices. Each of them had lengthy police records of assault, suspected murder, and thievery. And both had ties to occult groups.

A short while later, when Morgan Quincey walked through the hotel lobby, and didn't hesitate when being directed into the dining room, Officer Nicolescu's suspicions were relieved even more. He had his man escort Stoker and Clarise from the dining room and interrogated Quincey in private.

When Nicolescu emerged with Quincey, he was satisfied the shooting was justified for self defense.

Later, with the police satisfied and gone from the hotel, they all sat around a table in the empty dining room.

"I only found six of your horses," Quincey reported.

"That leaves us without a packhorse," Stoker sighed.

"We'll have the one I brought. That should do us well enough," Quincey said.

"Mr. Quincey, there is no way I can adequately thank you for what you did for my daughter," Professor Vambery said.

Stoker heard a low, indistinguishable utterance from Clarise. She was staring at Quincey with her arms crossed and a look of disapproval on her face.

"And I'm grateful for your returning my husband to me in one piece," Florence said.

Quincey glanced at the ground with honest humility. "I did nothing any of you wouldn't have done."

"I can't tell you how relieved I am that you're here," Sir Henry said. "I'd almost given up hope."

"Well, I didn't get your first telegram as quick as I should have. I was traveling on business and a good deal of the trip found me in wilderness country. I didn't see the message 'til I got back to my ranch in Colorado. But quick as I could, I made plans to join you and set about the trip."

"Oh, no, you had to chase us all the way from London," Stoker stated.

Quincey shook his head. "Not really. I got Sir Henry's second message, the one with your itinerary. That was a help. I think at the worst I was only three days behind you. I almost caught up to you in Varna. Good luck took me to the same hotel you stayed at. Ah, it wasn't that much luck. As soon as I saw the name *Grand English Hotel,* I headed for it. I figured with that name, somebody there was at least likely to speak English. Anyway, the clerk told me you'd checked out and headed here. I caught the next train, but the engine broke down about twenty miles south, some village so small I wonder if it even had a name. The conductor was saying it might be hours before they could get 'er going again, and well, I'm not a patient sort, so I gathered my possibles and got off the train."

"Possibles?" Stoker asked.

"My things. You know, my belongings," Quincey explained. "Anyway, it didn't take me too long to find horses. I was in the middle of farm country, so there was plenty to choose from. I made a deal for the two animals you saw, and the tack I needed, then rode the rest of the way."

"But how on earth did you find Stoker and Clarise in that alley?" Doyle asked.

"Now that was just plain luck. I was riding up to this very hotel to get me a room for the night when I saw Mr. Stoker and Miss Vambery walk into the alley. 'Course with the dark, I didn't know it was them at the time. And then I saw those two other men go in after you, kind of sneaky like. Thought I'd better take a look."

"Again," Vambery said. "I'm so grateful."

"I couldn't let anything happen to the little lady," Quincey said.

The comment drew a nasty glare from Clarise.

"We'll have plenty of time to catch up, but it's late and I think it best we get some rest," Stoker advised. "We have a long day ahead of us tomorrow."

Everyone rose from the table and exchanged their 'good nights.'

Quincey turned to face Clarise as she reached the dining room doorway with her father. "It's been very good to see you again after so many months, Miss Vambery. I'm glad you're unharmed."

She hesitated and then continued out of the room with a slight nod of acknowledgement.

Stoker and Florence were the last to leave the dining room with Quincey. The American paused in the hotel lobby, watching Clarise as she disappeared down the hallway at the top of the stairs.

"You have any idea what I might have done to rile that woman?" Quincey asked Stoker.

"Well, from what I can tell, you saved her life," Stoker sighed.

Florence shook her head with tired amusement. "You both have a good deal to learn about women," she said, and then proceeded up the stairs.

CHAPTER 33

S tochelo made his way through the forest, the three rabbits slung on his belt slapping against his side with each step. Since his fight with Jardani, Stochelo had been in a foul mood, and he hoped that getting away from the camp for a few hours would improve his disposition.

In all the many years of leading his people, he had rarely experienced any open opposition, and the few times there had been a grievance it was quickly and easily dispensed with. But this quarrel with Jardani felt different, and it troubled him. A mood of discontent wafted through the camp like an unpleasant odor. This time, he felt threatened by what had happened, and that feeling angered him.

As Stochelo neared the camp, he heard the sounds of daily activity. But then he heard voices as his wagon came into view near the edge of the clearing, voices that carried a tone of more than just idle conversation. He stepped out of the forest behind his wagon, removed the rabbits from his belt and hung them off the seat box.

The camp appeared normal. A few men attended to chores at their wagons. The women attended to their children or hung out wash to dry on lines strung between their wagon covers and nearby trees. Across the way a man was currying his horse, and at the wagon next to him, Jardani's wagon, there appeared a small gathering of perhaps a dozen or more.

"But what can we do about it?" a woman's voice reached him from across the clearing.

Another woman responded. "Yes, it's always been this way."

Stochelo made his way closer to Jardani's wagon, keeping the loose circle of wagons between him and the gathering.

"It grieved my heart to see that boy's body, knowing what had been done to him. The memory of it eats away at me. And seeing his parents gaze on him, I felt guilt and grief," Jardani said.

"You've nothing to feel guilt from," a man spoke up. "You did the boy no harm."

"Didn't I?" Jardani answered. "We've all served the Voivode without question. Do you not feel anything when you're promised safety and others in this valley live each night in fear?"

"It has always been so," Asena said.

Stochelo felt stung by betrayal. How could his wife see fit to take part in this conversation?

"What if that boy had been one of yours?" Miri asked. "What if it had been one of your daughters?"

"Why should we be concerned about the villagers?" a man asked.

"All my husband did was extend a kindness to one of them," Miri answered. "You saw the result of it. They came here with gratitude and no intent of harm or bickering."

Stochelo felt his anger increasing. He had made himself clear on this subject and yet his people still discussed it.

"You can't be saying we should somehow protect those who are not our own?" a woman asked.

"I wouldn't know how to protect them," Jardani said. "But just because we've served the Voivode for as long as we can remember doesn't make us right. I fear we'll face a reckoning someday."

Stochelo glimpsed Zache as he approached the group.

"You all know me," Zache began. "You know I hold strong to our traditions and believe in our people. But I've begun wondering if we should have concern for protecting ourselves."

"From the Voivode?" someone asked.

"Are we so arrogant to believe he will never turn on us," Zache said.

Stochelo could stand it no longer and stepped out from his concealment. All eyes turned to him.

"You can be sure he will prey upon you if he thinks we betray him," Stochelo said. "It is our loyalty that favors us in his eyes, but I hear no loyalty in any of this talk."

"Maybe some of us are beginning to think that such loyalty is wrong," Jardani responded.

"Do you wish to die?" Stochelo asked. "You think he cannot sense these things? You think he is unaware of your foolish talk?"

"I think there is more evil in what we do, in what we have done, than any of us want to think about," Jardani said. "But I'm no longer able to ignore it."

Stochelo turned his angry glare upon Zache. "And you're a part of this?"

"I'm concerned with the good of our people, just as you are," Zache answered.

"And you take Jardani's side?"

"I take no side," Zache said. "But I've given much thought to what Jardani has been saying, and I have found in recent weeks that I feel as he does."

Stochelo pointed an accusing finger in Jardani's face. "You stir up trouble, dangerous trouble."

"Has this become a tribe where a man cannot say what he feels?" Jardani asked.

"This tribe is my responsibility and this kind of talk will bring misfortune upon us all. It will stop or you'll have to leave," Stochelo shouted.

Stochelo watched Jardani as he looked over the crowd gathered around the wagon. They were silent, but not one of them looked away when Jardani's gaze met theirs.

"I think all of us have a great deal more to fear in our band than just talk," Jardani said.

Jardani took his wife's hand and together they climbed the steps to their wagon and disappeared inside.

Stochelo looked at the group that remained. "We will speak no more of this," he told them, and then watched as one by one they went about their business.

Only Zache and Asena remained. Zache hesitated, looking at him curiously for a moment, and then he, too, turned his back and walked away.

A feeling of unease began growing in his gut.

He looked at Asena, wishing she might offer some comfort, but knowing that she had no ability to do so. She walked the few steps to reach him, tugged at his coat sleeve, and then began walking toward their wagon. He followed her, consumed with his worries. Even Asena was questioning and doubting the old ways.

CHAPTER 34

P rofessor Vambery urged his horse up beside Stoker's. "We should reach the city before the day's end."

"Good." Stoker glanced up at the sky. "Sunset will be upon us in two hours, maybe less."

The first three days on the road had gone as well as expected. The horses were all in superb condition and they made excellent progress. They traveled only twenty miles their first day, an uninspiring distance Morgan Quincey attributed to everyone growing familiar with their mounts. The second and third days, they managed almost thirty. Now, at the end of their fourth day, they were nearing the city of Bacau.

"I mention it now because once we arrive, we must make a decision," the professor said.

"What's that?" Doyle asked, having overheard.

Vambery adjusted his position in the saddle. "Bacau is where the Sereth meets the Bistritsa. We're going to have to choose one or the other."

They had stayed on the road that followed the Sereth, a well maintained route that in some locations rose to elevations overlooking the river, and at others paralleled it just a few feet from the riverbank. Stoker preferred the road at its higher levels; it afforded a better view of the river itself as well as the surrounding countryside.

Each day they saw several boats, some with flat bottoms powered by poles thrust into the shallows by strapping men in billowing shirtsleeves.

Other crafts were rowed, and some were fitted with a sail or two. They even saw a few small steam launches chugging through the water, pushing aside the thin patches of ice that floated along in the current.

They had spoken to a few river men along the way, but none of those conversations had produced any helpful information. No one was familiar with the name of Grigor Ivankov, and no one had seen Tepes' box or noticed anything out of the ordinary.

"At this point, we're traveling blind. On what will we base that decision?" Stoker asked.

"Once we reach Bacau, we can make inquiries," Doyle said. "With luck, we may find someone who noticed the box during transport."

"That doesn't seem very promising," said Sir Henry.

"Let's not waste any energy worrying about it until we get there," Doyle said, adjusting the gun hidden under his long, wool coat.

Each of them carried one of the long barrel Colts supplied by Quincey, holstered on a gun belt secured around the waist. Even Florence and Clarise wore the sidearms which they concealed beneath their shin length cloaks. And everyone carried one of Quincey's Winchesters in a rifle scabbard secured to their saddle.

Stoker, riding next to Quincey, noticed the American show some interest in Clarise's horse, peering down at the left front leg of her mount.

Quincey was knowledgeable about horses and everyone had much appreciated his help with them. He ensured the animals were in good condition, and with his expert guidance, everyone could prepare their mounts quickly for travel each morning.

"Pull up a minute, Miss Vambery, if you don't mind," Quincey said.

"Would it be too much trouble to tell me why?" Clarise barely glanced at him.

"I think he may have picked up a stone or something. He seems to be favoring his left front hoof."

"I've been riding since I was nine, Mr. Quincey. I think I've developed the ability to tell when a horse is in distress."

Stoker wondered how Quincey would respond to the rebuke, and he didn't have to wait long to find out. Without a word, Quincey handed the lines of the packhorse he was leading to Stoker and then spurred his horse just ahead of Clarise's mount and cut her off. He swung to the ground, taking hold of the lines of her horse.

Everyone reined in their horses and turned to watch the young couple.

"I'm certain your knowledge of horseflesh is admirable," Quincey told her with a hint of impatience. "But we can't take a chance of our mounts going lame out here. God knows how hard it might be to replace them, and I can't abide to see an animal in discomfort."

Quincey kneeled down beside Clarise's horse and gave the animal's shin a gentle but solid thump with his fist. The horse raised his hoof. Quincey grabbed hold of it and gave it a careful examination.

It occurred to Stoker that the poor fellow might never again hear a civil word from Clarise Vambery if he was mistaken in this matter.

"Here we have it," Quincey announced, pulling his Bowie knife from its sheath.

Quincey used the tip of the knife to dislodge a small object from the groove of the hoof. He held it up so Clarise could see it.

"Looks like he got himself a thorn tip," Quincey said.

Clarise, her lips pursed, glared down at him. "Thank you, Mr. Quincey," she said, a tightness in her voice. "I'll have to take better care next time."

"Ah, now ma'am, uh, Miss Vambery," Quincey began.

Before he could finish, Clarise gave her horse a kick. Quincey had to jump back to avoid being stepped on as she moved past him up the road. Florence looked at him with bland amusement as she passed him, following Clarise.

Stoker met Professor Vambery's gaze. The professor communicated his puzzlement over the interaction between his daughter and Mr. Quincey with a shrug and then urged his horse onward.

Quincey swung back into his saddle as they all got underway again. He kept his gaze on the two women up ahead. "They do make a striking pair."

"They're quite capable as well," Stoker said.

"Miss Vambery, in particular." Quincey chuckled.

They had been fortunate to find themselves near a roadside inn or boarding house at the end of each day's travel, and Bacau was no exception. After consulting his Baedeker's guide, Professor Vambery directed them to an adequate hotel near the bank of the Sereth.

Whatever concerns any of them had over choosing the correct river route were quelled by another demonstration of Florence's odd behavior. During the evening meal in the hotel dining room, Florence rose from the table and made her way to the wall of French doors that faced the river.

The men all stood and waited. She seemed oblivious to them, gazing through the glass into the distant darkness beyond.

Stoker joined her. He could see her face reflected in the panes. The soft, diffused light from the dining room blending with the distant glow from the few gas lamps lining the riverbank to create a ghostly image. He drew closer to her. "Florrie. What is it?"

"I will travel the Bistritsa." Her voice was soft and clear.

Dumbfounded, he could only stare.

And then she said it again. "I will travel the Bistritsa."

CHAPTER 35

H is two wives begged to accompany him on his night's hunt. It was rare he permitted them, preferring solitude when seeking his nourishment. But they had not fed in several days. Tepes disdained their impertinence but understood their hunger, so allowed their company.

They had spent the first hours after sunset stalking through two of the small villages nestled at the foot of the Carpathians. It had proven an infuriating waste of time. Every door remained secured, and not a single soul ventured from the security of their home. Thin lines of lamp light seeped through the cracks of latched shutters, and through them wafted the disgusting, repellent odor of garlic hung around the window frames.

It was almost midnight when they discovered a gypsy wagon camped in a clearing off the main road on the outskirts of one of the foothill villages, a lone family engaged in travel. The small windows of the wagon were dark and strings of garlic were visible through the glass.

He could sense several hearts beating within; the travelers slept within the confined space of the wagon instead of risking that anyone fall asleep outside. While he remained in the shadows of the tree line, his younger wife approached the side of the wagon. Her sister, encouraged by this boldness, approached the back door, and took a position beside the steps to inspect the wagon entrance.

He was about to command that the women follow him away when a face appeared in the side window. It belonged to a young man of perhaps eighteen or nineteen years. Before the young fool could react, Tepes' young wife smiled invitingly at him, sending silent suggestions to his malleable mind of the unimaginable delights she could offer him.

The young man fixed his eyes on her as she touched her fingers to her lips, and then drew them down across her throat, bringing her hand to rest between her breasts. Her bosom rose and fell as she increased the deepness of her breaths. The yellowed gown billowed around her seductively moving body. All the while, she made silent promises of pleasure to the boy.

The young man's expression transformed from curiosity to excitement and hope. She parted her lips and tilted her head toward the wagon door, taking a step toward it as she did so. The hopeless idiot's eyes flashed with lust and he disappeared from the window.

In a moment, his young wife was standing at the bottom of the steps leading up to the wagon door. Her sister, eyes glittering with anticipation, moved to the rear wheel behind the steps, out of view.

He heard the latch drawn and watched as the door slowly opened. The young man, wearing only his trousers, hesitated in the doorway, his eyes fixed on the object of his desire waiting at the bottom of the steps. Strings of garlic draped down each side of the door frame inside and his young wife backed away as the stench reached her.

"Come," she whispered to him.

Smiling with anticipation, he stepped through the doorway.

From inside the darkened wagon, a girl's voice shouted, "Tomasis!"

The fool hesitated, and the figure of a girl came into view behind him. She took hold of his arm, fighting to pull him back within.

But his wives were faster and stronger. The younger one leaped forward, took hold of his arm, and wrenched him from the steps. The girl, still holding on to his arm, was dragged out behind him, and both tumbled into the snow.

In an instant, his younger wife was on the young fool. As he screamed, his sister made frantic efforts to get to her feet, but his second wife knocked her to the ground. As they began feeding, a woman's scream issued from within the wagon.

And then a man's voice screamed, "Tomasis, no! Kostana!"

The blood drawing him forward, he left the trees and reached the wagon as a work-hardened man jumped down the steps, holding a large crucifix in his hand. The crazed man brought the crucifix down across the shoulder of his second wife with substantial force. She screamed in pain as the cross seared her skin. She jumped upward. Flailing wildly, she knocked the crucifix from the man's hand.

He took hold of the fellow who struggled to free himself. Bending the man across the wagon steps, he fell upon him, taking his nourishment, as his wife returned to feed on the young girl.

A short time later, it was done. Each of them sated, the warmth of renewed strength filling them. The sound of anguished weeping reached them from the gloom within the wagon. Huddled on the floor at the front of the wagon was a woman.

His second wife gazed upon the woman with sympathy and beckoned to her.

"Come, they need their mother," she told the woman, extending her arm toward the corpses on the ground. "Come, give them comfort."

He watched as the woman struggled to her feet and staggered to the wagon door. His instincts and experience told him his wife's lies did not deceive the woman. But overcome by all she witnessed, she emerged from the wagon. Not to comfort her family in death, but to join them. In an instant, his wives were on her, and in a few slow minutes, the woman's cries were silenced.

CHAPTER 36

"It's as if we're in the middle of the Sahara without a compass," Stoker said to Doyle and Irving.

The three of them were riding alongside one another, leading the rest of their party down the road paralleling the Bistritsa River.

"It's a bit too chilly for the Sahara," Sir Henry quipped.

Stoker didn't find the remark amusing. "We're traveling blind. All we can say with any certainty is that we're following the river."

Bacau was six days behind them. The few travelers they had encountered and interviewed did not know of Tepes or his earth box. Not a single soul in the villages along the way could offer any information.

"You're forgetting that we have an excellent guide," Professor Vambery said from behind him.

Stoker swiveled in his saddle and looked back at the professor.

Vambery nodded toward Florence, riding just ahead of him beside Clarise.

Florence appeared oblivious to the conversation. Since leaving Bacau, her odd disposition had intensified. She rode in silence unless spoken to and seemed detached from any answer she might offer. Most disconcerting to Stoker was her eyes; he saw a gleam of anticipation in them.

He couldn't fault Vambery for referring to his wife as a guide, but it angered him. It angered him because in the epithet's truth there was immense uncertainty. They did not know where they were heading, but

Florence might very well know their precise destination. It was her uninten-
tional secret. His wife was being drawn into a dark and horrible vortex, and
he was helpless to prevent her from disappearing into it.

The countryside had grown less populated and more rugged with each
mile traveled, and the distances between the little towns and villages had
increased. Stands of beech trees, their branches bare and frosted with snow,
lined the road, and foliage running along the banks of the river was drab
and gray from the cold.

Quincey pointed. "Looks like a village up ahead."

Just over a mile away, chimney smoke rose above the trees.

"We should see to finding lodging for the night, then," Doyle said.

"There'll still be two hours of sunlight once we reach the place," Stoker
said.

"You're not suggesting we press on?" Clarise asked.

Stoker looked at his companions. He felt weary from the hours on the
road and he could see they were worn out as well, but he felt frustration
every time they weren't able to use every moment of the day.

"No," Stoker sighed. "Of course not."

"I could stand a hot bath," Sir Henry said. "It might provide some relief
to my aching muscles."

"Aching muscles? The horse is doing all the work," Doyle teased.

"As if you don't feel the same complaints," Sir Henry snapped back.
"I've got pain in muscles I never knew I had."

The village proved to be quite small; a community of farmers and their
families. There was no inn or any other type of lodging available, but a
farmer living at the far edge of the settlement had a large barn, which he
made available for both horses and riders.

The residents of the barn were two horses and a cow, all in stalls at the
front of the building. The stalls at the rear of the barn were clean and all
that was needed was to spread out an even bed of straw.

"I'm afraid we'll all be foregoing a hot bath tonight," Clarise said to Sir
Henry as everyone went about the business of finding suitable locations for
their sleeping blankets.

"At this point, my dear, I'm more concerned about not freezing to death
in this, this drafty bovine hotel," Sir Henry said.

"Hold a good thought that father will be successful," Clarise said.

Professor Vambery had left earlier to make payment to their host for the
accommodations, arrange for food, and see if he could secure additional
blankets to protect them against the snowy night.

Stoker was placing a vegetable crate in the stall Florence would occupy so she would have something to sit on when the clatter of a horse and wagon came from the yard. A cacophony of tinkling and clanging metal followed it. He and Doyle made their way to the front of the barn.

From the doorway Stoker saw Professor Vambery, his arms loaded with heavy blankets, standing next to an enclosed wagon in conversation with its owner. From the wagon hung a variety of farm tools, pots and pans, along with an impressive collection of other goods.

"Just a peddler," Doyle said.

The peddler was an old fellow with a full beard, wearing a heavy coat, and a substantial woolen cap. He gestured with his arms and pointed up the road he had just traveled. Vambery said something to the man who tied off the lines and then jumped down from the wagon. The professor was heading for the barn, and the peddler followed behind him.

The professor stepped into the barn, dropping the blankets onto the wooden cover of a water barrel. "You need to hear this. This fellow's just come from a district in northern Transylvania. He says everyone is talking about the killing there."

"What killing?" Stoker asked, as Sir Henry and Morgan Quincey joined them.

"A family, an entire family, gypsies. Every one of them murdered."

The old peddler began jabbering in Romanian, gesturing dramatically.

"He thinks they'd traveled from the south and were just passing through. A man driving livestock found them outside their wagon off one of the main roads, their throats ripped out and their bodies drained of blood."

"Well, that sounds familiar, doesn't it?" Doyle said.

"Do they know who did the killing?" Stoker asked.

Vambery translated. This time the peddler spoke slower when he answered, and in a somber tone. Stoker heard the word *voivode*.

"The Voivode Dracul?" Stoker asked the peddler.

The old fellow gestured at Stoker and then took a step back and crossed himself.

Vambery turned toward Stoker. "He just signed to ward off the evil eye."

"He's familiar with the name," Doyle said.

"Ask him if he thinks Vlad Dracul was responsible for these murders," Stoker instructed the professor.

Once again the man crossed himself, shook his head and addressed Vambery.

"He says you must not speak that name. You must never speak it."

"Will he at least tell us where these killings occurred?" Doyle asked.

Vambery translated the question and they all listened as the old peddler answered.

"He says the family was found off the main road about two miles north of Bistrita. It's at the edge of the frontier, right at the foot of the Carpathians," Professor Vambery said.

"It sounds like we should be heading to Bistrita." Quincey leaned against a post.

"How far?" Doyle asked.

"Let's say our goodbyes to this fellow and we'll find out," said Vambery.

The professor thanked the peddler with a few coins, sent the old fellow on his way, and then hurried to his satchel to consult his maps. Stoker and the other men gathered around him. They only had to wait a minute.

"By my best estimate I put us here," Vambery said, pointing to a spot on the map. "Bistrita is here, on the Bistritsa River. I'd say it's a long day's ride at best from where we are now."

"We could be there by tomorrow night?" Stoker asked.

"With an early start, yes," Vambery said.

A sound at the front of the barn interrupted them, drawing their attention. The farmer and his wife entered, carrying a large kettle of steaming soup and extra lanterns.

As Quincey and Irving stepped away to help their hosts with the provisions, Professor Vambery turned to Stoker.

"Yes, this holds promise, I think."

Stoker took in the professor's words and felt a spark of hope, and then a fresh tremor of fear. But with the fear came a strong sense of determination and purpose.

CHAPTER 37

The day's ride had taken them far from the flat farmlands, with the road slowly climbing upward. Bistrita lay ahead of them in the fading light, built at the base of foothills that climbed toward the mountains. Oak and acacia trees, dusted with snow, adorned the lower hills with stands of fir and spruce apparent toward the peaks of many of the higher ones. Beyond the town rose the Carpathians, the jagged peaks disappearing into the thick, gray clouds hanging heavy in the sky.

They had made excellent time with the horses performing well, but the sun was close to setting. The last of its rays were filtering through the clouds, and it concerned Stoker.

"We'd best hurry if we're to reach it before sundown," Stoker called out.

"We'll have to demand more of the horses," Doyle responded.

"You're not worried about being out after dark, are you?" Sir Henry prodded.

"I bloody well am, and so should you," Doyle answered.

"These are good animals," Quincey said. "I'd wager they've enough wind left for us to run 'em the rest of the way."

"Then let's do so," Stoker said.

Everyone pulled their coats tighter and then urged their horses into a gallop. Morgan Quincey led the way, followed by Doyle and Irving. Stoker, leading the packhorse, and the professor held back long enough to place Florence and Clarise ahead of them.

Stoker watched the two women, their long cloaks billowing out behind them as they raced along the road. Their riding skills had increased over the past days on the road, and now they leaned forward, close to their mounts' necks, the lines gripped in their fists.

Despite their efforts, the sun disappeared behind the mountains before they reached the town. Quincey reined his horse to a halt, and they waited while he retrieved two lanterns from the packhorse and lit them.

Florence was the only one of them who wasn't watching Quincey. Her eyes were distant, scanning the blackness oozing from the stands of trees on either side of the road.

"We'll be on our way soon enough," he told her.

She turned to look at him and favored him with another disturbing smile.

Quincey handed a lantern to Doyle and kept the other. Once Quincey was back in the saddle, he proceeded at a more cautious pace.

Less than a quarter of an hour later, they rode into the town, but for Stoker, that quarter hour seemed endless.

The streets at the outer edges of Bistrita were dark. The shutters and thresholds allowed only thin lines of light to escape, as every door and window were shut tight.

Progressing into the center of the town, Quincey spotted diffused light filtering through the night mist. He led them toward it and soon they turned onto a commercial street illuminated by gas lights.

"Thank God," Stoker said.

A minute later, Quincey leaned forward in his saddle and pointed. "Might that be a hotel up ahead?" he asked.

The American pointed toward a large building. Suspended over its front door on an iron bracket was a decorative wooden sign. Mounted to each side of the door burned two gas lamps.

As they drew closer to the building, Professor Vambery reined his horse up beside the American and read the sign. "It is. The Coroana de Aur."

"The what?" Quincey asked.

"The Golden Krone, Mr. Quincey, and it is indeed a hotel."

Like every building on the street, The Golden Krone's window shutters were drawn. The professor and Doyle dismounted and hurried to the door. Doyle grasped the latch to open the door, but it was locked. Without hesitating, he pounded his fist on the door. When there was no immediate response, he pounded again.

A few moments later, they heard activity behind the window to the left of the door. The shutter opened a few inches and in the lamplight within they could make out a man peering suspiciously out at them.

"We require lodging for the night," the professor said to the man in Romanian.

The fellow's eyes widened in disbelief. Without a word, the shutter slammed shut and a few moments later, a key sounded in the door lock. The door opened just wide enough for the man to fill the space. He was middle aged with a groomed moustache and gripped a simple crucifix in his hand suspended from a tarnished chain around his neck.

"English?" the fellow asked.

"Yes," Doyle told him.

"We have rooms for you, but you must come inside," the hotelier said in English, anxiety clear in his tone. "You must come in."

Stoker, Quincey, and Irving dismounted.

"Hurry. You must hurry," the hotelier said.

A woman Stoker took to be the man's wife appeared behind him, wringing her hands as she looked upon the open door.

Stoker acknowledged the woman with a nod, and then stepped around his horse to Florence's mount and helped her down.

Clarise began climbing down on her own, but the hem of her riding skirt became snagged in a stirrup buckle. Quincey hurried forward, intercepting her before she could lose her balance, and then eased her back onto the saddle.

"Mr. Quincey," Clarise began.

"For the sake of haste, Miss Vambery," he said with a softness that surprised Stoker.

The American deftly took hold of the tangled edge of the skirt and freed it from the buckle without damaging the fabric. He then took hold of Clarise, slid her out of the saddle, and placed her on solid ground.

Clarise stood facing him in silence with the oddest expression on her face. Quincey nodded to her and then turned away.

"We have stables behind us. There." The hotelier pointed.

"Can you show us the way?" Quincey asked him.

The man's eyes widened in fear. "No, no. I will not. I stay inside and so must you. You must hurry, it is just around back. Use the passage beside the hotel, just there."

"I'll help you," Sir Henry told Quincey as they gathered the reins.

"I as well," Doyle said.

The hotelier stepped back from the doorway as Stoker ushered Florence and Clarise inside. Professor Vambery followed them in.

The hotelier pointed at the door. "I lock the door. Knock again when you return."

Without further ceremony, the fellow slammed the door shut and threw the bolt.

The lobby was spacious and furnished with comfortable but roughhewn furniture. A dining room was visible through an archway to the left of the main desk. Guests eating their supper occupied only two tables in the dining room. Off to the right of the desk, beyond the staircase leading to the upper floors, was a generous sitting room with a fire burning in its hearth.

The hotelier's wife hurried forward to help Florence and Clarise out of their cloaks.

Clarise slipped off her gloves. "What about our things in the saddlebags and on the packhorse?"

The hotelier waved his arms and shook his head. "Leave them. You must leave them until the daylight," he told her.

"You're quite concerned about being out in the night," Stoker said, fishing.

The hotelier and his wife exchanged a troubled glance, then the fellow hurried behind the counter.

"It is of no concern now," the hotelier said, forcing a lighter tone. "Let us make you comfortable in your rooms."

They gathered at the main desk and, as Professor Vambery was signing the register, he asked, "Could it be the nosferatu that concerns you?"

The word had the effect of an electrical shock. Both the hotelier and his wife froze in their task of pulling room keys from the key box mounted on the rear counter and then turned to the professor. The woman crossed herself, her eyes wide.

"You know of such things?" the hotelier asked.

"We know a great deal," Stoker said.

"We should not speak of such things," the hotelier said, returning to the keys.

"Perhaps later, then," Stoker suggested.

A heavy knocking on the door sounded before the fellow could respond. He dropped the keys on the desk and hurried over to the window. He cracked the shutter open and peered through. Satisfied, he closed it and moved to the door. Throwing back the bolt, he pulled it open.

Doyle hurried in, followed by Sir Henry and Quincey. The men's arms were loaded down with the Winchesters still in their scabbards, and Quincey carried the extra weight of two saddle bags.

Quincey dumped his load of rifles on a nearby bench. "I've squared away the horses."

The hotelier closed the door and bolted it as Sir Henry and Doyle added their Winchesters to the bench. And then Stoker noticed Quincey approach Florence and Clarise with the saddlebags.

"I thought you ladies would want the comforts that might be found in these," he explained.

Clarise looked up at him for a moment with the same odd gaze she'd displayed when Quincey helped her from her horse outside the hotel and then smiled a shy smile. "How considerate, Mr. Quincey. Thank you."

"Indeed, Mr. Quincey," Florence said.

Clarise reached for her saddle bag but the American pulled them from her reach.

"I wouldn't think of it, ma'am, uh, Miss Vambery," he said.

"My wife will show you to the rooms." The hotelier gestured toward his wife. "Then you come back for hot soup to take the chill from you while the cook is still working."

The woman, her hands full of keys, started up the stairs, with Florence and Clarise following behind. The men gathered up the Winchesters and then made the climb to the second floor. Within five minutes, they were all settled in their rooms.

Stoker turned up the single gas lamp hung in the center of the room, and then lit an oil lamp he found on a table. He carried the lamp to the dressing table where Florence had seated herself as soon as they entered. Placing the lamp on the table, he rested his hand lovingly on her shoulder and looked at her face reflected in the framed mirror mounted on the table. She had that faraway look again and he couldn't help but feel saddened by it.

He looked around the room. "It's a nice enough room. We'll get some rest tonight."

Florence raised her eyes to look at him, the glow of the lamp creating a ghostly effect.

"I think that hot soup our host mentioned would be a good thing about now. Shall we go back down and get something to eat?" he asked.

"That would be nice," Florence said, her mouth parting in a soft smile.

The lamp light picked up the whiteness of her teeth. Stoker stifled a gasp. The tips of her two canine teeth were visible, extended just below her parted lips. He wanted to doubt his own eyes, but it seemed in the lamplight that they were longer than normal, and considerably sharper.

CHAPTER 38

O nce everyone had gathered in the dining room for supper, Stoker
seated Florence and Clarise with instructions to order for everyone,
then excused himself, with the rest of the men promising that they would
return shortly. Stoker led his friends to the sitting room on the opposite side
of the lobby.

The moment Stoker shut the sitting room doors, Professor Vambery
asked, "Are you certain of this?"

Stoker raised his hands in a futile gesture. "I know I haven't been myself,
but I'm not mistaken about her teeth."

"It may not be so unbelievable," the professor said, moving closer to the
warmth of the hearth.

"How do you mean?" Sir Henry asked.

"I think it's reasonable to conclude that the unusual changes we've seen
in Mrs. Stoker's behavior gradually increased with each mile we drew closer
to this place. If what Bram saw tonight is real, then it supports my belief.
The closer we get to Tepes, the greater his influence over her, and the more
we should expect her to transform."

"Are you saying that Florence is going to become a… become like him?"
Stoker asked, this time hearing the panic in his voice.

"You must calm yourself," the professor advised. "That's not the case at
all. As we've discussed before, his blood flows in her veins. If indeed this
tainted blood has caused changes in her demeanor, and as you've observed,

some physical changes as well, it doesn't mean her immortal soul is at risk yet. She must actually die if she is to become as he is."

Stoker felt his stomach tighten.

Professor Vambery continued. "We may be able to use this to our advantage. If Mrs. Stoker will allow me to hypnotize her again, we might learn more. And it might offer the opportunity to verify Bram's observation about her teeth. We could try first thing in the morning."

"But what's to be done now?" Sir Henry asked.

Doyle motioned toward the door. "We need to get back to our table and get something to eat. I'm well overdue for a meal, and I suspect the rest of you feel the same."

"True enough," Quincey said.

"After supper I suggest you take Mrs. Stoker back to your room and stay with her," Doyle said to Stoker. "We can't afford to leave her on her own, even for a few minutes."

"Is that all, then?" Stoker asked, frustrated.

"Once you have Mrs. Stoker safe in her room and Clarise has retired, the rest of us will have a conversation with our host," Doyle said. "Judging by his reaction when we arrived, he very well may have information that could prove helpful."

The hotelier appeared ill at ease as he watched Morgan Quincey close the doors to the sitting room.

"Why have you asked me here?" he asked. "I've much to do."

Doyle waited until Quincey sat down with the rest of them near the crackling fire. "We won't keep you long. We'd like to learn something more about this place."

"Bistrita?"

Doyle nodded. "Bistrita and the country north of it."

The man sat in silence, looking at Doyle with undisguised suspicion.

"We heard something about a murdered family," Doyle said.

"A terrible thing, terrible, and the reason we lock our doors and windows," the hotelier said. "All of Bistrita stays in at night behind locked doors."

"If you and everyone else here are locking their doors, then you must believe whoever did these murders is still nearby," Doyle said.

"Only a foolish man would act so careless with such a thing happening near his home. Locked doors and windows are a wise precaution."

"Do you have any idea who the murderer is?" Doyle asked.

The man's eyes narrowed. "I think you know what did the killing," he said.

"Nosferatu," the professor said.

"It surprised me that Englishmen would know this word and speak it as if they believed it to be real."

"So you believe, then?" Professor Vambery asked.

"I was born on a farm not far from here," the hotelier explained. "We are all raised with the reality of it, and taught how to protect ourselves against it. We have rarely had much to worry about here in this town, but of late it has grown to a matter of great concern."

"Because of the family that was killed?" Sir Henry asked.

The hotelier shrugged. "That happened on the road some miles north of here. Close enough to be of concern, yes, but there was a killing in the town two nights ago. A man too fond of his drink, too drunk to get himself home. They found him behind the tavern a block over."

"Nosferatu?" Doyle asked.

The man nodded.

"So the murders are the work of nosferatu. We agree on that, but I asked you if you knew *who* did them."

The hotelier shifted in his chair and looked at the fire.

"Perhaps the Voivode Dracul," Professor Vambery said.

The hotelier gasped and jumped up from his chair, crossing himself. "You must not say that name, you must not."

"So you *do* believe it was he." Doyle leaned forward.

"I must go now," the hotelier insisted. "My work—"

"Sit down, please," Doyle interrupted, as Quincey casually got up from his chair and positioned himself in front of the door.

The fellow looked at Quincey and then back at Doyle, and then returned to his chair. Doyle remained silent, observing the man.

The hotelier slumped in his chair. "I do not know. There are still many of them in the country. It might have been him, or just as easily not."

"Many of them?" Sir Henry repeated.

"The curse has been a part of our country longer than anyone can remember."

"If we wanted to find the Voivode, where would we look?" Doyle asked.

Once again, the hotelier looked horrified.

"But why would you want to do such a thing?" he asked.

"That is our concern," Doyle answered. "Where?"

The hotelier hesitated for several moments, and then said, "Anyone you ask in the region will tell you his castle is in the mountains above us, somewhere overlooking the Borgo Pass. But that is all they will tell you and all they know. No one wants to know where it is and no one right in his mind would dare go there."

"Looks like we got ourselves to the right place," Quincey said.

"The Borgo Pass," Doyle said to himself. "We'll leave tomorrow morning."

"No, you must not," the hotelier pleaded. "No one looks for that place and no one goes there. You must not."

"We have important business that we must see to," Professor Vambery said.

The hotelier rose from his chair and walked past Quincey to the door. He took hold of the door handle, but then hesitated and turned back to the room.

"If you do this thing," he said, his voice trembling. "You must know that you go to a place of death."

With that, he opened the door and hurried from the room.

CHAPTER 39

J ardani sat with Miri in front of the fire he had laid a few feet away from the foot of their wagon steps. The night was cold, but he was careful to keep the flames burning hot. Miri was sewing a new blouse of deep purple cotton by the firelight. He felt content to be doing nothing in her company.

Across the camp, a few of the men had gathered with their guitars and fiddles, and were entertaining themselves and the camp with their music. Some of the girls were dancing, laughing, and gossiping as they reeled around the fire. Some people had left their wagons to gather closer to the musicians and dancers, but most, like Jardani and Miri, listened from their own wagons.

Jardani could see Stochelo across the camp, sitting on the steps of his wagon, smoking his pipe with Asena nearby, cleaning up the pots from dinner. He had not spoken to Stochelo since the day of their fight, but he knew Stochelo blamed him for the talk of their ties to the Voivode that had grown more common of late. Some members of the tribe had begun questioning how God might view the alliance once they faced Him for their eternal judgment.

Miri held up the blouse to examine a stitch. "Stochelo can be hotheaded, but he'll see, someday, the sense in what you and the others have been saying."

He looked at his wife and realized that she must have observed him watching Stochelo. "Did I look that concerned about it?"

"I know it bothers you, husband. You don't have to tell me your heart for me to know it."

"He's been leading this tribe for years. And he's become used to the gold that comes from the Voivode. I think the gold is slowing his senses."

"That and his pride," Miri said. "He's hardly ever been questioned before, and almost never challenged."

"He's made it clear enough he doesn't like it."

Across the camp, Zache sat down in front of his fire with his oldest daughter.

"Zache's been careful with his words, but I'm sure he thinks as we do." The voice came from beside the wagon.

Jardani and Miri turned to find old Babik approaching their fire.

"He's been a friend to Stochelo for as long as I can recall," Babik continued. "He knows the Voivode is a curse to our people, not a benefactor, but in his loyalty to his friend, Zache does not speak out."

"Maybe that's the problem," Jardani said.

"There is no maybe. When men stay silent in the presence of evil, evil gains power from the silence," Babik said.

Miri placed her sewing on her lap. "We've not heard you speak of this before."

Babik shrugged. "I was once as Stochelo, happy with the gold we took for guarding the ruins or running errands, but I have not felt that way in many years. Maybe God is telling us it is time to speak out."

"I'd like it better if God would provide us with some means to rid ourselves of this curse," Jardani said.

"All in good time," Babik responded. "God does what He will do when He is ready to do it."

With that, Babik went on his way, walking toward the musicians and the dancers.

"Do you think there are more who think as we do but are afraid to say?" Miri asked.

Jardani shrugged.

Miri moved closer to him and put her arm through his, pulling him closer. "I'm proud of you for your part. You know that, yes?"

"My part?"

"You know what I mean and don't act as if you don't." She poked him playfully. "Speaking out was a good thing to do."

The music suddenly stopped, and a collective gasp sounded across the camp. A tall, slender man, dressed entirely in black, stood next to the tree line, his long coat settling around him as if he had just stepped out of the wind.

Jardani had never laid eyes on him before, but he knew with certainty he was gazing up at the Voivode.

"Get inside and bolt the door," Jardani whispered to Miri as he rose from his seat.

She hesitated, so he took hold of her arm and guided her up the wagon steps. She disappeared inside. Jardani heard the door slam shut and the bolt fall in place behind him.

All over the camp, the men were hurrying their women and children for shelter as the Voivode walked into the camp, his eyes absorbing every detail, every movement. Stochelo was already on his feet, walking to intercept the unexpected visitor.

Stochelo extended his arms in greeting. "You've never come to our camp before. Welcome."

The creature stood there, looking past Stochelo as if he weren't even there.

The Voivode turned his gaze upon Stochelo. "Am I?"

"Of course, yes, of course," Stochelo said, his voice tense. "Why would you doubt it?"

"Everyone shuts themselves away as if they've something to fear." The bewilderment in the Voivode's voice was almost convincing. "But after so many years of friendship, what would they fear of me?"

Stochelo hesitated. Behind him, Asena watched, fear in her eyes.

"Only a very few of our number have ever seen or spoken with you," Stochelo said. "You have taken everyone by surprise."

"Indeed," the Voivode responded, his eyes growing more penetrating and his cruel mouth parting in a humorless smile. "I was passing nearby, just now, and I heard certain talk. Troubling talk."

Jardani felt a wave of nausea roll through his stomach. He felt frightened for Stochelo, who stared back at the Voivode with complete confusion.

"I, I don't understand," Stochelo stammered.

The grim smile thinned as the Voivode stepped forward, forcing Stochelo to move from his path. Jardani feared that those terrible eyes could see everything.

"I thought we were allies," the Voivode said, a hint of disappointment in his voice. "Have I not always treated you with friendship?"

Stochelo stood frozen in silence. "Our dealings have always benefited all concerned," he said after a few moments.

"And yet I am certain I heard a young woman talk of pride for her husband who would speak against me." The Voivode turned to look at Jardani.

Jardani drew on every ounce of strength he could find to return the nosferatu's gaze without faltering.

Stochelo shook his head. "I heard no such talk from any woman here."

"No? My ears hear much more than your ears are capable," the Voivode said.

Again the Voivode paused and turned, this time to face Babik. "I also heard it spoken that I am a curse. Who would say such a terrible thing?"

Babik held the Voivode's gaze, glaring back at him with defiant eyes.

"Perhaps it was you." The Voivode extended an arm, pointing at Babik.

Babik remained silent, not shrinking from the Voivode's attention.

"No?" the Voivode taunted. "Then perhaps the young woman I heard earlier might tell me."

Jardani felt a shock of fear as the nosferatu began striding toward him, those terrible eyes locked on the wagon where Miri hid. He searched in desperation for something he might use to defend himself and Miri. The metal rod he had used to stir the fire lay next to the stones surrounding the embers. If he could reach it before the thing got any closer, he might stand a slight chance.

Babik stepped between Jardani and the Voivode.

"The great Voivode," Babik said, his tone mocking. "In all his strength and power, threatening a woman."

"I only wish to learn who said such terrible things about me," the Voivode said, his voice emotionless.

"You know it was me. I don't know how you know it, unholy fiend, but you know it well enough," Babik said.

"Perhaps you should choose your words more carefully," the nosferatu said, the menace in his tone unmistakable. "Make no mistake, for I am your master."

Babik spat. "Bah. God is my master. I've walked this earth more years than I can count. I've outlived my family and I've seen your kind bring more misery than I care to remember."

In a blur of motion, the Voivode was on Babik, his left hand clamped around the back of the old man's neck like a vise. Gasps of horror rose across the camp.

"Where is your God now?" the Voivode hissed.

The nosferatu's lips parted, revealing long, pointed canine teeth. He pulled Babik closer and clamped his mouth over the old man's throat. Babik gave a pitiful cry and tried to push the monster away. His breaths came in deep, short gasps as his body slowed.

Jardani had never felt more helpless. His instincts screamed at him to rush to the old man's aid, and at the same time warned him to take flight. It was all unfolding at such a swift pace he was helpless.

Babik's body twitched and went limp. When the nosferatu let go of him, he collapsed to the ground, as if his body had turned into old rags. Blood speckled the snow.

The Voivode looked up from the body, his eyes scanning the camp for any threat against him. Blood stained his moustache and dripped down his chin, but he was heedless of it.

"Do you see what your careless talk has brought upon you?" the Voivode called out, his voice strong and angry. "We've lived in harmony through the ages, but now you grumble and complain."

Jardani felt immense relief when the nosferatu turned away from him and walked toward Stochelo. Cowering behind her husband, Asena's face was frozen with horror, but Stochelo stood his ground.

"The English have come." The Voivode snarled at Stochelo. "You'll soon know what is to be done."

Stochelo nodded.

"And there will be an end to foolish talk," the Voivode said, turning to take in the entire camp. "For if there isn't, I will return. And then you will all learn what a true curse can be."

The great coat billowed up around the Voivode as he rose into the night. There was the brief sound of the garment flapping in the wind, and then nothing.

A chilling silence filled the camp, a silence so heavy that it could almost be touched. Behind him, Jardani heard the wagon door and a moment later Miri was clinging to him.

Stochelo walked over to Babik's body and looked down at it, his face heavy with sorrow. Then he looked up and his eyes found Jardani. The sorrow transformed into a burning anger.

"You!" Stochelo said to Jardani as he pointed at the corpse. "You did this."

Zache approached Stochelo and opened his mouth to speak, but Stochelo turned on his heel and walked away, his head down.

Jardani felt Miri give his arm a reassuring squeeze. But he felt no reassurance. He felt nothing at all.

CHAPTER 40

They left the Golden Krone just before nine in the morning. They decided that the best course of action would be to proceed toward the mountains in order to gather information that might help them pinpoint the castle's location.

The road climbed through farmland, and the farther they rode from Bistrita, the greater the distance grew between farms. Most of them looked forlorn under the gray sky. Occasional patches of brown grass pushed through the thin frosting of snow, and they saw only a few animals lolling outside the barns. With each mile they rode, the rolling hills became more formidable, reaching up to the foot of the jagged mountains that towered above them.

Stoker rode next to Florence, his fear for her safety growing with every mile. If the professor was right, then Florence might become capable of anything.

"Professor, what do you think?" Doyle called out from the front of the group.

Stoker forced his eyes away from Florence to see what prompted the question. Doyle, Sir Henry, and Clarise had stopped at a small, but well traveled path leading off from the main road. It wound through a stand of trees, and beyond the trees he could see several dwellings with smoke rising from their chimneys. Farther up the main road, he could see an orchard.

Professor Vambery, who had been riding with Quincey at the rear of the procession, trotted past Stoker to join Doyle at the head of the path.

"Well?" Doyle asked.

"A village. Worth visiting, I think." Vambery pointed. "Every person there has probably lived in this region their entire lives. Somebody will have information that might help us."

There was a sudden rustling from the trees several feet away from Doyle off the main road and a man emerged through the foliage. He wore a sheepskin vest over a linen shirt and trousers tucked into tall boots. A rather uneven hat tilted jauntily on his head, covering an abundant amount of straw colored hair. He carried a spade in one hand.

The fellow said something in his native language and Professor Vambery responded. The professor spoke his own name and the young fellow responded with, "Alexander."

"This is Alexander," Vambery said. "And this is his village."

Doyle rode forward to join the professor. "Ask him if we're near the Borgo Pass."

"I speak some English," Alexander said. "Just a little."

"Splendid," Doyle said.

"Borgo Pass is just there," Alexander pointed up the main road. "Maybe five miles."

"We'd like to ask you a few questions if you don't mind," Stoker said. "About this country."

Alexander looked confused, so Professor Vambery translated.

"Ah, yes," Alexander bobbed his head. "With hot drink, to warm you. Come."

A few minutes later, they gathered in the main room of Alexander's cottage. The central living area of the home was clean and neat, with everything in its place. A small kitchen occupied one end of the room with a variety of cooking utensils hanging over a brick hearth. A larger fireplace occupied the adjoining wall. Bright paint adorned the furniture, while the walls featured several holy pictures, painted on glass and framed in wood. There were only two other rooms; one Stoker assumed to be the couple's bedroom, and another that had a closed door. Strings of garlic hung down the center of each window and as well as the side of the door next to the latch.

The moment they had stepped across the threshold, their host's pretty young wife, smiling a genuinely warm smile, made them welcome and guided them to chairs. Alexander introduced her as Tatiana and then requested that she prepare tea. Tying back her long, dark hair in a scarf, she set about the task with Clarise's help.

Tatiana put the water on to boil and then said something that sounded apologetic, and hurried from the cottage.

"She doesn't have enough cups," Professor Vambery translated. "She's going to borrow some from the neighbors."

Several minutes later Tatiana returned, followed by a middle aged woman and man. The woman carried a large plate piled high with what looked like apple walnut cakes. The man carried a wooden box containing several china cups. Alexander introduced them as Marek and Lenka Tesar.

A minute later, another woman entered carrying a tray with several more cups. As the food was laid out, a few more of Alexander's curious neighbors joined the gathering, each bringing some kind of pastry or beverage.

Clarise delivered a cup of steaming tea to Florence who sat beside the hearth and had been staring at the fire in silence. She took the cup but said nothing.

Professor Vambery made introductions in Romanian, explaining to the villagers who they were and from where they had traveled.

Alexander took a seat opposite Stocker. "Most of them have never met any English."

"How did you learn English?" Doyle asked.

"My father saved a little to send me to school in Bucharest. An English school, but my father became sick and I could not stay. So my English, not so good."

"You do very well with it," Stoker said.

"Your guns have made them curious." Alexander gestured toward the Winchesters stacked against the side of the hearth, and then at his neighbors around the room. "They wish to know why you come here, to our village."

Stoker glanced at Professor Vambery who sat next to him.

The professor leaned in close. "I see no reason to withhold our purpose."

"We're searching for someone," Stoker said.

Alexander translated for his neighbors.

"We know him as Vlad Tepes," Stoker said.

An immediate reaction coursed throughout the room with several gasps and the name *Tepes* repeated in whispers. Stoker was certain that every villager in the room crossed themselves, including Alexander. Lenka Tesar sobbed. He watched as her husband put his arm around her, pulling her close.

Alexander nodded toward the Lenka. "The Voivode. He took a boy from them."

"The Tesar's boy?" An expression of horror lined Doyle's face.

Alexander nodded.

"When?" Doyle asked.

"Almost one month," Alexander said. "Revenge for some farmers that killed one of his wives."

"One of his wives?" Quincey repeated. "Are they like, like him?"

Once again Alexander expressed confusion and Professor Vambery translated. Alexander answered in Romanian.

"He said that there are several nosferatu still in this country, but none so old or powerful as the Voivode," Vambery translated. "It is believed he provides refuge to some of the others in his castle."

"Do you know where the castle is?" Stoker asked Alexander.

Alexander looked at Vambery, who repeated the question in Romanian.

Before Alexander could respond, a gruff looking fellow who had been leaning against the wall near the front door spoke to the professor.

"He wants to know why we want to know," Vambery translated.

"This is Branko Strnad," Alexander said, introducing the man.

"We've come here to kill the Voivode," Stoker answered.

The moment the words left his mouth, Florence pulled her gaze away from the flames and leveled it on him.

Alexander looked shocked by the answer. Branko addressed Alexander, shaking him out of his stunned silence. Alexander turned toward the man and translated.

Branko became angry and Stoker could see fear behind the anger. He spat out a sentence, paused and then kept talking, gesturing passionately. A few of the other villagers nodded as Branko spoke, their expressions showing concern.

"He said our guns will be of no use in this foolish errand," Vambery said, raising his voice to be heard over Branko's tirade.

Alexander interrupted Branko, and the two men exchanged several heated words. When Branko finally went silent, defiantly folding his arms, Alexander turned back to Stoker.

"My apologies for such rudeness," Alexander said.

Clarise gazed at Branko. "What on earth is he upset about?"

Vambery turned toward Clarise. "He says we are fools to try to find the Voivode, let alone try to kill him. Mr. Branko insists that we leave this village now. He claims the Voivode has ways of knowing things and that our intentions will get everyone in this village killed."

"He might very well be right," Sir Henry said.

"No one has ever tried such a thing," Alexander said. "Why would you?"

"Last year the Voivode came to England," Stoker said. "He murdered many people there, some of them people we knew and loved."

Quincey leaned back in his chair, resting a hand on the grip of his Colt. "Why haven't you people tried to kill him?"

"If only we could." Alexander shook his head.

"What's stopping you?" Quincey asked. "There are plenty of you and only one of him. Even with his abilities, together you're a greater force."

Branko addressed Alexander, who was now looking at the floor.

"He says that anyone who has ever raised a hand against the Voivode has suffered a terrible death," Vambery translated. "This has been the way for centuries, and these people have learned to live with it. They've learned how to protect themselves, and now only the foolish or the careless find themselves victims. They've no reason to risk their necks."

"But if you had a chance to put an end to it, stop living in fear—" Quincey began.

"Mr. Quincey," Sir Henry interrupted. "Perhaps this isn't the time."

"No, your friend's words have wisdom in them," Alexander said, raising his head. "And he is right. We are afraid."

Tatiana, standing at the end of the table, addressed Quincey in Romanian. Several of the other women in the room nodded and muttered in agreement.

The professor listened and then translated. "Tatiana says she doesn't want her man even thinking of such things. She says for any man to set upon killing the Voivode is like a mouse trying to kill a lynx. She prefers that her man live and someday give her babies."

"My wife speaks out of love, but sometimes she speaks out of turn." Alexander frowned at his wife.

Morgan Quincey's questions raised possibilities that Stoker had never considered. Perhaps Quincey was on the right path. Stoker decided it was worth a try.

"He has weaknesses," Stoker stated. "We chased him out of England because of them. If the able men of this village were to join with us, together we'd stand a good chance of ridding your village of this monster."

The shame that had clouded Alexander's face cleared.

"We have fought him before," Stoker said. "We can help you put an end to his hold on you."

Alexander nodded and then addressed his neighbors. There were a few exchanges between the men, and several of the women shook their heads while speaking to each other and giving heated opinions to their husbands.

Branko erupted with an intense flurry of Romanian accompanied by expansive, angry gestures. Alexander stood and faced him and the two men argued. The arguing ended with Branko storming out of the cottage. His neighbors soon followed him and in a short time the only villagers remaining were Alexander and Tatiana.

Alexander turned to face them, his face flushed. "Branko's view does not change. He insists that you must leave. That for you to stay means terrible things for our people. Some others agree with Branko, others do not."

"What about you?" Stoker asked. "Will you help us?"

Alexander looked at his wife and then back at Stoker.

"I want to, but Tatiana, she fears about me," Alexander said. "I too have much fear."

"Can you at least tell us how to find the Voivode's castle?" Doyle asked.

"And what will you do if I tell you?"

"I told you, we intend to kill him," Stoker said.

"You are either brave or fools," Alexander said. "I will take you to the castle road, but will go not beyond it." He then made his way to Tatiana and addressed her in Romanian.

The girl shook her head and began speaking with deep emotion in her voice. The husband and wife exchanged words, and Tatiana grew calmer. Alexander nodded at her final words and then kissed her on the cheek.

"Tatiana, she is much angry at me for taking you, and worried," Alexander said. "But she…"

Alexander trailed off, searching for the English words.

Professor Vambery intervened. "Tatiana predicts that if we return from the castle, it will be too late to risk traveling back to Bistrita."

"If we return?" Doyle repeated.

Vambery shrugged. "That's how she put it. There's no inn here, but Tatiana says that two of us can stay here tonight and that she will speak with her neighbors about finding lodging for the rest."

"Yes," Alexander nodded. "You mustn't be on the road at night."

"That's very kind, thank you, Tatiana," Stoker said.

At that Tatiana picked up a large knife from beside her stove and began waving it as she expressed herself yet again. Stoker thought he detected a note of finality in her tone and looked to Vambery for an interpretation.

The professor smiled. "She says that should we allow any harm to come to her husband that she'll kill us all herself."

CHAPTER 41

Less than an hour after leaving the village, Alexander reined in his horse and pointed ahead. Forty yards up the incline was a crossroads with a weatherworn signpost. "I go no more. The road there, with no sign, it is what you want."

Quincey rode up beside Alexander. "Thanks for getting us this far."

"Do not do this thing," Alexander addressed them all. "Come back with me."

"You'll see us back before sunset," Doyle said.

The look on the young man's face communicated he believed he would never lay eyes on them again. Without another word, he turned his horse and urged it back down the mountain at a fast trot.

Stoker couldn't help wondering if they should all be following him.

Quincey led them up to the crossroads and stopped in the center. The old sign pointing the direction they had traveled read, *Bistrita*, while the one pointing off to the right read, *Bukovina*. A third sign, dangling from a single rusted nail, was so faded Stoker couldn't make it out. As for the unmarked road, it looked only wide enough for a single carriage and was in shabby condition. Quincey led them onto it, and just over twenty minutes later, he reined in his horse and gazed upward.

The castle rested on the peak above them. The decay of the place set against the dull sky and gathering gray clouds created a sinister tableau.

"We've done it." Doyle pulled his Winchester from its scabbard.

The rest of them followed his example.

They urged their horses forward. A few minutes later, they rode onto a narrow stone bridge that led to what looked to be the castle's main gate. Judging from the castle's position on the edge of the precipice, Stoker knew it had to be the only gate leading into the place. He consulted his watch. "It's almost three. We don't want to be caught here at sunset."

"Sunset doesn't fall until after six," Doyle said. "We should have plenty of time as long as we don't dawdle."

A few moments later, they gathered their horses in front of the massive gate, its thick spikes protruding out from the alcove within the rampart above them.

Sir Henry looked upward, his eyes fixed on the heavy spikes. "I wouldn't want to be under that when it came down."

"I wouldn't want to be caught on the other side," Stoker said.

"Seems to be chained in place, least from what I can see here." Quincey pointed at a heavy chain wrapped around a large wooden winch spool. "I think we'll be safe enough."

Doyle urged his horse forward. "Well, let's get on with it."

They proceeded into the ancient courtyard and Stoker felt a surprising sense of pride, a feeling of empowerment that he had found the courage to enter this evil place of death.

The hooves of their mounts crunched through the snow and echoed eerily off the massive paving stones. They guided their horses up to a covered walkway and dismounted, tying the lines to the walkway's supporting posts.

Sir Henry shuddered as he surveyed the place. "Do you feel it? There's something, there's a horrible heaviness here."

Stoker had felt it as soon as they passed through the gates. The chilling air had an oppressive feel to it.

"I hate to admit it, but maybe that Alexander fella was right," Quincey said. "We might have shown more sense comin' up here in the morning."

"Let's see what we can learn about the place, since we're here," Doyle said.

"That looks like the only way in, at least from this courtyard," Sir Henry called out as he walked toward a narrow door set in the center of the main building.

Quincey's eyes scanned the structure. "There's not even a window on the ground level."

"It was designed for easy defense," Doyle said.

Quincey joined Sir Henry at the door and grasped the handle. He pushed on the door and put his entire weight into the task, but with no result.

"Locked," he announced. "There must be another door down here somewhere."

With ten minutes of exploration, they found doors at each end of the covered walkway, both locked. They discovered a third door at the base of the gate tower, but it was also locked.

"He's in there. He's in there somewhere." Stoker heard the quivering in his own voice.

"We need to get inside," Doyle said.

"The place is immense. Once we're in, it's going to take some time," Sir Henry said.

"It's unlikely his resting place is on the upper floors. We'll concentrate our efforts on the lower levels," Doyle said.

"What about the others?" Sir Henry asked. "Alexander said Tepes isn't the only one of his kind here."

"As long as we do what we came to do in the daylight, we should be safe enough," Doyle said.

Quincey took a position in the center of the courtyard, looking up at the windows in the main building and the adjoining towers.

Doyle stepped beside Quincey. "If you're thinking what I think you're thinking, I'd estimate the lowest windows to be at least twenty feet up."

"But look there." Quincey pointed. "Those vines have been there quite a spell. I'm guessing they'll hold me. Once I get up there, I'll go through the window, come down and get that door open."

Before anyone could respond, a gust of wind came out of nowhere. And then the gust became a steady blow, not strong, but ever present. As it blustered around the ancient stones and past the windows, it created a low, ghostly howl.

"If you're going to try this, you'd better get on with it," Stoker urged, beginning to feel uneasy.

They followed Quincy over to a growth of vines creeping up the castle wall about twenty feet to the right of the door.

"If you don't mind," he said to Sir Henry, handing the actor his rifle.

"Put the rifles here," Doyle instructed, leaning his Winchester against the castle wall a few feet from the vines. "We'll all need our hands free in case he slips."

Quincey took hold of a thick piece of the vine with his gloved hands and tested its strength. "Well, here I go."

Quincey started his climb, finding handholds and working the toes of his boots into the larger tangled branches. The progress was slow and he had gained about seven feet when the howl of a wolf drifted into the courtyard.

Stoker felt his stomach tighten. "Where'd that came from?"

"Impossible to say with the damned echo," Doyle said.

Sir Henry, his nerves on edge, back at the gate and the bridge beyond. "Hurry, Mr. Quincey. Hurry."

"That's what I mean to do," Quincey answered, pulling himself up another two feet.

Heavy gray clouds rolled in above them on the wind, darkening the sky.

Stoker's uneasiness grew; something was happening, something none of them could see. But he could feel it. The rifles were only a few feet away should any wolves appear on the bridge. Or would some other horror spring from the castle?

The higher Quincey climbed, the more difficulty he had, the greatest problem being his finding sturdy footholds to support his weight. He was about six feet from the bottom of the window now, his progress slow.

Another wolf howled in the distance and this time a second wolf answered it, and then a third. Their cries reverberated off the stone walls and then carried off by the wind.

Quincey struggled to get his boot into a small entanglement of branches. The wood gave way with a loud crack, and Quincey careened downward.

"Look out," Sir Henry shouted.

Quincey grabbed for the vine and stopped his descent before he had dropped three feet. His feet kicked in the air as he fought to find another foothold. A few seconds later, he did and resumed his climb without complaint.

"Are you all right?" Stoker called up to him.

"I'm fine. I best not do that again."

The wind blew harder as the American continued his ascent, and the howling of the wolves grew closer.

"He's almost got it," Doyle said.

Quincey was now only two feet from the window. Stoker couldn't pull his eyes away from the black opening above the American's head. What might be inside?

"I've made it," Quincey called down to them.

Stoker surveyed their surroundings, but saw nothing. He couldn't dispense with the growing, expectant feeling that knotted his insides.

As Stoker watched, Quincey reached up and gripped the window ledge with his right hand. With great effort, he pulled himself upward. Stoker, Doyle, and Irving all stifled gasps as Quincey let go of the vine with his left hand, transferring it to the window ledge. Now, with both hands gripping the ledge, he pulled himself upward.

The instinctive grip of fear intensified within him, a feeling that danger was imminent. "We must leave now!" Stoker heard himself yell.

"Stoker!" he heard Doyle shout.

With terrifying screeches, a half dozen large ravens swooped out of the window around Quincey. The American instinctively raised an arm to protect his eyes. Losing his grip, he slipped from the window, crying out as he hurtled downward.

Stoker, Doyle, and Irving pushed in closer to the wall. Halfway to the ground, Quincey grabbed hold of the vine again. His downward momentum swung him into the wall. He held his grip for only a moment longer and then continued to fall.

They managed to get their hands on him as he crashed down, knocking them all to the ground. Above them the shrieking birds circled, plunged down toward them, and then, as suddenly as they had appeared, flew out of sight over the battlements.

Stoker was the first to struggle to his feet. The fear within him grew, fear for all of them. "We're leaving. We're leaving now."

There were no arguments as they gathered the rifles and hurried to the horses.

"Are you all right to ride?" Doyle asked Quincey.

"Well, I didn't break anything. Couple of my ribs are kind of sore, but I guess that's all right."

The courtyard became darker as a cluster of clouds drifted over the mountain top, and the howling of the wolves stopped as quickly as they had begun. No sooner had they swung into their saddles when the horses began to whinny and pull against their lines.

"Of all the cursed luck." Quincey pointed.

Standing on the opposite side of the stone bridge was a large wolf. The animal lowered its head as it stared at them, its yellow eyes unwavering. A few moments later, a second wolf trotted up beside the first, then a third, and a fourth. In less than a minute, a dozen of the beasts had spread out across the road at the end of the bridge.

CHAPTER 42

Cradling their Winchesters across their saddles, they maneuvered the horses to a vantage point better suited to keeping the wolf pack in view.

"I'd favor any ideas that'll get us past them," Sir Henry said.

Doyle glanced at Sir Henry. "You're not nervous, are you?"

Sir Henry frowned at Doyle. "I have unpleasant memories of being pursued by wolves last year. And if I recall, you kept killing them, but they wouldn't stay dead."

"We'll see if these critters stay dead." Quincey fixed his gaze on the beasts gathered at the far end of the bridge. "I wanna get a bit closer first, though."

Quincey moved toward the gate. The wolves took a few steps toward them onto the bridge, then stopped.

"They only advanced when we moved closer to the gate. They're just trying to keep us in here," Doyle said.

"We can't allow that." Stoker shook his head.

"Let's see if you're right." Quincey urged his horse several steps closer to the gate.

The rest of them coaxed their horses forward, following him.

Snarling, the wolves moved toward them.

The moment Quincey stopped advancing, so did the wolves. "He can make these animals do what he wants, even when he's, even during the day?"

"We know he controlled the pack that attacked us in Regent's Park," Sir Henry said.

"If they attack, we'll be in real trouble," Doyle said. "There's nowhere to go here."

"What if we rush them?" Stoker asked. "Mr. Quincey, do you think you might keep them occupied with your Winchester?"

Quincey nodded. "I think rushing 'em is our best play here, but we'll better our odds with more than just me laying down fire. I'd say two in the lead, and two behind to shoot at any coming at us from the sides."

"Then no reason to delay any longer," Doyle said. "Sir Henry, are you all right riding in front with Mr. Quincey? I'll bring up the rear with Stoker."

Doyle looked at Stoker for an acknowledgement. He was pale as a ghost, his eyes wide and fixed on the wolves, his knuckles white from his unnaturally tight grip on the rifle. But he was keeping his head as he faced the growling threat in their path. "Stoker?"

"Yes, I'm ready," Stoker responded as snarls and low barks swept into the courtyard.

Good, Doyle thought. Whether Stoker realized it, he was overcoming the demons that had filled him with doubt and guilt.

"Everybody ready?" Quincey asked. "Let's run us some wolves."

As they walked their horses toward the gate, the wolves lowered their heads, and their snarls and growls increased. Those at the head of the pack advanced farther onto the bridge.

"Now!" Quincey yelled.

They kicked their horses and galloped through the gate and onto the bridge. Quincey raised his Winchester and fired the first shot. The loud report carried across the ravine and the bullet splintered the stone in front of the nearest wolf. The animal jumped to the side and then began charging toward them, with the rest of the pack following behind. Quincey cocked his rifle again.

Sir Henry fired next and his bullet struck the wolf Quincey had missed in the head. The animal yelped and fell dead. Before the sound of the shot could fade in the wind, Quincey fired again, this time killing the next closest wolf.

With the four horsemen galloping down on them, the pack circled themselves, barking and snarling in confusion. They then reversed direction, running back down the bridge, and jumping to the side of the road as the horses galloped past.

As the horsemen raced onto the road, Doyle looked back to see the wolves pick up the pursuit. One beast put on a sudden burst of speed and broke away from the rest of the pack, closing in on Doyle's horse.

The wolf drew up beside his mount and leaped. Doyle swung the barrel of his Winchester down, catching the animal on the side of its head and knocking it off balance. The wolf crashed to the ground and rolled, but scrambled back to its feet and continued the chase.

Stoker fired off several shots, and Doyle heard a wolf give a loud yelp.

The wolves divided ranks, with half of them taking the left side of the road, and the rest of them on the right. Quincey, Doyle and Irving opened up with their rifles, each man shooting at the wolves, leaping across the rocks and through the trees.

Quincey scored a hit and the wolf crumpled without a sound, but the rest kept up the pace. He cocked again and fired, wounding a second wolf that began yelping and quickly fell away.

Doyle estimated they were a little more than halfway to the crossroads and the road that would lead them back to the village. The wolves were still keeping pace with the horses, but now they seemed content to shadow the riders, keeping to the shelter of the trees.

The horses were growing winded and Doyle wondered how long they could continue. And then he noticed there were fewer wolves dashing in and out among the trees. The snarls and growls grew more distant as well.

"I think they've given up," he called out.

They continued their pace for another few minutes, and when they were about a quarter mile from the crossroads, Quincey slowed his horse to a stop. "Pull up."

They reined in their horses. Quincey turned his horse around with his Winchester on his shoulder, ready to fire, scanning the forest for any signs of the wolves.

"It looks like they've quit," Sir Henry said. "The bullets worked on this bunch, thank God."

Doyle looked up at the sky. The sun was less than an hour away from disappearing behind the mountain peaks. "We'd best keep moving. It'll be dark soon."

They set off down the road at a fast walk. They hadn't traveled far, just rounding a bend in the road when Doyle pulled his mount to an abrupt stop. His companions did the same and followed his gaze upward.

A group of men on horseback looked down on them from a ledge some twenty feet above the road and ahead of them. Doyle counted ten.

They were a tough looking lot with swarthy complexions. For the most part, they wore baggy trousers tucked into high boots, white linen shirts covered by heavy sheepskin vests, and coats. Black, wide brimmed hats covered dark, long, hair.

A big surly fellow wearing a wide, studded belt, and carrying an old rifle, appeared to be leading the band. Next to him was another man, one hand resting on the hilt of a wicked looking Kukri knife sheathed through his belt, the other hand grasping an old rifle.

Doyle raised his hand in a greeting. "Hello."

The men on the ledge continued to peer down at them, saying nothing.

"Gypsies, I'd wager," Quincey said, keeping his voice low.

"What do they want?" Sir Henry asked.

Quincey smiled warmly at the gypsies. "Can't say, but my hand's on this Winchester in case it's something we don't wanna give 'em."

"Hello," Doyle called up to them again. "English?"

Doyle couldn't be certain from his vantage point, but he'd swear the big fellow with the studded belt smirked.

Without turning to look at his men, the man said something to them that Doyle couldn't make out. The band reined their horses around and began riding into the trees.

One of them, a young man with a deep green feather stuck in his hatband, hesitated before following his companions. He looked down at them with a curious expression on his face.

Before Doyle could speak to him, the young man kicked his horse and rode off after the others.

"What on earth was that about?" Sir Henry asked.

"Something tells me it wasn't a chance meeting," Doyle said, his eyes still fixed on the ledge where the gypsies had been moments before.

"What makes you say that?" Quincey asked.

"I don't know, it's just a feeling," Doyle answered.

"If you're right, they might be lying in wait for us down the road," Quincey said.

"Whether they are or not, we better be on our way," Sir Henry said.

"I apologize for yelling like I did back there," Stoker said.

"Considering how events unfolded, I'd say it was a reasonable warning," Doyle responded.

"I could feel it," Stoker continued. "I could just tell that something wasn't as it should be."

"And it wasn't," Sir Henry said. "We were unwise to come here so late in the afternoon."

"Unwise or not, we've gotten a look at the place and learned something of it," Doyle said. "We'll return in the morning with everything we need to breach the place."

They kicked their horses into motion and continued down the road at a gallop. As Doyle focused on the road ahead, he found he couldn't get the group of gypsy men out of his mind.

CHAPTER 43

The sun was hovering just over the horizon by the time they returned to the village, the overcast sky diffusing its rays into a hazy line of red. A crowd of men had gathered in front of Alexander's cottage. Stoker's stomach knotted.

Sir Henry glanced at Stoker. "Now, what's this about?"

"Alexander's there, in his doorway." Stoker pointed. "Arguing with that Branko fellow."

A few moments later, they reined up beside the crowd. The faces in the gathering reflected anger and fear.

Stoker dismounted, carrying the Winchester with him.

The agitated men reluctantly moved aside as he pushed through them, with Doyle, Irving, and Quincey close behind him.

"What's happened?" Doyle asked, reaching Alexander.

"Inside," Alexander said, his voice tension filled. "Go inside."

Branko began yelling in Romanian and waving his arms at them.

"Go," Alexander repeated.

They entered the cottage. Alexander yelled something to the crowd, and then he followed them inside, slamming and bolting the door behind him.

Florence was sitting in front of the hearth where he had last seen her. Clarise stood just behind Florence holding one of the Colt revolvers while Professor Vambery stood nearby with his Winchester. Tatiana, looking terrified, huddled in a corner of the kitchen, grasping the cross that hung around her neck.

Hurrying across the room to Florence, Stoker leaned his rifle against the hearth and kneeled down next to her. "Are you all right?"

Florence turned her head to look at him with a serene smile. He couldn't help but gasp. Her canine teeth had grown. He stood up and stared down at her, feeling powerless.

"That's what caused the commotion," Professor Vambery said.

"They want you to leave," Alexander said.

"They want us to leave?" Doyle repeated. "Now?"

"About an hour ago Branko's wife stopped by to apologize for her husband's rudeness, and to bring something of a peace offering," Vambery continued.

"She'd baked something," Clarise explained.

"Go on," Stoker said with obvious impatience.

"The woman said what she came to say and then stepped over to Florence to present her with the cake. Florence looked up at her and smiled," the professor explained. "Well, and the teeth are quite prominent."

"It terrified her, the poor woman. She dropped the cake and ran from here as fast as she could," Clarise added.

"Crying out *nosferatu* as she left," Vambery added. "Her husband showed up with those friends of his about thirty minutes ago."

At the mention of *nosferatu,* Tatiana began sobbing. Alexander hurried over to her, and placing his hands on her shoulders, whispered to her. Whatever he said did little good, and he turned his attention back to his English visitors.

"All of them," Alexander gestured toward the front of the cottage. "They say you must leave here now."

"I assured Alexander and Tatiana that Mrs. Stoker presents no danger," the professor said. "I pointed out that if she were nosferatu, she wouldn't have been able to arrive here in daylight hours or sit at this hearth with the sun coming in through the windows."

"My wife is the reason we've come," Stoker said. "We must kill the Voivode so my wife can be free of this."

Alexander shook his head and continued pacing.

"Alexander took father's arguments to those men outside," Clarise said. "He's been arguing on our behalf ever since they arrived."

Morgan Quincey observed Alexander. "Maybe so, but it doesn't look like he's all that convinced himself."

"He's frightened," Sir Henry said. "They're all frightened, and it's hard to blame them."

"Alexander, if we're turned out now, with the night coming on, you know what that means," Doyle said.

Alexander remained silent, looking anxious and perplexed.

Professor Vambery repeated Doyle's concerns in Romanian, just to make certain Alexander understood. But before Alexander could respond, the crowd outside grew louder. Stoker heard Branko yell Alexander's name.

Alexander hesitated and then walked to the door and pulled it open. Professor Vambery joined him in the doorway. Doyle and Quincey backed them up, their hands resting on the grips of their Colts.

As Alexander and Branko exchanged heated words, Stoker noted that the sun was almost down. The men crowded around the cottage were aware of this as well, and it added to their fear and anger.

"Branko tells Alexander that his time is up," the professor translated. "We must leave now."

There was a commotion toward the back of the gathering. Stoker saw a fellow push through the throng carrying a rough shaft of wood. Old rags were wrapped around the end of the shaft and held in place with a coating of pitch. A torch.

Alexander and Branko exchanged more heated words, and the crowd grew more excited at hearing them. Alexander's tension turned to anger and he shouted his reply to Branko.

"This is very bad," Vambery said. "Branko says that if Alexander won't turn us out now, then these men will force us out and he and his wife will have to leave as well."

The man with the torch handed it to Branko as he pulled a match from his coat pocket. Branko tilted the head of the torch toward him. The fellow struck the match and touched it to the rags. In seconds, the pitch took the flame and the torch began burning.

Branko shouted more words at Alexander, and again Alexander shouted back, gesturing passionately.

"Alexander just told them that to do this is the same as doing murder," Vambery translated. "Branko says they have a right to protect their village. He swears he'll set fire to the cottage to make certain we all leave."

"Not if I have anything to say about it," Stoker said.

Another volley of defiant words between Alexander and Branko drew his attention.

Stoker stepped past Doyle and made his way for the door. As he stepped outside, Branko stepped forward and raised the torch toward the wooden shingles at the edge of the roof. Alexander leaped forward, knocking Branko to the ground and the burning torch from his hand.

Branko's friends rushed forward and pulled Alexander off him. Two of them held him by his arms as Branko retrieved the torch and got back on his feet. As Alexander screamed at him, Branko raised the torch and again advanced toward the cottage.

Stoker drew his Colt, cocked the hammer. Holding the gun above his head, he fired into the air. The exploding .44 cartridge drew everyone's attention and stopped Branko in his tracks.

"Tell them to get back," Stoker yelled at Vambery as Doyle stepped up beside him, his gun ready.

The professor did so, but the men held their ground. Stoker again cocked and fired, and this time the crowd backed away, but only a few feet.

"Tell them we'll go. We'll go now," Stoker instructed Vambery. "But they must leave these people in peace."

Vambery translated. After a few seconds of silence, Branko growled an order to the men holding Alexander. They released him, and then Branko questioned Vambery.

"He wants to know how soon?" Vambery told Stoker.

"We need just long enough to gather our things and get the horses ready," Stoker answered. "Just give us a few minutes. And tell them to get away from this house or the next time I shoot, it won't be in the air."

The professor again exchanged words with Branko. Branko called out to his men and they retreated from the cottage to gather around the well in the center of the square.

Stoker ushered Alexander back into the cottage with Vambery and Doyle following them.

"I'm sorry," Stoker said to his friends.

"I don't see where there was much choice," Doyle responded.

"But where will we go?" Sir Henry asked. "Back to Bistrita? It's a long ride."

Quincey shook his head. "We'd be sitting ducks if we're caught out on the open road. I say no to it."

"There's a shearing barn," Alexander said, defeat in his tone. "I will not take you, but it is easy to find. I tell you how."

Alexander provided the professor with directions in Romanian.

"Did you see an old barn on a hill north of here, near the river?" the professor asked Stoker. "He says it's just off the main road and less than a twenty minute ride."

"On the west side of the road? I think I saw that."

"West, yes," Alexander confirmed.

"He says that we take the main road north to the stand of pasture fence that borders the road. There's a new gate he says will be hard to miss," Vambery explained. "He thinks there should be lanterns inside. It should at least offer some shelter."

Tatiana, still crying, disappeared into the bedroom and returned carrying an armful of blankets. Clarise met her across the room and took them from her.

"Thank you," Clarise said.

Tatiana embraced Clarise and said something to her. Clarise looked to her father for translation.

"She says they are sorry. They are afraid, and sorry, and ashamed," Professor Vambery explained. "And she says she'll put together some food for us, though she doesn't have much to spare."

"Thank you, Tatiana," Clarise repeated, hugging her again.

"I'll gather up the Vamberys' and Mrs. Stoker's horses," Quincey said. In a few strides he was across the room, but he paused at the door, turning toward Alexander. "If your people had joined up with us, we'd have stood a better chance of killing this murdering monster."

Alexander looked downward as Quincey stepped outside, closing the door behind him.

Once the door latched, Alexander went into the kitchen, opened a bin next to the stove and removed several long strings of garlic. He took them to Professor Vambery and handed them over.

"Put these at openings," Alexander instructed. "Doors, windows, maybe big gaps in the wall planks."

"We appreciate this, Alexander," Stoker said.

"I am so sorry," Alexander said. "The sun is down now. Ride fast and stop for nothing."

CHAPTER 44

They galloped through the chilling night in near darkness; the moonlight hidden by the clouds. Two lanterns, carried by Doyle and Quincey, bobbed like fireflies at the front of the caravan.

Worry for Florence tormented Stoker. She was changing in a way that could only be described as supernatural. And now that they were outdoors, enveloped in the night, he felt keenly aware of their vulnerability.

"Wolves again," Quincey shouted.

The call pulled Stoker from his troublesome thoughts. He had heard no howls or growling; there had been no sound at all from the beasts. He strained to see through the darkness along the side of the road. At first he saw nothing, but then glimpsed two wolves darting in and out among the trees, pacing the horses. And then more of the animals appeared, their gray coats reflecting the light from the moon and the lanterns.

Stoker pulled the Winchester from its scabbard and cocked it. Sir Henry and Professor Vambery followed his example. He noticed Clarise was already gripping her Colt revolver.

"They're on both sides of us," Doyle called out.

Stoker turned to look and caught brief glimpses of the shadowy figures, yellow eyes and long, white teeth as they appeared and then disappeared among the timber.

"Hold your fire unless one of them charges," Quincey said. "We don't wanna start something that might be a mess to finish."

Stoker watched as Quincey pulled back on his reins, allowing Clarise to catch up with him. "Are you all right, Miss Vambery?"

"At the moment, I'm concerned about those animals running alongside us," she answered, a slight tremor in her voice. "Oh, and bolting along a road I don't know at all in the dark of night. Other than that, I suppose I'm fine."

Stoker watched the two of them exchange brief smiles.

"We'll get through it," Quincey assured her.

Quincey spurred his horse forward and took the lead beside Doyle again.

Stoker drew his mount closer to Florence. She seemed more excited by the wolves than frightened.

The pack stayed with them for almost ten minutes, but by the time the pasture fence came into view, there was not a single wolf in sight. They reined in their horses and did their best to see through the gloom.

"There's a gate," Sir Henry called out. "Can you tell if that's the one?"

"In this light I can't tell anything," Doyle said.

Stoker strained to see through the blackness. "It must be the one."

They rode through the gate and were soon back at a gallop as they followed the narrow path that wound up the hillside. Just visible against the night sky, Stoker could make out a building silhouetted against the horizon. Once they drew closer, he could see the barn was a single floor structure with a high, slanted roof. The double barn doors were wide open, and the blackness beyond them was daunting.

The first thing they heard when they dismounted in front of the barn was the sound of rushing water.

"Alexander said the place was near the river." Professor Vambery moved in his saddle, trying to locate the source of the sound.

"Mr. Quincey and I will take a look inside," Doyle said. "Mr. Stoker, if you would check around the building. Here, take my lantern. Sir Henry, professor, stay close to the ladies."

"Let's do it quickly," Stoker said.

Stoker set out along the side of the building, taking cautious steps in the unpredictable moonlight. As he approached the rear of the building, the sound of the river grew louder. He peered around the back corner of the barn and saw a single door set in the center of the wall. The ground behind the structure tilted downward and then appeared to abruptly vanish.

Holding the lantern high, Stoker made his way down the incline to a ledge that dropped off to the river rushing along below. The visibility was poor, but judging from the moonlight reflecting off the glimpses of white water, he judged it to be a forty or fifty foot drop.

"All's well in here." Quincey's voice came from inside the building. "Come ahead."

Stoker hurried around the other side of the barn and reached the front in time to help Florence down from her horse. Quincey was already assisting Clarise. Once the women were on solid ground, the men gathered up the horses and led them inside the barn.

Doyle and Sir Henry were lighting the lanterns they had found hanging inside the barn as Stoker pulled the front doors shut. Three rusted iron brackets were mounted on each door, with a long, equally rusty flat iron bolt slipped into the first two on the left door. The lock must have been installed to prevent sheep from pushing through the doors during the shearing process. With considerable effort, Stoker pushed the bolt through the brackets, securing the door.

Quincey approached from the back of the barn. "I checked the rear door. Looks like it was nailed shut years ago."

"Everyone, help with these." Professor Vambery pulled the strings of garlic from his saddlebags.

The professor handed out the aromatic vegetable to everyone, but when he extended a few strings to Florence, she recoiled.

"Get it away," Florence snapped, an ugly scowl on her face. "That horrible stuff. Get it away."

She retreated to a stall several feet away.

"I'm sorry," the professor said. "Mrs. Stoker, I apologize."

Without acknowledging the apology, Florence sat down on a small bench beside the stall, hiding her face in her hands. Stoker sat down beside her and took her hand.

"What's happening to me?" Florence whispered. "I feel as if I'm losing my mind."

"I'm sorry," he said. "I'm sorry you have to be here, going through this."

She squeezed his hand.

"Right now, I have to help get us settled in here, but I'll be back to you as soon as I can."

Stoker got up and made his way to the professor, who handed him a supply of garlic.

"I should have anticipated that," the professor said. "I do apologize."

"It's not your fault; none of it is."

They inspected every inch of the barn, searching for any openings through which Tepes or anything like him might gain access. The only window in the building had one shutter, and its twin was nowhere in evidence. The glass, however, was intact and in good condition. Doyle closed and bolted the shutter while Irving hung garlic strings to frame the exposed glass.

Stoker and the professor tied their strings of garlic to the main door while Quincey made his way, foot by foot, along each wall, placing garlic wherever he found any significant gaps. Clarise placed garlic strings around the back door, even though it was securely nailed.

"The roof looks as if it's in solid shape," Sir Henry said, gazing upward.

"Yes, I've been looking at it as well," Doyle said. "The light isn't good, but I don't see any holes or damaged spots."

"Not that we could get up there even if we had to," Stoker said.

"I'll get the horses squared away in those stalls at the back," Quincey said. "I can get 'em comfortable in what space we've got."

"We won't be able to build a fire in here. There's no opening for the smoke," Sir Henry said, his tone glum.

"I'll get the blankets," Clarise said. "Between our own and what Tatiana gave us, we'll still be cold, but we won't freeze to death. I'll see to getting some food together as well."

"The food will be fine for tonight," Doyle said. "I'll see about getting more when I go back to the village in the morning."

The comment surprised Sir Henry. "You're going back?"

"We need a ladder or a stout rope with a grappling hook if we're going to reach that window in the courtyard."

"You forgettin' they just ran us out of there?" Quincey asked.

Doyle shook his head. "If just two of us go back, I don't anticipate a problem. It's Florence they're afraid of, and in broad daylight they shouldn't have any objections to the professor and I making a brief visit."

"Do you think anyone will be willing to help us?" Stoker asked.

"I don't know, but I hope that at least Alexander might," Doyle said.

Sir Henry nodded his agreement. "I suppose it's the best course."

Doyle stooped, picking up a length of scrap wood from the ground. "And while Vambery and I are in the village, the rest of you can put your attention to making stakes out of whatever wood we can salvage from this place. We're going to need them."

"I suggest we devise a schedule to keep watch," Stoker said. "If each man stands watch for two hours, that should see us through the night."

"I'll take the first shift," Quincey said. "I'm not feeling all that sleepy, anyway."

CHAPTER 45

Q uincey got the horses settled in short order, even gathering up some hay for each of them from several crumbling bales scattered throughout the old barn. While he tended to the horses, the others went about the business of setting out what food they had and preparing places to sleep. He figured he'd get to that for himself once he'd stood his watch; but Miss Vambery approached him, pointing to a stall and explaining that she'd laid out blankets for him there. She then hurried off to help Mrs. Stoker get settled.

After modest portions of cheese, bread, and a few pieces of dried sausage, everybody had rolled up in their blankets. Although he considered it early, he couldn't fault them. The stress made them all tired, and anyway, the place was so cold that the blankets were the smart choice. He noted, too, that each of them had dozed off with the crosses Clarise had bought in Galatz within easy reach.

Quincey was nearing the end of his two-hour watch. He had spent the time bundled up in his heavy coat, roaming back and forth along the length of the building, twirling his cross in his fingers, occasionally peering through the window into the blackness, and listening for any sound that might signal danger. For the last fifteen minutes, he had settled in on a rickety bench near the rear door and was listening to the faint sound of rushing water rising from the river.

A muffled shuffling sound drew his attention. He tensed and reached for his Colt. Quincey relaxed when he realized the disturbance came from Miss Vambery, approaching him through the shadows, grasping a blanket around her. He rose as she reached him.

"Mr. Quincey," she greeted, keeping her voice low.

"Trouble sleeping?"

"A little, I guess. Please, do be seated."

"Only if you'll take a seat with me."

Clarise sat down on the bench, arranging the blanket around her. Once she settled, he sat down beside her. It was a small bench and they found themselves closer to one another than they had been the entire trip.

"Did you get any rest at all?" he asked.

"Some, but it's a bit of a challenge under the circumstances. You know, having that feeling of being, how do you Americans say it? Being a fish in a barrel?"

Quincey smiled. "Yes, it does kind of feel that way."

In the distance, a wolf howled. She pushed closer to him on the bench.

"They can't get in here," he said.

Clarise shivered. "It's not the wolves I'm worried about."

"Yeah."

They sat in silence for a while and listened to another howl. He couldn't be certain, but he'd swear this one was closer than the first.

"It's been a quiet night 'til now," he said. "I wonder what's stirring 'em up."

"I understand you charged an entire pack of them on horseback this afternoon." There was a hint of judgment in her voice.

"Yes, we didn't have much choice. Managed to shoot a few."

"I'm quite upset with you, you know." Clarise frowned at him.

"Yes, ma'am, I've been aware," Quincey said, feeling sheepish.

"I'm not talking about *that*."

"Maybe I'm just tired, but I'm having a hard time following you."

"Are you making some special effort to get yourself killed?"

"Ma'am?"

"I believe I've asked you not to refer to me as *ma'am*."

"I apologize," he said, wondering why he allowed her to talk to him this way.

"Sir Henry told me about that foolish stunt you pulled this afternoon, trying to climb up to that window. I can't imagine what you were thinking," she said.

"It just seemed like the only—"

"And he told me how those birds were almost the end of you as well," she interrupted. "Did you think of what might have happened if they'd flown into your face?"

"Well, they almost did."

"Those sharp beaks and claws. I can only imagine the wounds."

"There was no way anybody could've known those birds were in there," he said in feeble defense.

"At any rate, you managed to get through it without harm, though only by the grace of God. And certainly not by any use of your own wits. But then you decide to charge headlong into a pack of wolves."

Once again, the howls increased. It sounded like more wolves than before, and this time he was certain they were closer.

"Maybe that's them now, coming back to take their revenge," Quincey said.

"I don't think that's funny."

"No ma'am, uh, Miss Vambery."

She stared down at the ground for a few moments and then emitted a deep sigh.

"I'm sorry, Mr. Quincey," she said, her voice more mellow.

He did not expect to hear those words from her and couldn't mask his surprise.

Clarise turned toward him. "I know I've just come across as quite disagreeable. I don't mean to. But you know, I'd be truly upset if you came to any harm."

He looked over at her and she was looking up at him with a softness he had never seen in her.

"Miss Vambery, I'd like it greatly if you could bring yourself to call me Morgan."

She smiled at him. "I believe I can do that. But not until I apologize."

"You just did."

"I'm speaking of my behavior when you first found us in Galatz, and for those several days to follow. I was terribly rude. Rude and unkind, and for that, I apologize."

"I just figured you didn't take to me."

She shook her head. "It wasn't that. It wasn't that simple. You saved my life, and Mr. Stoker's. I should have been grateful. I am grateful, truly I am. But I'd never been through anything like that. That man holding me, his head just... the blood, so much... it was horrible."

"That fellow was holding a knife to your throat," he reminded her.

"Yes, and I still shudder when I think what might have happened if you hadn't been there. You had to shoot him, I know that. It was just that I was so afraid I couldn't comprehend what had happened. And then I was angry. Angry at being assaulted by those terrible men, and I think, angry at being so afraid."

"I would have taken you for a fool if you hadn't been afraid."

"I took it out on you. And you didn't deserve it."

She placed her hand over his and shifted her position to look into his eyes.

"Can you forgive me, Morgan?"

He gazed at her, the shimmering light from the lanterns adding an alluring glow to her lovely face. In that moment, he was pretty sure that he could forgive Clarise Vambery just about anything.

"There's nothing to forgive, Miss Vambery, not one thing." He took her hand in both of his.

"I'd like it greatly if you could bring yourself to call me Clarise."

He put his arm around her shoulder, feeling her body yielding to him as he drew her closer.

"Miss Vambery, I'm a simple man and I hope you won't think me a sizable dolt if I ask if I can kiss you."

"Clarise," she reminded him, touching her fingers to his lips.

As she drew her hand away, he bent her head back against his shoulder and lowered his lips toward hers. Her lips parted as he drew closer, and he could smell the sweetness of her breath.

A sudden cacophony of howling startled them out of the moment. The baying penetrated the old wood of the barn and reverberated off every surface. Clarise held him close as the racket continued, and the others roused from their sleep.

He and Clarise rose from the bench as the other men stepped away from their blankets. Only Florence appeared to be unconcerned by the yelps and cries. She had sat up but seemed content to remain where she was, her expression serene.

"It sounds like they're right outside," Stoker said.

Quincey glanced at the rear door, so close to the bench where he and Clarise had been sitting. Keeping his arm around her, he led her away from the door toward the center of the room.

The howling subsided and as the last echo of it faded away, the building took on a disturbing silence. They all stood where they were, afraid to make a sound, their eyes focused on the doors and window. The tension in the room was thick and the room had grown so cold that they could all see the vapor of their breath.

They stood, unmoving and silent, for almost a full minute. Quincey began thinking the worst was over. There was probably little to be concerned about.

The horses had been calm and quiet during the howling. But now, in the silence, they began to snort, shuffling and stomping in their stalls.

The main door of the barn suddenly shook and rattled, its hinges squeaking shrilly against some unseen force. Clarise squeezed Quincey's hand as the door shuddered, the metal of the brackets moaning as they strained against the bolt.

CHAPTER 46

S toker fought hard to contain the feeling within him. He stood perfectly
still, gripping the cross in his fist, his eyes fixed on the door shaking on
its hinges, the bolt straining against the locking brackets. Then a voice
seeped through the old wooden planks, speaking in what he was certain was
Romanian. It was a hollow, coarse voice with a quality of gritty sandpaper.

Doyle turned toward Vambery. "Professor?"

"He says he's cold, freezing. Please let him in to get warm. Show mercy."

As the door continued to rattle, Doyle hurried to the wall beside it and
moved his eye closer to a narrow gap between the boards.

"There's a mist that's come in and I can see one of them silhouetted
against it in the moonlight, some twenty-five feet away," he reported.

"That means there's two of them," Sir Henry said, alarmed.

At that moment, a scraping sound from the rear door reached them,
and the horses grew even more skittish.

"Three," Quincey said, as he and Clarise went to the horses to calm
them.

Stoker looked over at Florence, sitting among her sleeping blankets,
staring at the door as if they were back home and she had been expecting
visitors.

As the pleading continued from outside the front door, another voice
began a soft mewling from the rear entrance.

"More of the same," Professor Vambery said. "Have mercy on me. Don't let me perish in the cold."

At that moment, the professor's gaze met Clarise's. Stoker could only guess that the fear in his daughter's eyes did something to the man because he flushed with anger, strode to the rear door and hammered his fist against it.

"Părăseste acest loc, demon," he yelled. "Plecă ᾽n numele lui Isus Hristos."

A horrifying scream emitted from the opposite side of the door, so intense that Vambery staggered backwards several steps. A violent pounding against the door followed it, accompanied by a torrent of angry words.

"Dear God, man, what did you say?" Sir Henry asked, horrified.

Vambery took a moment to collect himself. "I ordered it to leave. To be gone in the name of Jesus Christ. I can't repeat what it's saying now."

"You've said they can't enter a place without being first invited. If that's so, then we should be safe in here," Doyle said.

"Yes, but this place is not a personal home to any of us, and I'm uncertain of how much protection it will afford. They may not require an invitation. I don't know."

"We're depending on the garlic then," Doyle said.

"And the power of God," Clarise added, lifting her cross.

Stoker gazed at the half-shuttered window with a fascination he did not want to have. He began making his way toward it. Step by step, as if pulled by some unseen force. Upon reaching the window, he positioned himself against the shuttered side so he could get an angle of view toward the front of the barn. At first, the visibility was poor; the blackness outside was overpowering. But then the mist seemed to fade into view out of the darkness, and in the pale moonlight he saw them.

"Can you make out anything?" Sir Henry asked.

"I can see four of them, all men," Stoker reported.

"And there's still one at each door, so six," Quincey said.

Stoker watched the creatures moving erratically back and forth along the building as if scouting for a way in, the fog swirling around them. Two of them brushed against one another in passing and they lashed out with wild, violent blows, and angry snarls. These things were little more than wild beasts and Stoker shuddered as he imagined what it would be like if they found a way inside.

He changed his position and drew closer to the glass. Moving his face closer to the windowpane, he hoped to gain a view toward the rear of the barn. A face suddenly smashed against the window. Stoker heard Clarise scream from somewhere behind him as he jumped back.

The feral, hideous creature glared through the window at them all. Its long hair was filthy and matted, making it difficult to tell the dirt from the dried, rust-colored blood smeared across its face. Dirt and dried blood also caked the collar and breast of the ragged, once white tunic, out of style now for some hundred years. Its mouth was curled open in an angry sneer that displayed a pair of long, pointed, and rotted teeth.

The creature's nostrils flared and its empty eyes surveyed the window until it spotted one of the garlic strings hanging against the side of the glass. The sneer seemed to deepen with recognition and then the thing raised a filthy hand and scraped a fingernail that better resembled an animal claw down across the glass. When it curled its fingers into a fist, Stoker realized it meant to strike the glass.

Stoker leaped back to the window and pushed the cross in his hand flat up against the panes. The thing emitted a blood curdling scream as it covered its face with an arm and jumped away from the window. Stumbling backwards, it tumbled to the ground and Stoker watched as it rolled out of sight into the blackness.

"God protect us," he heard Clarise pray as he lowered the cross from the glass and backed away from the window.

"It's gone now," Morgan Quincey assured Clarise.

"But for how long?" Doyle asked no one in particular.

"We only have to keep them out until sunrise," Professor Vambery said. "Bram just proved it possible."

The rattling and shaking of the front door was not as consistent as it had been, and the movement against the bolt was not as violent. As they stood watching and listening, the shaking became more and more sporadic, and then died away altogether. Almost immediately, the scraping and pounding at the rear door stopped as well.

"What are they up to now?" Quincey breathed.

Once again, a maddening silence fell over the barn. Each of them stood where they were, fearful to move, their eyes moving between the doors and the window.

Stoker sensed movement and turned to see that Florence had stood up and was staring at the front doors, an odd smile on her lips.

"Florence," he called to her.

Without acknowledging him, or anyone else, she walked toward the front entrance to the barn, stopping a few feet short of the doors.

"What is it?" Clarise asked.

Florence again didn't appear to hear. She cocked her head, as if listening, though the only sound in the barn was that of everyone's deep and anxious breathing.

Stoker found it difficult to turn his gaze from Florence, but curiosity drew him back to the window. This time exercising greater caution, he moved closer to the glass and peered out.

A light snow had begun falling, the delicate crystals fluttering down through the moonlight. The vampires were still out there; he could see three of them. They were just standing, looking at the barn. And then he noticed something else.

"Something's happening," Stoker called out.

In moments, everyone gathered around the window except Florence.

"There," Stoker pointed toward the front of the barn, and some ten feet above the ground, the snow was swirling within the beams of moonlight. The phenomenon was easy to make out, even in the dim moon glow, for the eddying snow moved in two distinct clusters while the snow surrounding them fell in an uninterrupted downward drop to the ground. Within the whirlpools of snow, the mist thickened, the snow seeming to become part of the mist and the mist becoming part of the snow. Each of the clusters grew in volume, lengthening as they floated downward, and as they neared the ground, they each took on form.

Stoker thought at first he might be hallucinating, but as he watched transfixed, the swirling snow took on the forms of two women. One was fair and one was dark, each was young and beautiful. The fair haired woman wore a long, flowing gown, once white but now yellowed with age. The dark haired one wore a similar gown, also terribly faded. Despite their diaphanous attire, neither of them appeared affected by the bitter night.

The two women moved with an alluring grace as they approached the window, stopping a few feet short of it. Stoker could make out their delicate features, their voluptuous red lips, and their dark, piercing eyes. The women gazed through the glass at him and their lips parted in horrible, obscene smiles.

And then they began speaking in their native tongue, one voice delicate and bright, the other sultry.

Stoker looked over at Florence. She was facing the window, her eyes bright with anticipation, her lips parted.

"Professor?" Stoker drew Vambery's attention.

"Come out. Come out to us, sister," Vambery translated.

"They're speaking to Florence." Stoker felt a rush of anger.

He turned to check on his wife. She stood motionless, staring past him toward the window, the odd smile still on her lips.

"Join us, sister. There is nothing to fear," Vambery continued.

"Bloody hell there isn't," Doyle said.

Like mythological sirens, the two seductive creatures captivated their attention. Everyone stood at the window, watching and listening. And with every passing minute, the tension in the barn increased.

"They're still only speaking to your wife," the professor reported. "Join us, be with us, open the door and be free with us. Disgusting dribble."

At the mention of the door, Stoker glanced in its direction.

"Florence," he shouted.

She was in front of the door; her face contorted with disgust as she tugged at the garlic string over the bolt and threw it away. Her fingers then gripped the rusted bolt, working to draw it out from the brackets.

Stoker saw the bolt moving as he raced across the room and grabbed hold of her. She resisted and grasped at the bolt as he wrestled her away from the door. Doyle reached the door moments later and shoved the bolt back in place.

"What does she think she's doing?" Sir Henry asked.

"She has no idea what she's doing," Professor Vambery said.

Stoker's anger grew to fury. The shameless endeavors of these vile, undead women to bring his wife to ruin were deplorable. With his arms still wrapped around Florence, he closed his eyes and prayed to God for strength, for direction, and for his wife's deliverance.

He expected no immediate answer from heaven; he expected no disembodied voice offering guidance. What he received was a sense of conviction so tangible as to startle him into awareness, a conviction *of* responsibility to defend his wife and his friends in these parlous circumstances.

Leaving Florence in the care of Sir Henry and Clarise, he made his way back to the window. As the two creatures came into view through the glass, their voices transformed from words into laughter, beautiful, mocking laughter.

Stoker again placed his cross up against the pane. The women's lovely smiles transformed into diabolical, leering grins while their laughter increased.

And then the two creatures began moving away. They did not turn and walk; they did not appear to be walking at all. They backed away, leaving no tracks in the snow. Flurries of snow began swirling around them, moving faster and faster, becoming crystalline whirlpools that pulled the two women into them.

Their scornful laughter grew more distant, echoing through the building as it diminished. The two women faded from view, becoming translucent as their forms merged with the snow and mist. And then they were gone.

Florence gave a soft moan and seemed to be more aware of her surroundings.

An unearthly silence enveloped the barn. Stoker moved closer to the window and peered out into the blackness. Once again, they were alone.

CHAPTER 47

S toker was sitting on the little bench at the rear of the barn, his tablet on his knees, writing down the nerve rattling events of the evening. Papers filled with notes occupied the bench beside him. The detailed descriptions flowed smoothly, the memories of the vampires, especially the two women, being so fresh.

He looked up as Doyle approached. "Trouble sleeping?"

"If anyone is truly sleeping, it isn't sound," Doyle said.

"Yes, of course."

"I suspect we've seen the worst of it this night," Doyle said.

"Dawn is less than a half hour away. And thank God for it."

"I knew you'd been writing again." Doyle gestured toward the tablet. "I've been meaning to ask you how it's coming along."

Stoker couldn't hide his surprise. "You knew? I believe this is the first time I've taken up my pen in your presence."

Doyle smiled. "The ink smudges on the tips of the index and third fingers of your right hand were revealing."

"Quite so."

"Do you have your ending yet?"

"I'm not sure at this point," Stoker answered.

"No?"

"I've been doing more journaling than writing. Jotting down observations and impressions of our journey. Perhaps some of it will find a place in my book."

"I still find it a mystery how the need to tell a story can consume us. Well, me, at any rate," Doyle said.

"I think it's well established that my book was born out of obsession," Stoker said, a hint of disdain in his voice.

"No need to revisit all that."

"No, of course not. But I was going to say that there's been something different in the writing for me over the last days."

"How so?"

Stoker gazed at his open tablet. "When I began the book, my only focus was on what I wanted."

"Fame, if I recall."

"And success. I'm ashamed to admit to that selfishness, and even more ashamed to confess that the same desire still exists in me."

"Normal, I think," Doyle said. "The human character of us all."

"But now, with all that's happened during this trip, seeing my dear Florence, changing like she is. Well, in writing it all down, I think I've come to realize certain truths."

"About your book?"

"If I live through what's coming, I suspect the book will finish itself," Stoker said. "No, I believe I've been hiding in the writing."

"Hiding?"

"I've buried myself in it, letting it distract me from my true purpose. The thought of failing at our intention was simply too terrifying."

Doyle nodded. "Ah, Florence."

"I'm finally able to acknowledge it again. My purpose here has always been to destroy the thing that threatens my wife's eternal soul. My greater purpose is to restore my relationship with her."

"And here is the charming lady herself," Doyle said.

Stoker looked away from Doyle to see Florence approaching.

"We need to talk," Florence said to him in a whisper.

Stoker flipped his tablet shut. "Of course."

"Then you'll both excuse me," Doyle said.

Florence placed her hand on Doyle's arm. "No, please stay if you would."

"If you like."

Stoker cleared his papers from the bench, and Florence sat down beside him. Doyle settled in, leaning against the wall next to them. Florence wore a calm expression and appeared to be well.

"Now, what is all this about?" Stoker asked, keeping his voice low.

Florence took a long breath, considering her thoughts. "We've been through a great deal together, all of us. You've all shown such courage. Through those terrible times last year, none of you ever flinched. Tepes would have destroyed us all, but you kept fighting. You, my husband, Sir Henry and you, Mr. Doyle. The Vamberys and even Mr. Quincey, a visitor who hardly knew any of us."

Stoker felt his concern growing. "Florrie, what's this all about?"

"You've shown me just how far you'll go for my welfare. I know you'd do anything for me."

"Of course we would," Doyle said.

"I love you, and you know it," Stoker said. "I'd sooner die than let anything happen to you."

She took his hand in hers. "I love you, Bram. And because I do, this is much more difficult than I expected."

"Just come out with it."

"Mr. Doyle, I want you to hear this because it's important that you bear witness to what I'm about to say."

"Then, please, say it."

"All right. Should I die—" Florence began.

"Should you die?" Stoker interrupted. "I won't have you speak of it. Don't even think such thoughts."

Florence pulled his hand closer to her. "If it even appears that Tepes might have his way, you must kill me."

"Florrie!" Stoker couldn't disguise his horror.

"How could you ask us to even consider such a thing?" Doyle asked, mortified.

"If it looks as if Tepes will have his way, you must kill me, and do so in the way prescribed by Professor Vambery. Should I die under any circumstances before any of you can intervene, then follow the professor's instructions on how to dispose of my body so I do not become, so I do not become one of *them*."

"That's enough," Stoker told her. "I can't stand any more of this talk."

"Mr. Doyle, you've heard me express my wishes. If it comes to where Bram must carry them out, you must speak up for him. I will not have anyone thinking that it was his idea to end my life. He must have the understanding and support of you all."

"My dear Florence…" Doyle began, disbelief in his voice.

"You both must promise me."

Stoker shook his head, feeling more miserable than he could remember. "No, I won't hear any more of this."

"You must hear it, and you must promise." Florence's eyes began glistening with tears. "My very soul is at risk, my eternal soul, and I know that you understand what that means. I've had so much time to think about these things and we must be prepared for the worst."

"But there's no need," Stoker said. "The night's been quiet since those terrible women disappeared, and the sun will be up within minutes. We've done it, Florrie, we've gotten through the night."

"Tepes can do us no harm during the day," Doyle reminded her.

"And as soon as we have daylight, Mr. Doyle and the professor will go back to the village. We'll get what supplies we need and then return to the castle," Stoker said.

"You'll stay here with Miss Vambery, of course, and Sir Henry will stay with you as well, or one of the other men," Doyle said, patting the grip of the Colt carried in the holster he had strapped to his waist. "You'll be nowhere near danger."

Stoker nodded. "Once we get inside, we'll hunt him down while he sleeps and can do nothing. We'll kill him and any like him. It'll all be over today, Florrie. Before the afternoon has passed, he'll be dead and you'll be released from his hold on you."

Florence dabbed her eyes and wiped a tear from her cheek with the corner of the blanket. "I want to believe that. God knows I want it to be as you've described. But I still want you both to promise. Should circumstance go against us, I want to know that you'll look after me as I've asked."

"I'll give you my promise, then," Stoker said. "Only because I'm certain I'll never have to deliver on it."

She nodded with optimism and started to weep. He wrapped his arms around her and pulled her close. He caused her misery and the time had come for him to make it all right. Opportunity would come with the sunrise.

A loud crash at the front doors jolted him to his feet. A moment later, with the sound of splintering wood and straining metal, the doors burst open.

CHAPTER 48

S ir Henry and the others jumped up from their blankets as a group of rough-looking men rushed into the barn. Most of them wielded wooden clubs, some had knives, and a few carried pistols.

Stoker recognized several of them as gypsies they had encountered the previous afternoon.

Morgan Quincey shoved Clarise and the professor behind him as several of the attackers closed in. The man leading them raised his club. In a blur of motion, Quincey's Colt appeared in his hand and he fired. The club flew from the gypsy's hand as he crumpled to the ground, blood spreading across the front of his shirt.

The fallen man's companions jumped on Quincey before he could cock the revolver again. At that moment, Doyle waded into the brawl to help the American. Together, he and Quincey fought fiercely. Quincey used his gun as a club until one gypsy twisted it from his hand. Moments later, both he and Doyle were wrestled to the ground.

Stoker pulled the Colt from its holster as quickly as he could, placing himself between Florence and the charging gypsies. Sir Henry already had his rifle to his shoulder, levered a cartridge into the chamber, and got off a shot. A man at the front of the gang grabbed at his shoulder as he dropped to the ground.

Florence screamed as the gypsies kept coming. Stoker thumbed back the hammer of his revolver and took hasty aim at another gypsy carrying a gun.

The Colt jumped in his hand as he fired, but his shot missed. Before he could fire again, two of the gypsies were on him. One of the men got a firm hold on his revolver, giving it a violent twist. Stoker felt a sharp pain shoot up his arm as the gun fell from his grasp. Seconds later, Stoker found himself pinned against the back wall by three men.

Stoker shouted a warning as several more of the gypsy men rushed toward Sir Henry. The actor swung his rifle, but one of the attackers blocked it with a club, providing his companions the opportunity to jump the actor and pull him to the ground.

And then Stoker saw the young fellow with the green feather in his hat, the one who had stared so strangely at them from the ledge the previous day. He advanced with the others and made his way to Florence, taking her by the arm and lifting her to her feet.

"Florence!" Stoker yelled, frantic and struggling.

As the young man looked at him, Stoker thought he saw sympathy in his eyes. He was keeping himself between Florence and the brawl. Protecting her.

At that moment, the big fellow with the wide, studded belt strode through the doors carrying a lantern. He stopped just inside, grimly surveying the room. He snapped an order and his men began herding Stoker and his companions from the barn. A second call from the man and several of his men led their horses from the stalls and gathered the guns. As they marched through the doorway, Stoker noticed the stern looking fellow with the big Kukri knife hanging from his belt watching from just inside the doorway.

The sun was not yet up, but Stoker could see its pale, red glow on the hazy horizon. Standing in front of the old barn, seeing the fear in the eyes of his friends, he began feeling the familiar twinges of shame and defeat. Despite all their planning and precautions, it had all come to this. This time, he could very well be responsible for their deaths. *No, no, no.* He couldn't allow himself to believe such things. He wouldn't allow himself to be pulled into this abyss of self-defeat again.

The gypsy leader began walking along his line of prisoners, dispassionate, as he gazed at each of them. When he drew near to the professor, Vambery addressed him in Romanian. The man mumbled a response and continued on.

"Professor?" Stoker called out.

"I asked him what he intends to do with us," Vambery answered, getting back on his feet. "He says that we'll find out soon enough."

BLACK HUNTERS' MOON 223

The gypsy leader yelled at them. There was no question he wanted their silence. And then the young man with the green feather guarding Florence began speaking to the leader.

Their conversation escalated to a heated exchange. As the young fellow argued, he released his grasp on Florence and took a step toward the leader.

"Professor?" Stoker queried.

"The young one doesn't like what they're doing," the professor began. "He fears God's judgment. The big fellow accuses him of being a coward and says he brings shame to them all. The young man says they should fight against this, that God will judge them all. He says that it is the big fellow who is the coward."

The gypsy leader, his face contorted with fury, jumped forward, smashed his fist into the young man's jaw, and then screamed another command. The young man had barely hit the ground before two of his companions yanked him to his feet. Another man pulled a length of rope from his horse's saddle and bound the young man's hands behind his back.

The gypsy leader swung into his saddle as the mutineer was dragged into the barn and shoved into one of the stalls. As the men exited the barn, one of them retrieved a broken wood plank from the ground. They shut the doors and slid the plank through the iron door handles.

Several gypsies saddled the horses they'd led from the barn. The animals were still skittish from all the commotion, and one of them attempted to get away from its handler. The man held tight to the lines, causing the horse to pivot off to the side. As its rump swung around, it collided with Quincey and the men holding him, knocking them all to the ground.

Quincey rolled away and jumped to his feet, retreating along the side of the barn. His two guards got to their feet and rushed at him. Quincey fought hard, but his guards forced back toward the rear of the building.

Stoker took advantage of his distracted guards, twisted out of their grasp, and sprinted toward Quincey. He could hear the pounding of footsteps behind him.

Quincey was running out of solid ground, landing blows on his opponents and then moving backwards toward the ledge dropping off to the river. One gypsy leaped forward again and Quincey delivered a powerful blow to his belly. The man doubled over and the American followed through with a vicious kick to his jaw. The man collapsed in a heap.

Stoker was almost there. In a few more feet, he'd be able to jump the second guard advancing on Quincey.

A shot exploded in the thin morning air. Quincey spun around and, with a painful cry toppled out of sight over the ledge.

Stoker heard Clarise scream somewhere behind him. He whirled around. The gypsy leader sat straight in his saddle, the old rifle in his hands, smoke curling from the barrel.

Shock and rage surged through Stoker as he turned back toward the river and raced to the ledge. Peering down into the shadowy gorge, he could see nothing. There was no sign of the American.

As he swore a silent oath that he would deliver his wife and friends from this horror, he heard advancing footsteps. He turned around.

His captors were almost on him. The sight of them infuriated him even more, and he charged at them, swinging wild punches. He was blind with rage. He could feel his blows landing, stinging his knuckles, but the only thing he could see was the gypsy leader sitting on his horse, holding that cursed rifle.

The gypsy was staring down at him, his expression scornful. Stoker swore to himself that he'd pull the big man from the horse and beat him to death with his bare hands.

Stoker's head exploded with pain and the face of the gypsy leader disappeared in a blinding burst of light. And then only darkness remained.

CHAPTER 49

His first sensation was of cold, and everything was black. The cold was emanating from beneath him. He opened his hand and felt the raw, hard stone beneath his fingers. And then he became aware of the throbbing pain in his head. He tried to open his eyes, but the blinding light intensified the pain. Closing them tight again gave relief.

"He's coming 'round, I think."

It was a woman's voice, but it sounded far away. And then footsteps sounded around him.

"Yes, he's waking up."

This time he recognized the voice, Clarise. Once again, he tried to open his eyes. She appeared blurry, but there she was, looking down at him, her face lined with worry. He turned his head, bringing Doyle and Irving into view.

"Thank God," Sir Henry said.

Doyle lay a hand on his shoulder. "Can you sit up?"

"Leave him be awhile," Clarise said.

"Florence?" Stoker asked.

"She's safe. Sitting right over there with father." Clarise pointed.

He tried to turn his head, but the pain came again.

"You need to get yourself together. We've little time," Doyle said.

He made another effort and this time managed to sit up with the help of Doyle and Irving. Another brief wave of pain struck him, but subsided to a dull throb. Reaching to the back of his head, he felt a sizable bump and winced.

As his vision cleared, he became aware of the hazy light filtering down from the windows set high in the walls. It fell upon the dusty floor and created a dim glow against the stone walls and pillars.

"The castle!" he gasped.

Doyle nodded. "I'm afraid so. We're in the main hall."

"And Florence is here?"

"She's here with me, and safe for now," Professor Vambery's voice came from behind.

Stoker turned to find the professor sitting next to Florence on the bottom steps of a narrow stairway that curved upward. Florence sat unmoving, staring vacantly into the shadows.

Feeling a wave of panic, Stoker reached for the small cross on the chain around his neck. It wasn't there.

"The gypsies took it," Clarise said. "They took them all."

"What happened?" Stoker asked.

"One of them clubbed you when you tried to get to the devil who shot Mr. Quincey," Sir Henry said. "We thought the blow had killed you, too."

At the mention of Morgan Quincey, Clarise uttered a small cry.

"They put us on our own horses, and threw you over a saddle, and brought us here," Doyle continued. "The sun was up by the time we arrived. They pushed us inside and closed the door."

"And locked it from the outside," Clarise added.

Doyle gestured around the vast room. "We've tried all the doors on this level. They're all locked, save one. Several have new padlocks on them. We were about to start looking upstairs when you came to."

"Several of the doors have new lumber on them as well," Sir Henry said.

"What about the one that's unlocked?" Stoker asked.

"It opens into a tower," Doyle said. "There's a stairway that goes downward, but it's pitch black in there. We couldn't see more than eight or nine steps before they disappeared in the darkness."

Clarise shuddered. "And there isn't a single torch."

"What about the windows?" Stoker asked. "What about the vine Mr. Quincey tried to climb?"

"Someone's cut down." Sir Henry gestured toward the window.

"There's nothing useful in this room, no furniture or anything else. We need to look over the upper levels, though I don't expect a better result," Doyle said.

Stoker struggled to his feet with help from Doyle and Irving. He made his way over to Florence and knelt down in front of her. She stared through him as if he wasn't there.

"She's been like this from the moment we stepped inside the place," Professor Vambery said.

Seeing Florence like this, and Quincey's murder burned into his memory, fueled Stoker with a new determination. "What time is it?"

Doyle retrieved his watch from his waistcoat and flipped it open. "Almost eleven."

"That gives us seven hours," Stoker said.

"To do what?" Sir Henry asked. "There doesn't appear to be any way out."

Stoker paced the empty floor, surveying the layout of the room, his strength returning with each step. "If we can't get out, then we've got to find Tepes and kill him, as quickly as we can, before the sun sets."

"And his wives and any like them," Doyle said.

"But how?" Clarise asked.

"We need to find weapons, and we need a way to get past the locks," Stoker answered.

Sir Henry reached inside his coat and around to his back. When he withdrew his hand, he was holding the Bowie knife gifted to him by Quincey. "I still have this. They were keen on relieving me of my gun, but they didn't bother looking for anything else."

"It's a start," Doyle said. "Now let's see what else we can find."

The actor moved the knife sheath around to his side and returned the blade to it.

"You say you've given this floor a thorough look?" Stoker asked.

"We have," Doyle said. "The upper floors, then?"

"As quickly as we can."

"I'll stay with Mrs. Stoker," the professor said.

Clarise moved toward Florence. "As will I."

"You should go with the men, my dear," her father advised. "The more of you searching, the better the chance of results. And we've little to fear as long as the sun is up. We'll be fine on our own."

"Very well."

"Call out should you need us," Stoker advised the professor.

Stoker led the way up the stairs. His head still throbbed, but at least he could stand on his feet. He prayed that he'd be able to stay that way.

CHAPTER 50

The passageway overlooking the main hall was well lit by the room's several windows, but the only light in the inner corridors came from a single window at the end of the passage. After pausing to get their bearings, Sir Henry stepped through a small archway just off the landing.

"Look here," Sir Henry called out.

They joined him on the small balcony.

Doyle looked down over the stone balustrade. "The chapel."

Stoker pointed. "The walls are crumbled there and there."

"But those broken sections are built to the edge of the precipice," Doyle said. "You can see it there."

"I don't see any doors," Clarise said.

"The door set under these stairs must be the chapel entrance. And since it's locked, there's probably another door that opens to the courtyard, though we can't see it from this position," Doyle said.

They searched the remainder of the second level only to find that the doors were all locked. Some of them had one or two pieces of new lumber replacing small sections, secured with iron straps bolted in place. They climbed to the third level and again found it poorly lighted, this time from a window at each end of the passageway.

They spread out down the corridor and began trying the doors. On the third try, they found one unlocked. The room was empty, with one tall narrow window opening to the south. Iron hinges were set into the wall on either side of the window; shutters had once hung on them.

Stoker leaned over the windowsill of thick cut stones and looked out. The view was dizzying and he could make out the silver reflection of a river flowing through the gorge below. "This wall is built right up to the edge of the peak. It's a terrible drop into the gorge."

They left the room and moved on to the next door. Clarise reached it first and tried the latch. It opened.

"Here's something," she said, stepping inside.

Stoker, Doyle, and Irving followed her to find what might have been a woman's bedchamber. Two windows filtered light into the room, each with empty iron hinges. Framing each window hung a pair of damask draperies secured on an iron rod bolted into the ancient stones. The second window was bare.

Clarise took up each of the draperies in her hands and examined them, pulling at each of them to test their strength. "Considering how old they must be, they're in remarkable condition. A little moth eaten, but we might find a use for them."

"Let's finish exploring and we'll collect them on our way back down," Doyle said.

The top floor proved even more disappointing than the floor below. Every door but one was shut tight and locked, and the unlocked chamber was empty. It was the last room in the corridor and much of the outer wall had crumbled away around one of its two windows.

Stoker approached the opening with care. As he drew near, the wind whistling past the gaping hole seemed to tug at him, as if it might pull him out through the opening at any moment. He quickly stepped back, unnerved.

"We've wasted valuable time," Sir Henry groused as they descended to the third floor landing.

Stoker hurried for the stairs. "I want to look at the room below again, the bedchamber."

The others followed after him.

"Why bother? We found little that might help us," Sir Henry said.

They reached the bedchamber and went inside. Stoker made his way directly to one of the windows.

"Someone take hold of me," he instructed, edging onto the sill in a sitting position. "I want to see what the exterior walls are like."

"What are you thinking?" Doyle asked, joining Sir Henry in finding firm holds on his coat and trousers.

"In a moment," Stoker said.

Gripping the outer edges of the sill, Stoker worked his way outward until he had a clear view of the exterior wall. To the right, he could see several more windows. There were two or three single windows, but most of them were set in pairs. He estimated the distance from each window, room to room, ranged between twelve to twenty feet. The wall itself was constructed of rough-hewn stones.

About three feet below the line of windows ran a ledge that jutted out from the wall some seven or eight inches. He couldn't tell if the ledge was decorative or served some structural purpose, but it was crumbling away in several places.

The view to the left was very much the same, though the room he was looking out from was closer to the end of the wing. He moved back, edging into the room.

"There are two unlocked rooms on this floor. This one, and the chamber to our left," Stoker said. "All the others are locked, and they wouldn't be locked if there wasn't something in them that might help us. What other reason could there be to keep us out?"

Clarise appeared doubtful. "You don't know that for certain."

"I think I can make it." Stoker pointed at the window. "It's not more than fifteen feet from the window of the room to the right of us. I think I can climb to it."

"You want to climb along the outside?" Sir Henry asked, shocked.

"There are plenty of handholds and there's a small ledge a few feet below the window sills. Once I get inside the room, I can probably open the door."

Clarise frowned. "Probably?"

"If I can't, I'll just have to return the way I came."

"No unsecured room has produced anything that might help us," Doyle said. "I agree with you. It's a reasonable deduction that the locked rooms contain something."

"It's insanity to even consider it," Clarise said.

"No one's asking that you do this," Sir Henry said.

"It's up to me to make all this right. Even if I die trying," Stoker said.

"Your dying won't do any of us any good, so let's take as many precautions as we can to assure you don't." Doyle pointed to the old draperies.

"Even tied together, these wouldn't come close to reaching the ground, but they'll reach the next window."

Stoker nodded with enthusiasm. "A safety tether. Yes, excellent."

Within a few minutes, they had wrestled the draperies from their iron mounts, laying them end to end across the room. Stoker stepped back and examined the total length of the two draperies.

"I think it'll do," he said. "With one end tied around my waist, there should still be enough to reach the window in the next chamber."

"Let's all pray it holds," Clarise said.

"It's all we have," Sir Henry said.

Clarise sighed and walked along the length of the draperies. "Well, then, if you insist on this insanity, then we might as well do it as smartly as we can. There's too much fabric as it is. Just the weight of it is dangerous; it could pull you right off the ledge. We need thinner strips we can braid together into a single, stronger rope."

"This should do the trick." Sir Henry pulled out his Bowie knife.

Forty minutes later they had assembled the fabric according to Clarise's directions. Using a tug of war, with two on each end, they tested the strength. The fabric held.

"Move with care and think every move through before you do it," Doyle advised, as Stoker tied the end of the tether around his waist. "Sir Henry and I'll have a firm hold on our end, so even if you slip the worst that should happen is you get scraped up a bit against the stones."

"As long as you don't let go," Stoker said, smiling.

"Don't even suggest that," Clarise scolded. "Dearest Lord, keep Your servant safe this day."

"No use putting it off," Stoker said.

Doyle and Irving picked up the trailing end of the tether, each finding a tight grip.

With a last pull at the fabric around his waist, Stoker edged out backwards onto the windowsill. He felt the cold air against his legs as he eased them downward. His heart beat against his chest as he held himself suspended there. And then, after what seemed a great deal of time, he felt his feet contact the ledge. With his own silent prayer to the God of heaven, he lowered his full weight onto the narrow stones.

CHAPTER 51

M organ Quincey became aware of a rushing sound in his head, and then a dull ache that pulsed through his temples. He opened his eyes to see the morning sunlight creeping over the edge of the steep hillside from which he'd fallen. The arm he'd thrown around the small hillside tree as he had plummeted down the incline ached like the devil. Even after he'd passed out, he had somehow kept his arm tight around the tree trunk; a lucky thing, since it had kept him from rolling off the small ledge upon which he had landed. As he got his bearings, he saw he was perched about thirty feet above the rushing river.

The side of his head ached and his shoulder burned like blazes. With a good deal of awkwardness, he kept hold of the tree while he worked his coat off. The gypsy's bullet had struck him high in the shoulder, but it looked like it had passed right through. Any lower and it might have shattered some bones.

He could do nothing for himself hanging off a tree. He would have to climb. Looking upward, he planned a route while he slipped back into his coat. The first few minutes of the climb he felt sick to his stomach, and stiff as an eighty-year-old farmer with rheumatism. But with each foot of progress, he felt a little better.

He struggled upward, but after almost falling twice, he made it over the top and collapsed on a frozen patch of ground at the rear of the old shearing barn. Lying there, his chest heaving, stark reality landed heavily on him.

He was pretty sure he knew where the gypsies had taken Clarise and the others. He knew what he had to do. But he needed a horse. And he needed to tend to his wound. It wouldn't do for him to start bleeding, for he'd need all his strength.

After resting for several minutes, he got to his feet. He made his way around to the front of the building. A length of wood lodged between the two door handles barred the door shut. He slipped it out and pulled open the doors. The place looked empty. He hadn't walked ten feet into the place when he saw the young fellow who had angered the head man of the raid.

Quincey had forgotten about him until now, but there he was, lying in the corner of a stall, trussed up like a calf ready for branding. A nasty bruise had formed where the big fellow had struck him; it covered most of his cheek and reached down across his chin. The man looked up at him, first with surprise, and then apprehension, and then began speaking. Quincey couldn't understand a word of it, but it was clear he was asking for help. And it made him angry.

Quincey glared at him, trying to think straight. The more he thought, the more he remembered that this man had opposed what his companions were doing. The man spoke again, and again the pleading was clear in his voice. If he cut this fellow free, maybe he'd be willing to give help in exchange. He pulled his Bowie knife from its sheath.

The young man's eyes grew wide and he tried to pull away.

"No, no. Just hang on there." Quincey forced a tone of gentleness into his voice. "I'm not gonna hurt you."

He knelt down and ran the knife blade under the ropes binding the man's ankles. He sawed at them and the hemp soon split. Looking relieved, the gypsy turned on his side to expose his tied wrists. Quincey cut through the rope.

The man jumped to his feet and began jabbering away and gesturing. Quincey shook his head and held his hands up in a gesture of helplessness.

The gypsy retrieved his hat and then, gesturing for Quincey to follow him, hurried outside the barn. He pointed up toward the pass leading into the mountains and spoke again, this time slower.

"The castle," Quincey said. "Your people took them to the castle."

The gypsy nodded. "Da, castelul."

"Voivode," Quincey said. "The Voivode's castle."

The fellow nodded and pointed up at the mountains. He then pointed at Quincy, and then at himself.

"You and me?" Quincey asked, pointing at the mountains.

The gypsy bobbed his head. "Da."

Quincey felt a twinge of fresh hope. Maybe this young fellow didn't like the idea of turning people over to the vampire for slaughter.

Quincey pointed at his wounded shoulder. The gypsy looked but didn't understand. Quincey slipped the coat from his shoulder, revealing his blood soaked shirt. Now the man understood, looking at the wound with concern.

Quincey pantomimed riding a horse, and again pointed to his shoulder, covering the wound with his palm. "Bandages and horses. We'll go to the village."

The gypsy was still confused, but Quincey could see that he understood enough. He waved to the man to follow him and began walking down the hill toward the main road. In a few steps, the gypsy was walking side by side with him.

CHAPTER 52

The sudden gust of wind swept along the castle wall. It tugged at him as if sent by Tepes with the express purpose of hurling him into the gorge below. Stoker dug his fingers into the crevices of the rough stones, held his position and closed his eyes, praying for the wind to subside.

His progress was slow, edging along the wall inch by inch. This was the third time the wind had gusted around him and it filled him with terror. The fabric rope tied around his waist might save him should he slip from the narrow ledge, but it might not. If he fell, it would be at least a hundred feet before his body struck any piece of terrain at all.

He listened to the wind whistling around him and felt the panic building inside him again. And then the wind subsided.

Stoker opened his eyes and continued inching along the wall, grateful that the throbbing in his head was subsiding. His fingers began bleeding from gripping the rough stone, and they stung terribly each time he moved them to a new handhold. He looked to his side and saw the window that was his goal, only about four feet away.

Inch by inch, he made his way along the narrow ledge. Suddenly, the ledge support fell away from under his left foot, and in a moment of terror, he thought he was done for. It was by God's grace he had solid hand holds when it happened. He regained his footing and listened to the pieces of stone as they clattered against the castle wall, and then the rocks a hundred feet below.

"Are you all right?" Doyle shouted from the other window.

"Yes," he shouted back. "I'm almost there."

He had made another two feet of progress when he felt the tether around his waist tug at him. Turning his head, he saw that the fabric rope was taut.

"I need more line," Stoker shouted.

A moment passed, and then he saw Clarise's head emerge from the window.

"That's all there is," she called to him. "Only just enough to keep a hold on."

He clung to the stone wall, his mind racing. He had come too far and risked too much to go back now.

"I'm only two feet short," Stoker called back. "I'm going to untie it."

"No!" Doyle shouted.

"You can't let go of your end. The wind might catch it and pull me off," Stoker shouted again. "This is the only way."

"Don't be a fool," Doyle said.

Stoker released his left hand from the wall and lowered it to his waist. He felt for the knot and began working it with his aching fingers. It took more than a minute, but he felt the knot loosen. He widened the knot and pulled the fabric through it. In another minute, the fabric came free and fell away from his waist.

He quickly returned his left hand to the wall and found a hold. Gripping the wall tighter than ever before, he began moving along the ledge again. Another six inches, and then another. The window was only a foot away. Closer and closer he drew to it.

The wind gusted again, worse than before, as he edged in front of the casement. Stoker thanked God. The window was open. He reached over the sill, found a firm grip and pulled himself in.

"He made it," he heard Clarise's voice follow him on the wind.

Stoker immediately saw why the room was locked. It had once been a bedchamber and the bed lay in pieces against the wall at the end of the room. Some of the wood had rotted with the ages, but much of it was intact. With Sir Henry's Bowie knife and some sweat, they could fashion several sturdy stakes from the scraps.

In a corner of the room there was what Stoker first thought to be a pile of rags, but upon closer inspection he realized he was looking at bedding. It was full of moth holes and stained with rat droppings and he had a thought of how it might prove useful.

"Stoker." Sir Henry's voice came from outside the padlocked door. Stoker moved closer to the door. "I'm here."

"Can you open the door?" Doyle's voice filtered into the room.

"I don't know yet. Give me a moment to look around."

Stoker began looking over the room and got to moving the old bedding aside with his foot. He made contact with something heavy that scraped the stones under the rotted fabric. Moving the bedding aside, he found the end of a heavy four-sided iron shaft a little over an inch thick. He dragged it out from under the bedding. It was just over four feet long and had two large, bent and rusted metal hooks around it.

"What're you doing in there?" Doyle's voice penetrated the door.

"I think I've found a curtain rod," Stoker said.

"What good is that?" Sir Henry asked.

Stoker carried the rod to the door and examined the portal. He tried sliding the iron rod in between the latch and the door frame, but the shaft was too thick. Stepping back, he stood gazing at the door, looking for a point of weakness that he might exploit. His focus centered on the hinges. They were large and heavy to support the dense wood of the old door. The thick hinge pins had slight heads on them that extended just over the hinge barrel.

Stoker stepped closer to the door, grasped the curtain rod, and thrust it up against the exposed edge of the top hinge's pin head. The clang of metal against metal reverberated hollowly through the room, but the pin held fast. He adjusted his grip, took aim, and tried again.

"What's that?" Clarise called out.

"Just wait."

Stoker rammed the end of the curtain rod up against the hinge pin several more times. Finally, the pin moved. Again and again he struck with the iron rod until the pin came free and clattered to the floor.

The lower hinge presented more of a problem. Its proximity to the floor meant he wouldn't have the distance or the angle to strike the heavy hinge pin with any force. Lowering himself to his knees, he adjusted his grip on the curtain rod and went to work. The work took twice as long as it did for the upper hinge, but the pin loosened enough for Stoker to pry it free.

"All right, I took out the hinge pins," Stoker called through the door. "Try pushing the door in."

He watched the door as Doyle and Irving caused it to move inward.

"Stand clear," Doyle shouted.

Stoker moved back and heard his two friends slam their bodies against the door. It moved more than it had before.

"Again," he heard Doyle say.

A loud thump sounded against the wood, and this time the door flew off its hinges and fell into the room where it dangled from the padlock that had secured it.

A moment later, Doyle, Irving, and Clarise joined him in the chamber.

Stoker pointed at the old bed. "There's wood there we can use for stakes."

"And perhaps crosses," Clarise added.

"We'll take those rags as well," Doyle said.

"What on earth for?" Sir Henry asked.

"Torches," Doyle answered. "Soon enough, we'll need something to light our way."

"What do you plan to light them with?" Sir Henry said. "Those thugs took what matches I had, and I assume everyone else's as well."

Doyle knelt down, and reaching into the top of his riding boot produced a small matchbox. "I managed to slip this into my boot."

"Resourceful as ever," Stoker said.

Clarise set to shaking out the old bedding and folding it for carrying while the men began pulling the wood from the old bed frame. Stoker led them back down the stairs with the first armful of the treasure.

Professor Vambery saw them coming down the stairs with their arms loaded. He took Florence by the arm, helped her to her feet, and then escorted her out of their path.

They placed the wood and bedding on the floor. With one more trip upstairs, they claimed everything that might be of use.

Clarise gazed upon their bounty. "It doesn't look like much, considering you risked your neck for it."

"Sir Henry, can you inspect the wood and single out the sturdiest lengths?" Stoker asked.

"I can, and will." Sir Henry began sifting through the pile of wood.

"Then use your knife to sharpen them to points," Stoker said.

"While he's doing that, I was thinking we might see where that tower stairway leads," Doyle suggested. "We can tie the rags around this curtain rod for our torch."

"We need to be fast about it," Sir Henry said. "It's almost one thirty."

Fifteen minutes later they had assembled a crude torch. Doyle led the way to the tower door and pulled it open, revealing what seemed like an endless blackness beyond.

"Wait here," Stoker said to Clarise.

She peered through the open door into the darkness. "You don't have to ask me twice."

"But stay near the door in case we call," Doyle told her.

"Of course."

Doyle withdrew the box of matches from his pocket, opened it and took up a match. "Let's hope these are flammable. I don't have many left," he said.

Stoker tilted the rod, so the rag wrapped end was pointing downward.

Doyle struck the match and held it below the rags. The little flame danced around the fabric for what seemed a long time. Just as it died out, another piece of rag began to smolder and then flame.

Stoker rotated the shaft, making sure the flame spread around the torch head. In a few seconds, the torch was burning well. "Let's hurry. This won't burn for long."

They stepped through the doorway. The flickering flame made the shadows move along the curved wall as they made their way downward. The torch provided enough light for them to move at a steady pace. Before long, they found themselves at the bottom of the stairway in front of another door.

"There's no padlock on this one." Doyle pointed.

Stoker stepped up to the door and took hold of the handle. It wouldn't budge. "It's locked all the same."

"I don't suppose you see the key lying about," Doyle quipped.

Stoker lowered the torch close to the door and moved it around the primitive lock. "Look here."

Doyle moved in closer.

"This plank, just to the right of the keyhole plate, it looks loose," Stoker said.

"Where?"

Stoker pointed. "Here, you can see where it's raised above the others."

"The gypsies bolted new lumber over the loose wood on the other doors," Doyle said. "How did they miss this one?"

"It's hellishly dark down here. It'd be easy for them to miss it," Stoker answered.

Doyle tried to grip the plank with his fingers.

"I can feel it give a little, but I can't get enough of a grip on it to do any good," Doyle said. "We'll need Sir Henry's Bowie knife."

"All right," Stoker said. "But we must make better headway. By my estimation, I don't think we've got more than four hours left."

CHAPTER 53

Jardani led the way through the forest with Alexander and the American Quincey on either side of him. They rode horses borrowed from reluctant farmers. While Alexander's wife, Tatiana, cleaned and bandaged the foreigner's bullet wound, Alexander had introduced each of them, a courtesy their language differences had previously prevented.

The American's presence in the village had created a substantial amount of curiosity and suspicion, and many of the men gathered at Alexander's house. Fear among the villagers was still strong, just as it was among his people. Arguing and heated shouting dominated many of the conversations. The fighting ate up valuable time and with every word spoken, Jardani felt more anxious.

But Alexander and the American had argued with more passion than anyone else, and their arguments were based on pushing fear aside and doing right. And then Jardani made promises he prayed he'd be able to keep. In a very short while, he'd find out.

They broke from the trees well after noon and Jardani led his two friends straight through the middle of the camp, heading toward his wagon. His people, going about their work, stopped what they were doing when they saw him. He recognized several faces of the men who had taken part in the early morning capture of the English. Some of those faces wore expressions of fear and some anger, but every one of them shared the look of shame.

Asena sat on her wagon steps folding a length of cloth, watching Stochelo examined the guns he had stolen from the English piled on the little table he kept beside the steps of his wagon. Nearby, in a tangled pile, were the crosses taken from the English. Stochelo's face registered surprise and then turned red with anger when he looked up and saw them riding past.

Jardani ignored Stochelo's angry glare, instead focusing on his beautiful Miri, who was already running toward him, tears in her eyes. He swung down from his horse and pulled her into his arms.

"Thanks to God, thanks to God," she said.

"I'm unharmed."

"Stochelo said you'd betrayed us," she said, crying freely now. "He wouldn't say what he'd done with you, but then Zache came and told me you were safe when he last saw you. What happened?"

"Face me, coward," Stochelo's voice roared from across the camp.

Jardani turned to see the chief striding toward him, but before Stochelo covered ten paces, Alexander and Quincey swung out of their saddles, positioning themselves in his path. Stochelo slowed, surprised by the opposition, but his surprise soon turned to defiance, and he pulled the long knife from his belt.

Jardani gave Miri a gentle nudge. "Get back to the wagon. Get inside."

Miri, with reluctance, retreated to their wagon and opened the door, but did not go inside.

Quincey stepped closer to Stochelo and spoke. Jardani couldn't understand the words, but there was no mistaking the grim tone.

Stochelo stared at Quincey for a moment, and then looked at Jardani and Alexander.

"Tell me what he said," Stochelo said.

"He knows you're the man who shot him," Alexander said.

Stochelo's look of contempt was unmistakable. Turning toward Quincey, he spat on the ground.

"I didn't shoot him good enough," Stochelo said. "And you, Jardani, you betray your people and then come back to camp with *them* to defend you?"

Jardani felt the heat of anger rush through him. He pushed past Alexander and Quincey.

"You call me a coward?" Jardani said. "You, who carry helpless people to that, that place of death, and lock them inside. People who have done nothing to harm you and only wished to help us. And you do this all for more gold in your pocket."

"I do what I must do to keep my people safe, but you cannot under-stand," Stochelo shouted. "And that gold you have such contempt for fed us when work was scarce or animals had died."

"We are no better than that monster if we serve him to make the evil he does easier," Jardani responded in equal volume.

Stochelo gestured to men watching from points around the camp, and several of them gathered around him. "What you understand or don't understand is no longer a concern to me. And before this day is done, you and your friends will join the English in the castle."

Alexander grabbed the sickle he had secured to his saddle as he spoke in English to Quincey. Jardani saw a knife appear in the American's hand as if by sorcery, its wicked blade glistening in the early sunlight.

Stochelo looked around at his men in the camp and raised his own knife. "Take them."

Stochelo's men started forward.

"Stop!" Zache shouted, pushing through the crowd, his big knife and old revolver still in his sash from the morning's work. He came to a stop facing Stochelo. "I heard what you've ordered, and this I can't allow."

"It is for me to decide," Stochelo said.

Zache shook his head. "I have been at your right hand. I have supported you through much. But I will not go along with this. Ever since we left the castle this morning, I have felt nothing but shame. None of us should agree to this."

The sound of horses drew everyone's attention and ten riders from the village burst out of the trees armed with axes, hatchets, and sickles. Two of the riders had several crude, sharpened stakes tied in a bundle across their saddles. The riders slowed their mounts to a walk and reined up behind Stochelo and his men.

"What is this, more betrayal?" Stochelo shouted.

"This is what I came back for," Jardani said. "This is what I would have told you, but you don't listen."

"What did you come to say?" Zache stepped closer to Jardani.

"The English came here to kill the Voivode," Jardani said.

The words had only just passed his lips when gasps came from everyone listening and then subdued murmurings. Jardani waited for them to quiet.

"If we join together, we can help do this thing," Jardani said.

"Kill the Voivode," Zache repeated, his voice thoughtful.

"The English asked me to do this when they first arrived," Alexander added. "But I was afraid, all of us were afraid."

"Fools," Stochelo screamed. "You will break a trust centuries old. He will kill us all."

"Not if we kill him first, and yes, perhaps some of us will die," Jardani shouted. "But is that worse than living every day with the shame of what we've done, or with the threat of being killed, should we dare to do what's right?"

Jardani heard several of the men voice agreement, and the sound of it angered Stochelo even more.

"You men, any of you who do this thing must leave this camp," Stochelo said.

Every Szgany in the camp reacted with audible disbelief.

"For the sake of our people, you must leave," Stochelo repeated.

"This man calls Jardani a coward," Alexander shouted. "But what about the rest of you? I am nothing but a farmer. My neighbors are farmers, and yesterday we did a shameful thing, forcing the people who would help us to leave our village, putting them in danger. But now we face our shame. Now at least we know what must be done. What about you?"

"None of us are cowards," Zache said.

"There is no time left for talk. Those of you ready to join us, arm yourselves and gather your horses," Jardani said.

Several of the men dispersed. Jardani watched just long enough to be certain that he had support and then turned and began heading back to his wagon.

A bellow of rage came from behind him. He whirled around. Stochelo was charging at him, his long knife held high and ready to strike. Jardani had nothing to defend himself, and Stochelo was almost on him. He dropped into a defensive crouch, hoping he could avoid the blade, ready to take the impact of Stochelo's attack.

Quincey appeared in Stochelo's path, moving fast, keeping his body low. He ran full force into Stochelo, and as he made contact, he thrust his shoulder upward, striking the man's knife arm. Stochelo kept his grip on the knife but tumbled backward, landing hard on the ground.

As Stochelo scrambled to his feet and leaped forward, slashing his knife at the American as he closed in. Quincey jumped away and then lunged forward again. Stochelo spun away, but not before the American's blade cut through his shirt, staining the linen with red.

Stochelo roared with pain and charged Quincey. This time, Quincey ran straight at Stochelo and dived toward the ground, swinging the full force of his body against his opponent's legs. Stochelo's feet were swept out

from under him and he hit the ground hard, the knife flying from his
hands. He scrambled to recover the knife, trying to rise to his feet at the
same time.

Quincey didn't let him get far, grabbing hold of Stochelo's leg and dragging him backwards. The American tossed his knife aside and then threw
himself on Stochelo, landing a fist on the man's jaw. Stochelo returned a
blow so hard that the American was knocked off balance again.

Zache picked up each of the knives from the ground and handed them
to the man nearest him.

Quincey and the gypsy leader fought fiercely, delivering blows to one
another in one moment and wrestling, rolling across the cold ground in
another.

Quincey was younger than Stochelo, but his bullet wound saddled him
with a disadvantage. Both men were now cut, bloody, and bruised, but the
American was now landing more blows than Stochelo. Stochelo was tiring,
fighting more wildly and with less effectiveness.

The American moved in, landing a powerful blow to Stochelo's jaw.
Stochelo yelped with pain and drew his hands up to his face. Quincey
followed with a punch to the man's stomach. With a loud grunt, Stochelo
staggered backwards, collided with one of the villager's horses and fell to the
ground next to Zache.

Stochelo lay on the ground for several moments, his breathing labored.
He struggled onto his hands and knees, and then reached for Zache, using
his friend to pull himself to his feet. Zache, expressionless, gazed upon
Stochelo in silence.

Moving fast, Stochelo grabbed the grip of the old revolver tucked into
Zache's sash. He jerked the gun from the sash as he shoved Zache away from
him. Before Zache could recover, Stochelo whirled around with the gun and
leveled it at Quincey.

Shouts and warning cries rose from the onlookers as they scattered to
get out of the way.

As Stochelo advanced on him with the gun, Quincey ducked under one
of the horses, rolling to the other side of the animal. It bought him a few
seconds of time.

Quincey made his way toward the guns outside of Stochelo's wagon, zig
zagging to present a poorer target. But Stochelo was taking aim. He pulled
the trigger and the shot rang out across the camp.

The shot went wild, but Quincey ducked and changed his direction. He
was closer to the guns now and Jardani could see that Stochelo was aware of

the American's intentions. As Quincey charged toward the table, Stochelo fired once again. The bullet splintered the corner of the wagon's door frame.

Stochelo closed in on Quincey and fired yet again. Quincey dived for the table, grabbing one of the revolvers from its holster as he rolled to the ground. As Stochelo extended his pistol to fire again, Quincey pulled the trigger.

The roar of the exploding cartridge filled the air. Stochelo staggered backwards as a red stain spread across his chest. He raised his gun once more, and once again, Quincey pulled the trigger. Stochelo spun around as the bullet shattered his shoulder and dropped to the ground, dead.

Quincey rose to his feet, his eyes sweeping the camp for any potential threats, his gun still ready in his hand. But all eyes were on the body of Stochelo. A few people glanced warily at Quincey as they walked toward the body, but that was all.

Jardani felt Miri next to him and she took his arm, drawing close to him. Together they watched Asena walk to her husband's body and drop to her knees beside it with tears welling up in her eyes and grief lining her face. Zache stood beside her, looking down at the man who had once been his closest friend. In a short while, Zache helped Asena to her feet, putting her in the care of several women who had gathered to help her.

Quincey walked through the crowd, joining Alexander and Jardani. His bullet wound had opened again, and his face was cut and bruised. He looked at each of them, and then fixed his gaze on Zache and spoke in a resolute tone.

"What is he saying?" Zache asked.

"He says this is not what he wanted," Alexander translated. "But there is no more time. We must all decide."

CHAPTER 54

S toker held the torch near the door. "Is it working?"
"It's loosening, I think," Doyle said. "I don't want to break the blade."

The uneven light from the guttering torch cast ghostly shadows that traveled over the door and crawled up the stone walls of the tower.

"The sun's going to set in—"

"I'm doing the best I can," Doyle interrupted, his voice amplified with stress.

"Yes, sorry," Stoker said.

The creaking of wood echoed through the tower as Doyle used the knife blade as a lever to dislodge the plank.

"I think I've got it." Doyle put the knife on the floor beside him. "Give me a hand."

Stoker moved the torch to his left hand and took hold of the wood that Doyle had pried up from the door.

"On three," Doyle said. "We'll pull it back slow and steady."

At the end of the count they pulled and Stoker could feel the plank moving, the creaking and moaning of the wood reverberating up the tower. Less than five minutes later, the plank broke free with its remaining nails screeching in protest.

"Bring the torch lower, as close to the opening as you can," Doyle said.

Doyle peered into the opening, trying to see into the blackness beyond the door. He drew his right hand up to the opening and hesitated.

"*He* might be in there, you know," Doyle said.

"They all might be in there," Stoker replied, hearing the anxiety in his voice.

Doyle inserted his hand through the opening. A few moments later, he pulled it back.

"There's no latch," he said. "We'll have to try to draw the bolt back inside here."

After another few valuable minutes of using the knife, Doyle worked the bolt back. He rose from his crouch beside the door, gripped the handle, and pushed against the door. The hinges creaked, but the door moved only a little.

"Here we go," Stoker said, moving forward and taking hold of the door handle.

Working together, they had little difficulty in pushing open the heavy door. They instinctively drew back from it and stood in silence for several moments, gathering their nerves.

With a nod to Doyle, Stoker raised the torch and moved through the doorway. At first, all he could make out were a few stone steps. A few seconds later he and Doyle were standing on the main floor of the room, the torch's inadequate light revealing ancient artifacts. Seeing these artifacts, Stoker felt tangible hope.

"This was the armory," Doyle said.

"No wonder it was locked," Stoker said.

They spent the next few minutes walking the length of the circular room, examining the various weapons.

"We can use several of these things," Doyle said.

"We'll need help," Stoker said. "Let's get back upstairs. We need to re-wrap the torch, anyway. It's about done, judging from the flame."

They climbed back to the main floor and discovered Clarise had constructed three crosses, joining the vertical and horizontal pieces with scraps of cloth stripped from the old bedding. She had also wrapped two additional torches.

Professor Vambery remained with Florence, taking over sharpening wooden stakes from Sir Henry. Stoker, Doyle, Sir Henry, and Clarise returned to the armory, and with a marked sense of urgency.

"Look here," Sir Henry called out, holding up a crude spear. Once about eight feet long, a portion of the shaft had broken off, leaving a five-foot weapon, including the metal tip.

"It's a pike," Doyle said.

Sir Henry held up a second pike. "There's three or four of them here. All broken like this one."

"They're a perfect replacement for the iklwas we lost," Doyle said.

"There's a broad ax here in this corner." Stoker pointed. "And another here."

"Can you bring the light closer?" Clarise asked. "Over here, please."

Stoker accommodated her with the torch.

"Arrows," Clarise said, excitement in her voice. "Most of them are warped or broken, but some are still in good shape. Now, where are the bows?"

They found the bows a short distance away, leaning against an oak rack. Most of them had rotted away and some cracked. Clarise began sifting through them.

"This one looks quite good." Clarise lifted a long bow and examined it closer under the torchlight.

"It still has its string," Clarise continued. "It's only attached at one end, but maybe I can restring it."

"I'd be wary of that after all this time," Sir Henry said.

"Well, with God's grace it won't snap the first time we try it," Clarise said.

Working as quickly as anyone might, they gathered up their supplies. By the time they climbed the stairs with the last load, the distant howling of wolves greeted their ears.

Professor Vambery stood in the middle of the main hall, staring up at the tall windows, listening to the mournful baying. Florence still sat silent on the steps.

"I wish those bloody animals would stop," Sir Henry groused.

"We've got enough to do without worrying about wolves," Doyle said.

With each of them forcing down the feeling of panic caused by the setting sun, they hurried along, organizing their weapons and making whatever repairs might be necessary.

In less than an hour, Stoker finished with the last of the pike tips he had been sharpening.

"We've got enough here to arm all of us," he announced.

"The pikes will render the same result as a stake, and those arrows,"

Professor Vambery said. "And the axes should separate the vampire's head from its body, a method just as effective as the stake."

Doyle completed restringing Clarise's bow and handed it to her. "Here you go."

Clarise gripped the bow and tested the string. "This should do very well."

Stoker watched the dimming light casting distorted shadows through the windows. "We've no more time."

"Dear God, it's already six," Doyle said, consulting his watch.

"No more putting it off, then," Stoker said.

"The only door that leads downward besides the one opening to the armory is that one there, near the corner under the balcony," Doyle pointed. "And it's padlocked."

"Look," Clarise pointed up at the windows.

Only the faintest glow of light was visible, and as they watched, it gradually dwindled.

"We'll take the stakes you and the professor made and those battle hammers to drive them," Doyle said.

"I'm bringing this," Sir Henry said, holding up a sword he'd been sharpening.

"What of the lock?" Clarise asked.

"I've an idea about that," Doyle answered.

He picked up a broad ax, testing its weight in his hands.

CHAPTER 55

The ax blade striking the heavy padlock shackle sent a loud clang echoing through the shadows of the main hall. Once again, Doyle drew back the ax and hurled it down on the lock. There was a sharp, horrible sound as the ax handle snapped in two and the blade clattered onto the stone floor, throwing centuries of dust into the air. In the same instant, the shackle separated and the lock clattered to the floor with the remains of the ax.

"All right," he said.

Stoker gazed down at the lock. "I hadn't thought through this before, but we can't risk taking Florence with us."

"Of course not," Doyle said.

"I'll stay with her." Clarise stepped forward.

"Not on your own," Professor Vambery said. "I'll remain as well."

"We're going to need every man," Doyle said. "There aren't enough of us as it is."

"You can't be suggesting that we leave the women here on their own?" Sir Henry asked.

Doyle shook his head. "No, I can't say I'm comfortable with that at all."

"To say no one's thought this out is an understatement," Clarise said. "All you men must go, and quickly."

"But, my dear—"

Clarise stopped her father with a raised hand. "If you accomplish what we came for before the sun can set, then none of us should have reason to worry. If the sun sets before you can do the work, well then, I don't suppose it'll matter much if Mrs. Stoker and I are in your company or not."

"I still don't like it," Stoker said.

"We'll be fine," Clarise said. "I'll keep one of the pikes along with my bow. Now, let's get on with it."

Preparing for the hunt was a somber affair and few words were spoken as each man outfitted himself. In less than ten minutes Stoker, Doyle, Sir Henry, and the professor reassembled at the door.

Stoker took charge of a torch and carried a battle hammer, while Doyle carried a battle hammer and a pike. Besides his Bowie knife carried in its sheath on his belt, Sir Henry brought along the arming sword and carried a second torch. Professor Vambery took charge of carrying the bundle of wooden stakes.

Clarise picked up one of the crude wooden crosses she had made. "I'm afraid that after all the stakes, we only had wood enough for four of these."

"That's one for you, then, and one for Mrs. Stoker," Doyle said. "We'll make do with the other two."

Clarise handed two of the crosses to Doyle and Stoker. They tucked them into the waistbands of their trousers.

Stoker reached for the heavy iron door handle. "I suppose we're as ready as we can be."

"Don't take another step." Clarise slipped her head through the fabric loop that suspended the homemade cross around her neck. "Not until we ask God to help us with what we are about to do."

The men turned toward her and bowed their heads as Clarise knelt at the top of the three stairs.

"Heavenly Father, we do not pretend to know your will or purpose for our lives, but we find ourselves in a terrible place today, in danger of losing our mortal souls," Clarise prayed. "For reasons we cannot comprehend, You have allowed us to be in this place, and in this danger, and so we know that it must be according to Your will. Please be with these men, Your servants, as they seek out the evil that dwells in this place. Cover them with Your love and Your protection. Give them the strength and courage to accomplish what they set out to do here. Please Lord, keep them safe, keep us all safe this day. We pray these things in the name of Jesus Christ, Your Son."

"Amen," the men echoed.

Clarise picked up the last torch from the floor and extended it toward Doyle, who produced his match box and set it aflame. The men waited until

Clarise walked back across the hall to join Florence while Doyle lit the remaining two torches.

Stoker turned back toward the door and took hold of the handle. The hinges creaked horribly as he eased the door open, revealing a chasm of darkness. He paused, looking back at Florence for what he wondered might be the last time.

She was standing now, and even in the dim flickering light of Clarise's torch, he could see her eyes glistening with anticipation. Clarise, unnerved by Florence's sudden interest in the open doorway, encouraged her to sit down again.

Stoker turned back to the doorway. "May God be with us."

Stoker stepped through the doorway, with the others following close behind.

A foul, musty odor assaulted their senses. The fluttering torch light revealed narrow stairs curving downward along a wall shrouded in cobwebs and heavy with dust. Each stone step, too, was blanketed in dust, and it plumed into the air with every step.

"Another tower," Stoker said in a whisper.

They traveled down the stairwell, their footsteps echoing in the dingy tower, making them more anxious with every step. Some thirty steps down, Stoker slowed his pace, forced to use the torch to clear a wide swath of cobwebs draped from a timber support.

"These stairs haven't been used in years," Doyle whispered.

"Not by anything human," Professor Vambery said.

"Do you smell that?" Sir Henry asked, his voice low.

It was impossible not to smell. The odor had grown worse, transforming from mustiness to the stench of decay and death.

"We're close," Stoker said.

In another ten steps, they arrived in a small, vaulted chamber. Set in the wall opposite the stairs was a doorway set in a gothic arch. The heavy oaken door leading into the adjoining chamber was wide open.

Moving as quietly as possible, they made their way to the doorway. Together, Stoker and Sir Henry extended their torches through the portal. The flickering light revealed three wide steps descending to a dirt floor. Holding the torches high, Stoker and Henry led the way down the steps.

The torchlight illuminated a low ceiling not more than two feet over their heads, supported by a network of gothic rib vaults that faded away into the darkness. Cobwebs were everywhere, spanning from the keystones in the archways to the supporting pillars. The blackness was so complete as to be stifling.

Stepping with caution, they ventured deeper into the crypt. They saw piles of human skulls stacked at the base of several pillars, while others littered the dirt floor. They passed two complete but broken skeletons; the bones yellowed with age, scattered in the dirt.

They had not gone far when Doyle stopped and pointed. "There."

Almost invisible in the pathetic light, resting beneath one of the arches, was a heavy wood coffin. It was dull with age, matted with dust, and spotted with worm holes. They made their way to it.

Stoker took a position at the head of the coffin and Doyle at the foot, pulling his cross from his waistband and holding it ready. Sir Henry lowered the torch closer to the coffin. With a coordinating nod, they took hold and lifted the lid.

The body inside was that of a young woman, quite beautiful, perhaps in her late twenties when she had died. She wore a faded, yellowing gown that outlined her body. Her hair was dark and her lips were crimson red. Her mouth was slightly open and the needle sharp points of her canine teeth protruded beyond her upper lip. The woman's eyes were half open, but completely without life. Despite her beauty, this was an insidious, loathsome thing.

"She's one of them from the barn," Stoker said, realizing he feared the sound of his voice might wake the odious creature.

Stoker handed his torch to Sir Henry and then took the stake that the professor offered him. Moving tentatively, he positioned himself and placed the point of the stake over the woman's heart. The horror of what he was about to do caused him a moment of hesitation. But in a sudden fluid motion, he raised the battle hammer, took aim, and hurled it down upon the stake.

With the sound of a mallet splitting a melon, the sharpened point of the wood plunged into the woman's chest. Her eyes opened wide, and a blood-chilling scream rushed from her lungs, reverberating throughout the vaults. She grasped the stake with her hands, gripping it desperately as a pool of blood bubbled from her open mouth. Her limbs went stiff for what seemed like several seconds, and then her fingers fell away from the wood, her arms collapsing at her side. Then, before their eyes, the body decomposed.

Within seconds, all that remained was a skeleton with bits of rotted flesh clinging to the bones.

"God have mercy on us all," Sir Henry gasped as Stoker backed away from the coffin.

"We must move on," Stoker said. "Any objections to splitting up, two men to a torch? We'll cover more ground."

No objections were voiced, so Stoker ventured off to the right side of the crypt with Professor Vambery while Doyle and Sir Henry took the left.

Stoker and the professor had not gone far when they came across another coffin.

"Just like the other one," Vambery observed.

Stoker handed the torch to Vambery and set the hammer down on the dirt floor. Gripping the coffin lid, he lifted it open.

"Empty," the professor stated, surprised.

"Look, the soil's displaced along the bed," Stoker pointed.

"Stoker, Vambery," Doyle's voice reverberated through the darkness. "Over here."

They followed the dim flickering of Doyle's torch and found him with Sir Henry standing beside a large, stone coffin. Crude decorative engravings decorated its sides and adorned the top of the lid.

"It must be his," Doyle whispered.

With his cross in one hand and the hammer in the other, Stoker leaned the heels of his palms against the head end of the coffin lid. Sir Henry did the same at the foot end while Doyle took a position between them, his cross and pike ready.

Together, Stoker and Sir Henry began pushing. The lid began moving inch by inch, the grating sound of stone against stone deafening to their ears in the dark, silent tomb.

Stoker felt his heart pounding in his chest as they displaced the head end of the lid enough to see inside the coffin. There lay Tepes, his arms folded across his chest, his complexion waxen. The thin lips were pulled back in a horrible grimace, revealing the sharp elongated teeth. But most disturbing were the eyes, wide open and as black and empty as the night.

Stoker and Sir Henry put their backs into it and shoved the lid off the far side of the coffin. It crashed to the ground, throwing dust into the fetid air. Professor Vambery hurried forward with a stake.

Not a sound filled the deathly still air as Stoker positioned the stake over the body. He felt the beads of perspiration dampening his brow.

A deep, rasping gasp suddenly issued from Tepes' body, and his chest began to rise and fall. As the four men watched, transfixed with shock and revulsion, Tepes' eyes focused with sight. Seeing Stoker leaning over him, he emitted a threatening snarl, his face contorting in a vicious sneer.

Tepes sat up, and with a powerful sweep of his arm hurled Stoker away from the coffin. Stoker tumbled across the floor and collapsed in the dirt as Doyle, Sir Henry, and the professor jumped back.

Tepes rose, and in a fluid leap stood beside the coffin, his long, black coat making him almost invisible against the blackness of the crypt. He surveyed each of them, his eyes glowing with hatred.

Stoker got to his feet, pulling the handmade wooden cross from his waistband. But before Stoker could draw another breath, Tepes was gone, retreating into the depths of the crypt, disappearing into the horrible darkness.

CHAPTER 56

D umbfounded, they stared past the stone coffin at the blackness extending into the catacombs.

"He's gone!" Doyle exclaimed, baffled.

Stoker pointed the stake into the blackness. "He went back into the vaults."

"But why?" Doyle asked. "He had the advantage."

Every muscle in Stoker's body tautened in alarm. "Florence!" he cried. "We must get back upstairs."

Professor Vambery paled. "Clarise."

They all turned, hurrying back in the direction they had come. They hadn't covered twenty feet when, out of the darkness, the torches picked up a shimmer of white ahead. The fair haired woman they'd seen the night before came toward them, her long hair draped across her shoulders.

She smiled at them, a loathsome, perverse smile, and then tilted her head as if she were appreciating a fine piece of art.

"There's no time," Stoker said with desperation.

The woman was very close now, and her smile transformed into an awful sneer, her lips pulled back in an ugly gash, revealing the two long, sharp teeth.

Stoker and Doyle raised their crosses. The woman uttered a horrible cry and backed away, turning her head. They advanced on her as she continued backing away.

The creature's eyes were now looking past Stoker and Doyle to Sir Henry.

"Sir Henry!" Doyle cried.

The woman passed between them in an instant and hurtled full force into the actor. He gave a yell of surprise and hit the floor hard, the woman on top of him, pinning him down. She began clawing at his collar, working to bare the skin of his throat.

Stoker and Doyle fell upon the woman, thrusting their crosses against her back and arms. She screamed in pain and rage, pulling away from Sir Henry and thrashing to fend off the cleansing fire of the cross. Taking advantage of her distraction, Sir Henry grabbed hold of her ankles. Stoker and Doyle pulled her off balance and the creature fell hard onto the dirt floor.

Before she could twist free, Stoker and Doyle pinned her down. As she twisted and thrashed under them, Professor Vambery struggled into position with a stake and battle hammer. She began shrieking.

Stoker fought to keep hold of the thing. "Hurry."

The professor raised the hammer and brought it down. The stake penetrated her chest, but not enough. As her screams increased in volume, he raised the hammer again and struck. With the sickening sound of the wood parting flesh, the stake passed through her heart. A few seconds later, all that was left of the monster was a skeleton and remnants of decayed flesh.

The crypt was once again silent.

"Sir Henry?" Doyle asked.

Sir Henry climbed to his feet. "I'm all right. She just scratched me a little, I think."

"Wait. Do you hear that?" Stoker cocked his head.

They stood in silence and listened. There it was, a muffled scuttling sound coming from the blackness of the crypt. It grew louder, and now they could hear what sounded like panting breaths. Whatever was moving through the darkness was drawing nearer.

"We've got to get out!" Stoker said.

They ran as fast as they could through the darkness. The torches fluttering, in danger of extinguishing. The arched doorway came into view and they rushed toward it. In another moment, they were through it.

Staying next to the wall, they climbed the stairway as fast as they dared in the inadequate torch light. The encroaching sounds spurred them on.

Stoker saw the door at the top of the stairway come into view. With the sun gone, there was nothing but darkness beyond the portal. After a few more steps, they reached it and hurried into the main hall.

They came to an abrupt stop. The blackness in the immense room was disorienting. The little light that was in evidence came from the pale moonlight filtering through the tall windows, and from Clarise Vambery's torch.

"Clarise." Professor Vambery called out.

Clarise stood with her back against the wall, holding a torch in one hand while struggling to place the wooden cross she'd made around Florence's neck with the other. Florence stared with unnatural intensity at the windows, and without as much as a glance toward Clarise, pushed the cross away.

Stoker looked up. A large bat, outlined in the moonlight, circled just outside. It swept around several times and then shot through the center window, diving downward into the gloom of the hall. A moment later, Tepes stepped out of the shadows.

CHAPTER 57

Tepes advanced toward the two women as Clarise struggled to hang the wooden cross around Florence's neck. Florence resisted and when the cross brushed against her cheek, it glowed red. Florence shrieked and shoved Clarise away, jarring the cross from her grip. It clattered to the floor. Florence touched her hand to the angry welt raised by the cross, and then began walking, trancelike, toward Tepes.

Clarise gripped the cross around her neck and pursued Florence. But Stoker could see that Florence was beyond Clarise's influence.

He broke into a run, thankful to hear the footsteps of Doyle, Irving, and the professor running behind him. Professor Vambery made his way to Clarise, pulling her back to put more distance between them and Tepes. Reaching the narrowing space between Florence and Tepes, Stoker, Doyle, and Sir Henry formed a defensive line. Stoker and Doyle held their crosses in front of them.

Tepes stopped, his eyes trying to avoid the cross. Still, he studied them as if they were insects on display under glass. And then his mouth formed a contemptuous sneer.

Stoker felt a rush of heat spread over him; the monster's arrogance and mocking demeanor made him furious.

"You must have known I'd be waiting, that I have brought you here," Tepes said, mocking.

And then Tepes moved his eyes past Stoker, resting them hungrily on Florence.

"It is so good to see your lovely wife once again," he said. "I have thought of her often since leaving England."

"Steady," Stoker heard Doyle say.

But he didn't need Doyle's caution. The anger churning within was fueling him with strength and purpose. And he was more certain of what he must do now than ever before.

Stoker raised his cross and stepped forward. Tepes glowered at him, but stepped back.

Stoker advanced again, this time with Doyle, the crosses held resolutely before them. Doyle held the pike in his hand, ready to strike, and Sir Henry tightened his grip on the sword.

Tepes smiled, that terrible, superior, loathsome smile that Stoker had grown to hate.

The scuttling sounds that had followed them out of the crypt grew in volume. Tepes turned his head to look at the door leading to the catacombs.

Coming through the door were the feral vampires Stoker had seen gathered outside the shearing barn the night before. Now, so close, he thought them to be the most odious creatures he had ever seen; five, six, eight, he lost count. They were vampires, but these *things* were nothing like Tepes. Dried blood stained their cadaverous faces and the rags they wore. Long, matted, filthy hair fell across their brows. Dark, soulless eyes gaped wide in a wildness Stoker had observed once in the inmates of an insane asylum. The fetor of death permeated the hall.

"There!" Sir Henry called out.

Heads of several more of the monsters appeared over the stone stools of the tall windows. Their arms reached over and downward, and then the whole bodies slithered through the window. Face down, they descended toward the floor with the movements of reptiles crawling across a wall.

The vampires reached the floor and began advancing while the group that had come from the catacombs closed in from the side. Tepes extended an arm and the vile band of undead stopped, holding their position but shuffling and hissing with impatience.

"I will not give you to them until you've watched me take your wife for my own," Tepes said. "A small pleasure in return for the trouble you've caused me."

Stoker started toward Tepes again. Tepes took a single step and leaped into the air, passing over the heads of Stoker and his friends, and landing next to Florence. He pulled her roughly to him, his long, thin fingers circled around the back of her neck, a look of sinister triumph on his face.

Florence offered no resistance.

The feral vampires stirred with excitement, shuffling, restless.

Again Stoker advanced on Tepes. Tepes tightened his grip on Florence, jerking her closer to him.

"Stand where you are," Tepes commanded as Stoker stopped in his tracks. "I began something with this one before leaving England, something I did not have time to finish."

Tepes ran his free hand across her cheek and up through her hair. He sniffed her like a dog taking in the aroma of a piece of beef.

Stoker heard himself scream as he dropped the torch in his hand and threw himself on Tepes. He glimpsed Tepes' arm moving and then felt a terrible blow land across his chest. He went flying backwards and felt the air forced from his lungs as he tumbled down hard on the stone floor.

Tepes gazed down at him with imperious, victorious satisfaction.

Doyle and Irving, furious, began advancing.

"Not another step," Tepes ordered. "Or I will let them take you."

The feral vampires moved forward a few more feet and then stopped again.

Stoker, fighting to catch his breath, raised himself up on his elbows, struggling to get up.

Tepes glanced down at him with indifference and then turned back to Florence. He forced her head backwards, exposing her throat. Drawing closer to her, his lips parted wide, exposing the long, needle sharp teeth. He paused, his lips lingering just above the soft, white skin. And then he lowered his lips to her throat.

Clarise screamed, and a deafening crash echoed from the main door.

Tepes' head jerked upward.

Another loud crash, and then another. And then the door burst open, swinging back violently, crashing into the wall.

CHAPTER 58

Doyle whirled around as a group of men burst into the hall, the first of them dropping the heavy timber they'd used as a battering ram. On their heels flooded in some twenty men carrying a variety of weapons. Many of them held torches, and all of them wore crosses.

At their head was Morgan Quincey, gripping his Bowie knife in one hand and a makeshift wooden spear in the other. Beside him came the villager, Alexander, flanked by the young Szgany whom had mutinied against his leader. The older Szgany, carrying the Kukri knife, rushed in beside them.

"Quincey!" Doyle shouted.

Tepes shouted out a command as he shoved past Clarise and the professor with Florence in his grip.

The vampires rushed forward.

Sir Henry swooped up the cross dropped by Clarise, taking a defensive position.

The room, now alive with torchlight, erupted into a nightmarish melee, echoing with the shouts of men and the snarls and screams of the ravenous vampires. Torches appeared to lurch through the terrible blackness on their own, casting shadows made by the swinging scythes and axes.

A group of villagers and gypsies fell upon a vampire, first with one man hacking away with an old military saber to hold it at bay, and then with the rest overwhelming the monster, wrestling it down to the ground. One of the band raised a broken shovel handle he had sharpened to a point and plunged it through the creature's heart with all his weight behind it.

No sooner had the creature rotted away before their eyes than a pack of the vampires fell upon the men. A villager screamed in terror as one creature jumped upon him, knocking him backwards before his companions, occupied with fending off the other monsters, could offer any help. The torch he held was jarred from his hands, falling into the pile of the old drapery remnants Clarise Vambery had left bundled against a wall.

Both vampire and villager scrambled to get away from the flames as the fighting spread throughout the hall. Doyle observed the monsters were wary of the crosses, but only to a point, maneuvering around their intended victims until they saw an opening to strike from behind or from the side. Anything to avoid contact with the symbol of Christ. It mattered little for villagers, and Szgany alike rushed to engage the undead predators with intrepid energy.

As the flames began climbing up the supporting beams toward the roof timbers, Doyle realized he had lost sight of Tepes. His eyes darted desperately around the room. There, on the stairway, Tepes was almost at the second level landing, with Florence in his grasp. Leaping up the stairs some twenty feet behind was Stoker, his wooden cross in one hand and a pike in the other.

Morgan Quincey pointed toward Stoker. "Go! We'll carry the fight here."

Doyle set off at a run for the stairs. Hearing footsteps behind him, he looked back to find Sir Henry keeping pace with him. Together, they reached the stairs and started up.

Stoker ran up the stairway, taking the steps two and three at a time. Tepes had just disappeared from his line of sight off the second floor landing and he was desperate to close the distance between them.

He reached the landing as flames that had climbed up the vertical support beams began licking at the roof timbers. In the flickering firelight, he spotted Tepes and Florence at the far end of the passage, turning into a connecting passageway.

Stoker broke into a run. "Florence!"

Moments later, he turned into the passageway and recognized it as the one with the locked doors. Tepes and Florence were already three quarters of the way to the end, where a precipice dropped off into the valley below. Tepes could escape by that route, but he wouldn't easily be able to take Florence with him.

"Stop!" Stoker yelled.

To Stoker's amazement, Tepes did stop, and then turned to face him. The dancing light from the fire was dim, but Stoker could still see the hatred and contempt contorting Tepes' face.

Stoker raised his cross before him and began to advancing. Tepes pulled Florence to him, and bending her head back, curled his long fingers around her throat.

"I'll snap her neck," Tepes said, void of emotion.

Stoker stopped.

Smoke from the fire began making its way down the corridor and there were wisps of it seeping out from under the doorways.

"Let her go, please," Stoker pleaded, knowing that he sounded pathetic, and that Tepes would never heed the request.

"I kill her now as you watch, or you come to me," Tepes said.

Stoker knew heeding the command would do neither of them any good.

"You are already dead. Come."

Stoker suddenly felt the urge to move toward Tepes. He felt himself take a single step.

"Come," Tepes repeated.

He took another unwanted step again. No, no, he must not. He must not give in. Stoker drew his cross up to his chest and placed it across his heart, gripping it as if he might fall into hell should he let it go. "No."

A scowl darkened Tepes' face. He left Florence in the middle of the passageway and began advancing toward him.

"Your will was always strong," Tepes said.

Stoker held the cross up before him. His body quaked as Tepes drew closer.

Tepes pointed a clawlike finger at the cross. "Cling to it if it brings you comfort, but I can withstand its flame long enough to break you in two."

Tepes was almost on him now.

Stoker raised the pike, but Tepes reached out with the swiftness of a striking snake, grabbed the weapon and hurled it away.

Footsteps sounded behind him.

"What about the flame of three crosses?" Stoker heard Doyle's voice from behind him.

Tepes' contempt transformed to wariness.

In another moment, Stoker found himself flanked by Doyle and Sir Henry.

CHAPTER 59

M organ Quincey, struggling to hold down a writhing vampire with the help of two Szgany men, had never seen so much gruesome death in his entire life. He had been in his share of scraps, but nothing like this. A villager armed with a stake placed the wooden point over the creature's chest and drove it through the heart with a heavy hammer. Quincey had lost count of how many monsters he had watched die and rot away to a disgusting heap of bones. He doubted that he'd ever be free of the memory.

Quincey picked up his wooden spear from the floor beside him and readied for the next skirmish. The fire had grown worse, climbing up and across the roof timbers and burning along the wall supports. The smoke made it difficult to breathe and even more difficult to see.

Off to his left he saw the Szgany, Zache, decapitate a vampire as it charged toward him.

Alexander fell upon the corpse with a wooden stake while one of his neighbors hammered it home, just to make certain the thing remained dead.

Jardani was dragging a wounded villager to safety when two of the monsters cornered him. Two other villagers, aided by several Szgany, got to him in time.

Across the room he could see Clarise stringing arrow after arrow into her bow, and letting them fly with practiced fluidity. She had killed two of the monsters already. Her father stood protectively next to her, wielding a large wooden cross to keep the vampires at bay.

Quincey saw one monster rushing out of the smoke toward Clarise.

"Clarise!" he shouted.

She saw the thing and, with practiced haste, strung the arrow already in her hand.

The creature was almost on her. Clarise drew back the arrow, and with only an instant to aim, released it. The shaft hissed through the air, striking the vampire and penetrating its heart only five feet from her. The thing twisted in the air and was nothing but rotting bones when it hit the ground at her feet.

Quincey was about to give her an encouraging wave when a vampire knocked him to the ground. The hit forced the air out of him and jarred the spear from his hand. Foul breath preceded the full view of the salivating monster, beginning to claw at his collar.

The small metal cross worn around his neck must have slipped under his coat. He clamped his powerful hand around the vampire's throat and began scrambling to find the cross with the other.

He felt the chain of the cross and pulled at it. The vampire snarled in protest and moved backwards.

Quincey shoved the thing away with all his might and scrambled to retrieve his spear. The vampire, crazed with bloodlust, was already coming at him again, and Quincey realized he'd never reach the spear. As the monster reached for him, an arrow suddenly appeared in the creature's throat.

He glanced at Clarise to see her eyes fixed on him while she strung another shaft.

As the vampire began clawing at the arrow, Quincey reclaimed his spear and rushed forward. He took aim and drove the shaft through the thing's heart. The vampire emitted a horrifying scream and dropped to the floor. Quincey waited until it morphed to rotted flesh and bones before recovering the spear.

Turning back toward Clarise, he saw her drawing back the bowstring, her eyes focused beyond him. He whirled around to see another vampire rushing toward him. As he leaped out of the way, Clarise released the arrow.

He heard the hiss of the shaft cutting through the air and then turned to see the vampire clawing at the arrow driven through its heart. The monster toppled over as it decomposed.

Quincey turned back toward Clarise as a beastly vampire lumbered toward her, blood dripping from its jaws.

"Daughter!" Professor Vambery yelled.

She saw the thing coming and knew there was no time to string another arrow. Panicking, she began backing away, but in her haste tripped over her own feet. She went down hard, landing on her stomach, her body covering the cross hung around her neck. In an instant, the vampire was on her, pinning her to the ground.

Quincey was already at a full run when he saw Professor Vambery hurl himself upon his daughter's attacker, thrusting the cross down upon its back.

The vampire bellowed in pain and jerked around, hurling the professor off of him. Vambery landed several feet away, the cross thrown from his hand. The monster closed in on the professor, fell upon him, and sank his fangs into his throat.

Quincey grabbed the creature's filthy hair with his left hand and jerked its head back with all his might. In the same instant, he slashed across the vampire's throat and pulled back hard with the Bowie knife's ten-inch blade.

Blood spewed everywhere, and Quincey fought off a wave of nausea as he felt the creature's head loosen from its neck. With another stroke of the knife, the head separated from the thing's body, and Quincey let it fall to the floor. In another moment, both head and body turned into putrefied remains.

Clarise rushed to her father's side, and Quincey intercepted her. A moment later, Jardani and Zache joined them. The professor was unconscious, with a terrible wound in his throat.

"Will he be all right?" Clarise asked, desperate for a kind answer.

"God willing," Quincey said.

He looked around the great hall. The roof was alive with flame and wouldn't last long. The air was growing thinner each moment and the smoke thicker. Several villagers and Szgany alike were wounded or dead, but the last two or three vampires were being disposed of.

"We need to get them out of here," Quincey said to Jardani, pointing toward the outer door.

Jardani understood and translated for Zache. They picked up the professor and began making their way toward the exit.

Quincey walked beside them, holding Clarise close. He could only pray that Mrs. Stoker was still safe, and that her husband and the others were still alive.

CHAPTER 60

The moment Doyle and Irving rushed to his side, Stoker felt a fresh surge of hope. Tepes was backing away, wary and furious. He turned, and then half carrying, half dragging Florence, retreated to the far end of the passageway.

Stoker, Doyle, and Irving went after him, running with all their might.

Tepes paused in front of the last door. He gripped the iron handle and the sound of moaning, straining metal filled the air as he ripped the lock from its bolts. Wisps of smoke made its way out of the doorway as Tepes and Florence disappeared inside.

Stoker and his companions rushed through the portal only moments later and came to an abrupt stop. They found themselves on a narrow landing in one of the circular towers. There had once been a restraining railing, but most of it had rotted away. Another step and they would have toppled over the side.

The stone stairway wound down along the curved walls to a floor over thirty feet below, where flames consumed every wooden surface it touched. Several of the cross beams reinforcing the tower walls were already burning. Only ten feet below them, three of the massive beams devoured by the flames broke away from the wall and crashed to the floor. Heat and smoke rose through the tower as if it were a chimney.

Above them, Tepes had almost reached the landing on the floor above, dragging Florence along behind him. Stoker charged up the narrow stairs, closing the distance between them. Doyle and Irving stayed close behind him.

Tepes gained the landing above, pausing long enough to peer malevolently down at them, the flames far below reflecting in his dead eyes.

As Stoker neared the upper floor, Tepes released his grip on Florence. She crumpled to the floor against the closed door and lay still. And then Tepes turned toward him.

Stoker realized he had no weapon. At least, if he were going to die now, it would be while trying to put right this terrible evil he had brought upon his family and friends.

Hoping for comfort, he looked down at the cross in his hand and saw something he hadn't noticed before. The long end of the cross had torn away, resulting in a jagged splintering of wood that tapered to a sharp point.

Keeping the cross behind him, he began climbing toward Tepes.

"Lord God, bless and protect me now, I beg of Thee," Stoker prayed silently.

Tepes was just above him now, glaring down at him. Stoker would only have one chance.

Tepes was reaching for him now, his clawlike fingers opening wide to take hold of him. Stoker dipped into a crouch and then leaped upward and forward with all his might. In the same instant, he brought the cross around, thrusting upward with its jagged, sharpened tip with every bit of strength he had left. The abrupt attack caught Tepes off guard. Stoker felt a moment of resistance and then felt the wood penetrate the monster's body.

Tepes bellowed in rage, but did not falter. Stoker's aim had been low. He'd missed the heart.

Tepes grabbed Stoker by his neck and lifted him onto the landing.

"Stoker!" Doyle shouted.

Doyle and Irving were close at hand, but the stairway was narrow and the landing small; there was little his friends could do to help.

Tepes locked his fingers around Stoker's throat. He felt the piercing sting of the long, sharp nails. There came a painful pressure as the fingers tightened and burning seared his lungs as he tried to find breath. Dark blotches began floating in his vision.

"Oh, Father, forgive me. Your deliverance from this, Your deliverance," Stoker prayed.

Tepes bellowed again, but this time in pain as whips of smoke rose from the wound where the cross had entered his body. The vampire's grip loosened. Stoker caught a cloudy glimpse of Doyle and Irving just below him on the stairs, struggling to find a means of attack. And then Florence came into view, unconscious on the landing at Tepes' feet, fueling him with new determination.

He grasped the wooden shaft of the cross and pushed, then twisted it with all his might, struggling to force it upward toward the monster's heart. Tepes' clothing smoldered.

Tepes snarled with fury and released Stoker. Seeing his chance, Stoker threw all of his weight again against the wooden shaft. Tepes thrashed in pain and rage. He bellowed again and spun Stoker around toward the edge of the platform. Stoker dug his boots into the rough stones, pushing back with all his might, but Tepes easily forced him backwards, closer and closer to the sheer drop.

Stoker felt the old wooden restraining rail press up against his back. It gave under his weight and he heard a cracking sound. He looked down. Over forty feet below, burning, twisted beams and shafts of jagged wood reached out of the cauldron of smoke and flame.

Tepes' face was only inches from his own, the empty eyes glowing red with hatred, the thin, red lips pulled back in a horrifying grimace, the sharp teeth menacing. A flicker of distraction appeared in those eyes and Stoker felt the heat against his chest.

Tepes roared again as small tongues of flame rose from the wound made by the cross. Still maintaining a vice like grip on Stoker, he struggled to pull the cross free.

The wood creaked again, and Stoker felt the railing break. He thrust his leg outward, his boot lodging between Tepes' boots.

The instant he did it, Stoker realized his mistake. Tepes fell forward against him. As they both tumbled backwards, Stoker glimpsed Doyle and Irving lunging forward.

As they hurtled over the landing, Tepes released his hold, trying in desperation to free himself from the cross. Stoker felt the nauseating pull of gravity, reaching up through the air at nothing.

He felt something grip at his leg and then an instant later a hand grasped his wrist. Doyle and Irving held on to him with all their might as his body swung against the side of the stairway, pounding the air from his lungs and sending a sharp pain through his back.

Tepes fell, face upward, the cross still dangling from his chest. And then for a moment his body seemed to change, transforming in shape and size. In a fraction of a second there was the outline of jagged wings through the heavy smoke, and then in the next second Tepes struck a pile of burning timbers.

A horrific scream shot up from the bottom of the tower as spikes of charred wood erupted through Tepes' chest. His transformation reverted and his hands grabbed at the smoking wood.

"Pull," Doyle yelled.

Stoker forced his gaze away from the horror below and looked up to see Doyle and Sir Henry hovering above him.

"Almost," Sir Henry called out. "We've got him."

It hurt like the devil as they wrestled him back onto the stairs. He lay there, trying to catch his breath, every muscle in his body aching with dull pain.

Sir Henry pointed downward. "He's still alive."

They peered down through the thickening smoke.

"Bloody hell!" Doyle cursed.

As the fire burned around him, Tepes fought to free himself from his impalement.

A wall timber, burning just below them, gave way with a groan and plummeted down. It landed near Tepes, increasing the flames and spreading burning debris everywhere. As they watched, the fire began spreading, moving toward Tepes. He thrashed, clawing at the wood rising from his chest.

Stoker could see the vampire's eyes, full of evil hatred, and then a flicker of fear.

Tepes unleashed a bloodcurdling howl. It echoed throughout the tower. A moment later the heavy smoke shrouded his body. The screams died away, stifled by the smoke and finally silenced by the flames.

"He's dead?" Stoker asked, uncertain.

"He has to be," Doyle said.

Above them on the landing, Florence emitted a soft moan.

Stoker scrambled up to her side and helped her sit up. As he did, the ugly welt where Clarise's cross had touched her skin faded away before his eyes.

"Florence," Stoker whispered to her. "You're safe now, you're safe."

Her face brightened with recognition, and she held tight to him.

"He must be dead or he'd still have a hold on her," Sir Henry said.

Stoker peered down into the smoke and flames. "I want to see the remains."

"As do I," Doyle said. "But is that possible now?"

"What's happened?" Florence asked, still a bit dazed.

Before Stoker could answer, another timber broke loose and fell into the flames below.

"We need to get out of here before the whole place comes down on us," Stoker said.

He helped Florence to her feet and together they all hurried back down the stairway.

CHAPTER 61

Q uincey and Jardani intercepted them as they stumbled through the tower door into the second floor corridor.
"Thank God," Quincey said. "We've been looking for you. Mrs. Stoker, is she all right? And what about you fellas?"

"She's unharmed. I'm a bit bruised, but alive," Stoker said.

"What about *him*?"

"Dead," Stoker said.

"You're certain?"

"We saw him burn."

Quincey looked around at the smoke and flames. "We're gonna be next if we don't hurry."

Without another word, they rushed along the passageway, avoiding burning timbers and covering their mouths against the smoke. Florence took everything in with eyes wide, as if seeing it all for the first time.

Descending the stairway to the main floor, Stoker could see that the flames had found every inch of wood in the stone structure. Large sections of the roof had collapsed and what remained were now glowing embers, illuminating the entire room in a reddish orange glow diffused by the smoke.

The place was a carnage house. The grotesque remains of the vampires were scattered everywhere. Blood stained the walls and floor. Small groups of villagers and Szgany were removing the last of the wounded from the building.

"The Vamberys?" Stoker asked.

"Already outside," Quincey said. "Clarise is fine, but the professor is hurt bad."

"Take me to him," Doyle said.

They stepped out to the courtyard and Florence appeared awed by the surroundings. Stoker realized that, aside from the dreams, she was seeing it all for the first time.

Men, many with torches, occupied the courtyard. They talked amongst themselves as they readied their horses. Others made the wounded comfortable in a large wagon, where Clarise knelt beside her father. The fire roared and crackled from behind the ancient stone walls, its orange glow illuminating the entire area, while ash and smoke swirled down around them.

"Mr. Doyle, here!" Clarise called out upon seeing him. "Please."

Doyle hurried to the wagon with Quincey close behind, and climbing up beside Clarise, began examining Professor Vambery.

"If anyone was responsible, it was I," said Stoker, "but it's behind us now."

"You all stayed with me," Florence said.

She noticed Sir Henry peering at her mouth. "Whatever are you gaping at?"

"Your teeth," Sir Henry answered, and then reddened with embarrassment.

"My teeth?"

"I, uh, your smile. You've always had the loveliest of smiles," Sir Henry said.

Stoker couldn't help a chuckle at the relieved glance Sir Henry gave him.

Clarise leaned over her father, holding back tears. "Will he be all right?"

"He's been unconscious since the attack?" Doyle asked.

"Yes, I think he hit his head when he was knocked down."

"The wound is still seeping," Doyle answered.

"Oh, no." Clarise sobbed.

Doyle held up a cautioning hand. "If we can get him back to the village with all due haste, I can attend to him better, and he just may have a decent chance."

"It's gonna be fine," Morgan Quincey told her with gentle confidence. "You spend enough of your time talkin' with the Lord Almighty that there's little question in my mind that He'll see to your father for you."

"You think so?" She looked at him.

"You know, they say the clean Colorado air is good for healing the worst of ailments," Quincey said. "Once the professor is feelin' a bit better, maybe you'd consider letting me take you both to my ranch. He can get some good rest and I'll be able to better keep an eye on you."

"It sounds wonderful," Sir Henry said.

"I believe the invitation was directed to Miss Vambery," Doyle said.

"Uh, yes. Of course," Sir Henry said. "Nothing escapes your keen powers of observation. If only your business ethics were so astute."

"Will there be no reprieve for me, Sir Henry?" Doyle asked with a sigh. "We've been through a lot together as friends, and I value that. I'd hate to see it all gone over the matter of a play."

"Well, I suppose I'll find it in my heart to forgive you… someday," Sir Henry said, the hint of a smile on his lips. "Besides, I'll always have the satisfaction that you'll come to realize I would have made the superior Holmes."

A few minutes later, the entire party made its way through the courtyard gates and across the stone bridge leading to the road. Doyle remained in the wagon with Clarise to tend to the professor. The rest of them rode behind them on horseback.

Stoker saw another wagon toward the front of the procession driven by the Szgany man who carried the Kukri knife. In the torchlight, he could make out covered bodies.

"How many?" Stoker pointed toward the wagon.

"More wounded than dead," Quincey said. "Only four didn't make it. It's a damned miracle if you ask me. Could've been a lot worse."

"I have strong suspicions that you'll finish it now," Doyle addressed Stoker from his place in the wagon.

"Finish it?"

"Your book."

"I suspect it will be an easier task now." Stoker reached out and took Florence's hand. "But there are more important things that require my attention first."

A roaring groan from the fire drew their attention.

A smoky orange glow outlined the ruined fortress against the night sky. Fire consumed the roof of the main building and tongues of flame reached through the narrow tower windows. With a loud creaking and moaning, what remained of the roof collapsed, sending a rain of sparks and burning embers into the air. Huge flames leaped from the windows of the main hall as the roar of the fire sounded across the valley.

"Hellish," Stoker said to himself.

Doyle looked back at the castle. "A most accurate description."

EPILOGUE

Although Arthur Conan Doyle and Henry Irving quelled any animosity between them, Doyle proved adamant in his decision not to produce his five act play, *The Adventures of Sherlock Holmes*, at the Lyceum. And, of course, Irving never played the role of Sherlock Holmes.

Doyle proceeded with his plans and sold the rights to his play to an American theatrical agent named Harold Frohman. One of Frohman's clients was the very successful American actor, William Gillette. Frohman and Gillette secured Doyle's permission for Gillette to both rewrite and star in the play.

The Adventures of Sherlock Holmes opened in Buffalo, New York, on October 23, 1899. It debuted the following month at New York City's Garrick Theater and became a tremendous hit.

In 1901, Gillette took the production to London, where it enjoyed a success equal to that in America. Performed in several London theaters, the play eventually found its way to the Lyceum. A young man by the name of Charles Chaplin played the role of Billy the pageboy in the London production.

Bram Stoker remained Henry Irving's friend and business manager at the Lyceum Theatre until the end of Irving's life. Stoker's loyalty to his friend was unquestionable. Especially in the final years, that loyalty was often tested.

The Lyceum's decline began late in 1896 when Irving injured his knee by slipping on the stairs. For the first time in his life, he was an invalid and unable to appear on the stage.

Stoker had to close the Lyceum for a month and search for someone to replace Irving for the already scheduled productions. The financial consequences drove the company into debt.

Two years later, a devastating fire destroyed the Lyceum's storage facility in Southwark. The building housed all the scenery and props for the theater. It had been presumed fireproof, so Stoker had drastically underinsured its contents. The Lyceum sank even further into debt.

Financial difficulties continued until the company's directors took action. The chairman proposed forming a new company that would convert the Lyceum into a music hall. The board voted to salvage what they could, and it was done. Henry Irving became an actor without a theater in which to perform.

Irving's physical energy began fading and he became plagued with several health problems. He died in 1905 with Walter Collinson, his long-time valet and friend, at his side.

Bram Stoker completed his manuscript of *Dracula* and saw it published in 1897. His books generally failed to draw much attention or make much money, and *Dracula* was no exception. At least the book did not financially benefit Stoker in his lifetime.

Florence, however, made out well with *Dracula*. She lived until 1937, and after her husband's death in 1912, she sold the dramatic rights to an Irish producer named Hamilton Deane. Florence opted for a percentage of the profits instead of an outright sale.

Deane authored a stage version of the tale and the play first appeared at the Grand Theatre in Derby, in 1924. It became an overwhelming success. In fact, Deane was compelled to present *Dracula* year after year in order to satisfy audience demand.

In 1931, Florence sold the rights of *Dracula* to Universal Pictures for $40,000. The studio's landmark production starring Bela Lugosi launched dozens of *Dracula* films. The films continue to be made, cultivating an interest in each new generation for Stoker's original writing.

Bram Stoker never knew it, but his book established one of the most successful and enduring characters in literature.

DID YOU LIKE THIS BOOK?

You Can Make A Big Difference!

Reviews are the most powerful tool I have when it comes to getting attention for my books. Honest reviews of my books help bring them to the attention of other readers.

If you've enjoyed this book, this writer would be very grateful if you could spend just a few minutes leaving a review (it can be as short or as long as you like).

Simply visit the *Black Hunters' Moon* book page where you made your purchase (Amazon, iBooks, Barnes & Noble, or Kobo) and look for the "leave a customer review" link.

Sincere thanks in advance, P.G. Kassel

ALSO BY P.G. KASSEL

Black Shadow Moon
Stoker's Dark Secret Book One
(A Supernatural Vampire Thriller)
Siphon
(A Cayden March Thriller)
Phantom Kill
(A Cayden March Thriller)
Dark Ride: A Novella
Get your FREE digital copy at www.pgkassel.com
(paperback for sale only)

ABOUT THE AUTHOR

P.G. Kassel (Phil to his readers) is a former film and television writer-director turned novelist. With over 30 years working in the entertainment industry his teleplays have been produced for television, and his feature length screenplays optioned by major studios and production companies.

Phil is married to an amazing and beautiful woman who puts up with all his artistic moodiness. They make their home in Los Angeles, California.

If you have any questions or comments for Phil connect with him online:

phil@pgkassel.com
www.pgkassel.com
facebook.com/pgkassel
bookbub.com/authors/p-g-kassel